Chapter 1

They were known throughout the castle as Aerigard's brats. Dark Lord Aerigard was a powerful sorcerer who had no time for marriage--who, rumor had it, had never even touched a woman. Unlike his ill-fated sister who had died of a wasting sickness, Lord Aerigard's single-minded devotion to the magic arts had made him rich, powerful and feared. Most shuddered at his name, and thought that he had sold his heart long ago for more power.

Whatever the rumors said about him, he had enough compassion to take in his poor sister's orphans at her death and feed them. But there his compassion ended. He thoroughly neglected them, spending all his time in the tower crafting rare spells and potions. Like most children, starved for attention, Jannis and Lance Solaran started causing trouble. The only problem was, they never grew out of it.

"AHHHhhhh!" Lance screamed, jumping back.

His sister looked up from where she was sitting at the window, expression flat and bored, staring out over the fog. "What's the matter, did a rat scare you, little brother?"

"Oh no," Lance replied, shaking, "I just forget how ugly you are until I see your face in the morning."

Jannis's brush paused in its path through her silky silver hair and her violet eyes narrowed for a moment. She was a rare beauty, and they both knew it. If she lacked for suitors, it wasn't because of her looks.

"What are you up to this early? The sun's not even up yet." She replied, her voice neutral.

"Arms practice." Lance replied, hefting the heavy dull metal sword he carried as if it were a stupid question.

"Before dawn?" Jannis glanced at him, and one delicate

silver eyebrow arched.

"Well you know, Uncle was up until ungodly hours of the night constructing a new homunculus; his regular alarm can't possibly wake him up after that. I thought I'd give him a hand."

"Oh, of course, who could sleep through all the clanging. Very considerate." She turned her attention back out the window, methodically brushing through her long silver hair, and Lance smirked, continuing down the stairs out into the fog.

It was always foggy around Aerigard's castle before dawn, one of the side effects of living in a swamp. Lord Aerigard had no tolerance or time for the goings-on of politics or cities, so he had chosen an extremely remote and impassible location for his secret fortress. Built by magic in a week's time, it was a towering structure of black marble and obsidian in the center of a very large and deadly swamp. Just in case a determined visitor avoided the hazards of the swamp: the hidden bogs, the deadly serpents, and the strange diseases, Aerigard had placed a number of nasty spells on the land surrounding the castle to avoid being disturbed.

A shrieking metallic clang rang out through the pre-dawn air. Birds cried and scattered from the marsh below. A second clang followed the first. If possible, it was even louder. Jannis placed her brush back on her vanity and yawned. She stretched idly. Another, unexpected clang caused her to flinch. She started down the steps into the keep, as the sounds grew louder and more frequent. Once in the kitchen, Jannis helped herself to the last of a particularly potent Turkish coffee that their Uncle favored and a small apple. Her uncle Lord Aerigard came storming down out of his tower as she sat quietly in the kitchen.

Aerigard stormed over to the coffee pot, attempting to pour it into a mug. Finding it empty, he hurled it at her head. Jannis ducked without changing her expression, and sipped her coffee.

"Does a demon possess your brother? What on earth is he thinking causing such a racket so early?!"

Jannis shrugged. "Since you're awake anyway, I'll go join

him." She rose gracefully, finishing her coffee. Jannis neatly deposited the apple core in the trash and selected a second apple from those in the wicker basket by the fire. Aerigard snorted, and towered forbodingly over the poor kitchen girl scrambling to make more coffee.

Jannis grabbed a suit of armor and a beaten metal practice blade from those lined up in the armory and strode out into the fog. Lance appeared suddenly from the fog, sword raised and an expression of manical glee on his face. His sister stared at him expressionlessly for a moment, and he lowered the sword.

"What took you so long?"

"I needed some coffee. How can you practice without even eating breakfast yet?" She hurled the apple at him, and it hit his metal helm with a dull thunk.

"You brought me breakfast? Thanks!" The grin from the shadows of the helm was broad and unconcerned.

"Not that you deserve it." Jannis started strapping on the cloth and leather padding that went under the heavy plate armor they both favored.

It irritated their Uncle no end that despite the fact that both Solarans had inherited considerable magical talent with their sorceror blood, they almost completely ignored magic, and imitated the castle guards, training with heavy plate, shields and swords.

"Girls always take so long to get ready." Lance whined, grounding his sword blade.

"I'm not late. You started early." Jannis replied accusingly, her voice slightly muffled through the armor.

"This is why I'm better with a sword than you are." Lance replied. "Practice. Dedication."

"No, it's because you're a man, fathead. More strength, longer arm reach." Jannis hefted her shield.

"Exactly! Girls are weak and stupid. I don't know why I put up with you."

"And who else would train with you? Herman stopped after

you broke his arm, and he was the last of the guards who would." Jannis swung the heavy metal practice blade at Lance, who parried it easily.

He countered, his blade clanging fiercely against her scarred metal shield.

"Not a big loss. I outpaced all those out-of-shape meatheads years ago."

Neither of them were built for the heavy armor they wore. Both were tall, painfully lean, and delicately boned like their Uncle Aerigard. At first sight you might think that the weight of the armor alone would make them fall over, for it surely weighed more than they did. Which is what made it so surreal how fast Lance could be in that armor. He struck lightning-quick, like some kind of viper.

If it were possible, Jannis was even less physically suited to the armor than Lance, but struggled gamely to keep up with her brother. She was soaked in sweat, eyes narrowed and determined, as Lance danced around her, attempting to knock her over onto the cobblestones that paved the courtyard.

"Come on, at least give me a work-out before you end up on your back like a turtle!" He taunted her, his sword darting in, as Jannis barely blocked it with her increasingly heavy shield.

With a sickening sensation in her chest Jannis saw the sword blade coming again and knew she would never block it in time. Time slowed as it headed for the side of her helm, knocking her senseless. She barely realized that she was falling before she blacked out.

When she awoke it was to the sickening scent of smelling salts. Lance had her out of her metal shell, and was cradling her head in his lap, the bottle below her nose.

"Ready for the second round?" He asked cheerfully. Jannis groaned and touched the bump on her temple. The helmet had absorbed most of the impact, but not enough, and Lance never held back in practice.

"My lord? My lady?" A servant appeared meekly from the

fog behind them both. "The master wishes to speak with you."

Lance and Jannis perched in their chairs at the large dark-stained oak table in the dining room. Both had shed their metal armor, but still wore the leather padding, and dripped with sweat. Jannis clenched a wet rag to her temple. Aerigard glanced at them both, a pained look in his eyes and sighed. His coveted coffee sat steaming in a mug in his grip, and it did not appear he intended to let go of it for anything.

"If this is about having practice too early, it was Jannis's idea." Lance grinned, leaning back. Jannis shot him a dark look.

"As if I would bother talking to you about that, Lance." Aerigard sipped his coffee, a distant look in his eyes.

"Then what do you need, Uncle? Another fruitless attempt to teach us some magic?" Lance stretched, rubbing his shoulder with his left hand.

"No." Aerigard seemed quite preoccupied. He stared at Jannis, a strange look on his face.

"I've had an offer for your sister's hand."

Lance raised one eyebrow. "You want me to cut it off?"

"In marriage, you twit." Aerigard replied, irritated. Jannis glanced at Lance, a worried look on her face. Lance howled with laughter.

"Marriage? Who would want her? And all these years I thought you didn't have a sense of humor, Uncle!"

"It's not a joke. The king of Harderior wants to marry her."

"It sounds like a joke. No one could possibly want my sister, especially a king!"

"It's not for her personality, that's for sure. It may surprise you Lance, but your sister is really quite fetching until she opens her mouth." Aerigard paused. "But it's her magic talent the king wants. He's always dreamed of being a powerful mage, and since he can never be one, he wants his children to have that ability. He offered to marry Jannis, and I accepted."

"What? Why?!" Jannis turned pale, and reached for her brother's hand.

"He gave me the Tome of Ellis Caerig."

"You traded my sister for a book?!" Lance reddened and surged to his feet. "There is no way I'm gonna let you send her off without me!"

"Wonderful, then I can be rid of both you headaches at once." Aerigard drank his coffee, a satisfied expression on his face. "I'm not going to stop you, if you want to go, too, Lance. Think of it this way, your sister will be well provided for, taken care of--just like I've taken care of the two of you all these years. It's really nothing to get all worked up about. But please, go with her, protect her... or whatever. I'm going back to bed." Aerigard rose and strode out of the room without another word. Jannis and Lance stared at each other in shock.

The lad was only seven years old. He could barely stand, and yet the determination that caused him to cling so desperately to his nurse's arm was reflected in his gray-green eyes. General Fredrick's heart went out to the boy, as it rarely did to the many mageborn children the king's breeding program had produced. The fact that the boy was the king's favorite grandson might also have affected his opinion.

"Do you need to rest, your Highness?" The general inquired quietly, displaying a small part of his concern. Young Prince Darien was the only one of the mages on the hilltop still standing. The army medics bustled about them, attempting to care for the small children lying in the grass, many of them unmoving. A line of white wrapped bundles behind them stood silent accusation to the price of the day's efforts. Unfortunately, most of the mage children still alive would probably join them before the night was through.

"I will stay as long as I can." The boy's clear voice quavered with exhaustion and the barest hint of fear, but there was no doubt in his words.

"The next target is to the left of the ravine, near the point where the forest thins." The general turned from the boy, taking his brave claim at face value. The small handful of mages still fighting linked their powers to call down a ball of fire on the approaching catapult. A girl of about eight or nine years of age fell forward from where she had been kneeling in the dirt at the prince's feet. A pair of stoic-faced medics rushed in and lifted her small form effortlessly away.

"I need some tailwind to increase our archer's range." The general said, his voice expressionless. Prince Darien took a deep breath, and the general noticed that the wind had changed direction.

"Ready archers!" The general shouted to the waiting aides. "Can you give me a little more, your Highness?" The prince lost his hold on his nurse, falling to his knees, but the wind picked up.

"Fire!" The general watched the thick cloud of arrows slam into the enemy before glancing down at the prince.

"Your Highness?"

"Please... help... me... up..." The words were slurred with exhaustion, and his eyes were starting to lose focus. The general gently grabbed the prince under his arms and lifted him back to his feet. Prince Darien clung to his nurse's arm weakly, and the general motioned in one of the hovering medics to help hold the prince up before letting the boy go and stepping back.

"We have another piece of siege coming up slightly to the right of that last catapult."

Fire suddenly tore through the offending wood and iron on the horizon.

"General?" The boy glanced at him, and for a moment that fierce determination waivered and his eyes looked all too deep and far too young.

"Yes, your Highness?"

"I hope... the battle doesn't last... much longer..."

"Report?" General Fredrick looked up from where he was studying the maps in his tent to the young man standing rigidly right inside the tent flap.

"Four of the mages are still alive, including Prince Darien."

"Thank the goddess, the king wouldn't be happy if the boy came home in a wooden box. When can we get more mages?"

"There will be another batch in from the capital with the next major supply, about eight days."

"Hmm." The general frowned. "We're under too much pressure here, we need to fall back to our alternate position, at least until we can get more mages. It will take at least a day or two before the mages we have now are recovered enough to use in battle."

"At least." The man standing near the flickering oil lamp was one of General Fredrick's advisers, the commander of the support and medical forces. "They're only children, and you are working them to death."

"You can keep your complaints to yourself." General Fredrick raised one eyebrow.

"It's not a *complaint*. Look at the bodies my men are hauling away to mass graves - It's a *fact*. You have to let them rest. Four little children, their powers spent, aren't going to make much of a difference anyway."

"You aren't telling me anything I don't already know, Gregor. I already said we were going to fall back. Just keep those mages alive and try to get them back on their feet as soon as possible."

Gregor sighed. "Yes, sir." His voice was submissive and he appeared resigned, but the general knew he would hear the same complaint again a dozen times before this campaign was finished.

Jannis packed her bags as if she were going to a funeral. Her escort would be arriving later that day, according to the servants.

Just something her uncle had neglected to mention, probably to avoid her tantrum about the whole affair. A nasty snicker behind her alerted her to Lance's arrival at her open door.

"Don't say a word." Jannis said flatly, not bothering to turn around.

"Wouldn't dream of it, dear sister." Lance eyed her up and down, a huge grin on his face. Jannis slammed her leather satchel down on the bed in disgust

"I hate this!"

"Getting married... or wearing the dress?" Lance's eyes sparkled with merriment. Jannis smoothed the heavy silk self-consciously, frowning.

"You actually almost look like a girl in that dress, if you ignore the hair, and the ears... and the nose..." Lance commented, eying her appraisingly.

"If you like it so much, I'll be sure to have a dress made for you as well, I'm sure you would look just as nice in one." Jannis retorted. She eyed the padded leather and cloth that sat on an armoring stand in the corner longingly.

"Give it up sis. No one wants to see the queen soaked in sweat and covered in metal. You have to look all pretty and dainty and show off how incredibly masculine your husband must be."

"I don't want to get married to anyone, let alone a complete stranger. Who is this king anyway? Does he just take whatever he thinks he might want?"

Lance shrugged. "Most kings do. The idea that you can have whatever you want kinda goes hand-in-hand with that whole supreme royal power thing." Lance toyed with the brush she still had sitting on her vanity. "You might like him you know, or at least, not hate him any worse than Uncle. Being a queen probably isn't half bad, with all that power, money, and random people grovelling at your feet."

"You don't seem all that disturbed. Whatever happened to rushing to my aid, Lance?"

"Hey, I'm just trying to keep an open mind. Might as well give this guy a sporting chance before we decide to ruin his life." Lance grinned and put the brush down. "At least, ruin it any worse than it is already. Who knows how bad his life is if this guy wants to marry you, of all people?"

"If you're going to loiter here, you might as well make yourself useful. Take these packs down to the main gate." Jannis began shoving leather bags of various sizes and shapes at her brother.

"Ack, no, don't treat me like a pack mule! Go find some servants, you lazy beast!" Lance lost his balance for a moment, attempting to juggle the pile of bags that had been handed to him. "What is it with women and luggage? Can't you go anywhere without bringing your entire wardrobe?"

"I have to bring my entire wardrobe because I'm never coming home again, you insensitive monster."

"Just get your new husband to buy you new dresses when you get there, so you can look all frilly and whatever." Lance said, tossing aside one of the bags in disgust. "He's a king, he can afford it."

———————

Jannis spent most of the ride out of the swamp complaining about the bugs, the damp, the smell, the soreness in her rump and her thighs, and Lance in general. She did it for more than one reason. First, she was in a foul mood and inclined to find fault with everything around her. Second, being miserable about things like biting insects prevented her from thinking about where they were going, and, more importantly, what was waiting for her there.

Jannis was torn between several very strong emotions. Elation: That she was finally getting out of the swamp she had been trapped in most of her life. Fear: The uncertainty of her future, and going to marry a man she had never met. Outrage and humiliation: That her Uncle would do this to her without so much as asking.

Confusion: Not knowing what was ahead and not having time to think any of this through. Jannis had never had a serious relationship, so the idea of something like marriage was not only foreign but terrifying.

The net effect of all these conflicting emotions was that she really didn't know what to do or what she wanted, so she just delayed thinking about it at all. Lance provided a welcome distraction.

Jannis was an old and known target. Their honor escort was new and interesting. So Lance entertained himself by tormenting their temporary traveling companions.

One of the royal guards' horses spooked suddenly.

"Lance!" Jannis accused, glaring at her brother.

"You really do blame me for everything." Lance said calmly, leaning forward in the saddle. "Do you ever stop complaining?"

"Maybe if you would behave, I could stop complaining so much."

"I always behave. Just not the way you want me to."

"It's your fault I'm here." Jannis added.

"Oh, really? Explain how that makes any sense. This was Uncle's stupid idea."

"But you were the one who talked me into it."

"All I did was ask you to keep an open mind. You keep your mind sealed shut pretty much constantly."

"You were just as upset as I was when Uncle first told us. And then a sudden change of heart. Why do I get the impression that you are just using this whole business to get out of that filthy swamp?"

"And you aren't?" Lance challenged.

Jannis flushed, and yanked hard on the reins, causing her horse to pull up abruptly, sidestepping.

"No, I'm not! I don't know what I am doing!"

"Like that's a change."

"I can't stand you!"

"That's why I came." Lance concluded, satisfied.

Chapter 2

Jannis eyed the room she had been led to doubtfully. The perky young lady-in-waiting who had led her here followed closely behind her, still rambling on about some people Jannis didn't know and their recent exploits.

She was beginning to regret letting Lance talk her into giving this king a chance. Maybe she should have just cut her hair off and become a mercenary. But that would have meant risking sleeping on the ground, missing meals, maybe getting raped or killed in battle. Not exactly the most tantilizing option. She still had serious doubts about this whole marriage business.

Jannis went over to the large fireplace that burned along one wall. The fire was small for the size of the fire pit, and all along the finely crafted stone mantle were various trinkets of gold, silver, iron and carved wood. A pair of comfortable hide-covered chairs sat near the fire, and Jannis plopped down into one of them with a sigh.

"My lady, isn't the lesser audience chamber lovely? The king wanted to receive you in style, but he was so afraid that a sheltered girl like you might not want to suffer through the whole court until you had a chance to adjust. I'd be happy to bring you some dinner if you would like?"

Jannis waved the woman away. "How long until the king gets here?"

"Oh, my lady, the king is very busy with matters of state, he wanted me to make sure that you were comfortable while you were waiting. There is some lovely carved roast in the kitchen. Or rosemary chicken if you prefer. We might even have some mushroom soup. Mushroom soup is the chef's specialty. He uses a blend of six different kinds of wild mushrooms minced finely and fresh crea..."

"No, thank you." Jannis cut the woman off.

"But you must eat, my lady. The king is always very concerned for the health of his mages, and for his bride he must be doubly concerned."

"I'm not hungry." Jannis replied, eyes narrowing and a headache beginning to form behind her temples.

"You must eat, my lady." The lady-in-waiting whined, looking up at her pleadingly. "It is my responsibility to take care of you. The king cares about nothing so much as your well-being."

Jannis eyed the young noblewoman doubtfully.

"I'm really not that hungry."

"But you will be waiting here for a long time. I insist, you must eat something. The king ordered me to take care of you. If I should fail, he may have me beaten."

Jannis sighed and rubbed her temples where this incessant little woman was giving her a headache. She doubted the king would have the lady-in-waiting beaten just for failing to get dinner, but why argue the matter?

"Oh very well, just get me whatever you think will suit. I don't like turnips or peas."

"Of course, my lady! I know just the thing, wait here and I will have your dinner momentarily!" The young woman practically bounced out the door, bubbling with enthusiasm. Jannis sighed, and rubbed her temples again.

Jannis suspected the king would make her wait for a very long time. Royalty did that sort of thing to demonstrate their power and importance. Jannis decided to examine this room she had been left in to pass the time. It was very plushly appointed, clearly a place the king spent a lot of time in. That was a good sign. He wasn't likely to leave her in a room he frequented if he suspected her of being, an assassin, for instance.

The walls and floor were paneled in dark-stained wood, and tapestries graced the walls showing the typical themes of brightly colored hunts and royal balls. An old, well-kept banner and a shield enameled with the Harderior royal coat of arms claimed pride of place above the mantle. A small wooden bookshelf was built into one wall. Jannis rose, and let her curiosity draw her to it. She scanned the spines and was not surprised to see a collection of books on warfare, philosophy, and a handwritten ledger or two--probably copies of the castle accounts.

Near the bookshelf was a small table, like a desk, only oval rather than square. Paper was stacked neatly on it, and a dry inkwell sat ready with a pair of pens. A few more padded chairs circled the table. One of the chairs was noticeably more plush than the others, and had been carved intricately. Upon closer inspection of the chair Jannis discovered silver inlay and some onyx paneling.

"Oh, my lady, here you are! I bet you are near faint with hunger." The lady-in-waiting bustled back through the door like a whirlwind leading a pair of servants loaded down with various trays and bottles. Jannis looked up as the woman entered, and sighed.

"I take it this is the king's chair?" Jannis said, gesturing to the inlaid one.

"Oh yes, a masterwork that, hand-carved in the time of my grandfather. You have such a good eye, my lady. We will set up your dinner here on the table, but please be careful not to knock the papers all over the place. That's right, just move them over to the bookshelf neatly." The young noblewoman directed the servants as they laid out what seemed to be a dinner for three or four people, not just one. Jannis debated objecting, but decided against it.

"Just don't expect me to eat all this." She said, sitting down in one of the chairs and selecting a fork.

"Of course not, my lady. Feel free to eat as much as you like. I'll have the servants remove anything left. Now there is just one more thing I must take care of and then you may eat in peace." Jannis paused, her fork poised above a tasty-looking baked fish. The woman picked up a small wooden chest that had been placed on the table with the rest of the food and opened it to reveal a strange dull gray stone. As soon as the chest's lid had opened, the stone began glowing with a sullen red light. Jannis sighed, and set her fork down.

"Weyrstone? So your king doesn't really believe I'm a mage, or does he just want to be sure he's gotten the full benefit of his bargain?"

"Don't be upset, my lady, I'm certain the king does not doubt your lineage. I am merely following his instructions. Place your hand on the stone, please."

Jannis sighed and reached for the box. As her hand approached the softly glowing stone, it brightened and the color changed first from red to orange, then to yellow, then to white, and as she placed her hand on the stone, it flared brilliantly blue, illuminating the whole room.

The lady-in-waiting gasped. Jannis removed her hand from the stone and lifted one eyebrow.

"Problem?" She enquired delicately, one deliberate glance at the waiting food.

"No, no, my lady, please eat now. I apologize, I've just never met an archmage before. I never would have guessed it from looking at you, you seem so... robust, so strong. Just eat; I'll be back to clear the dishes."

"Robust??" Jannis asked no one in particular, confused and quite frankly insulted, as the lady-in-waiting and the servants fled the room, taking the offending weyrstone with them. Free at last to eat in peace, Jannis did just that.

Two hours later she was still waiting in the lesser audience chamber, dinner had been finished and the table cleared, and Jannis was analyzing one of the castle accounts to pass the time. She had already discovered three minor accounting errors. The infernally perky lady-in-waiting burst in irregularly to see if there was anything she needed, and probably to ensure that Jannis was still waiting where she was supposed to like a good little girl and not out wandering the halls.

For a long time as she waited, Jannis entertained the idea

Lance had planted in her head back in the swamp. Maybe marrying this king wouldn't be so bad. Queens had a lot of power, and a lot more freedom than most women. It was, in fact, just as likely that he wouldn't want her, as that she wouldn't want him.

Jannis smoothed her dress self-consciously and wished for a mirror. Though she had washed her face as soon as they arrived at the castle, she still felt grimy with the dust of travel, and wished that she had taken the time to change her gown.

You never get a second chance at a first impression. She thought sourly.

"Your uncle says you're quite a handful." The voice that echoed from behind her, near the door, was rich and commanding. Jannis turned at the sound, and fell to the floor in a graceful courtesy. The king examined her appraisingly with his gaze, walking forward until he was within arms reach. He reached down for her hand, lifting it, and with it her, to her feet.

"Your Majesty." Jannis replied, keeping any fear or hesitation from her musical voice.

"'Stubborn, capricious, irritating and entirely too clever and beautiful for her own good.' Were his exact words, if I recall." The king paused, and a smile teased his lips. "You aren't going to deny it?"

"My uncle is unfailingly accurate in his appraisal, your Majesty." Jannis kept her eyes down, to keep the flash of irritation hidden. Of course Dark Lord Aerigard would tell the king all about her, and ruin any chance she had of making a good first impression.

"He said it would be difficult for any man to keep you in line. But he also said you were worth the effort, and I'm inclined to agree with him." The king stared at her in a way that made Jannis feel very uncomfortable. "Turn around." He gestured with one hand, and Jannis obediently rotated in a circle. The longer the king stared at her, the more uncomfortable she felt.

"Stop. It's remarkable. You look so healthy, like an ordinary woman." Jannis bit back a comment at the unintended insult, confused and increasingly disturbed.

"Ordinary? What do you mean, your Majesty?" She kept the bite from her words, and curtsied again just for good measure.

"Well, just look at you." He replied, unhelpfully. "I never would have guessed that you were an archmage just as strong or stronger than your uncle. Do you tire at all?"

"I was riding for ten hours today before we reached your castle, your Majesty, I confess I am a little tired."

"Simply remarkable. And did you tire at home, or take ill?"

"I am rarely sick, your Majesty, though I do admit, I was exhausted on a regular basis at home trying to keep up with my brother."

"Brothers have a habit of doing that. You brought yours with you, as I recall. I'll have to meet him when circumstances allow." The king dismissed further thought of Lance and smiled possessively as he stared.

Jannis fidgeted, unable to contain her discomfort any longer.

"Your Majesty, if I may be so bold, it makes me somewhat uncomfortable when you look at me like that."

The king laughed, amused. "Of course. I forget how sheltered you are, growing up in the middle of nowhere, in a swamp of all places. You don't have to worry, I'll take good care of you. Of all the girls I've encountered in my lifetime, you are the rarest." He reached out one hand to stroke the side of her face. Jannis looked down, afraid to meet his gaze.

"Your uncle also said you have noble blood from both parents."

"I did not know my father, he left when I was very young."

"Noble blood makes this a lot easier, not as good as royal, mind you, but my nobles can get very difficult when I take a lowborn wife. You look the part too: elegant and regal, just like a queen should. Even that isn't the most important consideration though. You're healthy, so much healthier than my last wife."

"Your... last wife?" Jannis asked.

"She died in childbirth." The kind said dismissively.

"I'm so sorry to hear of your loss, your Majesty."

The king shrugged philosophically. "Most mageborn girls are so fragile, it's almost to be expected. They hardly live to adulthood let alone through childbirth."

"I see..." Jannis said, at a loss for words.

"You don't." The king said, frowning sympathetically. "You, your uncle, and your brother are all mages, and perfectly healthy. It must come as a nasty shock for you to realize that most mages don't share your fortitude. No one knows why, but they are weak from birth, prone to illness, and easily exhausted. Their skin is often pale or yellowed, and their hearts beat erratically and even stop."

Jannis frowned, her mind quickly calculating.

"Iron." Jannis said, insight suddenly dawning.

"Excuse me?" The king asked, irritated at the unexpected interruption.

"Iron interferes with magic. The mere touch of iron can kill some rare fae creatures. But iron isn't just in sword blades, it's also in our food, and in our blood. If I were to hazard a guess, your mages can't eat red meat, can they? They become nauseated and vomit. But our bodies need iron to produce blood. Your mages are suffering from a blood disorder because iron makes them ill, which is why they are so weak and sick."

"Can that possibly be the reason?" The king looked skeptical. "I think your uncle is right--you are entirely too clever for your own good. Do you always trot out your book learning to prove that you are smarter than everyone around you?" He shrugged. "It doesn't matter what causes the condition, only what can be done about it. Do you have any ideas, clever one?"

Jannis blushed, and shook her head.

"I thought not." The king concluded, and then smiled condescendingly. "You don't need to prove to me how clever you are. Don't worry so much about matters that don't concern you. Our wedding is in three weeks, you should have more than enough to keep you occupied until then. Now, it is time to retire..."

"Your Majesty, may I ask one question?"

He frowned. "A quick one."

"May I know the name of my husband to be?"

"No one's told you?"

"My uncle was in a hurry to see us off, and the guards simply call you His Majesty or the king, no one has bothered to enlighten me until now."

The king laughed, amused. "Eduardo Malifest the Fourth. You can call me Eddy, but only when we're alone." The king reached up to kiss her gently on the cheek before turning and heading out the door.

"Thank you for coming." The man stood up from where he had been sitting behind a very large and impressive-looking desk of dark wood covered in various stacks of papers. He was dressed luxuriously, if somewhat excessively, in robes of plush burgundy velvet and heavy lined silk satin, embroidered in thread-of-gold. Heavy chain links of gold rested on strong shoulders, and the man's hair was going ever so slightly to gray on his mustache and around his temples. Lance hid a smirk, and smiled graciously, reaching out to shake the offered hand before they both sat.

"I appreciate you making time in your busy schedule to visit with me, Duke Tellis. And so quickly. After all, I only got here yesterday evening. I was a bit surprised to receive your invitation so soon after arriving." Lance kept his gaze on this oily nobleman, deliberately ignoring the lush and well appointed office that the Duke had received him in. It seemed almost deliberately crafted to overwhelm whoever visited it with the wealth of the owner. Lance recognized wealth, but he wasn't impressed by it. Lance was impressed by very little.

"I think we're all surprised. I was pleasantly surprised that you had so graciously and unexpectedly accompanied our queen-to-be."

"Surprises are generally unexpected." Lance smiled secretively.

"But not pleasant?" The duke inquired, his forehead furrowing in mild confusion.

"Let's just say that my presence can be a bit overwhelming for some close-minded and lesser individuals." Lance replied loftily, shrugging his shoulders. "I'm sure that you don't fall into that category, Duke Tellis."

The duke let the comment pass, already taking a different tack.

"I hope you slept well last night." He commented, pouring himself a glass of white wine from a bottle on the table.

"Well enough." Lance replied. "I can't say I think much of your security though, I had a late night intruder."

"Really?" The duke asked with feigned interest. "I hope it wasn't too much of a shock. I'll have to talk to the guard."

"Don't worry, I already took care of it." Lance replied flippantly and dismissively.

"I'm glad to hear it was resolved so quickly. Let's hope there are no further problems." The duke sipped his wine. "Would you like some?" He offered, gesturing to the bottle.

"No, thank you, it's a little early in the morning for me."

The duke laughed. "Oh come now, a vigorous young man like you must have a healthy appetite."

"Actually, I already ate breakfast. Thank you, anyway, though."

"A man needs more than just food."

"Are we talking about the wine? It's really quite kind of you, but I don't drink this early."

"Of course." Duke Tellis forced a smile. "You have remarkable self-control for a man of your age. It's a pity self-control comes at such a heavy price. You don't get to enjoy life nearly enough." The duke sipped his wine with an expression of pure pleasure.

"That must be one hell of a vintage for you to obsess over it so much. Maybe I'll sample it if you invite me over in the evening."

"I was in the welcoming party when you arrived yesterday. Your sister is really quite lovely, unusually colored, but lovely. I see you have the same violet eyes. Is that a family trait?"

"Maybe." Lance smiled. "I don't have her ugly gray hair though." He ran a hand through his own blond hair.

"So you prefer blondes?" The duke asked.

"I'm prettier than my sister if that's what you're asking. She's so thin and tall, like a stick." Lance commented, ignoring the fact that Jannis's height and build were traits that he shared.

"It's not very fair to criticize your sister so. Beauty comes in all sorts of shapes and sizes. I do admit though that it is pleasant to have a lady that gazes up at you, rather than staring you in the face."

"My sister is also entirely too self-controlled. I wish I could meet a gypsy sometime, I read about them in books when I was a child and I always thought they sounded so beautiful, wild, and free." Lance warmed to his subject, his face animated. "But the absolutely most beautiful girls in the world, are the ones without a leg." The duke had been listening intently, while feigning disinterest, but he sputtered at that last comment. "Excuse me? Without legs?"

"Oh the girls without any legs are alright I suppose," Lance said dismissively, "But it's the ones with only one leg that are really incredible."

"So, your idea of the perfect woman is a short, one-legged gypsy?" The duke asked, incredulously.

Lance sighed, as if pained. "I know, it's tragic, isn't it? You have no idea how hard they are to find. At this point I've just resigned myself to a life of enforced celibacy. So if you've got any daughters falling in love with me, you better disabuse them of the notion quick, I don't want to break any more hearts than I have to."

"Do you break a lot of hearts? I would have thought it was hard to meet ladies, in a swamp."

Lance ignored him. Glancing around the room he noticed an small and ornate footed chest on the shelf along the far wall. It was filled with stones, pulsing with a soft red glow. "Hey, neat!" He exclaimed, rising to his feet and moving over to the chest. "You collect the same funny glowing rocks Uncle does!" Reaching into the chest, he picked up a stone, which began not only to glow a fierce blue at his touch, but steam and hiss at the same time.

"I love these things! Watch this!" The stone was hissing even louder now, and it began to whine, an irritating shriek that grew louder and more piercing with every moment until the stone unexpectedly sputtered and cracked into pieces, falling silent and going dark. Without hesitating a moment, Lance dropped the shattered pieces on the duke's desk and reached for another stone. The whining began again.

"I really wish you wouldn't..."

"You have no idea how rare these things are!" Lance remarked excitedly, ignoring the duke. "Expensive, too!" The stone's wail reached a hair raising pitch and snapped into pieces. Lance quickly grabbed a third stone. It flared and started to smoke, the wail beginning again. "Uncle was so mad when he found out what I did to his rocks, I thought he was going to spit fire!"

"Your new bride's brother is a headache."

"Excuse me?" King Eduardo looked up from his desk as the Duke of Tellis bowed formally before him.

"At first, I'd have thought he was nothing more than one of the dozens of worthless, self-absorbed lordlings that hang around the court... but he's a lot smarter than he lets on. Either the most powerful mage on the continent really is a self-avowed celibate obsessed with one-legged gypsies, or he suspected all along I was responsible for the young ladies in his room last night and was toying with me for his own amusement."

"On the continent? You better have some kind of proof before you start making claims like that." The king frowned, disturbed.

"Oh I have proof, enough shattered weyrstone to finance a heavy cavalry legion. To think I had planned a plausible excuse for getting him to touch it, and then he wrecks half of my supply on a whimsy. Apparently our young lord Lance can shatter weyrstone at a touch, accompanied by the most irritating noise imaginable."

"Not to ignore your feelings, Duke Tellis, but we have higher priorities. This is an opportunity that we cannot ignore. Do what you can to recruit him to our cause."

The duke sighed. "Of course, your Majesty." He bowed deeply and turned to leave.

The king spoke to his departing back, and the duke immediately turned at the sound and bowed again.

"Can he really," the king paused, surprised as what Duke Tellis said finally sank in, "Shatter weyrstone? I've never heard of a mage that powerful."

"Yes, your Majesty." The duke replied evenly, keeping the irritation out of his voice. He couldn't help thinking of the pile of broken rock that had been taken out with the trash, worthless rock that had once been worth more than its weight in gold.

"What an unexpected bonus." The king's sharp green eyes narrowed possessively. "My bargain with the Dark Lord is paying off far faster than I could have expected. It appears your concerns were unfounded."

"Perhaps." The Duke of Tellis bowed again, respectfully, his velvet doublet straining around the slight paunch of his waist. "But we had no way of knowing at the time whether the Dark Lord would deal fairly and keep his side of the bargain. That sorcerer has a fearsome reputation, after all." The duke carefully didn't mention that he still had doubts about this bargain with Lord Aerigard. Young Lord Lance was clearly more than he seemed.

"It's a pity." The king commented at last. "I would have liked to recruit that sorcerer as well, but he simply wasn't interested. I'll have to settle for his nephew, it seems."

The duke debated whether he should voice his concerns again, but decided against it. The king clearly saw Aerigard's nephew as an asset, not a problem. Tellis suspected though, that the king was terribly wrong.

The insufferable lady-in-waiting Jannis had already been exposed to, she later learned was named Lady Charlotte Doucee. Lady Charlotte, as court rumor went, despite being the younger sister of the dowager Duchess Felivoit, had few marriage prospects. Lady Charlotte had engaged in some indescrete relationships in the first year she was at court, including a couple of affairs with older, married men. Though she was the model of proper conduct now, the specter of her past behavior continued to haunt her.

"Are you ready to dress now, m'lady?" Lady Charlotte asked for the fourth time. Jannis resisted the urge to grind her teeth. She loathed the elaborate court gowns that she was now forced to wear, and tended to put off putting them on as long as possible.

Jannis continued brushing her long silky, silver hair, perched like a bird on the wrought metal stool in front of her vanity, and contemplated the reflection of her own face in the mirror. She was already garbed in the shift and underdress that went under the more elaborate court gown, and so she was hardly indecent.

The ladies-in-waiting were scattered around the room, pretending to have something to do, but every one of them had her attention fixed on Jannis. It was stiffling being the center of so much attention all the time, and in her own room, no less!

Besides Lady Charlotte, the head lady-in-waiting, there were four others. One however, was absent with some kind of sickness. It was a slight relief that there were only five women crammed into the room instead of six.

"What can you tell me about relations with Kalen?" Jannis asked smoothly, trying to start some kind of conversation as she put off the moment the hated dress would come on.

"Excuse me, my lady?" Lady Charlotte asked hesitantly, a smile frozen on her face.

"You know, Kalen, the kingdom Harderior is at war with," Jannis clarified needlessly.

"I don't think.." Lady Charlotte began hesitantly, but Jannis cut her off ruthlessly.

"I mean, if I am going to be your queen, I have to have a basic knowledge of the kingdom and I would think knowing about a war going on counts as basic."

"I'm not sure his Majesty would approve..." Lady Charlotte said plaintively, "Of this particular type of discussion."

"Alright, what about accounting techniques. What kind of administrative controls does the royal accountant emply against embezzlement?" Jannis asked next.

Lady Charlotte had the look of a hunted animal. Her smile was drooping despite her best efforts to keep it pasted in place.

"Right.... So, what about magic theory, are you familiar with any of archmage Diagras's theories about field forces?" Jannis arched one eyebrow at the now quivering lady-in-waiting. Lady Charlotte looked ready to flee.

"Sweet goddess, can I talk about anything besides dresses without horrifying the entire court?" Jannis finally asked, setting her brush down on the vanity somewhat too firmly.

"Embroidery!" Lady Charlotte replied happily, a beautific smile reappearing on her face.

"Embroidery?" Jannis repeated, incredulous.

"And dancing!" Another lady-in-waiting added, coming to Lady Charlotte's rescue. The second voice seemed to open the floodgates and all four ladies-in-waiting started chattering at once about dances, embroidery, new slippers and gossip about people Jannis had never heard of. It was like being in a hen house with a bunch of clucking chickens.

Jannis rubbed her temple where a headache was already starting to form. And she had thought being around Lance was frustrating. At least he wasn't this tedious.

"Are you ready to dress now, m'lady?" Lady Charlotte asked again, with a smile.

"I'm here to see my sister." Lance declared, striking an exaggerated pose and using every inch of his imposing height to stare down on the two hapless guards in the hallway.

"I'm sorry, my Lord, no visitors." The older and more senior of the two guards, a grizzled veteran who was surprised by very little, and impressed by even less, met Lance's demand without pause. The other guard, far younger and less experienced, stared at Lance in shock.

Maybe if Lance had wanted to, he could have gotten up to his sister's quarters the normal way. But that would hardly have been challenging, and what's more, Lance had nothing but contempt for the lousy security that had allowed three scantily clad chamber maids to hide in his bed the night before. After he had chased the poorly dressed girls out of his room, Lance's sharp mind had begun plotting ways to repay whoever had humiliated him, and anyone else who might be convenient.

Maybe it was divine inspiration that had led him to the spider crawling up the side of the windowsill. Lance didn't know and didn't care. The spider had the right idea. With catlike agility he had lodged a grappling hook in a windowsill near the top of the keep and swarmed up the rope along the outside of the castle. With suitably dramatic flair he came crashing through the heavy iron filigree that both ornamented and guarded the window to land in front of the two hapless guards in the hallway, his arrival accompanied by the heartrending crash of shattering glass.

The young guardsman stared at the wrecked window, then at

the twisted metal lying on the floor of the hall, then at the imposing young man towering over him. He gulped, and looked to his partner for support. The other man simply stared at Lance, unimpressed, and shifted the grip on his spear threateningly.

"I told you, my Lord, no visitors." The grizzled man repeated, when Lance showed no sign of leaving. Lance sighed and eyed the two men.

"Oh all right," He said airily and turned back to the broken out window, reaching up to grasp the rope that still dangled outside the wall.

"My Lord, what do you think you are doing?" The old guardsman asked, suspicious, as Lance heaved himself up onto the windowsill with the rope.

"I could kill you, but it would be a waste of time," Lance replied without looking back, "I'm just going to go in through my sister's window instead. It's so much more dramatic to come in through a window than a door. Anyone can use a door." He swung out the window as he spoke, and the two guards, alarmed, ran to the opening.

"I told you, sir, no visitors!" The guardsman shouted after the disappearing blue and blonde blur that was Lance, far too late to stop him. The guardsman turned to the door he had been guarding, and quickly opened it.

The old veteran was greeted by the sight of Lance smashing once again through an iron grilled window, twisting the metal, sending fat shards of broken glass flying, and landing in a tumbled heap atop the king's poor bride.

Jannis didn't scream delicately like a noblewoman should, but rather in full-throated rage as she felt herself knocked to the floor by an all-too-familiar weight.

"Are you glad to see me?" Lance asked, grinning, not even bothering to get off of her.

"You, you beast! You half-blood Gorgon!" Jannis sputtered, trying desperately to get out from underneath him, hampered both by her elaborate gown and Lance's unhelpful efforts.

"Now, now, sister. My blood is your blood too, so there's really no point in insulting my lineage." Lance smirked, finally standing.

Jannis staggered to her feet, her beautiful silver hair in disarray, her dress torn in places, and a bloody gash on her leg where the twisted iron grill from the window had struck her. The two guardsmen dashed into the room without hesitation, seizing the young man from both sides.

"You again?" Lance asked, glancing at the two of them.

"I tried to tell you, young Lord, no visitors. The king isn't going to be pleased by how you treated his future bride. You'll have to come with us."

"Wait. Let him go." Jannis brushed the hair out of her face, grimacing at the damage that had been done to the beautiful sea green silk dress.

"I'm sorry, my Lady, we have our orders from the king."

"Trust me, you'll be sorry if you don't let him go." Jannis's violet eyes were calm, but certain.

"My Lady, there is no need to threaten us," the younger guardsman smiled at her winningly, "No harm will come to your brother, I'm sure, he just needs to learn some decorum."

"It wasn't a threat. Let Lance go, or you will regret it."

"Compliments, big sister? I'm blushing, really." Lance shrugged and smiled, seemingly oblivious to the two armed guards clutching his arms.

"You're an idiot." Jannis snapped, her eyes flaring at him and her face flushing.

"You're so ugly when you get mad, you know." Lance replied, his eyes alight with mischief.

"That's enough. You're coming with us, Lord Lance." The two guards started dragging him out of the room, but Jannis didn't miss the irrepressible twinkle in his eyes. She sighed and closed her eyes, waiting for the inevitable.

"You could have avoided this, you know," Lance said. "I just wanted to see my sister. It's not very smart to separate us."

"Whatever." The older guard seemed unconcerned.

A sickening crack. Jannis didn't look. A meaty thud, a grinding scrape, and another sickening crack. Her eyes were still closed. One slow soft thud, followed shortly by another, the sound of two bodies hitting the carpet that covered the stone floor. She sighed again, and rubbed her temples.

"Not much of a challenge," Lance commented, pulling the door to the hallway closed. He used his foot to shove the body of the unconscious guard closest to him in front of the closed door.

"Was that really necessary?" Jannis asked, walking over to sit in the plush chair nearest the window. She lifted her leg and inspected the cut there, the blood was already starting to dry in little brown-red streaks down her leg. She set the leg back down in disgust.

Lance didn't bother to respond. He strode across the room, finding another chair there. It was a heavy carved wooden chair, but he lifted it easily and carrying it across the room set it down a few feet from her with a thud. Lance sat without saying anything else, and just stared at her, that irritating grin still on his face, eyes alight.

"Are you just here to irritate me?" Jannis finally asked, frustrated.

"Why do you keep asking questions you already know the answer to? I'm your brother, it's my job to irritate you."

"We aren't little kids any more, Lance. When are you going to grow up?"

"When are you?" He countered. Jannis sighed and was silent for a long moment.

"I'm glad you're here, Lance." She said finally, sincerely. "Irritating as you are, you're so much better company than the flutterbrained airheads I've been putting up with." He just smirked.

"What's your new husband like?" He asked finally, changing the subject. "Not that he is worthy of a Solaran, even if he is a king.

Still, I'd like to know if I need to be on my manners. So I need to know if you've fallen hopelessly in love with him or something."

"Hardly." Jannis shuddered a little. "He scares me. The way he looks at me scares me."

"You've got to be kidding me." Lance stared at her. "A basilisk's stare wouldn't scare you. He must be one ugly guy if a single look could do that to my fearsome sister!"

"Could you, you know, not be yourself for five minutes? I'm not joking, Lance. He scares me. Uncle said something about this guy wanting to breed a mageborn heir, well I'm not his first attempt at it. Apparently the king has had four previous marriages, all to mages, and all of his wives are dead. The king had a number of children with them, but they are all dead now. His last living daughter died giving birth to his grandson Prince Darien. There's a lot more to this business than we first believed. It scares me."

"Actually it explains a lot." Lance said thoughtfully.

"It does?" Jannis asked, surprised.

"Yeah, I wondered why the Duke of Tellis bothered to smuggle three chambermaids into my room last night."

"He did?" Jannis blushed. Lance arched one delicate blond eyebrow at her.

"I am terribly insulted that he would think I would engage in questionable activity with women of that quality." Lance replied in hurt tones, his voice dripping with disdain.

The women in question had been quite lovely actually, and their lack of clothes had displayed their ample assets to full effect. In the end, however, their substantial feminine wiles had been no match for Lance's unfaltering arrogance and icy disdain.

"A man has to have standards." Lance finished with an air of insulted pride.

"Out of curiosity, what kind of woman would meet your inflated standards?" Jannis asked mockingly, unimpressed by Lance's attitude.

"A goddess." Lance replied without hesitation. "But only if

she came down from heaven and groveled at my feet." He added, as if an afterthought.

"You're never going to get married, you know." Jannis commented, her chin in one hand.

"As if I care, women are a waste of time anyway. Especially sisters."

"It sounds like you have a problem then, Lance. I doubt the king's cronies are going to stop flinging women at you."

Lance groaned, and put his head in his hands. "It's my curse to live with, to be so undeniably desirable." He mimed a heartfelt sob, before a strong strain of irritation set into his shoulders. "Seriously though, it's terribly insulting that they think I'd be interested in women like that. I mean it's like the Duke of Tellis just assumed I'd fall all over a bunch of lowborn hussies like a rutting animal or something." Irritation, and something stronger, hurt pride, flashed in his normally carefree eyes.

Jannis glanced at him out of one eye, pretending to look out the window. Lance was dangerous in this mood, more dangerous than usual.

"How old are you?" She asked finally, as if it didn't matter.

"Are you suggesting something?" He asked, irritation heavy in his voice.

"Just answer the damn question."

"You know how old I am, sis. Ten months younger than you. And you are a damned old maid. You are lucky the king wanted you, because at this point no one else would take you."

"You are eighteen years old." Jannis snapped, eyes narrowing as his barb hit home, and she was forced to answer her own question. "The duke's assumption wasn't all that far fetched. Most men of your age would in fact go at it 'like a rutting animal' as soon as they were given the chance. He could hardly have known what you are like, since he'd never met you before."

"See, this only makes it more insulting," Lance whined, gesturing halfheartedly with one hand. "That bastard probably thought he was doing me a favor, as if I couldn't find a woman of my own, if I actually wanted one. Which I don't." Lance added the last quickly, and glared at Jannis. Wisely, she didn't say anything.

The silence stretched between them for a moment as Lance finished his uncharacteristic pout.

"I suppose you want me to look into this then?" He asked finally, cocking one eyebrow at his sister. "This whole mage breeding thing?"

Jannis nodded, and Lance uttered a long-suffering sigh.

"Typical. I finally get the chance to get out of that damn swamp to see the world, and what happens?" He paused for effect. "The idiot king of this pathetic country decides to try and turn me and my sister, the great and noble Solarans, sorcerers of an ancient line, into breeding stock. That bastard isn't going to get away with it." Lance grinned then, a feral kind of smile and bowed low from where he sat. "Do not fear, my Lady, you may leave the matter in my capable hands." Lance stood then, and Jannis stood as well.

Unfortunately, Jannis couldn't resist getting in the last word.

"You're still a virgin, aren't you?" She asked as he climbed into the broken windowsill. Lance paused.

"That's a matter of opinion." He replied in dignified tones.

"How is it a matter of opinion?" Jannis couldn't help asking.

"Well, I've never been with a human woman." He replied, stepping off of the sill and putting his weight on the rope.

"That's a terribly disturbing thought." Jannis shuddered. Lance smirked and started sliding down the rope, but Jannis caught his reply.

"I know."

In the end, Lance always got the last word.

Chapter 3

"Report?" General Fredrick looked up to the soldier standing rigidly at attention right inside his tent flap.

"Prince Darien is awake, sir."

The general's adviser Gregor frowned from where he was seated by the general's cot. "Sir, you wouldn't send him into battle again before he recovers."

General Fredrick granted Sir Gregor one contemptuous glance.

"Of course not. Prince Darien is irreplaceable. Besides we will have our new mage reinforcements tomorrow. Somehow we've managed to hold on this long." The general eyed a map laid out on the folding table within the command tent. He had not liked losing ground to fall back to a more defensible position. He had liked it even less when the king's grandson had failed to wake after the two days he had expected. One of the other three mages who had survived the battle hadn't woken up at all. The child's heart had stopped and the sleep became eternal.

"You know I don't approve of your methods, Fredrick." Gregor said finally after the reporting soldier had left the tent. He would never have called his old friend by name in front of the troops, it undermined discipline.

"Yes, I know. Which is why I don't know why you keep repeating yourself." The general reached for the battered metal cup on the table and gulped down the contents. Only water--he grimaced but did not wish for wine, not while there were still battles to fight. "I don't like this any more than you do, but we don't have a choice. Without their sacrifice, we would have been overrun months ago. It's a matter of numbers. I sacrifice dozens to save hundreds, and I'll sacrifice hundreds to save thousands, without hesitation."

"They're children, not soldiers." Gregor protested. Fredrick sighed and slammed the metal cup back down on the folding table.

"Enough! Be quiet or get out. If we were overrun, those children would be dead anyway. You know how the kingdom of Kalen feels about our king and his mages."

"A problem that Eduardo caused himself," Gregor muttered, irritated, and General Fredrick did not correct him. "By refusing an alliance marriage with Kalen's princess royal. Maybe it wouldn't have been taken as such an insult if our beloved king hadn't turned around and married a commoner less than a month later."

"A commoner with remarkable mage powers, but common nonetheless." Fredrick sighed as he finished the thought. The king of Kalen wasn't the only one who was angered by the lowborn status of Eduardo's second wife. Many of Harderior's own nobles had been outraged. Relations with Kalen had quickly gone sour after that, a series of unpleasant incidents that descended into all-out war as the years passed.

"He's obsessed." Gregor said, voicing the silent thought that was even then going through the general's mind.

"He's our king. Don't talk treason in the command tent of his Majesty's armies." General Fredrick cast one significant glance towards the dangling tent flaps. Gregor flushed and looked down, though he had spoken too quietly for anyone else to hear. They were the sort of words it wasn't wise to voice, true or not.

"Well the problem seems to have solved itself." Gregor said finally, helping himself to the barrel of water sitting next to a tent pole. "His Majesty found a new bride, apparently both noble enough and mage enough to satisfy."

"I still wonder where he managed to find one. At this point every king, noble, and mage school in the region knows what King Eduardo is up to. He's already managed to work his way through four wives. Any mage within reach is already fled or in his control." The general paused, knowing that Gregor had more information to share, or he wouldn't have brought the subject up.

"It's the sorcerer Aerigard's niece."

There was a long silence in the tent.

"Seriously?" The general asked, at last impressed. Dark Lord Aerigard had a fearsome reputation indeed. Even powerful demons knew and respected his name. He'd never heard of the Dark Lord having any family though.

"She's supposed to be a powerful archmage in her own right."

"That could be an immense help." The general said, as if to himself. "We could throw back Kalen if we had an archmage here."

"Sir," Gregor said, alarmed, "There's no way His Majesty would risk his new wife on a battlefield!"

"Why not? He sent his only grandson out here." The general eyed his old friend and shrugged. "His Majesty knows, just as we do, how desperate our situation is. I think though, that the time has come to send Prince Darien home. He took far too long to wake up after the last battle. He needs more time to rest and recover fully, and he can't do that here." Unspoken was the thought they both shared that next time the prince might not wake up at all. Fredrick sighed, disappointed. The prince was one of the most reliable mages he'd worked with in the last few months. Gregor wisely didn't comment. He had been asking Fredrick to send Prince Darien home for weeks now, and wasn't inclined to argue now that his request would be granted.

Jannis curtseyed deeply, and remained there on the floor in a pool of silken skirts. King Eduardo barely glanced at her, his eyes examining the twisted metal still hanging from the edges of the windowsill. The captain of his palace guard was supervising the men carrying the two guards out in litters, and his chatelaine was standing to the side, wringing his hands in despair.

"Lady," the captain finally said, turning to her as the wounded men were removed, "Your brother was responsible for this?"

"Yes sir." She replied evenly, still on the floor.

"Were you harmed?" He asked next.

Jannis flushed, glad that her face was down. "Just a scratch, sir."

The king finally noticed her at this point, turning suddenly. "You were harmed?" He asked, face darkening. "Show me."

Jannis stood and lifted her skirt slightly to show the white wrapped bandage stretching along her left calf, stained with a couple spots of red.

"Your Majesty, it isn't a concern truly. I've been injured far worse playing with my brother before."

His face darkened further and Jannis shut her mouth.

"Your brother needs to learn to control himself, it seems. I've already heard about he destroyed Duke Tellis's weyrstone for his own amusement, and now apparently he is climbing the walls and smashing through windows. I don't suppose you know where he is now?"

"No, sire. But..." Jannis paused, and didn't finish the thought.

The captain of the guard finished it for her. "But he can't be that hard to find, Your Majesty. He's a pretty distinctive young man."

"Well, its hardly appropriate for a man of his age to be acting like an overgrown child." The chatelaine interjected finally, outraged at the cost of replacing the two iron grills.

Jannis sighed. "Believe me, good sir, I've been telling him that every day since he was twelve."

Ironically, Lance was in the very last place that anyone bothered to look. He had decided, with a kind of pragmatic wisdom, to go drinking in the middle of the day with the jailers in the dungeon below the castle. After all, sooner or later, he'd get thrown in one of those cells for one of the very many nasty little surprises he was planning, and it was better to have the jailers on his side. Nothing works quite so well to get a bored jailer on your side as a few bottles of fine brandy and a game or two of dice or cards. Hence, with one stop to break into a castle storeroom and steal some of the finest brandy, he made his way unconcerned down into the dungeons, and spent the rest of the day getting horribly drunk and playing cards.

In fact, no one bothered to look in the dungeons at all. It was only after Lance had left the dungeon that the guards found him staggering down the hallway, smelling of liquor. The guards didn't hesitate to seize him and drag him before their increasingly irritated ruler.

"You, sir, are a disgrace." King Eduardo said darkly, eying the disheveled young man before him.

Lance shrugged, unconcerned. The king's face darkened. They were standing in the lesser audience chamber, a handful of uncomfortable guards hovering over their precious prisoner. The king had not been pleased by how long it took to locate the young man.

"Forgive me, but I can't really take the opinion of a man dumb enough to marry my sister seriously," Lance said, blinking stupidly.

The king literally spat with rage, and backhanded Lance across the face, sending him crashing to the floor.

"Unexpected side bonus!" Lance declared delightedly from the floor as he realized that the massive amount of alcohol he had consumed was blunting the pain. "In all seriousness, Your Majesty, if you get this mad over a couple of broken windows and a couple of bottles of brandy, you'll die of a heart attack." Lance wiped his mouth, halfway amused to see blood.

"You assaulted my future queen!"

"Assault is such an ugly word. It was just a fall, an unfortunate accident. Its not like I broke her arm... again... or stabbed her in the chest... again... or, well, suffice it to say my sister is a lot more durable than you give her credit for."

"You stabbed her?!" The king asked with increasing rage.

"It's an almost weekly occurrence," Lance replied dismissively. "You see, that's your problem--you just don't appreciate the kind of relationship I have with my sister. Quite sad really, since you're going to be my future brother-in-law."

The king started to strike him again, and resisted with a

visible effort. "What is wrong with you?" He spat finally.

Lance arched one eyebrow and shrugged. "If the great Dark Lord Aerigard couldn't figure that out after fourteen years of agonizing, I seriously doubt you have the brain power to figure it out. Let's just say that I'm bored."

The king eyed Lance again, disgust clearly written across face. The young man was tall and thin like his uncle and his sister, almost impossibly lean, with a shock of pale blond hair and delicate features. He was also covered in dirt and cobwebs, stank of alcohol, and had a thin trail of blood running down one corner of his mouth.

"It's impossible. This... ruffian.... can't possibly be an archmage. During all his antics, has anyone even seen him cast a spell?"

"Actually, I don't do magic." Lance commented. He grinned mischievously and continued with enthusiasm, "There's actually a really fascinating story behind that. It all happened when I was seven years old, and I broke into my uncle's library...."

"Just, shut up, you moron." The king cut him off with a violent gesture. Lance shrugged and went silent. The king would have been wiser to listen, if he had only known it.

"Chain him and take him to the compound." The king said finally. "As irritating as he is, he's too valuable to kill out of hand. At the very least it would upset my wife. Just keep him out of trouble until the wedding."

The guards bowed deeply and dragged Lance out of the king's presence, not at all inclined to be gentle. Lance looked amused, of all things, at his situation and it only further irritated the guards.

"What the hell is wrong with you?!" The captain of the guard finally snapped, as a not too gentle shove sent Lance sprawling and he responded with amused laughter.

"A miscalculation on my part, how clumsy of me. I thought for sure that the king would throw me in the dungeon. I was looking forward to the torture. And instead I'm getting shipped off to some 'compound'. Do they do torture there?" Lance asked hopefully.

The guard captain looked at Lance silently, unwilling to share any knowledge he may have had, which only invited Lance to continue.

"The best torture my uncle ever did to me was after I shattered his black diamond demon summoning wand." The guards shoved Lance forward as soon as he got to his feet and he continued without pause. "It really took an effort let me tell you, diamond is hard to break! Anyways suffice it to say it involved chili peppers and flesh eating hurricui worms. I still have the scars, do you want to see?"

"No." The captain replied, in clipped tones.

"Took a long time to heal, not as long as the hell hound claw marks though. Did you know that hell hounds are allergic to green onions?" The captain didn't respond, they were almost to the castle gates at this point.

"Sneezing hell hounds can tear holes in the fabric of reality. At least Quilizzoiti can. They are a kind of hell hound, only bigger, hairier and smellier than the usual. They almost smell as bad as decomposing flesh, which is to say, slightly better than the average street beggar."

"Do you ever shut up?" The captain finally inquired. Lance simply shrugged and shook his head.

"Gag him." The captain ordered, already busy speaking to the quartermaster.

———————

The wagon rolled up to a large well-guarded building. It appeared to once have been the country estate of some nobleman, but additional outbuildings changed the character of the building. It was now surrounded by a deep trench, the earth having been piled high to form a kind of embankment studded with sharpened wooden spikes. Dozens of quiet, steely men patrolled in pairs around the grounds. Lance grinned to himself, unable to share his joy vocally with an old rag stuffed in his mouth. He shifted slightly, his chains scraping wood on metal, and without even looking behind him, the guard on the wagon seat slammed the butt of his spear into Lance's gut. The guards had enjoyed Lance's company for several hours now, and the slightest sound from him was liable to provoke violence.

"What do we have here?" The gate guard looked skeptically into the wagon at the chained and gagged man. He was lean and tall, dressed in fine clothes that had seen better days, currently rumpled and covered in dust and dirt, and had pale blonde hair and strange violet eyes. Those eyes sparkled with amusement despite the bruises that were already starting to darken on almost all of his exposed skin. Several streaks of dried blood and newly inflicted gashes were scattered across his skin as well.

"Spawn of misfortune." One of the two guards on the seat commented sarcastically, before the other hushed him.

"Mage. We came from the palace on the king's orders."

"Right. Report to Lord Firin then. Get moving." The gate guard waved them forward, and the wagon started rolling again as the guards urged the mules on.

Lord Firin was a significant part of the king's special project despite his relatively low rank for several reasons. He shared the king's unusual preoccupation with mages and magic in general, but more tellingly, he also possessed a very minor magegift of his own, something he had inherited from his mother. He was also a terribly serious and dedicated kind of person, and despite the tendency to take ill easily, one almost all mages shared, worked very hard to further the king's goals.

He was a very lean man, of average height, and his skin was yellowed and sallow. Although he was only in his late thirties, he looked far older and his sorrowful and serious expression only added to the impression of greater age. He dressed in somber robes, of appropriate quality for a lord of the realm, but unadorned with the gold or embroidery that someone of a greater rank might consider necessary.

The wagon that rolled up in front of Lord Firin was unexpected. Unexpected in Lord Firin's small world meant suspect. His eyes narrowed slightly as the guard hopped down from the seat and saluted.

"Who are you, and what are you doing here?" He asked, eyebrows furrowed.

"Here on the king's orders, brought a new mage. Here he is, and you are welcome to him." With those words, the other guard already hauled Lance out of the back of the wagon and dumped him unceremoniously on the ground at Lord Firin's feet.

Lord Firin gazed skeptically at the young man on the ground, before returning his attention to the two guards. They were already back on the wagon and ready to leave. One of them tossed Lord Firin the keys to Lance's chains.

"Excuse me, but how can you be sure this man is a mage? And if he were one, why is he beaten and chained like this?"

The wagon was already moving. One of the guards called back over his shoulder.

"It's the new queen's rotten little brother--Dark Lord Aerigard's nephew. Good luck; you'll need it."

Lance and Lord Firin regarded each other silently for a few moments, and then Lord Firin pulled the gag out of the other man's mouth.

"Are you truly the new queen's brother?" Lord Firin asked, unconvinced. "The Dark Lord Aerigard's nephew?" Both claims seemed equally outrageous, especially considering the bad condition the young man was in. Lord Firin didn't even know that the sorcerer Aerigard had a nephew.

"That's right." Lance replied, smiling.

"And you are a mage as well, I suppose?"

"Archmage actually. But I don't do magic."

"An archmage that doesn't do magic? How... odd." At this point Lord Firin didn't believe a word the young man said.

Archmages were exceptionally rare, and one certainly wouldn't appear out of the blue like this. Lord Firin had searched in vain for years for an archmage, on the king's orders.

"There's actually a really interesting story behind it," Lance said, warming instantly to the story that had been interrupted earlier. "It happened when I was seven years old and I broke into my uncle's library. He was always a rotten liar, and telling us that the sixth floor was only cookbooks, I mean, please. Of course I knew that's where he kept his copy of the Necromonicon." At this point Lord Firin held up his hand for silence, and for the second time Lance had to halt his tale. Lance sighed. It really was such a good story too.

"Well you're quite a creative liar, young man. But I really don't have time to listen to your tales. Get up and follow me. Even if you aren't a mage, you look strong enough to do some work around here. Tell your friends not to use me for their practical jokes next time. I take it you are one of the castle guards?"

"You could at least pretend to believe me." Lance said, sighing. "And I got into so much trouble after I broke into the palace storehouse and stole that brandy. The Captain got pissed, let me tell you! Maybe I shouldn't have told him that I was tortured by flesh eating worms."

"Getting beaten and chained up is probably getting off easily for theft. The palace guard captain is one strict commander. How long have you been at the palace anyway?"

"Only a couple of days, but I'm afraid they already have me pegged as a troublemaker." Lance shrugged. "It won't be the first place I've been thrown out of."

Lance followed Lord Firin inside the main building, his eyes taking a few moments to adjust as they went from the bright light of the afternoon sun into the dimly lit interior. What windows were there had been barred or shuttered, preventing much light from entering. Lord Firin led Lance to a shrewish fat woman commanding a force of harried-looking sexless young drudges and a handful of stronger, slightly older men.

"This trouble-making soldier needs a little hard work to curb his lying tongue," Lord Firin said, by way of an introduction.

"I'm an archmage." Lance said, irritated. "One more powerful than the Dark Lord Aerigard, who happens to be my miserable two-faced uncle."

"Right," the woman said, eying him like a piece of meat. "Get those shackles off, and then get to work."

Lord Firin wordlessly handed Lance the key and left, too much of his valuable time already wasted. Lance turned the key in the lock, and dropped the shackles on the floor, looking up at the woman expectantly. She growled at him.

"No, you idiot, get those damn chains out of here! Too much iron, it will make all the mages horribly sick if they get close to it. I don't know what you were thinking even bringing those in here! Lord Firin won't be able to eat tonight after being in close quarters with so much iron."

"Your mages must be singularly useless if the mere sight of iron makes them sick. How are they supposed to function on a battlefield, for example?" Lance said, as he gathered the chains back up and stalked back outside.

At his return, Lance discovered that the fat old woman and her crew had already christened him with a not-quite-loving nickname.

"Well, Archmage, I have a pile of firewood that needs chopping behind the South building near the ovens. I hope that's not too far beyond your considerable ability."

"My lady, nothing is beyond my ability." Lance replied, smiling and bowing mockingly. He turned to find the firewood.

———————

Jannis found her days more and more restrictive. After two weeks at the castle, she had not heard one word from her brother. The king would not permit her to leave the suite of rooms he had assigned her. Supposedly to ensure the safety of his new bride, he had assigned a personal physician to her, in addition to the troupe of irritating ladies-in-waiting.

They followed her around like a bevy of startled birds, hanging on her every word and movement. Standing and walking were apparently too difficult for a delicate lady of breeding, and the slightest cough resulted in a detailed examination by her ever-attendant physician.

In other words, Jannis was going slowly mad with inactivity, both physical and mental. The result was almost inevitable.

She coughed delicately and mimed a swoon. A moistened cloth quickly replaced the one that fell off her forehead. The hovering physician checked her throat gently and shook his head, concerned.

"I'm not ill, truly, good sir. I'm simply allergic to peas."

Jannis wasn't at all allergic to peas, though she hated them passionately. Tonight's dinner had to her disgust strongly featured peas. She had tried valiantly to avoid them all, but she was sure she had accidentally eaten at least a few.

"You should have told us that, my Lady. I saw how you tried to eat around them, but there is no excuse. I'll be sure the kitchen knows straight away to keep peas out of your food."

"I will be fine, doctor." Jannis coughed again, and tried to look pathetic. "I just need some rest." She paused for dramatic effect.

"Could you all, please, leave so I can rest?" She widened her eyes pleadingly, and she thought, pathetically.

The physician smiled down at her, consolingly. Jannis resisted the sudden urge to laugh. She carefully kept her face schooled in the expression of exhaustion and weakness.

"Of course, my Lady, your health is of the utmost concern. Please, get as much rest as you need. I'll make sure no one disturbs you."

Jannis sighed and closed her eyes. All of her ladies-in-waiting filed silently out of the bedroom wringing their hands, the physician closing the door as quietly as possible behind them, and Jannis was finally alone.

She faked sleep for a few more minutes until she was certain they were all gone and then rose stealthily from the bed, pulling off the elaborate gown that she had been wearing. After all, she had been so ill that the ladies-in-waiting hadn't even bothered to undress her. It was like unwrapping a package, unlacing all the ties and pulling off the petticoats. Jannis was sweating and tired by the time she was finally standing there in her shift.

She searched in the layers of bedding for the dark brown tunic and leggings she had hidden there, finding them after some effort and pulling them on in place of her elaborate gown. Now the only thing that marked her as the king's new bride was her startling silver hair and her violet eyes. Patiently, she braided her long silver hair, wrapping it up around her head and out of the way before pulling on a light-weight cloak of the same dark brown.

Wordlessly, Jannis considered the heavy iron filigree on her window, paned with colored glass to keep out the night's chill. And keep her in, she thought, irritated. She snapped a few arcane words, sliding one finger around the edge of the window pane.

The windowpane slid effortlessly from the stone of the wall, surprising her with its weight. It was heavy! All that glass and metal weighed her down and almost made her drop it. She eased it down to the floor as quietly as she could, biting her lip with the effort of ignoring her sore fingers.

Jannis glanced out the window. It was another hour before the sun set, but she didn't think she could wait that long. Jannis decided to risk it, considering. The wall was rough hewn stone, and she would have preferred to use a rope to get down, but there wasn't a rope in her rooms so she didn't worry about the matter further.

Instead, Jannis muttered a few more strange words under her breath and crawled out onto the wall. A spell that temporarily lightened her body weight would let her climb down the wall without too much effort as long as she was careful. In any case,

Jannis already knew where she was going.

It was time to get some exercise.

Chapter 4

"I heard your uncle sold his soul to the devil," one of the other workmen commented as Lance sat down next to him with his lunch.

"Really?" Lance said, unsurprised. "The devil, himself? Sounds like an exaggeration to me. The devil rarely has time to make pacts with mortals personally. It was probably just an arch-demon."

The others laughed. Lance ignored them.

"So you ever summon a demon, Archmage?"

"Well, yeah. I've summoned Maliad Heriophant, the Demon of Perpetual Flatulence."

Half of the men listening started laughing, and the other half sat there confused. Lance sighed as his superior wit fell wasted on the uneducated ears of his listeners. One of the brighter men clarified for the rest.

"That's the Farting Imp, you morons, flatulence means fart!"

"You see," Lance began in hurt tones, "It's not as funny if you have to explain it."

"Kid, you're really a hoot. It's like you believe your crazy stories." The workman next to him slapped Lance on the back. Lance simply arched one eyebrow and didn't bother to clarify.

"So why don't you do some magic for us, Archmage? Snap your fingers and make sparks fly out of Callie's fat bum." Snickers and grins accompanied the comment and Lance ignored them all.

"How many times do I have to tell you? I don't do magic."

"Right, an archmage that doesn't do magic." This voice was full of scornful amusement. None of them believed a word he said, and quite frankly, Lance wasn't inclined to correct them. Years spent under the watchful eye of the most powerful dark mage in the world had taught Lance one thing: the absolute best lie was the unvarnished truth. Tell someone the truth without hesitation and that person would automatically assume you were lying. It helped that the truth about Lance's life was particularly unbelievable. He sighed and accepted the inevitable.

"I'd turn her into an elephant if I thought it would help." Lance said instead, grinning.

"What's an elephant?"

"Extremely large, ugly gray animal with wrinkled skin and a horribly long nose."

A scrawny, rheumy-looking mage was watching him now, so Lance stopped there and finished his food without further comment. Lance didn't say another word as he got back to work, vanishing quickly down the hallway, taking trays of food to those mages too weak to leave their rooms.

Callie noticed the mage's gaze and hurried over to him.

"Did the Archmage do anything to bother you, m'Lord?" She asked, concerned.

"No," he replied absently. "I was just listening to his stories."

"Oh that," Callie rolled her eyes, "Such an imagination. That's why we all call him 'Archmage.' First day, he was claiming to be one."

"He seems to be an interesting fellow, I think I'll go have a word with him."

———————

The mage caught up to Lance easily, especially since Lance had to stop constantly, moving from door to door with the food he carried. The trays were made of a lightweight wood, each with a kind of footing on it that stacked on top of the other, allowing Lance to carry half a dozen trays with ease.

"You're a lot smarter than you look." The mage said, as he

approached the tall young man in the hall. Lance regarded him with bored eyes.

"Don't you have better things to do than follow people to randomly insult? I happen to believe that I look very smart indeed."

"Of course," the mage replied, forcing a smile. "That wasn't what I meant. I just haven't heard of the elephant since my studies in zoology. It doesn't even live on this continent. I'm surprised you know of it."

"The benefits of a classical education." Lance droned, his face emotionless.

"And then there's Maliad Heriophant..." The mage began, stopping suddenly at Lance's upraised hand.

"The wise mage doesn't speak the name of a demon outside of a warding circle, lest he accidentally summon it. Are you a moron or something?" Lance asked, irritated.

"And yet, you did."

"I'm not a mage, I'm an archmage. Besides which, I don't do magic. Imitating me is dangerous. Don't blame me if there is a sudden increase in uncontrollable gas in the compound." Lance turned and walked to the next door, the smaller mage following in his footsteps.

"I've got work to do," Lance protested, irritated.

"Just who are you?" The crippled-looking little mage gazed up at him curiously, and Lance sighed.

"I'm Lord Lance Solaran, the most powerful archmage on the continent and nephew of the sorcerer Aerigard. My sister is marrying the king in a little over a week. The king, Eddy, got a little irritated when I stole a few bottles of brandy and smashed a window. He slapped me and then sent me here in chains. If you ask me, he has a serious personality disorder."

The two of them stared at each other wordlessly for a moment, and then the mage looked down at the two trays still in Lance's hands.

"And you're serving lunch."

"Life's strange that way."

"Are you a lunatic?"

"I get that question a lot." Lance smiled winningly. "Especially from my sister."

"You are definitely an interesting fellow. Have you already met Lord Firin?"

"Of course. I met him the first day I got here."

"And you told him you were an archmage."

"Naturally."

"And you told him you were the new queen's brother and Dark Lord Aerigard's nephew."

"Indeed." Lance stopped at a door and knocked, opening it slightly to place the tray just inside.

"What did he say?"

"That I was a very creative liar." Lance delivered the last tray in his hands and started back towards the kitchen. He smirked at the mage trailing him, and couldn't help but add, "It amuses me no end to let you idiots believe what you want to believe."

"I don't believe you either." The mage said at last.

"Right. Then why are you following me around like this?"

"It's just my sense of morbid curiosity. You're a fascinating fellow."

"Are you going to follow me all day?"

"Maybe. It's not like I have anything better to do." The mage replied, grimly.

"I suppose you can lessen my boredom then. Are you familiar with hurricui worms?"

"Flesh eating worms from the western nation of Kalen? I've heard of them, but I've never seen one."

"They gave me a really neat looking scar, would you like to see it?"

———————

Jannis found the barracks of the castle guard quite easily, and the small well-used practice field outside of it. A quick can-trap to change her hair and eyes a mousy brown for a few hours and no one would be the wiser. More elaborate illusion spells could be quite a bother, but a brief color change was an instant's work. She smiled softly to herself as she walked out onto the practice field, a heavy wooden practice sword in one hand, and shield in the other. At this time of day there were quite a few of the palace guard hacking and slashing at the crude wooden practice dummies lined up along one side of the field.

Jannis ignored them. Finding an unoccupied spot, she did a handful of test swings to get the feel for the unfamiliar wooden sword. She didn't attract any more attention than a few curious glances, and so Jannis started into a more advanced set of movements. Maybe if she'd been really good with a sword she would have attracted more attention, but Jannis was fighting against the double handicap of her painfully lean body structure and her gender. As such, she was only average as a swordsman, and not of enough importance to attract much attention.

There were a handful of women in the palace guard, but not that many, and if she did get a glance or two, it was probably only because she was a woman, and an attractive one at that. An hour later, sweating and exhausted, the sun setting, Jannis returned the practice equipment to the room she had found them. Unwilling to return to the stuffy embrace of her rooms, instead she followed one of the other guards into the barracks and down to the common room.

———————

Lord Firin had a very disturbing message on his desk. It had arrived earlier that morning with the latest batch of supplies and mage children that the king had managed to round up. He frowned, and a deep furrow appeared in his wan face. Lord Firin sighed heavily, and put his elbows on the desk, resting his chin in his hands.

This is what the message said:

Firin:

I hope that worthless sot hasn't caused you too much trouble. Please stop beating him now so that he will look presentable for the wedding. My bride will only get upset if she sees her brother covered in bruises. Send him back to the palace with the wagon we send you the day before the wedding. Also, my grandson arrived back from the front lines to recover, apparently they are having a hard time of it and need more mages.

Eddy

The informal nature of the message didn't bother Lord Firin. At this point he and the king had been working hand-in-hand on Eduardo's private obsession for years, and a certain degree of camaraderie had sprung up between them. No, what bothered Lord Firin was the content.

The door swung open to admit the man Lord Firin had been waiting for, one of his most valuable mages, a man who had lived to, what was for a mage, a ripe old age. He wasn't much to look at, being scrawny, even for a mage, and only of about average height. He looked permanently ill, with dark circles under his eyes and his skin overlaid with a perpetual shade of gray.

"Where have you been?" Firin demanded, rising as he entered.

"Nowhere important, just chatting with an unusual young man."

"Well, we're in the middle of a crisis. Apparently, the king sent his new wife's brother out here to the compound and now no one knows where he is."

"Chopping firewood." The other man supplied, helping himself to the chair across from Lord Firin.

"Excuse me?" Firin stared at the other mage.

"The young man in question, Lord Lance Solaran, just finished serving lunch and now Callie has him chopping firewood. Not exactly what I would call appropriate work for an archmage, but nothing seems to dampen his mood, or his ego."

"Then, he's safe? Wait, you just said 'archmage'?"

"Honestly, Lord Firin, I'm surprised you didn't notice when you first laid eyes on him. He's so powerful he distorts magical energy around him. And it's interacting with something, some spell of frightful complexity. Of course, it's a very localized phenomenon- you wouldn't see it unless you were very close."

The door opened then, and the young man in question walked in. Wordlessly, he placed a large, obnoxious-looking hat on the desk.

"You left that on the woodpile." Lance remarked, arching one eyebrow at the scrawny mage. Without another word he turned and walked back towards the door to leave.

"Stop!" Lord Firin called, torn between relief and panic. Of course, now that he knew what he was looking for, he could see it with his mage sight-- a shell of flowing magic just above the young man's skin, dense, delicate and immensely powerful. It was a spell of some sort, a master's work, clean and flawless. Lord Firin forced a smile.

"Please, come sit down."

Lance stood there for a few moments longer, expressionless, and then turned back towards them. He took two measured steps and sat in a third chair, also across from Lord Firin's desk. Lord Firin tried to smile more naturally. He reached for the pitcher of wine on the upper left corner of his desk and poured three goblets, handing one to each of his two guests.

Lance took the goblet wordlessly, held it up to his nose and sniffed it, then set it back on the desk untouched.

"This must be a country of raging alcoholics. Don't you people drink coffee, or tea, or globis?"

"Globis?!" The scrawny mage next to him looked at him with an expression of horror.

"Okay, okay, I know it's made from demon's blood and crushed marsh lizard eyeballs, but it isn't half bad. It's a far cry better than half the potions Uncle's shoved down my throat over the years. My sister prefers Turkish coffee like Uncle, but I can't stand the stuff, reminds me of boiled boot leather." Lance crossed his arms in front of him, and shrugged.

"I see." Lord Firin said, setting his own goblet down, also untasted. "I remember you now. You got here almost two weeks ago. You were... claiming... to be the nephew of the sorcerer Aerigard... and an... archmage..." Lord Firin paused, flushing. He had never even considered the possibility that the young man had been telling the truth. His claims had simply been too far-fetched, and no mage would have stood the touch of cold iron so easily. No mage would have been beaten by the guards when the king horded them and sheltered them like rare treasures. No mage would have looked so healthy and strong. Would he?

"See, I feel insulted. I never lied to any of you. Is it really that hard to believe that I'm an archmage?"

"No one's ever seen you cast a spell." The scrawny mage added helpfully.

"I. Don't. Do. Magic." Lance said with finality, biting off each word. "Not like my suck-up sister, she learned a bit just for the hell of it."

"Then what's that spell?" Lord Firin asked, gesturing to Lance.

"Just some of my uncle's work," Lance replied dismissively. "It isn't important."

"Is that what keeps you so healthy?" Lord Firin asked, immensely curious.

Lance laughed. "No, that's a family trait. My sister doesn't have a spell like this on her, and she's as healthy as a horse, or a goat, or whatever other hairy, smelly animal you want to compare her to. In fact, I don't think the sickliness of mages affects any archmage. How many do you have here?"

There was a long pause. There weren't any archmages in the king's breeding program, and not for lack of effort. Archmages were not only extremely rare, but smart, elusive, and not particularly interested in falling into Eduardo's hands.

"Right." Lance commented helpfully into the silence. "Well I've met other archmages before who came to visit Uncle over the years, and none of them looked sick, well, except one, but that wasn't sickness, it was poison. A rather long story I don't want to go into right now," Lance paused inconsequentially, about to stand up on the spot with or without Lord Firin's approval. "Can I go now?"

Lord Firin was at a loss for words for a moment, he had never considered the possibility that archmages wouldn't suffer from the same malady as common mages, but it made perfect sense now that he thought about it. Lance's last comment finally pierced the fog of his contemplation and he started.

"No, no, I'm afraid that's not possible." Lord Firin's mind was frantically working. He'd had an archmage here for almost two weeks without even knowing about it, and that same archmage was leaving in less than a week to return to the palace. For all these years he had been trying to find one, suddenly one had just appeared out of nowhere. It was as if some diety was playing a cosmic joke on them all. "The king will send a wagon for you in another five days. You'll have to stay here until then."

Lance looked at him as if he were an idiot. "I meant this room. Callie asked me to clean out the kitchen fire pit. Quite frankly, you aren't a great conversationalist. If you were intelligent you would have realized what I was the first day. If you had half a brain you would have at least checked my story and found out a couple of days later. The fact that you are only now realizing it tells me you are a complete moron. I've got work to do. Good-bye."

Lance stood then, and stalked towards the door despite Lord Firin's feeble protests behind him. He actually made it almost all the way to the kitchen before the guards seized him from behind.

"Good afternoon. Can I help you?" He inquired mildly of the four men who had grabbed his arms in a vice-like grip and started dragging him back down the hallway towards Lord Firin's office. None of them replied, so Lance simply shrugged and decided not to resist. Resisting might have been fun, but he had been working too hard to restrain himself over the past two weeks to ruin it now.

Lord Firin stood out in front of his desk now, the other scrawny mage gone. There was a strange light in Firin's eyes, one that Lance had seen many times before in his Uncle's eyes. Lance sighed to himself. If you've seen it once, you can always recognize it. That light of madness: Obsession.

"He's beautiful." Lord Firin said quietly to himself, staring at Lance possessively.

"Why thank you, Lord Firin. But you really aren't my type." Lance replied flippantly. "Callie's going to be really upset if that fire pit doesn't get swept out. Is this really necessary?" Lance glanced at the armed guards still clutching his arms.

"That fat sow has more than enough help. It's appalling to think of an archmage doing such menial labor."

Of course, Lance had been thinking that very same thing the entire time he was at the compound, but he wouldn't have been a very good spy if he had refused to do work and been found out. Sometimes you have to make sacrifices for the greater good. So he didn't bother arguing with Lord Firin's very well-made point.

"If I wanted to run," Lance added helpfully, "Don't you think I would have done it while you were still thinking I was the hired help? Or do you really want to rough me up? It might be fun, if you don't mind your guards getting a little damaged in the process."

Lord Firin was still staring at the young man with that disturbing look in his eyes, possessively, but his eyes narrowed in consideration at Lance's words.

"Release him. He can't escape, and I'd like to talk to him more privately."

The guards removed their hands and Lance half-halfheartedly rubbed his arms where they had been holding him. He'd have bruises there, if he cared.

"I'd really rather not talk to you. As I've already said, you're a lousy conversationalist. This may come as a surprise to you, but I hate mages and magic in general. I'm actually a swordsman, and a damn good one. If you want to talk about magic, you'd have to talk to my uncle, he loves that nonsense."

"You really are an odd young man. An archmage who hates magic? It's like a bird that hates to fly or a fish that hates to swim. Just have a seat, Lord Lance."

"Whatever." Lance shrugged and sat in the same chair he had sat in previously, this time putting his feet up on the desk. Lord Firin turned, taking a step forward so that he stood within arms reach right in front and slightly to the side of where Lance sat. Lord Firin bent down, reaching out and grasping Lance's wrist, and running his other hand up the younger man's arm.

"What do you think you're doing? I'm not a doll." Lance commented flatly, but did not resist. Firin was shocked at the hard, wiry muscles that covered the younger man. Obviously the comment about being a swordsman had not been a jest. Just because Lance was lean did not make him weak. He simply had the kind of body that didn't bulk up with physical labor. But when Firin's hand touched Lance's chest, the younger man slapped it away.

"Look, you really aren't my type, Lord Firin, and there is only so much pawing I'm going to tolerate. Is there a point to this?"

"Of course. I didn't mean to offend you." Lord Firin resisted the urge to touch the young man again, smiled tightly, and walked back around his desk, finally taking a seat. Two of the guards were still by the door, but the other two had disappeared.

"It's just that you are in far better physical condition than I would have expected."

"Hours of sword practice a day have that effect," Lance interjected dryly. "And even since I've been here, I haven't exactly been doing light work."

"How old are you, if I may ask?" Firin looked sincerely curious.

"What is this strange facination with my age, lately? I'm eighteen, if it matters."

Firin blinked, but his expression did not change.

"Not that it applies to you, as an archmage, but most mages don't live that long. The majority die during childhood from wasting sickness. I'm sure you know what we are trying to accomplish, since you've been working here for almost two weeks. This is a breeding facility."

Lance knew. Most of the mages in the building were so weak they could barely stand. There were girls barely teenagers lying sick in beds, their bellies swollen with pregnancy. There was a graveyard behind the northern building where he had been assigned off and on to digging graves for the sick children who died of wasting disease. It was appalling. Lance said nothing.

"We have an unfortunate shortage of adult mages because so many die young. You are a very rare commodity, Lord Lance."

"You know," Lance said, crossing his arms, "I'm not very impressed with your facility. Quite frankly, it's a death sentence. I've been on grave digging duty a lot. Callie tends to give it to people who annoy her." Lance was good at annoying people.

"An unfortunate reality, I'm afraid." Lord Firin smiled sadly. "Mages simply aren't hardy enough to live very long. Most mages, anyway. You don't seem to have that problem. I really wish they wouldn't die. We do everything we can to try to save them." That much was true, there was a large staff of physicians on hand at the compound to shove various potions down the mages' throats all day long.

Lance and Firin sat for a long moment, silently regarding each other. Lance knew what Firin's oddly possessive look meant, and sighed again.

"You're wasting your time, you know. I'm not interested in any of the thin, wasted, miserably sick, barely pubescent girls here. Quite frankly, it's disgusting and offensive that you are even thinking it."

"It would be so much easier for everyone if you would just cooperate, Lord Lance."

Lance shrugged. "That really doesn't concern me. I'm not a very cooperative person by nature."

Lord Firin didn't seem very concerned by Lance's refusal.

"Take him to his room," Lord Firin said to the guards still waiting by the door.

———————

Lance waited until they were out in the hallway and outside of hearing range of Lord Firin's office before he slammed their heads together. Just another sign of the sheer contempt these people had for his substantial skills. Lance shook his head sadly. The fact that he had been deliberately cultivating that underestimation didn't change his opinion. It really was just an indication of how stupid they all were for not realizing it sooner.

The two guards drifted noisily to the ground, making a series of soft thumps and clangs as their arms, knees and helmets hit the floor. Lance sighed and contemplated again the sad fate of wasting his brilliant combat skills on such unworthy opponents. He could have easily taken all four of the guards earlier, let alone two.

The problem now was what to do with himself for the five days until the wagon came to take him to the palace. The most obvious answer, to escape and return to the palace early, he dismissed at once. He didn't dismiss it because of difficulty, actually Lance didn't think it would be that hard to get out of this place, but rather because it was a waste of time. There was still a lot of information he needed, and not much time left.

In the end, the answer was a simple one. Lance found his way, stealthily, to the room of a particular mage, the same scrawny, sickly looking mage who had been so interested in elephants and flesh-eating worms earlier. Obviously the man was well educated, and knew something of what Lord Firin and the king were up to.

The door was locked, but Lance had no problem letting

himself in. The room was empty; obviously the mage was busy elsewhere. Lance philosophically stretched out on the mage's bed and took a nap. Somehow he suspected that he would need to be well-rested once Lord Firin's thugs found him.

While Lance indulged in stolen sleep, Jannis contemplated her fate. She sat, nursing a cup of poor watered wine, in the common room of the castle barracks with the off-duty guards. The room was about half full, but for some strange reason no one sat near her. Irritated, her beautiful face twisted into a very unladylike snarl.

Her arrival in the common room was inevitable. After sparring with practice dummies for about half an hour, Jannis had challenged a likely off-duty guard to a friendly bout. They had thoroughly bludgeoned each other with the dull, weighted practice swords, and then Jannis had followed the pack of guards as they left the practice field in search of something to drink. Anything had to be better than going back to her room. What she couldn't understand was why everyone avoided her like the plague. She would drown her vague dissatisfaction in her cup, if the wine were better quality. Instead, she sipped at it, and grimaced.

A heavy wooden chair scraped at the rough stone floor very loudly, very close. Jannis startled, as one of the guards sat down next to her. She eyed him critically, noting that his uniform was clean and relatively free of wrinkles, his face regularly shaved, except for a carefully cultivated goatee. Deciding that he looked halfway intelligent, she resolved not to give him a hard time, and maybe she could get a decent conversation out of him.

He chuckled, amused, and sipped at his own mug.

"Do I pass?" His voice was mellow and full of good humor.

"Excuse me?"

"I feel like I was just weighed, measured, and stamped with that look. You could give gorgons lessons." The smile on his face took away the sting of the insult. "So do I pass?"

"I suppose so." Jannis said casually, turning back to her watered wine. "Better company than the wine. And better than most in this room."

"You haven't been here long I take it."

"No, only arrived recently. Why?"

"Well, I make a point of knowing all the guards on my shift, and your face was unfamiliar. Very attractive, despite the ice princess act, and you're halfway decent with a sword. Surprising really, you're so thin and delicate I would have thought you would snap like a twig."

"I'm trying to decide if you are complimenting or insulting me."

He chuckled again, genuinely amused. "Lieutenant Flemming. And you are?"

"Disgusted with the quality of this wine. Name's Lydia. And I haven't been here very long at all, as you already guessed."

"What's with the attitude? You would be far more attractive if you were a little less thorn and a little more rose."

"I don't have an attitude. At least I don't think I do. Have you ever met my brother? Now he has an attitude."

"No, and somehow I don't think I want to. It was nice to meet you Lydia, and I just hope you thaw out a bit once you get to know us. The guard is a group of halfway decent guys--you should give them all a chance. If you do, you could make a lot of friends here. It's always better that way, comrades in arms, all that stuff. Consider it an order." Lieutenant Flemming winked at her, and pushed back his chair to leave.

"Wait." Jannis flinched internally, cursing herself for her weakness. She sounded pathetic. "You could stay, and talk a little more... I mean, if you wanted to."

"Not used to people much, are you?" Lieutenant Flemming sat back down, smiling.

"I grew up in a swamp. So, no, didn't get much opportunity to talk to people."

"Well, I'm sure you're a really sweet girl somewhere under there. Here, try a smile."

"A... smile?" Jannis paused, confused.

"I'm sure you have a beautiful smile. You don't have to look so sour all the time. Is life really that bad?" Lieutenant Flemming's face was warm and open. Jannis resisted the urge to snap back that indeed life was that bad, which is why she had snuck out of her room, disguised her hair and was currently hiding in the castle guard's common room drinking lousy wine.

"I can try." She said instead, and twisted her lips upward.

"A little more natural; you make it look painful. I take it you don't smile much. Try thinking of something that makes you really happy, or something really funny, and just let your face move the way it wants to."

"You make it sound so simple."

"It is that simple, just try it."

Jannis took a deep breath and imagined the funniest thing she could think of, which was Lance fallen flat on his face in the mud, with his rump in the air. The thought made one corner of her mouth creep upwards in amusement.

"There, now that's a smile." The lieutenant flashed his own gleaming smile at her and winked again. "A little one, but it's a good place to start. I think we might just thaw you after all, ice princess."

Jannis smiled then, a real, genuine, honest-to-god smile like she hadn't smiled in a very long time. Of course, it was at that moment that a door slammed and shouting began, ruining it. Feet and chairs scraping the floor sounded all over the room. Jannis hesitated, unsure and confused.

"What...?"

"Get up, everyone's being called to duty. It's an emergency." Lieutenant Flemming was brisk, efficient and military in his movements and his words. He started gesturing and shouting over the crowd, and the guards vanished at his direction through every doorway. Jannis set her mug down on the table and stood, still confused and waiting for direction.

"What happened? What do I do?"

He paused for a moment. "The king's new bride has been stolen from her room. The window was removed with magic. If you're unfamiliar with the castle, I doubt you would be much help with the search, but if you go relieve the guards protecting Prince Darien's room, they could help with the search."

"Right. Where do you want me?"

Jannis found herself in a tower. The lieutenant's decision made a solid kind of military sense. The previous two guards on Prince Darien's room were older, seasoned veterans more suited to a large scale search than an untrained guard. Prince Darien couldn't be left unguarded, but any idiot could watch a door.

Jannis debated returning to her room or turning herself in, but the fear of what the king might do kept her there at that door. If she waited until after the frenzy died down, she could find one of the search parties outside of the castle walls and blame Kalen, that kingdom that Eduardo was at war with, for kidnapping her and claim she had gotten away. Or, if that would cause too much trouble, blame Lance. He was always good for that.

A weak voice from the other side of the door startled her out of her thoughts. She was really going to have to start paying more attention to what was going on around her. Jannis grasped the bronze door handle and cracked the door open quietly, so she wouldn't disturb the sleeping prince inside, if he was still asleep.

"...water..." A hoarse, barely audible voice croaked from the bed. Jannis gingerly slid the door the rest of the way open, slid herself into the room, and slid the door back closed.

"Your Highness? Do you need something?" She inquired, glancing around the darkened room. It was so dark she could barely see the darker bulk in the corner that had to be the bed.

"Water." He repeated, louder, his voice cracking. Jannis

strode over to the window, heavily draped in what looked like brocaded silk, and thrust back the curtains, letting the last of the setting sun pour into the room. The light fell on a large dark wood four poster bed, plump with downy pillows and blankets.

It looked like the bed had been made for the pillows and not for its occupant at all, a tiny, weak boy almost unnoticeable in the pile of blankets. A silver pitcher sat on a small mahogany table to the left of the bed, tiny beads of water clinging to its outside. A lovely silver goblet sat next to it, and an assortment of tiny vials of various colors. Jannis wrinkled her nose at those, but strode over to the bed and poured water into the goblet. She started to hand the goblet to the boy, and then stopped, unsure.

"Your Highness, can you sit up?"

He shook his head weakly. Jannis set the goblet back down on the table and gently slid her hands under Prince Darien's shoulders. She lifted him up into a sitting position and stuffed a few of those plump pillows behind his back to help hold him upright. Then she retrieved the goblet and held it to his lips, letting him drink slowly.

"Don't you have attendants or something?" Jannis asked, surprised that the boy would be abandoned like this. He gulped the water like someone near dying of thirst.

"They didn't expect me to wake up so soon." Darien said softly, and coughed, his whole body spasming. "The medicine makes me sleep."

"Well, it must not be working very well, you look horrible." Jannis said without thinking, and then blushed.

Darien laughed weakly. He was very sick, his face pale, his skin tinted an unhealthy yellow, large dark circles under his eyes, and he was so thin that he almost looked more like a skeleton than a boy.

"That wasn't a very nice thing to say, but don't worry, you didn't hurt my feelings. I'm just glad to be home. It's so much better than being out with the army. And Grandfather comes to see me every day."

"Do you need anything else?" Jannis was genuinely concerned, the boy looked like he needed food, sleep, water, medicine and anything else at hand to keep him alive.

"Just someone to talk to. It gets lonely, and I'm too tired to play."

"I suppose I could sit a minute and talk."

"You're very pretty, I don't think I've seen you before."

"Well, I'm kinda new in the palace guard," Jannis hedged, blushing slightly. "And they've never given me the duty guarding your door before."

"Where is the other guard?"

"He was called away to some emergency," Jannis said offhandedly, and shrugged, as if she didn't know anything more about it.

"You don't act much like a guard, but I guess you can't be a spy or anything, cause you would have killed me already if you were." Darien said it in a matter-of-fact way, and Jannis was momentarily shocked. But then she paused, and realized that even a small boy had to grow up fast if he were a prince in a kingdom at war.

Darien started coughing, and his whole body shook with the effort. Jannis grew very concerned.

"You really don't look well, are you sure I shouldn't fetch the doctor?"

Darien laughed, weakly.

"All mages are sick; it's nothing special. And I'm a lot better now than I was."

"You said earlier that being here was better than being with the army. What were you doing with the army?"

"Magic. They need mages bad. It was really horrible. I think killing people was worse than the being scared all the time, but that was pretty bad too. I hated it, but I had to. At least General Frederick was nice to me."

"I guess I just find it hard to believe that the king would send his only grandson, a little boy, to the front lines of a battle."

"I'm not that little." Darien said, his pride wounded. "I'm almost eight years old."

"Right, I'm sorry. It just sounded like your grandfather really loves you, so why would he put you in danger?"

"I don't think he had a choice." Darien said, with surprising insight. "We're losing. Lots of mages are dying, and we don't have enough. Kalen's going to win. And then, I'd die anyway." He finished, sadly.

"You can't think like that, your Highness."

"Maybe the woman who is marrying my Grandfather can help. People say she's an archmage. I know they are getting married soon."

"I'd heard that too, actually." Jannis said, straight-faced. "But do you really think the king would let her go? I mean, he has to want to keep her safe."

"You're probably right," Darien said, deflated. "And she's only a girl anyway. How could she help?"

"Oh I don't know, girls can do a lot more than you might think." Jannis said, and Darien flushed.

"I'm sorry, you're a girl, too, aren't you? I didn't mean to be rude."

"I'm used to it, but that doesn't mean it doesn't hurt." Jannis said.

"What's it like to be a girl and a soldier?" Darien asked, his eyes bright.

"I guess, its like always trying to be the best and always knowing you never can be, because you will always be weaker and slower. But, you don't stop trying. Do you know what I mean?"

"I do, I do actually." Darien said, and he seemed to be seriously considering what she had said. "It's like being a kid on a battlefield with adults all around. I'm not strong enough, not good enough, but I try and try and try."

"Why do you try so hard?"

Darien shrugged. "Because I have to? Maybe? Or because I want to make Grandfather proud?"

"It must be hard to be a prince."

"Yeah, I guess." Darien looked pretty upset, and Jannis didn't know why.

"Are you alright?"

"I guess."

"I know something's bothering you. What is it?"

"It's a secret."

"I see." Jannis paused and the silence hung heavy between them.

"Promise not to tell anyone?" Darien asked hopefully.

"Of course." Jannis made a crossing motion across the surface of the leather armor covering her chest.

"I have to save Harderior. I have to. Because my mom died so I could live; I have to do it for her." Darien pulled a small locket out of the collar of his nightshirt. He opened it and looked fondly at the contents. Jannis couldn't make it out but she presumed it was a tiny portrait of his mother painted inside.

The silence was painful between them. Jannis struggled awkwardly. She really didn't know what to say.

"So, um, what do you like to do for fun?"

Darien looked at her sorrowfully and Jannis flushed a little. He really was a serious boy.

"I guess, well, I don't have much time to play, really. When I'm not really tired, they have me learning magic and reading a lot of books."

"You have to have fun sometime." Jannis pressed.

"Well, I guess I like to ride horses. And give them apples and carrots. We have a lot of horses in the palace stable, even a couple of ponies." He looked wistful. "When I was out at the battlefield, I used to pet the warhorses whenever I could."

Darien paused, and continued somewhat relentlessly.

"I don't have time to have fun though, we are at war, and I have to save the people."

"You have to know that you can't save the whole country by yourself. There is no way one small boy, even if he is a prince, can save the whole country." Jannis hated saying it, but she felt compelled to.

Darien deflated; he looked so sad and so helpless. Her heart went out to him. He really was quite brave for such a little boy.

"I suppose though, you could do it if you had help. I mean, no one expects you to do it alone, right?"

He looked up at her, and hope warred with dispair on his face.

"But who could help me?"

"Well, maybe I could help you." Jannis offered.

"You're just a guard."

"Am I? I thought you said earlier, that I didn't act much like a guard."

"So you aren't a guard." Darien said, his eyes narrowing slightly, but there was a firmness to his voice that indicated a puzzle solved. "Who are you?'

"It's a secret. You can keep a secret can't you?"

"I give you my word." Child he may have been, but there was a finality to what he said- he was a prince and he knew what his word meant.

"Just watch." She mustered her magic and cast the can-trip that turned her hair and eyes from an ordinary brown back to their natural silver and violet coloring. Darien's eyes widened, not at the color change, but at the play of magic, which, as a mage, he could also see. She could see his mind furiously working as he finally put all the pieces together.

"It's you, isn't it? You're gonna marry my Grandfather. What were you doing guarding my door? Dressed like that?" He gestured to the leather armor Jannis had tossed on over her tunic and leggings. A common steel sword was slung at her hip, courtesy of the castle armory.

"I snuck out. I was going crazy stuck in those rooms."

Darien paled. His eyes were wide and his mouth formed a little o.

"Do you have any idea what Grandfather could do...."

"I know. That's why you can't tell anyone."

If Darien looked sick before, he looked even sicker now. Jannis doubted that Darien had ever been on the recieving end of the king's displeasure, but he surely had to have seen it in action. It did nothing to help the fluttering that was already in her stomach.

Darien was examining her closely and he seemed puzzled by what he saw. He was looking at her like she was a strange, walking fish. "I've never met a mage like you before.... you don't look sick at all. What are you? You can't be a mage. But you were doing magic!"

"Archmage actually, not a mage at all. I don't get sick like you do." Jannis paused. "Well, I get sick, but like a normal person, not like a mage. It's complicated."

The prince was getting really worked up, and Jannis was worried about him. He looked like he was on fire from the inside, a sudden flurry of activity in that sallow husk of a body.

"Calm down a little, I'm not going anywhere."

"You can't stay here. They'll find you if you stay here." Darien shook his head and swallowed. "Grandfather is going to be angry. You don't want him to find you while he's still angry." Darien's voice fell to a whisper.

"Not for a while. You aren't even supposed to be awake yet, remember? Just quiet down a little."

"Alright." Prince Darien glanced at the door and swallowed again, his eyes narrowing. "What do you want to talk about?"

"I can't let Harderior be overrun just because the king thinks I'm some sort of delicate lady that needs to be sheltered and protected." Jannis shuddered. "I've had more than enough of that. I'm going out to the battlefield to find this general of yours, and I'm not going to tell the king or anyone else. You're going to show me the way."

Prince Darien stared at her, clearly disbelieving.

"What? I can't even walk yet. You're getting married in less than a week, and the front line is farther away than that." Jannis pursed her lips to better concentrate on the problem. Her forehead furrowed.

"What other option is there? Do you want to see your country overrun? Do you want to die? Do you want to see all the people you care about die?"

"No." The young prince lowered his head and stared at his hands, folded in his lap. His eyes had lit with a kind of fierce determination, almost uncanny in that young, sick face. "We don't have a choice, do we? And I'll probably end up dead either way." He finished that last almost as an afterthought, his voice bitter and resigned.

"I'm not going to let you die, Darien." Jannis's voice was just as fierce, and her eyes sharp, but the prince found her words oddly reassuring. Maybe they could do something to help, after all.

Chapter 5

Lance was startled awake by the sound of the door opening. The mage he had been waiting for was paused motionless in the doorway, apparently struck speechless by the sight of Lance stretched out on his bed.

"Yes, I know, I do have that effect on people." Lance intoned arrogantly, stretching slightly, and sitting up.

"What are you doing in my room? Lord Firin's been searching the entire complex for you!"

"Well, I enjoyed our chat earlier so much, I wanted to talk to you again. And, since I didn't know where you went, I thought I would wait in your room."

"You were asleep in my bed."

They stared at each other. Lance didn't bother to reply.

"How did you get in?"

"The locks on the doors in this place really aren't that hard to pick." Lance said dismissively.

"They're all sealed by magic."

"Oh, really? I didn't notice."

The mage finally moved from the doorway, closing the door silently behind him and falling into the nearest chair, probably from exhaustion. Most people found Lance's presence exhausting.

"I'm surprised you're still here. I would have thought you would run for it."

"I did give it some thought." Lance commented helpfully. "But decided against it. Not that it would be that hard to get out of here."

"If you stayed, maybe you're considering cooperating with us after all."

"You wish. I just stayed to see the library. Oh, and talk to you. You're the only halfway intelligent person in this whole crazy country, at least that I've met so far."

"I thought you didn't 'do' magic. Why would you care about a mage library?"

"Well you know, being an educated man, I happen to like reading. Not that I practice magic or anything, but it amuses me to know more than everyone else about everything. I'm always game to dig through a library, but I haven't seen the one at the compound yet. Callie wouldn't let me go in there. She wouldn't even tell me where it was!"

"We don't let anyone in there except mages. Not even to clean. Some of the younger mages take turns using magic to clean up the library from the dust and dirt that slowly builds up over time. It's just easier to do it that way, we wouldn't want the common folks that do our cleaning to ruin some of these books by mistake."

"If I were Eddy," Lance said contemplatively, "I would hide

my rarest and most valuable books on magic out here at the compound. After all, he already managed to anger a large number of mage schools and foreign archmages with his little project here, and they might get it in their heads to raid the library at the castle just to get even. I didn't even know this compound was here until I was dragged out here. It just makes sense that this little place is a secret from them as well."

"Maybe," the mage replied. "You sound awfully sure of yourself."

"That's only because I'm always right. It's a curse you know, to always have to listen to everyone around you try to tell you something wrong, when you already know you are always right. Have you ever heard of the Tome of Ellis Caerig?"

"Oh my, a very rare and eclectic book indeed. We actually had the original volume here, but the king removed it, so now we only have a copy. There aren't many copies, of course, magic texts of that power can only be copied by hand, and only by a skilled mage."

"And then there's the problem of the parchment."

"Yes, indeed, you are very well versed on the matter. Magic texts such as these cannot be written on paper, or even ordinary parchment. The power of the enchantments written on the pages will slowly destroy the pages over time."

"My uncle favored using Selkie skins to make parchment for recording his most powerful spells."

The mage looked green. "Your uncle is a very sick man. And a very powerful man indeed, if he is using Fae skins to make parchment. They take that kind of thing personally."

"The great Dark Lord Aerigard can handle himself." Lance shrugged. "Lots of people try to kill him all the time. I think it amuses him. I even tried to kill him a couple of times, just for fun."

"I see..."

"But about that library. I bet you could get me in to have a look." Lance gave the mage a winning smile.

"I doubt Lord Firin would allow it."

"Now, now. Lord Firin has his priorities. And his top priority at this point has got to be making me happy. After all, you aren't going to find another archmage just lying around somewhere. You really want me to cooperate, don't you? And I really don't want to cooperate with you people. You should doing everything in your power to... convince me to aid your cause."

The wizened little mage looked torn. He glanced back and forth, distress on his face. Clearly he didn't want to expose his beloved library, but just as clearly Lance's comment had struck home.

"Well..."

"Don't make up your mind right now, you interrupted a very pleasant nap. I'll just stay here and get some more sleep while you go ask Lord Firin." Lance laid back down, his arms stretched behind his head and closed his eyes.

"On... my bed?" The mage slowly stood, speechless.

"Why not?"

"I..."

"Go on, go ask him. I bet he will be so relieved that you found me. He's still looking everywhere, isn't he?"

The mage started and flushed. "By the goddess, you're right! I've got to go find Lord Firin." He turned and headed out the door, propelled by new urgency. Lance just sighed and chuckled slightly to himself. This was almost too easy.

———————

King Eduardo Malifest the Fourth, absolute ruler of his particular corner of the world, was fuming with rage. His intended bride, who had come at an unusual and high price, was missing. The possibility of her kidnapping was very real, but King Eduardo knew it was just as likely that Lady Jannis had left on her own. An archmage of considerable power in her own right, Jannis possessed the ability to break the wards on the walls and remove the window from its sill on her own, without any outside assistance. And after Lord Aerigard's warning, he should have expected it.

The most frustrating aspect of this whole fiasco was that Eduardo had genuinely believed that Aerigard was exaggerating. Despite a somewhat icy and arrogant attitude, Jannis had seemed quiet and pliant. She had hardly seemed like the reckless trouble-maker her uncle had painted her to be. And besides, her younger brother Lance had been far more of a problem, and had quickly become the center of attention. It was easy to ignore Jannis when her brother was around, a mistake Eduardo was now paying for.

He ground his teeth in frustration, flinging a handy inkwell at the nearest wall, where the soft soapstone shattered with a reassuring crack and left an ugly black smear on the stone. Duke Tellis kept his face carefully schooled. He didn't want to remind the king that he had warned Eduardo about trusting the Dark Lord Aerigard or his bargains. In this mood who knew what the king might do?

"Anything yet?" The king snapped at a hapless servant carrying a pitcher of chilled wine as he entered the door.

"No, your Majesty." The servant set the tray down carefully on the desk and disappeared as fast as he could. The king was in a dangerous mood.

"The guards are almost done searching the castle. We've organized search parties and quartered the land immediately surrounding the castle. Captain Schrander has pretty much scoured the north out about four miles. The south will take longer because of all the homes and shops to search. Please, Your Majesty, calm down, the lady has only been missing for a few hours. We'll find her."

"And if she left on her own?" Eduardo snapped, eyes narrowed. "There is no way our soldiers can subdue an archmage as thinly stretched as they are, even if they do find her."

"I hardly think she would just abandon you like that." The duke replied, reassuringly. "You've treated her with the greatest respect, given her the most comfortable suite of rooms in the castle, given her every courtesy."

"Maybe. And maybe she just went out for a walk to get some fresh air. Capricious and stubborn, hmm, Aerigard? You didn't tell me the half of it, you dark-hearted bastard."

Duke Tellis didn't have to say anything to that. Dark Lord Aerigard's reputation preceded him, and if this was the worst of it, Tellis believed they had gotten off easy. He had never approved of approaching the sorcerer in the first place. But it wasn't something a wise man would mention to the king right now.

"She won't have gone far, even if she did sneak out to spite you. But perhaps you should calm down, Your Majesty, before you do yourself some harm. Think instead about how you will deal with her when she's found. And as you just said, the lady is an archmage in her own right. Punishing her for any indiscretions might prove... difficult. But this is all supposition. I think it is far more likely that her brother stole her. The sot did make a point of breaking into her rooms before, banging up the guards in the process. And he is also an archmage, and a known trouble-maker. I think the brother is the most likely suspect."

The king paused, eyes wide, glancing down at his desk. Duke Tellis followed his gaze down to a single sheet of paper in the scattered pile on the desk, glowing ever so faintly green.

"By my word, that's a rare enchantment." Duke Tellis lifted the page from the desk, turning it over carefully. "I doubt that there are a handful of human mages that can perform that particular fae enchantment."

Oh, shut up!" Eduardo snapped, snatching the paper back from the duke and glancing over the page quickly.

This is what the note said:

My Lord King:

I fear I was in desperate need of some fresh air, and so I took a walk around your castle. By happy chance, I met your grandson Prince Darien and we spoke about the kingdom's troubles. I am sorry, but I cannot ignore the threat to your lands and people, with an invading army at your doorstep. Darien and I are going to the front lines to face these foes and drive them from your borders. With a little luck, I'll be back in time for the wedding.

Jannis

King Eduardo stroked his chin, closing his eyes while Duke Tellis read the note and then snatching the note back from the duke to read it again, as if he could not believe it.

"Well," Duke Tellis commented unhelpfully, "At least you know where she is."

"I…" The king was momentarily at a loss for words. "I don't know how to feel about this."

"You were raging a moment ago; aren't you angry at her for her high-handedness?"

"She's infuriating and maybe I should be outraged. At the very least she should never have left without my permission. The problem is: she's right. As much as I hate it, she's doing the best thing for the kingdom. It's hard to argue with necessity."

The duke and the king stared at each other for a moment, not saying what both were thinking, that at least the lady had not been kidnapped, or run away, or run off with her brother.

"Aren't you worried for her safety?"

The king's brow furrowed. "Of course. The thought of her in danger is horrible, but so was the thought of Darien in danger, and yet necessity forced me to send him to battle. The hardest part of being a king is making those choices. And in all honesty, I don't know if I would have been able to order her into battle myself, despite the fact that an archmage could turn the tide of this war." King Eduardo paused for a moment, and his face hardened. "That doesn't mean I won't punish her for her flagrant disregard and insolence. A man has to control his wife, and a king doubly so. At least Lord Aerigard warned me about her before I agreed to wed her."

Duke Tellis carefully did not comment. He still had considerable doubts, but was in no position to voice them. Instead he chose a safer topic.

"This is a remarkable piece of work she performed. If nothing else she could be invaluable for communications alone. This fae magic of distance writing would let us communicate directly with General Frederick."

"And it has the added bonus of keeping her away from direct fighting." The king mused.

"Perhaps. I'm more concerned that the wedding might have to be postponed. A considerable amount of time and money are already tied up in it. What do you want to do, sire?"

"Continue with the wedding as planned. Without more information, it's just not possible to know when my wayward bride will show up. Send a messenger pigeon to the general."

"Of course."

Her spell complete, Jannis packed the scattered components back up into her satchel and smiled at the serious young face beside her. Darien had watched her spell-work with all the avid curiosity of any seven-year-old, but twice the discipline.

"That's a strange magic." He commented finally, when she was almost done repacking. "I've never seen it before. Where did you learn it?"

"From my uncle."

"I suppose Dark Lord Aerigard would know some pretty rare magics." Darien concluded.

"More than either of us could learn in a lifetime, I bet." Jannis replied, standing, and slinging her satchel over her shoulder. She was still dressed in the leather armor and sword borrowed from the castle armory, and despite a pretty face and her odd silver hair looked far more like a common mercenary or village watchman than a powerful mage. "My uncle has been studying the arcane arts for longer than I've been alive. It's all he cares about, and he's amassed rare books, spell components from all over the world… He's a lot better than I'll ever be."

"Someday you'll be just as good." Darien offered innocently.

"No, I won't." Jannis sighed regretfully.

"Why not?"

Jannis stopped and considered her answer before replying, finally just giving the stark, simple truth.

"Because I just don't care enough."

"I don't understand. You don't care about what, about magic?"

"Exactly. It's always been more of a hobby than a study to me. Something to deal with boredom and pass the time. I really only do it because I can. And Lance can't, so it bugs him when I do magic." Jannis declared, amused.

"You only study magic to make your brother angry?"

"Pretty much."

"How can you not care about magic?" Darien asked plaitively. He looked somewhat disturbed. Jannis supposed with the king's obsession with magic and mages, her own opinion on the matter must be bordering on heresy in this kingdom.

"It's a part of you. A part of who you are. How can you not care about it?"

"It's complicated."

"'It's complicated.' That's what adults always say when they don't know the answer or don't want to say it."

Darien sighed, distressed. Jannis was starting to become concerned herself, because the prince was wasn't in the best health, and he kept looking worse and worse. He hadn't been fully recovered when they left the castle, and this trip was taking its toll on him.

On their way out of the castle, Jannis had stolen, that is, 'borrowed', two horses from the castle stables. Darien had taken a moment to give both horses a number of apples from their supplies while Jannis got their tack ready. One of them was loaded up with supplies: food, water, rope, a lantern, a small cooking pot, a tent, a knife, and other assorted supplies. Darien rode the other. Jannis had elected to start this journey on foot, since her long legs could keep up with a walking horse, and she was still mad with inactivity from all the time cooped up in her rooms. By the time she was sick of walking, she could start riding the packhorse, because they would eat through some of the weight it was carrying.

Jannis had done some pretty reckless things in her eighteen years of life, most of them incited by her brother, but dragging a small, sick child out of bed and on a quest to defeat an army was probably the worst. She felt guilty. But that wasn't a new experience for her, and so she dealt with her guilt the way she always did—she ignored it.

"You don't think very much of me, do you?" Darien said, as they started moving again.

"That's not true." Jannis replied. "You are very brave to come along with me. I wouldn't be able to find the army without you."

"Don't lie to me. You could have found the army by stealing a military map, or kidnapping a guard. Why didn't you just leave me in the castle? Why take me along?"

"I really don't know. Maybe I just didn't think this through very well."

"Would you have left me behind if you had?"

"Maybe: you're still sick, and you would be safer and better off back in your bed."

"You really don't think much of me, do you?" He repeated, frustrated.

"Why do you think you have to save the whole country by

yourself, anyway? You're just a little boy, not a great warrior, or a trained mage." She snapped back, without thinking.

"'Just a little boy,'" he repeated, voice heated. "I'm a prince and I have to protect my people."

"I doubt anyone expects that of you."

"I do. I have to do it, because there isn't anyone else."

"You're just being silly." Jannis retorted. "I'm here, and I can help. Even my brother would be willing to help if I tricked him into it. There have to be other people out there too. The army has a general doesn't it?"

"Frederick." Darien supplied, tartly.

"Who?"

"General Frederick is running the army. I think he likes me. He gave me a little carved horse for working so hard the last time I was out there."

"I see. Well, I bet General Frederick is working to try to save your people. You don't have to do it all yourself."

"But I *do* have to help. Even if you help, even if General Frederick helps, I have to help too. You didn't make a mistake by bringing me along. I can help with my magic." Darien paused, and finally voiced why he was upset. "But you don't think very much of magic, do you?"

Jannis stopped and looked at Darien. The boy prince was pale, his eyes sunken in, his body curled up as best it could atop the gray gelding he rode.

"If I offended you…" Jannis began, but Darien cut her off.

"You did. Magic isn't just a part of who you are, it's also a part of who I am, and it's not funny to treat it like a game. Just something to tease your brother. It's a part of both of us. Who we are."

"I see," Jannis replied noncommittally. She turned and started walking again. Darien followed on his horse. The packhorse trailed the two of them, its long leather lead in Jannis's hand.

"I really do admire you, Darien. It takes a lot of courage to fight at any age, but especially at yours. War is horrible."

"I was scared, but in a way I liked it better out there than at home." Darien replied, stiffly.

"Really? Why?"

"Because on the battlefield, people care about you for what you do, not who you are. The soldiers, General Frederick, they all cared about me because of what I could do, not just because I was a prince." Darien paused. "And because I got to stay in a tent. It was like camping."

"Well, at least you can stay in a tent again." Jannis changed the subject. "Now, no one knows where we are, and we are in the middle of nowhere, so start looking for traps."

"Why would there be traps?"

"Because Lance—that's my brother—is about to show up."

"How would you know that, and why would he set traps?"

"My entire life, whenever I think Lance can't possibly be anywhere nearby and I let my guard down, he plants some kind of nasty surprise. Nothing particularly... dangerous, just unpleasant. Like a pit trap full of fresh horse turds... or a hive of angry marsh bees... or, well, just stay alert and keep your eyes open."

"There is no way your brother is out here. We aren't even following the main road." Darien pointed out as Jannis knelt down and carefully eyed the ground in front of them. "This road can't be used by that many people; it's practically a game trail." Darien gestured at the narrow dirt road they had been following. Weeds happily overgrew the sides of the road, and had started their steady creep into the road itself. Birds called in the distance, and apart from that and the buzzing of some annoying horseflies, there was no other sound.

"Everyone underestimates Lance; he likes it that way. But I'm not going to fall for his tricks again. I'm not that stupid." Jannis declared, moving slowly forward, and crouching every few steps to examine the ground anew.

"Your brother is miles away. This is just slowing us down."

Darien protested weakly, coughing. Jannis examined the ground.

"Sis, what on earth are you doing, looking for a grub or a worm for a nice mid-afternoon snack? You know they're better with salt and rosemary." The man that broke through the high weeds to the left and onto the road in front of Jannis was all too familiar.

"Lance." Jannis said, by way of greeting. "I was looking for traps."

"Traps? Out here in the middle of nowhere? Why?"

"Never mind." Jannis forced a smile and turned. "I'd like to introduce you to Prince Darien, the king's grandson."

"Wow, you kidnapped the king's grandson? I guess you win this round; the guy I kidnapped isn't nearly as impressive. I'll introduce you anyway."

Lance vanished back the way he came and reappeared leading a pair of horses. One was saddled, the other was loaded up with some bulging saddlebags, and had a middle-aged man, dressed in dark robes, slung like a sack of vegetables across its back, tied and gagged.

"Ah, um, what's your name?" Lance asked, while at the same time Darien exclaimed.

"Master Emrys!"

"Oh, so that's your name." Lance nodded sagely.

"Lance!" Jannis rebuked, "You kidnapped a man, without even knowing his name?"

"Well, knowing his name isn't that important. And besides, kidnapping a complete stranger gives you the same kind of delightful guilty pleasure as crushing fresh strawberries under your boot in front of starving children. You know I just couldn't resist."

Darien was already out of the saddle and standing, or more accurately tottering, as he didn't stand very steadily, near the other horse, untying the hapless mage.

"Master Emrys, are you all right?" Prince Darien asked, as he finished untying the man and removed the gag.

"Your Highness, what are you doing out here, and what is

going on?"

"Lance, just what have you been up to?" Jannis demanded.

"You know, the usual…" Lance said dismissively. "You shouldn't worry your pretty head about it, sis. Go ahead, find yourself some grubs, we can use the break anyway."

"Let me help you down," The prince reached for the older mage.

"No, no, your Highness, I'll be fine, thank you." He patted the prince on the hand and climbed down from the horse's back on his own.

"I can't believe you, Lance. Why are you always getting into so much trouble?"

"Why are you always getting into so much trouble?" Lance parroted, in an annoying whine. "Why are you such a pain? I can never seem to get away from you, and you are always whining and moaning about everything. I swear there is nothing more useless or annoying than a sister."

"No matter how hard I try, I can never be rid of you."

"It touches my heart, really, how happy you are to see me."

"Why don't you go crawl back into the hole you came out of?"

"What, because you want me to go find you some yummy grubs? They wriggle, you know, as they slide down your throat… If you're lucky they're even slimy."

"You're sick, you know that? Absolutely sick! What are you even doing out here, Lance? And where have you been for this, what, two weeks you've been gone?"

"Aww, you missed me."

"More like worried out of my mind not knowing what disasters you're brewing."

"Compliments again? You know, I really missed you too." Lance flashed his sister his best winning smile.

"Just for once, I wish you would be of some use, instead of just a walking, talking headache."

"Now, now, that wasn't fair. I've been working very hard this whole time."

"Doing what? Making people miserable?"

"Of course! But I don't have to work hard to do that. No, I've been investigating Eddy's private obsession. My little friend here was one of Eddy's mages on his private mage torture facility, also known as Lord Firin's eastern estate."

Jannis eyed the older mage. He was late middle-aged, but looked far older because of his health and the wasted state of his body.

"Aren't there any healthy mages in this whole bloody country?" She asked, exasperated.

"Apparently not. Haven't you been paying attention, at all?" Lance rolled his eyes.

"I was just wondering if this is normal. I mean, what's normal for the rest of the world, a mage being like me, or being like him?" Jannis gestured at the wizened little man.

"You're a freak. It's hard to accept I know, but there you have it." Lance concluded, patting his sister on the shoulder.

"I don't suppose there is a point to all this?"

"Oh yes, how silly of me. Eddy's been a very naughty boy. Lots of dead people, dead children, torture, rape, so on and so forth. But what's worse, he actually slapped me! Slapped me, can you believe it??"

"What a shock." Jannis replied, her voice dripping with irony.

"So I was thinking, despite all the trouble I've caused in my life, I've never tried regicide…"

"Hold on, stop right there Lance. You are not going to kill the king, my future husband, just because he slapped you."

"Oh come on, it's not just because he slapped me, he chained me up too! And admit it, you don't really like him. He doesn't deserve you."

"You could be arrested for treason for talking that way about my grandfather." Darien interjected fiercely. The two Solarans paused, and glanced at each other. Lance's face started to crawl as if he were going to burst out laughing. Jannis sighed, closed her eyes and put her head in her hands.

"Treason? Really?" Lance asked brightly, trying to keep his face under control. "That's even better!"

Darien shook his head, disbelieving. "What's wrong with you?"

"Don't bother." Jannis interjected. "Far older and wiser minds have struggled with that particular riddle."

The Solarans looked at each other, and Jannis pursed her lips.

"I mean, we were raised by an evil sorcerer. I think, all things considered, we could have turned out worse. In his case, I don't know how, but I think so. I think he could have turned out worse."

Lance sighed heavily. "I'll just have to work harder then." Lance conveniently did not mention regicide again, and hoped that the others dismissed his comment or forgot it.

"Darien is leading me to General Fredrick's command post on the battlefront." Jannis said, changing the subject. "I was going to try to take on the enemy army."

"Just you and boy wonder here?" Lance said, gesturing to the seven-year-old.

"You're welcome to come along, Lance."

"It's suicide! Sounds like fun. I'm in."

"I'm coming as well," Emrys said firmly. "I cannot allow his Highness to go into such terrible danger alone."

"Hey, I'm with him, he's not alone." Jannis objected, miffed.

"The more the merrier." Lance offered. "Let the elephant mage come along. If nothing else his gruesome death might provide a valuable distraction, letting us get away."

"I will protect Prince Darien with my life."

"Ok, fine. Everyone's coming, now do we have a plan?"

Jannis continued, irritated.

"Of course, sis. I always have a plan."

"Which is?"

"I'm going to march up to the enemy commander and demand their immediate surrender."

Jannis shrugged. "All right, let's go."

"Wha-wait." Emrys protested. "That's it, that's your great plan?"

Lance shrugged. Darien looked at Jannis.

"He isn't serious, is he?" The prince whispered to her.

"Completely." Jannis replied, deadpan.

"That's crazy."

"That's Lance."

"We're all going to die, aren't we?" The prince asked with surprising calm.

Jannis shrugged again. "Maybe. Lance has a way of surprising people. His plans never work, but strangely, everything always works out in the end."

———————

The battle front was once near the border, far from the capital and the king's palace. Years of steady attrition had moved the front first one way and then another until it snaked oddly into Harderior, like a balloon about to burst from the pressure applied to it.

Between Prince Darien and his friend Master Emrys, the small party was headed in the most direct way to the front, that is, over a small, ancient mountain range, raggedly covered with an assorted mix of spiny trees and meadows full of thick, tall grasses and mangy weeds. In past years the area would have been alternately controlled by either locals out hunting or fishing, or the odd pack of bandits who would loot and pillage and run amok until they caused enough ruckus to attract the city guard. The guards would clear out the bandits, and the locals would take the area back over until the next bunch of thieves moved in.

This natural cycle had been disturbed by the nearby warring, and both the locals and whatever bandits usually roamed the hills were all staying clear of this particular patch of territory. There was an odd silence over everything, broken occasionally by the loud cries of some oblivious bird, and the harsh buzzing of insects.

If anyone controlled these hills, it was the insects. Jannis slapped her neck.

Jannis sighed again.

"I don't want to talk about it, sis, so just forget it." Lance said, infuriatingly, at her latest attempt to find out just what he had been up to. Finally she just gave up.

A determined look on her face, Jannis urged the horse forward to where Master Emrys rode beside Prince Darien. With an apologetic smile for the young prince, Jannis pushed her horse between them and addressed the older mage.

"Master Emrys. Just what happened with my brother while I was at the castle?"

"Well," Emrys glanced back at Lance, who made a rude gesture.

"Can't leave well enough alone? Women are such horrible gossips!" Lance called forward at them.

"When he first got to the estate, he was working for Callie doing menial labor. Chopping wood, cleaning the floors, delivering lunch, that sort of thing."

"He was… what?"

"Well," Emrys looked embarrassed. "No one really believed he was an archmage. I think it was the manacles that did it. Any mage would have been unconscious in the presence of so much raw iron, but he wore them as if they weren't even there. And of course, as long as he was wearing them, they distorted the magical energies that naturally flow around any powerful mage."

"Right," Jannis pursed her lips, thinking. "But didn't the guards who brought Lance tell you who he was?"

"They might have, yes, but it didn't seem plausible, and Lord Firin thought it was just a joke the guards were playing on one of their own. No one has seen an archmage in Harderior since before King Eduardo took the throne. To have one just show up, seemed as likely as finding a lump of gold in a pig sty. And then when Lance told us he was the sorcerer Aerigard's nephew, everyone thought it had to be a joke."

"I've noticed that despite my uncle's fame, my brother and my existence seems to be completely unknown." Jannis offered helpfully. "You would think more people would know about us, if only because of our relationship with him. On the other hand, he might have kept us a secret deliberately. Why, I have no idea. My uncle isn't what I would call an ordinary person. Sometimes the workings of his mind seem completely alien."

"Greed, most likely," Emrys hazarded. "Magical energy is finite, and you can run out of it just like you can run out of anything else. Drawing off energy from another sorcerer or wizard is first of all extremely difficult, and second extremely dangerous, but your uncle probably had the skill and the lack of ethics to try. In fact, when I first saw that spell on Lance, that's what I suspected it was."

"Oh yes, that spell." Jannis glanced back. "You're mistaken, it's not a spell to drain off magical energy, exactly… Although I can see where you might make that mistake."

Emrys immediately perked up, his interest piqued.

"Then what kind of spell is it? The sheer complexity of it makes it hard to examine, and Lance doesn't help, since he is constantly on the move. I've never seen anything like it."

Jannis forestalled the rush of questions with a raised hand. "Look, it's my uncle's work, and it's very advanced. I really don't know enough magic to be able to explain it to you, sorry. I'm sure if you like, Lance will tell you the whole sordid story about it, since he is always taking every opportunity to try to tell anyone who will listen. Not that that will help you understand the magical energies and how they are constructed, only how Lance managed to get our uncle mad enough to cast the spell in the first place."

"It's not the story about the hell hound is it?"

"Ah, so you are already familiar. Have you heard it, then?"

"Not all of it. I'll admit, the way he tells it is so far-fetched, I just couldn't keep listening."

"Most people have that reaction. But, it's all true, I'm afraid. I was there." Jannis paused. "You know, you never finished answering my first question, about what Lance has been up to."

"It's very easy to get distracted while talking about him isn't it?"

"It's even worse if you are actually talking to him." Jannis remarked.

Emrys took a deep breath and gathered his thoughts again.

"Well, almost two weeks after he arrived, the king sent a message about Lance to Lord Firin. It was at that point we realized he had been telling the truth the whole time. There was a bit of a scuffle between Lance and a few guards, he disappeared, and an hour later I found him in my room asleep on my bed."

"Ah, typical of Lance. Stirs up the hornet's nest, finds a hole to hide and giggles to himself while chaos rages. Then he strides out into the middle of the mess he caused, smooth and calm as silk, laughing at all the disarray."

"Your brother is a very unique character."

"You have no idea."

"After I found Lance in my room, he suggested that maybe he would be willing to cooperate if I did something for him."

"Which was?"

"Show him the library."

At this point Jannis put her head in her hands again. "You didn't."

"It seemed fairly innocent."

"At this point, you should already have had enough exposure to Lance to realize that word doesn't belong in the same sentence."

Emrys' face twisted in grim amusement as he continued. "So

we went to the library. I'll spare you the details I think, except to mention that Lance knows a lot about magic books, and he knew exactly which ones were the rarest and most valuable."

"Please tell me he didn't destroy them..."

"He didn't. They're in the saddlebags." Emrys gestured. "I... objected to their theft, quite violently, and your brother slammed my forehead into, or through, a wood paneled wall. I was unconscious after that point, but I can guess what happened next. I just hope he left the guards bruised and unconscious rather than dead."

"Lance doesn't believe in what he calls 'soiling his hands on the worthless,' in other words, in killing people who aren't a challenge. So the odds are good that the guards survived."

Emrys wore dignity like a cloak, he looked at Jannis, serene and serious as he chose his words. "Just so we understand one another, my lady. I'm going to protect the prince. And I'm going to protect these books, both from the enemy army, and that maniac you call a brother. It's not my place to harm an archmage, when the king so desperately needs every mage he can find, but if I had the power your brother would be in irons right here, right now."

"I'm not offended. Anyone who isn't actively trying to kill Lance I'd say falls into the friendly category. The only thing I find curious is why Lance bothered tying you up and dragging you along. It means he must think you have significant value, because he has zero patience for anything that he can't get use out of."

"I can't imagine what use he thinks I will be." Emrys said stiffly.

"You're the best mage in Harderior." Prince Darien chimed in at this point. Both Jannis and Emrys turned their attention to the prince with surprise. Of course, Darien had been listening closely to the whole conversation, but he was so quiet, it had been easy to forget him.

"I don't know if I would say that," Emrys protested dismissively.

"You were the best tutor I ever had," Prince Darien countered with conviction.

"Yes, well, the ranks of Harderior's mages have been somewhat... depleted over the past few years. Because of the war, you know." Emrys paused as a thought occurred to him. "Actually, your Highness, you're a far more powerful mage than I am."

Jannis snorted.

"If power is the only measure, then Lance is the best mage on the continent," she commented dryly.

"I don't do magic," Lance pouted behind them. He was uncharacteristically quiet, and Jannis spent one disturbing moment wondering what he was up to.

"So your brother feels the same way about magic as you do," Darien said softly and sadly.

"Well, not exactly. Lance doesn't 'do' magic. I do."

"He said the same thing earlier, that he doesn't 'do' magic, what is that supposed to mean anyway?" Emrys asked. "You would think he would say he can't do magic, or doesn't practice magic, but he specifically said that he doesn't 'do' magic."

"Oh, it's complicated. Let's just say it's not fair to say Lance can't do magic because he can, but it's just as unfair to say he can do magic, because he can't... so whether he can or can't isn't the issue. He just doesn't 'do' magic."

"I get a headache just trying to understand what you just said." Emrys said finally, after trying to work out Jannis' convoluted logic.

"Finally! Someone who understands!" Lance declared from behind them.

"It's tragic." Darien commented, "That you have so much power and so little regard for it. It seems terribly unfair that the goddess gave the two of you such a great gift and you don't even use it."

"Aha, but!" Lance said, riding into the weeds at the side of the trail to squeeze up beside Darien. "The goddess also gave each of us a life, and the vast majority of people squander theirs. You would think they would treasure their lives, since we each only get one, but most people spend theirs drinking, or chasing women, or obsessing about worthless nonsense like magic!"

"Spending your life doing what you love isn't wasting your time." Emrys pointed out mildly.

"I think you would find that most people don't love what they are doing, they just hate doing something else more." Lance concluded, regally.

"Arguing with Lance is like trying to drink the ocean, Darien." Jannis said nastily, glancing at her brother. "And you will never make him stop hating magic; it's too deep a wound to heal now."

"Shut up, you! All of you, all you ever talk about is magic, magic, magic. It isn't everything! I feel like the lone voice of reason in a pack of madmen. Listen to me… Magic. Isn't. That. Important!" Lance shouted at her, throwing his hands to the sky.

Chapter 6

"Lance, we need to talk."

"Uh-oh." Lance paused, and sighed, and rubbed his chin in a exaggerated manner as if he were an old, old man stroking his beard. "Whenever you say that, what it really means is 'I'm gonna try to use guilt to stop Lance from doing something.'"

"Try to be serious for once in your life."

"Not interested."

"Just… hear me out, Lance. Please, this is important."

"Translation: 'I'm going to talk to you whether you want me to or not.'"

Jannis's eyes narrowed, and she paused for a moment to recollect her thoughts before continuing.

"You aren't seriously thinking about killing the king?"

Lance sighed, give it to his sister to remember that earlier comment. Darn.

"Whyever would you think that?" Lance said, the picture of innocence.

"Let's skip all that; the fake innocence, the witty banter, the clever comments. I just want to talk, Lance. This is serious."

"You're always serious. Sometimes I wonder who shoved what so far up your butt. Mothers don't tell their children to sit up straight-- they tell them to sit like Jannis."

"You can't kill the king of Harderior."

"Why not? Because it's wrong? Because it hurts your delicate sensibilities the thought that I might eliminate that creep and put him out of both our miseries?"

"Honestly, whether killing people is wrong or right, I would sleep better if Eddy the Creep were no more. But that's not the issue. You can't kill the king of Harderior."

"I thought that was the issue, said creep and the king are one and the same, after all."

"That's not what I mean, Lance." Jannis scowled at him. "You can't kill the king because it will have far-reaching consequences. Whether or not Eduardo deserves a knife in the back, his people don't deserve the chaos that his death will bring. You are talking about putting Darien on the throne."

"I still don't see the problem. He'd do a much better job than the current king."

"He's seven!"

Lance shrugged. "He'll be a king sooner or later, regardless of anything I do."

"Do you even bother to consider the consequences of your actions?"

"Of course I do. I just don't care."

Jannis's eyes narrowed, and her voice took on a new sharpness. "Lance, you have to take responsibility for your actions, especially when the lives of so many innocents are at risk. You just can't do whatever you want, however you want, with no thought for anyone but yourself!"

"Wrong!" Lance countered, his own eyes narrowing and flashing with distaste. "This isn't about taking responsibility at all. It's not my fault that Eddy is a madman or got his kingdom into a war. If anything, me killing the king would be the natural consequence of his actions. Any time you have a mad little despot running around, sooner or later their life ends, quite messily. If it wasn't me, it would be someone else."

Lance paused, and Jannis opened her mouth to retort, but Lance wasn't finished yet.

"I think you have the opposite problem, dear sister. You always accuse me of not taking responsibility for my actions, but you are always trying to take responsiblity for everyone and everything else around you, even stuff that you had nothing to do with! Look at where we are right now; going to try to stop a war that we didn't start, between two kingdoms we don't belong to, to help people we don't really know. You think I'm being rediculous and irrational, but you are just as bad as I am. Actually, you're worse! Because I at least admit that I'm doing what I want to for no particular good reason. You think you are on some kind of noble, holy crusade or something, like a hero in shining armor come to save the day. It makes me sick."

"Because trying to do the right thing, to save lives and stop wars is fundamentally irrational and rediculous."

"Absolutely."

"But its totally alright to kill people for a superficial reason like that they slapped you?"

"Exactly."

Jannis put her head in her hands and screamed at the world in general, Lance in particular. Lance just shrugged.

"If you have such a hard time grasping reality, let me spell it out for you. The world itself is fundamentally unfair. Innocents are always being forced to pay for the actions of others. It's simply a part of life. It isn't my fault that others are forced to pay for my actions, it's a part of life. You can't hold me responsible for those collateral consequences, because I didn't plan it, I didn't design it, it is just the way the world works. And quite frankly, I don't care."

"You're a monster!"

"Now, now," Lance replied. "I prefer to think of myself as 'ethically challenged.'"

"How is what you are doing any different from what Eduardo did to you?"

"Completely different, because he was dumb enough to leave me alive after he insulted me. It would all have been a lot cleaner if he had just killed me to begin with."

Jannis clenched and unclenched her fists, breathing heavily. "There is no talking sense with you, is there?"

"Totally unfair of you to say, since you were the one who wanted to talk about this, and I wasn't interested. You can't expect me to cooperate when you try to force me into something. Speaking of which, I have a question: Why do you care so much about this now, anyway?"

"There is too much at stake, Lance. You're actions would affect the entire country."

"Wrong. That's not why you care. It's about Darien, isn't it? I have no idea why you are attached to that annoying little brat."

"Lance calling someone annoying? Will wonders never cease."

"Ha ha. You don't even know this kid, and suddenly you decided to make him your cause? What is with that anyway? You don't want his beloved grandpapa to get axed because it will hurt his widdle feewwings?"

"Well I certainly don't care about your feelings, since you apparently don't have any. No feelings of sympathy for others, no feelings of remorse for all the chaos you drag in your wake..."

"Plenty of feelings of irritation at my annoying sister trying to guilt me into doing the right thing. I'm pretty sure those count."

"And what about my feelings? Do you care about those? No wait, forget I asked."

"Actually I do care."

"Really?" Jannis was more than just skeptical.

"Really. As your brother it is my perogative to be irritating, frightening, angering and depressing you. Anyone else who tries is treading on my territory and must pay the price. Like Eddy. That bastard must pay."

"It would be touching if it wasn't so aggravating."

"I'm your brother, it's my job."

Jannis sighed and rubbed her temples. "Don't kill the king, Lance."

"Of course not, whyever would I do a thing like that?" Lance asked, his expression the model of innocence.

General Frederick examined the map before him with a dull sense of frustration, fast approaching apathy. Decades of military experience underlined one key fact: they were losing. Defeat was inevitable. All their efforts, noble sacrifices, struggles only slowed the enemy's advance.

It was enough to make a less-experienced man throw up his hands and surrender. But the general had too much experience with battle. Buying time sometimes meant buying enough time for the situation to change; for some unknown, unforseen element to arrive on the board. The only thing the general didn't understand was why he still held onto that vague, faint hope that some mysterious something would turn the tide of the battle. It was an irrational hope, unworthy of the nation's greatest military strategist, and yet, it was the only hope he had left.

General Fredrick sighed and turned his back on the map. It loomed large in his consciousness, and he deliberately banished it from his mind long enough to mop his forehead with a dry cloth.

The heat of the day was slowly, too slowly, seeping away as the light vanished from the sky. He sensed more than heard his old friend and comrade approaching.

Gregor held back, instinct and ingrained military courtesy granting the general time to gather his thoughts. Fredrick smiled slightly, at least he wasn't alone in this spirit-sapping struggle.

"General." Gregor finally said, quietly. "The last of the mages woke up a few minutes ago. Two days of rest and he should be ready for combat."

"You didn't have to come yourself, you could have sent your aide, or a messenger," General Fredrick replied gratefully, glad for the news. "But thank you."

"I knew you could use some good news." Gregor resisted the urge to glance at the map on the table. It loomed large in both their minds, he knew.

"Yes. And the messenger is almost as welcome as the news. Sit down. We haven't just talked for a long time."

"Thank you. You know I don't hold it against you if we seem to be butting heads every time we see each other. It's just the nature of war. We both have a job to do."

"And honestly, I need someone to disagree with me from time to time," Frederick laughed, "It's too easy for military men to simply accept their orders, regardless of the consequences, because that is what they are trained to do. Even I need someone to question me now and again." Frederick paused, and his voice took on a steely edge. "Just not in front of the troops, that would undermine discipline."

"Of course." Gregor's return smile was uncomfortable. There were some things they would never agree on, but Frederick was the one in command, which meant in the military way that he would always be right. History would judge, not a subordinate military officer. Frederick was kind to forgive Gregor's marginal insubordination, but they both knew where they stood, what was expected.

"I need to pick your brain. I've considered every possible angle, every option. We need something to change the rules, something to give us an edge. Something to steal victory from the enemy."

"If you've considered every option, I doubt I see something you don't." Gregor protested mildly.

General Frederick snorted. "So diplomatic. Now tell me what you really wanted to say."

"We both know enough to know that the easy answer is rarely the right one. The easy answer in this conflict from the beginning has been magic. Magic is such a game-changer, it can be the critical element that snatches victory from defeat. But what if that assumption was the problem from the beginning? What if magic is the problem, not the solution? We've become dangerously dependant on magic tactically. That means that our mages are being worked to exhaustion, and then when they collapse, we lose ground."

"Not this again. I know how you feel about those children..."

"This isn't about feelings," Gregor corrected. "It's about tactics. We have become so dependant on magic it has become a critical weakness in our strategy. Be honest with me, what you have been hoping for is a really powerful mage to show up from King Eduardo's searching."

"Maybe." Fredrick hedged.

"Magic has become your solution, your hope. Maybe that is the root of the problem."

"But even if true, that doesn't provide a solution. We may be dangerously dependant on magic, but not carelessly or stupidly so. Magic has become the solution because we have no other solution. It's a matter of necessity."

"You've known all along?"

"I'm not a fool, Gregor, and it's somewhat insulting that you would think so." Fredrick said tightly, then smiled. "Magic is a major part of our problem, but I can't see a way out of our dangerous dependance on it."

They both sat in uncomfortable silence for a time, the buzzing of night insects outside the tent even louder for the silence within. The lantern flickered, scattering patterns of light on the walls of the tent.

They had been traveling for the better part of two days, making a rough camp in the brush beside the narrow path for the night. One of their horses still carried all the gear and the books, with Lance and Jannis each on one, and the last horse shared by master Emrys and the young prince.

"We have a problem." Lance declared, suddenly coming to a halt. Because he was in front that forced both Jannis and Emrys to pull their horses up fast. Jannis pursed her lips.

"How observant." Jannis observed dryly. "We *are* going to go try to stop a war, after all. With no real plan, I might add."

Lance rolled his eyes. "Another problem--a more immediate problem." He turned, glancing back and forth as if searching for something.

"Well, enlighten us already." Jannis replied, Emrys wisely choosing to stay silent.

"We are riding into battle without arms or armor, or well, anything except the castle guard rejects you're wearing." Lance gestured at the leather armor Jannis was in with a look of disgust.

"So where do you propose we find armor, Lance? Common armor isn't going to fit, you know. Most soldiers or guards are a lot more, well, *built* than either of us." Jannis's observation was well-made, since both of the Solarans were so lightly built and slender it almost made it ludicrous the kind of armor they favored. In fact, the only armor likely to fit either of them was their own, still safely packed away in their uncle's keep, deep in the swamp, and days away.

"I'm still working on that," Lance replied, thinking.

"Great." Jannis urged her horse forward around Lance.

"Hey! Don't ignore me! I'm thinking here."

"Think on the road. We are under some rather tight time constraints, remember?"

"Why does it matter?" Darien asked suddenly, interested in the brief conversation.

"Why does what matter?" Lance asked amicably, for him at least.

"Why do you need armor, and why wouldn't common armor work?"

"Oh that. Well, you need armor, because if you've got a sword, or a spear, or something else designed to kill you coming right at your heart, the armor stops it, and you aren't dead. And you need armor that fits, because while you can wear loose clothes, clothes don't rub you, or scrape you, or trap your arm or leg to prevent it from moving. Armor has the tendancy to do that if it doesn't fit."

"Really." Darien seemed unfamiliar with the idea, which being a mage, may have been the case. Mages are not that fond of heavy metal armor, especially anything made of iron.

"Yes, really. Do a fast calculation. Think of every warrior you know; guards, soldiers, generals. Now I'm willing to bet the older, more experienced, more important or richer a warrior is, the more and better armor he wears. There's a reason for that: armor keeps you alive."

"I'll admit it, Lance, I'm stumped." Jannis said finally, interjecting herself into the conversation again. "I have no idea how we are going to come up with armor. There isn't anywhere nearby where we can find armor that already fits, not even when we get to the miltary encampment, and we don't have the time to do the necessary alterations to armor that doesn't fit. We can't even use magic to do alterations because steel is made with iron, and it will resist any magic we try to use on it."

Lance shrugged. "You aren't telling me anything I didn't

already know; but really, that is no surprise, I always knew you were useless."

Jannis' eyes narrowed but she didn't say anything else, and the four of them continued forward in an uncomfortable silence, the hills around them entirely too quiet for comfort. In fact, it almost felt like they were traveling through a graveyard. It was almost midday, but the sunlight seemed thin, wasted, and dimmed. Darien shuddered, his thin form tightly wrapped in his cloak. It wasn't cold, but it seemed cold. He clung to Emrys' back as if seeking warmth. It was still early in the year for the first hard freeze, but the heat of summer had already passed.

Dead grasses, their long shaggy stems leaning like drunkards, blocked their view and gave the feeling that something could be hiding there, almost within arm's reach, watching. There was green scattered in amongst the brown, nettles happily growing, unaffected by the recent searing of late summer. The occasional patch of tiny buzzing gnats flew into Jannis' face.

Lance swatted a particularly annoying horse fly with the flat of his hand on the horse's rump and his horse startled, sidestepping slightly with a frightened whinny. Jannis rolled her eyes and shifted in the saddle, trying to ease the cramps that inevitably started whenever you rode too long.

The path they were following, for it had long since ceased to be a road, was entirely, eerily, too quiet. It was the sort of place that you found in ghost stories. Jannis listened, listened attentively, for any sound. The creak of leather--saddles, bridles. The muffled clop of horses' hooves on dirt. In the distance, a crow's harsh call echoed out over the still air.

Darien shuddered again, his face bleak. Lance was oblivious to it all, still deep in contempation. Jannis sighed, and wished she was somewhere else. Suddenly something fell from the sky right at her.

It actually swooped more than fell, and its movement was all the more startling because of its complete silence. Automatically

Jannis held out her left arm as the gigantic owl stretched out its claws to land. Everyone else flinched instinctively away as the owl fanned its wings and gained its balance on Jannis's arm.

Jannis tensed, her muscles strained at the sudden, living weight, and the need to hold her arm steady under the grip of sharp claws. Thank all that was holy for leather armor.

"Looks like your boyfriend found us." Lance smirked. "I wonder why Delilah won't ever come to me."

"Delilah is too smart; she knows what happened to all the other familiars." Jannis said, scratching lightly under the soft feathers of Delilah's neck ruffle. It was a gesture of familiarity that would cause anyone else to lose a finger. Delilah was not a small bird, and her claws and beak were razor-sharp, perfectly designed to tear apart her prey.

Aerigard's current apprentice, a quiet, studious man in his early thirties, had come to the keep with a small grey tabby cat as his companion. That poor cat had vanished within a week of its arrival. The toad that followed it had similiarly disappeared. Then the lizard, then the crow. He began to realize why Aerigard kept a basilisk as a familiar, and not just to look commanding and impressive. Lance had a way of.... wearing out familiars. In a way that reqiured frequent replacement.

Instead of choosing a similarly dangerous and magical familiar, that apprentice had chosen to take a Great Grey Owl as his familiar. Delilah was quite capable of defending herself from Lance's many pranks, not only with her razor claws and ability to fly safely away, but with her uncanny intelligence.

It was that intelligence that Jannis saw when she looked in the bird's eyes. She felt an deep, personal bond with the bird. Both of them forced to suffer Lance and his nonsense. Both exiled to a rotten castle in the middle of the swamp and suffered to deal with magic day in and out. Both natural born killers, cold, quiet, elegant.

"What does that bloody stupid bird want?" Lance scowled.

Both sadly underestimated and underappreciated, Jannis

finished thinking sourly.

Jannis examined Delilah's leg for the message tube she knew had to be there. And delicately attempted to remove the message tube, one handed, while holding up the considerable weight of the bird with the other arm. Delilah shuffled, wings outstretching as her arm perch dipped and swayed, and dug her claws in to keep her balance as Jannis fumbled with the tube. Jannis bit back a sharp cry as the claws dug through the leather covering her arm and into her skin beneath.

Rolled parchment safely in hand, Jannis grimaced sourly. It was all Lance's fault. Somehow, even if he had nothing to do with it, it was still his fault.

The owl blinked at her, as if waiting for an apology, her feathers up in a ruff around her neck. The bird was more than half feathers, and hardly bird at all, but it didn't make her any smaller, or any lighter. With great dignity and silent elegance, Delilah swept her wings out, and crouched against Jannis' arm as she gathered herself and threw herself into the sky. Soundlessly, but it didn't change the fact that those claws had dug in again right before that leap into the sky. Jannis rubbed her arm lightly, trying not to get any blood on the paper.

The owl circled them once before winging her way back towards the swamp and her waiting master.

"What does your boyfriend want?" Lance asked, reaching for the rolled parchment. Jannis snatched it back, out of his reach, and Lance pursed his lips, thoughtfully.

"Mobius isn't my boyfriend." Jannis reminded Lance for the hundredth time, as she unrolled the tiny cream-colored parchment.

"Maybe you should tell him that, instead of me." Lance muttered as if to himself, though Jannis could hear him clearly.

It was a problem for another day, and one that Jannis had hoped to side-step completely with this marriage with Eduardo. Mobius, the quiet, soft-spoken man who was their uncle's current apprentice had, what was to her mind at least, an unhealthy facination with Jannis. He was a subtle man, but no less dangerous for all that. Being a sorcerer, his quiet and subtlety made him that much more dangerous. He was neither attractive nor unattractive, of average height with dark brown hair and eyes. Completely forgettable, until or unless you remembered that he was a powerful sorcerer in his own right. Jannis didn't feel anything for him, except maybe a vague disquiet.

He had left her flowers, unremarked, without a note, and other gifts. Jannis had no idea what it was about her that attracted him, whether it was her relationship to Aerigard, or her own rather odd beauty, but she found his attentions terribly uncomfortable. And it didn't help that her uncle's eyes narrowed at the sight of one of those flowers in her hand. It was entirely possible that their uncle had arranged this marriage with the king specifically to stop that nonsense before it became more serious, rare book or not.

Lance found the whole situation uproarously funny, when he didn't find it threatening. He had eyed Mobius more than once, with a dark, considering look.

Jannis unrolled the tiny parchment and read carefully.

My lady,

I am ever your devoted friend. I strongly suspect that you are in trouble, or soon will be, with your brother there to make certain of it. Use this parchment as a component in a summoning ritual to make a gateway back to the castle. The ink in which I write contains my blood as well as your uncle's, do not ask how I obtained that. I have already prepared a magic circle here to act as an anchor for your spell. You will need the blood of three powerful mage-born virgins to make the spell work, but I am sure you will find what you need if your need is strong enough. I trust your discretion.

Always yours,
Mobius

Jannis pursed her lips and rolled the scroll back up. It gave her the creeps even reading it. Having an admirer was odd enough to make her uncomfortable, that it was one like Mobius would have made any woman run for the hills. Sorcerers.

Jannis drew a small dagger from her boot and before Lance could give her any trouble or even react she slashed it at him. He dodged, but not fast enough, and blood beaded up along a thin line on his left cheek.

"What the hell was that for?!" Lance demanded, grabbing her arm in a tight, angry grip.

"Virgin blood," she replied emotionlessly. Pure necessity, for the spell, and not at all because hurting Lance was immensely satisfying.

"Honestly, I don't know why I didn't kill you a long time ago. All women are vipers, but you could give cobras lessons." Lance grumped as Jannis wiped the blood on his cheek onto the outside of the parchment in her hand.

The same dagger across her own palm, and Jannis added her own blood to the parchment.

"Darien, this spell requires the blood of three virgins." Jannis said, looking at the young prince.

Darien flushed, but asked gamely, "What spell?"

"Gateway. It opens a door and connects two far distant places. Not an easy spell to pull off; it takes a lot of preparation, and some rare ingredients; but Mobius, thats my uncle's apprentice, has his end all set up. All we need on this side is some blood."

"Absolutely not!" Emrys declared, moving his horse in between Jannis and the young prince. "You won't touch the prince, especially not with a steel dagger. Do you have any idea what that would do to him, in his present weakened condition? It could kill him! He shouldn't even be here, he should be back at the palace, safely in bed."

"Well I doubt you are volunteering to take his place," Lance said dryly. "So tell me, did you enjoy raping those little girls back at the compound, or did you just tell yourself it was for king and country? It's amazing the horrible things people will do for the sake of duty. Don't try to take the moral high ground with us, hypocrate."

Emrys looked green around the edges, as if he were about to be sick, and clearly disturbed at Lance's words.

"No, I..." Emrys started, and then stopped, licking his suddenly dry lips. It was hard to tell which emotion was strongest on his conflicted face, rage or shame.

"That's enough both of you." Jannis said, interrupting what might turn into a very ugly discussion. "Emrys is quite correct about the dagger. My apologies, Darien, I forgot about how strongly mages react to iron. I have a silver dagger in my bag with the spell components. Would that suit you?" She directed that last question at Emrys as much as at the prince.

Emrys shot one last murderous glance at Lance before turning to Jannis. "That would work better, my lady, but even so, I don't think the prince should have to suffer for your spell. Even a tiny cut can become infected out here." His brief gesture indicated the wilderness that surrounded them.

"What good would casting this gateway do?" The prince asked finally, quietly.

"Well for one," Lance said with satisfaction, "We can retrieve our armor through the gateway, and our weapons. And I'm sure uncle has some nasty little surprises hidden throughout the castle we could use. Mobius might already have scrounged some up, and have them ready to toss through the gate."

"He was probably intending for us to escape through the gateway, Lance. I doubt he would have dug through Uncle's storerooms." Jannis interjected, before Lance got carried away.

"Hmm, that may present a problem then." Lance rubbed his chin with one hand. Even days out in the wilderness, he was still clean-shaven, without a trace of stubble, but then, Lance took rediculous pains with his appearance sometimes. And he had the nerve to call her vain!

"What kind of problem?" Jannis asked, heart sinking.

"Mobius might try to come along with us, once he finds out you are on a crusade to stop an army. Or even worse, if you go through the gateway, he might decide to close it and keep you there, you know, safe and out of danger." Lance was quite correct, and what was more, Mobius wasn't likely to care which side of the gateway Lance and the others were on when the gate closed. Mobius didn't have any kind of unhealthy obsession with Lance, except the usual: a healthy, perfectly normal desire to tear Lance into small pieces.

"But it doesn't matter." Lance concluded. "I still want my armor, and that means we need some royal blood. Actually virgin blood." Lance added with a signficant glance at Emrys, who turned facinating colors but said nothing further. "Just don't go through the gateway, sis. Stay on this side to maintain it, and I'll go through. If Mobius wants to come along, well, three archmages are better than two, right?"

"This Mobius is an archmage, too?" Emrys asked, overwhelmed. Years of never seeing an archmage and now it seemed like they were springing up out of nowhere.

Jannis and Lance favored him with identical looks of ironic amusement, as if he were asking a stupid question. "Why would the Dark Lord Aerigard take an ordinary mage for an apprentice?" Lance asked quietly.

Put that way, Emrys could see just how stupid the question was, and he flushed again before visibly taking control of himself. At the very least he should have realized that this Mobius had to be an archmage because Lance and Jannis had both been completely ignorant of the limitations of normal mages before coming out into the world. It was only logical that their only exposure to mages of any kind had been to archmages like their uncle.

But that wasn't the last of the surprises.

"If you want my blood to make the gateway," Prince Darien said solemnly, "I want to go through."

The three adults shared one horrified glance before the

torrent started again.

"Absolutely not, your Highness..."

"I doubt Mobius would hesitate to kill a stranger, even a child..."

"Gateways are pretty dangerous..."

"What would happen to Harderior if the heir apparent vanished?"

"What if you collapse on the other side? You aren't in the best of health, your Highness..."

"If you want my blood," Prince Darien repeated, "I want to go through the gateway."

The three of them exchanged identical looks of worry and dismay, instantly unified at the prince's absurd demand.

"And I have another question. This gateway, can we make one to get to the army camp?"

"Sadly no," Emrys answered before either of the Solarans could respond. "A gateway has to be anchored from both sides by an archmage, and both archmages must possess the blood of the other to use as a spell component. A gateway also requires an immense amount of power, usually drawn from several different people, not just the two archmages anchoring the spell, unless of course the archmages are willing to die to cast the spell. It is a significant amount of power."

"But gateways can also be used to link together different worlds." Jannis said, taking on a lecturing tone. "If two archmages from two different worlds work together, they can link our world to the world of Haerg Nerue, also called Tir Na Nog, where the higher Fae still make their home, or to the realm of demons. Not that it is an easy task, since a lesser transportation spell to exchange blood must precede it."

"Stop, stop. If I have to hear one more word about magic, I think I'll be sick." Lance whined, clutching his belly in an exaggerated manner.

Jannis pursed her lips again. "Would you be able to keep an

eye on the prince if he went through the gateway, Lance?"

"I'm not a babysitter." Lance replied flatly.

And almost as immediately Darien chimed in with, "I'm not a baby."

"Just tie up his royal Highness, take his blood and get the gate up. We don't have time for this nonsense." Lance suited word to action, and grabbed the prince's horse's reins with one hand, and Darien's shoulder with the other.

"Unhand him!" Emrys shouted, leaping out of his saddle at Lance, clinging like a burr to Lance's back, while the horses beneath them tried to dance away at all the commotion on their backs.

"Prince Darien is the future king of Harderior, and you may not treat him with such disrespect!" Emrys cried as Lance flung the hapless mage, like a sick, wizened spider into the tall grass on the side of the dirt trail they followed. His words followed him as he flew through the air.

Jannis sighed.

"Fat lot of good you are, sister, just sitting there and letting me do all the work." Lance complained, as he drug the prince bodily out of his saddle and lashed his arms behind him with a length of strong cord, probably the same cord that had held Emrys when Lance had first appeared on the road. Prince Darien protested the entire time, and attempted feebly to struggle against Lance, but a sick, wasted seven-year-old had no chance against a healthy, full-grown man.

The older mage was still protesting Prince Darien's treatment at the top of his lungs from the tall grass alongside the trail, but he had not moved, or even stood up. Jannis realized with a sickening feeling that Emrys might have been seriously injured by his fall.

"Why do you have to make everything worse, Lance?" Jannis asked disparagingly as she dismounted from her own horse, and went into the tall grass to find what was left of Master Emrys.

"Me? Me? Maybe if you would give me a hand instead of sitting there like a lump, his mighty mageness wouldn't have ended up in midair. You could have pulled him off me, you know."

"And you didn't have to manhandle a sick little boy." Jannis replied, on her knees in the grass besides Master Emrys. He seemed mostly uninjured, at least there were no bones broken, though Jannis would have bet on a number of large, brightly colored bruises appearing within the next day. Master Emrys was spitting mad, literally, his vehement protestations at the prince's treatment punctuated by spittle flying from his lips.

"Do you need some help up, sir?" Jannis asked Emrys mildly, before shooting a dark glance at Lance.

"Thank you, my lady. It's just my back." Master Emrys replied, taking her offered arm and slowly getting to his feet with a number of winces and flinches. He immediately began rubbing his lower back with his free hand, a pinched expression of pain on his face.

But whatever injury his back had suffered, it did not stop the wiry, middle-aged mage from lunging, or was it staggering, at Lance, with every intention to continue protecting the honor of the young prince bodily. Jannis could not understand it in the slightest. If Master Emrys really was the best mage in the country, why was he brawling like a street-fighter? And against a far superior opponent?

Lance slid sideways and Emrys fell in the dust at his feet. Lance planted one boot in the middle of the other man's back, just to make sure he stayed down, and finished trussing up the prince before turning his attentions back to Master Emrys.

They were both soon tied hand and foot, and tied together atop the prince's horse, when Lance turned to Jannis, his face flat and blank and demanded in a voice just as flat. "Silver knife."

"Lance..." Jannis began, but Lance was having none of it.

"Or I can use my own belt knife. Steel, but the kid should survive it all the same."

Jannis dug the silver knife out of her pack in a huff, shoving both it and the scrap of parchment into Lance's hands with narrowed eyes.

"Always so gracious, my lady." He said in reply, one eyebrow arched in irony.

"I need to set up for the spell." She replied, just as flatly, stalking off with her saddlebag through the long grass. Lance watched her disappearing back for a long moment before turning back to the two bound together atop the horse.

"You know," Lance said consideringly. "It's even money whether leaving you two alive or killing you would cause me more trouble. You might want to keep that in mind whenever you decide to give me more trouble." He advanced on the two of them slowly, deliberately, and sliced the back of the prince's forearm in one clean motion, dabbing the blood onto the parchment as it welled up from the shallow cut. His mild, considering look seemed positively villianous with that bloody dagger in his hand.

Two sets of cold, angry eyes followed Lance as he followed the way that Jannis had went, leading the horses behind him.

Chapter 7

Aerigard sipped his turkish coffee, still steaming from a minor cantrip that kept the silver mug at the perfect temperature and sat back in his heavy cushioned chair. He was in one of several reading rooms in his library, this one on the second floor, and with large leaded glass windows all along one wall that took full advantage of the afternoon sunlight. One large, aged tome sat on his lap, and a stack of others waited within arm's reach on a low dark-stained table to his right side.

There were dozens of oil lamps in the room, should the sunlight fail, and also small glass globes designed to hold mage lights if he did not wish to risk fire around his precious books.

Aerigard placed a bookmark made of crimson ribbon in the book on his lap to mark the page, and closed it with a dull thud, placing it on a table to his left, this one also holding a fair number of books. Selecting the next book in the stack to the right, Aerigard opened the leather cover to scan the table of contents briefly and turned to page 236. He picked up the tray also on the table to his left, that held a few sheets of parchment, two already crammed with notes in his small precise handwritting, an ink well, a blotter of tan cloth and several pens.

Aerigard distributed his attentions equally between the book he was studying, the notes he was taking, and his coffee.

He had come to the reading room on the second floor two hours ago, migrating from the reading room on the fifth floor to take advantage of the better light. He had been in the library, day and night, for the better part of two weeks now.

A lot of sorcerers neglected their studies once they came into any kind of real power, focusing on the hands-on aspect of their work. They lived in workrooms, and sadly, never realized that they were stale and stagnant, repeating the same few steps over and over again, like a man who never learned how to finish the dance he started. That was Aerigard's opinion.

Unfortunately, Aerigard had had to neglect his own books for years now, only able to really read or research with any success for a matter of two or three hours at most. It had been most trying to have his relatives in his house, children inclined to cause trouble at the slightest opportunity. Full grown they may have been in body, the Solarans were still children to his mind.

But his niece and nephew's timely absence gave him the opportunity he had longed for, to finally get some serious research done, and lay the theoretical foundations for a whole new line of sorcery. The workroom would come, later. At the moment he was ecstatic just to be in a quiet house, with nothing to disturb him.

And what he was studying was very dry reading indeed. Aerigard was looking at the most fundamental and abstract qualities of magic. He was examining the nature of elements.

The idea of elements had originated in Greece, with the Greek Elements: fire, earth, water and air; sometimes called the material elements in modern magic. Most schools of magecraft taught only these four elements, but some schools also held that lightning, wood, metal, light, spirit, music or darkness were also elements equal to the classic Greek Elements.

Aerigard had been examining one theory that actually removed water as an element and replaced it with ice, and that held that lightning opposed ice rather than fire, a quaint variation on the classic elemental matrix that had him reaching for another book that claimed that the element of wood was actually a variation of the element of void.

That particular book was more philosophy than any real magical framework, but the ideas seemed similar and they seemed to spark something in the back of his head. Sometimes ideas came quickly and sometimes they had to simmer for a while before they became whole. He recognized the feeling of an idea forming. It almost... itched... inside his head.

Aerigard scanned the page in front of him again, and made a few more notes before closing the book with a thud and selecting the next from the stack. He had a lot of work to do, and his head was buzzing with the feeling of a new idea coming together.

A hesitant knock on the door hardly drew his attention at all, but Aerigard was aware of the presence of another sorcerer, the barely perceptable auras and ripples that surrounded any archmage as obvious to him as the sun rising. Mobius was so quiet, and quite focused and studious, a decided improvement over some of his past apprentices. That also made him more dangerous. Aerigard would have to be a fool not to know that.

"Magic theory." Mobius remarked, running one finger along the stack of books to Aerigard's left. He sounded impressed. Mobius understood why Aerigard would 'waste' time on something like that.

Aerigard didn't look up, finishing the notes he was carefully penning, marking his place in this book with another strip of ribbon, this time a deep purple, and closing it with a thud.

Mobius wasn't a fool. He wouldn't be here, disturbing his master, if it wasn't important. Thus there was no point in getting angry at the man for disturbing him, even if any other entering this reading room would have earned a nasty transformation. Mobius was waiting to be acknowledged by his master before addressing his concerns. Two more marks in his favor; patience, deference.

"What is it?" Aerigard said finally, setting his tray of notes back on the table and sipping at his coffee. He turned that flat, cold basilisk stare on his apprentice, not intended to accuse, merely to remind that if he was disturbed, it had better be important.

"Your niece..." Mobius began, and Aerigard's eyes narrowed. A problem for another time, the man's poorly disguised interest in Jannis. And maybe King Eduardo would solve that problem for him. Maybe. "I've sent her a..." The man actually paused and flushed with embarrassment. Not a good sign. "A stigma notandum."

Aerigard favored him with an even colder stare, his eyes narrowed. The man was surely besotted if he was sending Jannis a letter written in his own blood. It was a foolhardly thing for any sorcerer to do, because there were a large number of very nasty spells that could be cast if an enemy only had the sorcerer's blood to use as a spell component. Most of them fatal. Or worse.

"Please tell me you weren't fool enough to send it by courier." Aerigard commented finally, setting aside his book, and giving Mobius his undivided attention.

"I sent my familiar." Mobius replied stiffly.

Of course, even besotted, he wouldn't be so much of a fool as to leave his blood in the hands of an unknown messanger. Though sending his familiar couldn't be much better, as it put the familiar at risk as well. Aerigard scowled, then his face took on its smooth, emotionless mask.

"What's done is done." Aerigard said finally, as if he were discussing something of no import. "You had cause." The way he said that was half statement and half question. Aerigard required explaination, but a master did not ask an apprentice for information. The relationship between them was often a tightrope.

"I've just completed the preparation for a para-dimensional gate in the south third floor workroom." Mobius said evenly.

"Para-dimensional, not trans-dimensional?" Aerigard asked pointedly. Mobius nodded, he would not make a mistake like that.

"A bi-modal persistant para-dimensional gate," Aerigard mused. "Well that explains why you would need to send the stigma notandum." Though Aerigard still wondered where Mobius had gotten any of Jannis' blood. He would have to have some to link the gate.

"I was wondering, sir," Mobius began almost hesitantly, "Whether you would assist me with the gate."

Aerigard had expected the question: para-dimensional gates required an immense amount of magical power. It didn't make the question any less insubordinate though. If Mobius had been planning this and expecting Aerigard to aid him, he should have told Aerigard from the start about his plans. Aerigard was the master, not Mobius. How Aerigard chose to expend his magical energy was his own business. It didn't need to be squandered for some apprentice's irrational, romantic notion.

"No." Aerigard stated with finality. He turned away from Mobius and selected another book from the table to his right.

"But sir," Mobius persisted, sounding desperate, "It's for your niece."

"Use Lance." Aerigard replied, just as bluntly, growing tired of Mobius's peculiar obsession, and wondering if he wasn't just as flawed as all the other apprentices who had come before him and met singularly spectacular ends. "The boy has to be good for something."

Mobius colored and bowed deeply, excusing himself. "Of course, sir. Sorry for disturbing you."

What Mobius didn't realize of course, as he carefully closed the towering wooden doors as silently as a whisper, was that

Aerigard had every intention of participating in the gate spell. But Aerigard had to remind Mobius just who was in charge.

It was a constant battle of course, between master and pupil, when each was quite powerful in his own right. Experience taught Aerigard to keep a tight rein on his apprentices to make sure that none made the mistake of challenging him directly. Only the first two ever had, and they were still out in the swamp... somewhere. Not in human form; the price of challenging a superior sorcerer.

Aerigard set his silver mug down, and picked up a pen. That idea was still simmering in the back of his mind, and the itching made him irritable.

Jannis finished her own preparations with little effort. The way the gate was designed, the full preparations only had to be performed on one end.

Still, she had to do some minor work, setting up a warding circle, for example, so that changes in local magic wouldn't disturb the carefully crafted weave of magic that formed the gate. Disturbing a gate... caused problems. And she had carefully banked the coals in her tiny brazier, made of bronze with silly clawed feet. An ordinary campfire would have worked, but a constant temperature was better. Jannis didn't like taking chances. Not with a gate, gates were dangerous.

"You do realize," Lance added helpfully from where he lounged on top of the pile of saddlebags a few feet away. "That when you cast this thing, it is going to be felt by any mage with even a hint of magegift for, well, miles in every direction. Gates aren't exactly subtle."

And Lance was quite correct. The enormous amount of magical energy it took to make a gate also made gates visible for miles in every direction to anyone with the magesight. They were currently about three days from the frontline. It was entirely possible that when the gate went up both Harderior's and Kalen's battle mages would sense the gate. And either side could send scouts to investigate. Or assassins. Gates always meant archmages.

"I wish you hadn't said that." Jannis replied, nervous. She really hadn't wanted to be reminded of the collateral consequences of this spell. She just wished things would work out right for once. Somehow that had to be Lance's fault, too.

"I'm not just talking about the armies." Lance continued, as if instructing an idiot. "I'm talking about the Fae."

"What Fae?" Jannis found herself asking. She certainly hadn't been thinking about Fae. They hadn't seen any since they left the swamp.

"Oh right, because, if they were here, you would definately know, and you would see them, right?" Lance asked, voice dripping with sarcasm. "Sometimes I wonder how someone so stupid could live to adulthood. Just because the swamp Fae were familiar with us, and would show themselves, doesn't mean strange Fae would do the same. I'm pretty sure there have to be some around, even if we haven't seen them."

"Right. I guess I better set up another ward." Jannis said weakly, and Lance rolled his eyes. Neither Emrys nor Darien had anything to add, probably because they were both gagged. Lance had gotten tired of their protestations.

"I don't know if I'm comfortable with letting a rank ameteur use me in an extremely complex and dangerous spell." Lance continued, eyeing his sister. "Have you ever even cast a gate before?"

"Well, no." Jannis admitted. "But I've watched uncle do it, and I've read a number of books."

Lance snorted. He could be so crude sometimes. "My blood is on that parchment." He said pointedly, levering himself up to gesture at the scrap of parchment sitting quietly on a cloth with the rest of her spell components. "That means I'll be linked to the spell just as much as you are, and so will our friend the ever-cooperative little prince. Our lives will be in your hands. I don't like it."

Jannis sighed. "Well, what do you want me to do, Lance? Just forget about casting the spell? Go on to the battle as we are? I'm game if you are. It's not like you, or either of those two could cast it in my place. You don't do magic, and neither of them is an archmage."

Lance frowned. "You could at least consult the elephant mage to be sure you're doing it right."

"Maybe I would have, if he wasn't bound and gagged!" She burst out finally in frustration.

"Oh, this is all my fault, is it?" Lance asked coyly, sitting up and crossing his arms in front of his chest. "You are the one who snuck out of the palace, kidnapped the king's grandson, and decided to go harring off to a battlefield."

"But, I..." Jannis attempted to interject, but Lance wasn't finished and he kept going right over her.

"You are the one who has been leading Mobius around by the nose. You are the one who has been dabbling with magic far beyond your skill for years, and for what? You'll never be as good at magic as uncle, and even if you could be, he would never tolerate it. You'd be a rival then. And besides which," Lance added, looking thoughtful. "I don't think you have the ruthlessness you would need to be a good sorceress."

"Ungag Master Emrys." Jannis ordered, teeth clenched.

"Finally going to start listening to me?" Lance asked, raising one eyebrow.

"Of course not!" Jannis hissed. "Half of what comes out of your mouth is utter nonsense and the other half pure spite!"

Lance laughed to himself, dragging the poor mage up, still bound and gagged, and dropping him unceremoniously next to Jannis before pulling the gag out of his mouth.

Master Emrys' eyes flashed daggers at Lance but his mouth was pursed in a tight line. Jannis sighed.

"Please Master Emrys, would you examine my wards and see

if I missed anything?"

"Lady, your brother is a monster." He said instead, tightly, glaring at Lance. And the gaze he turned on her was little better.

Jannis almost screamed in frustration. Was everyone going to start being difficult now?

"What do you expect me to do, Master Emrys? Tie Lance up like he trussed up you and Prince Darien? I've never been able to beat my brother one-on-one."

Lance had the nerve to smirk at her.

Master Emrys paused and the look he cast on Lance this time was more considering than murderous. "I suppose not. And even an archmage couldn't subdue him with magic, not with that enchantment." The look he turned back on her was considerably more polite.

"Your wards are solid enough, if oddly balanced. Why did you use an eight-pointed pattern instead of six or twelve?"

"Well the energies of the wards themselves might interfere with the gate if they aren't harmonized with the gate's energies, which means I have to base them on fours instead of sixes."

"I thought gate energies were based on sixes."

"Only trans-dimensional gates, not para-dimensional gates." Para-dimensional gates were rarer and took more power--they linked two distant locations in the same plane allowing someone to travel great distances instantly, while trans-dimensional gates linked two different planes, two different worlds. In many ways it was easier to make a gate into the world of demons than it was to make a gate like the one she was about to attempt that crossed distance within their own world.

"And there is no reason you couldn't have used a base twelve pattern, since that would be harmonious with either four or six." Emrys continued, looking at her.

Jannis flushed. "I guess I didn't think of that. Do you think I should change it to a base twelve pattern then?"

"No, I don't think its necessary." Master Emrys said after a moment's more study. "With this many layered wards, changing their harmonics might muck everything up. You didn't try to shield the energy from view."

"An exercise in futility, as we both know. Wards strong enough to shield the gate would be strong enough to be sensed in their own right. Just a waste of magical energy, really." Jannis concluded. Master Emrys gave her a grudging nod of approval.

"I can't say I'm happy with the idea of the prince being at risk for this spell," Emrys glanced at her and then over at Lance, eyes narrowing. "But I think you will do well enough. I'd hardly call you an ameteur." He was looking pointedly at Lance, who shrugged.

"Compared to the Dark Lord Aerigard, everyone is an ameteur." Lance said dismissively. "And when did magic become math? Though I suppose one is as useless as another."

"If you knew anything Lance, you would know there is math in everything from building ships to making flutes." Jannis commented dryly.

"Everyone may use math, but no one dithers on about it except scholars." Lance said dismissively.

Mobius stood on the second floor of the library looking up at the painting hanging in the hall, fingering a small vial concealed in the folds of his robe. The hall was poorly lit, the large, glass-paned windows almost covered by heavy maroon drapes.

The weak afternoon light barely scraped the shadows that hung throughout the space, making it seem small and dark despite the high ceilings and polished stone floors. The magelights that lined the hall were unlit save for a couple further down the hall near a door that lead into one of the library's many rooms.

The poor light did little credit to the subject of the painting. An enormous painting, easily the height of a man, it hung high on the wall. In the dark, it had an aura of neglect, like something forgotten, but Mobius's sharp eyes noted the lack of dust, the loving care with which the frame had been polished. The master of this keep spent many lonely minutes standing in this hall, apparently in thought, and certainly only when he thought he was unobserved.

For the painting was of his beloved, dead sister Ciara. Her hair hung, raven black, with a slight sideways curl that seemed quite natural, past her smoothly sloping shoulders. Her gown was fine, of a demure blue-grey, with cream-colored seed pearls worked into the cuffs and neckline in a pattern of winding vines and leaves.

But the thing about the painting that was truly shocking was the face of his master's little sister. More and more each day it seemed that if hair and eyes could somehow change color, it would be Jannis in that picture. There was an uncanny resemblance between Jannis and her mother. Where Ciara was dark, very dark, Jannis was pale, so very pale. But apart from that, they could have been twins. The slope of their necks, the height of their cheekbones, the angle of their eyes... identical.

Mobius stared at the picture in quiet contemplation, the only sign of the intensity of his consideration the tiny furrow across his forehead. This uncanny resemblance was something he could use, something of value, a source of power.

She isn't my weakness, old man--but yours. Mobius allowed the barest hint of a smile to touch his lips. His master had precious few weaknesses, and Mobius knew that well, for he had spent a great deal of effort to discover even the smallest of cracks in the great sorcerer's armor.

Patience. A sorcerer had to have patience. So much was waiting. Wait, and wait, and wait. But then, a great sorcerer had to know when to strike. Long months waiting, and a swift and decisive stroke when the time was right.

Lance would have made a great sorcerer if his uncle hadn't

neutered him. The boy had more than enough audacity, and was capable of great patience when it suited him. Jannis would never have made a good sorceress. She had patience and audacity in measures to rival her brother, but a horrible sense of timing and even worse luck. She wouldn't have lasted a year as a real sorceress.

The Dark Lord Aerigard had had to look elsewhere for an apprentice, rejecting his own kin. But then, very few sorcerers dared risk an apprentice, a possible challenger to their own power. Was it pride or foolishness, the need for another pair of hands to help with the work, or a deeply hidden need for companionship that had driven the Dark Lord to take an apprentice?

Mobius was not the first, only the latest in a long line of apprentices. The Dark Lord Aerigard had never gone without an apprentice for more than a few months. An oddity that could conceal another weakness.

Mobius hadn't decided yet what he would do when he finally tipped the balance of power in his favor. It was barely possible that Aerigard might tolerate becoming subordinate to his former pupil. Far more likely that he would need to die, but for a moment Mobius savored the idea of his master serving him instead. Death was so… final.

Mobius let go of his musings reluctantly. There was still much waiting to be done. Now was only the time to test his master's patience. If Mobius did not do so soon, his master would suspect Mobius's true purpose. Better, far better, to do as the Dark Lord Aerigard expected. Let the master believe he was still in complete control.

Wait for the right time to strike. Mobius was, after all, one of the most patient sorcerers in the world. That was what made him dangerous.

He turned from his contemplation and strode down the hall with a firm, measured step, neither hurrying, nor dallying. Most of the preparations were already in order, but he wanted to check everything one last time before beginning. Someone may have ever so slightly tampered with his careful preparations. Not paranoia, no, but gates were dangerous, and Mobius was careful.

He strode purposefully through the library and out into the stairwell, traveling up one flight of stairs to the third floor. There he unlocked the magically sealed doors with a strange medallion made of a rare faerie metal, orihalcum. Where his master had obtained the metal he did not know, but the Dark Lord had his ways. And making keys out of orihalcum was almost a necessity. Orihalcum was extremely difficult to work with magically, but once enchanted, virtually impossible to tamper with.

He passed through the third floor of the library without pause, past shelves and shelves of rare manuscripts and treatises on magic and philosphy. Aerigard had a great many books that were not strictly magical, especially books on religion and philosophy, many of which had been banned as heresy in one nation or another.

His goal was the work room in the south tower, where his preparations were already complete. He had left a golem there to protect his work, but that would not have stopped Aerigard if his master had intended to tamper.

Mobius slipped through another large doorway, the magical seals springing back into place as he left the library, and walked down a short hall to the workroom. It was floored in stone as many of the workrooms were, though Aerigard had others floored in different enchanted woods, and even one made entirely of iron-- floor, walls and ceiling.

This particular room, and another like it on the second floor, had been set aside for Aerigard's apprentice. The Dark Lord himself had active projects underway in five different rooms in different parts of the castle, some of them heavily warded. Mobius had only been inside two of them.

Mobius checked his preparations carefully, the hulking stone golem in the corner as motionless as a statue. The warding patterns, the ingredients carefully laid out, the mage focus he had spent the last four days charging... everything was in order. And then he replayed the steps of the spell in his mind, outlined in his own handwriting in notes on the table in the workroom. Mobius had cast gates before, but with the power required, no sorcerer cast them frequently.

Finally satisfied, Mobius pulled the last component of the spell from the pocket inside his robes, a tiny glass vial filled with dark red liquid. Jannis's blood. He had not let it out of his sight since the odd day when her half-mad little brother had given it to him.

A terrible risk, that. Mobius could have killed her, enchanted her, done almost anything to her, had he so desired. A slight smile appeared on his face. Lance appeared to believe that Mobius's pretended infatuation with Jannis was real. Enough perhaps, to trust Mobius with her blood, sure he would do no harm? It was hard to tell with that one. He may even have given Mobius the blood intending his sister to come to harm.

They were all so facinating, so unpredictable. It made the game more interesting. Predictable people were easy to control, but they were also boring. It really was too bad that Lance would have to die eventually. The young man had so much promise, but he was, quite frankly, impossible to control.

It was two days after Lance had left the compound, when Lord Firin's guards and workmen were cleaning up the mess he left of the library, that they began to realize just what Lance had been doing while he was there. Lance had had the run of the compound for almost two weeks, digging graves, chopping wood, serving lunch, cleaning everything and anything before that fateful letter from the king had unmasked him and ruined it.

The library itself was structurally intact, the only real damage done to the building were a few cracked support beams. The blood, smashed shelving, scattered and torn volumes, they were easily cleaned up, and it appeared at first that the consequences of Lance's recent stay were resolved.

It was a chance inventory error that led to the missing supplies. Someone started counting and checking the contents of a kitchen storeroom and realized that food was somehow missing. Further inspection revealed a small tunnel, dug in a corner under a pile of empty potato sacks, that led out to the field where Lance had been digging graves.

At that point, Lord Firin, in keeping with his need to monitor and control every aspect of his little corner of the world, ordered a complete inventory of every storeroom.

That was how they discovered the missing supplies in the mage components storeroom in the other building. There were a massive number of unrelated items missing, some of them frightfully valuable. Close inspection revealed another tunnel behind a floor-to-ceiling shelf on the far wall. It also led out to the field.

Lord Firin was so upset between the stolen supplies and stolen books that he started to take ill. Mages are notoriously prone to illness, and Firin, being a mage, was no exception. He also was in ill-favor with the king due to the whole mess. Being in charge of the operation meant he was responsible for the losses.

Given Lord Firin's illness, the stress of leadership, and the problems cleaning up Lance's thefts, he could probably be forgiven the length of time it took him to notice the results of Lance's other activities.

Lance had decided, with his sociopathic curiosity, that if the king and Lord Firin were going to provide him with an entire compound of sick mages, he would use them as test subjects in an enormous human experiment. This sickness the mages of Harderior had—it could not be typical of mages everywhere in the world—or Lance would have read about it in one of his Uncle's books. As such, it must be a local phenomenon, and he was interested in studying it.

Some of Lance's test subjects suffered no ill effect to the substances he had hidden in their food, some actually improved, and there were a handful of mage children who pulled back from the brink of death, put on weight, and had considerably less trouble breathing. The vast majority, however, suffered symptoms that ranged from the comic, like uncontrollable farting or facial warts, to the disastrous.

It wasn't until after the third death that Lord Firin connected the missing magic supplies to the strange malady.

"And you say his heart exploded?" Firin asked the doctor as he examined the corpse.

"Not what I would call an ...ordinary cause of death. But yes, it exploded." The doctor replied, shifting his glasses and cleaning his tools.

"And the last one, Gavin, he died of his organs expanding?"

"As I reported. Yes, sir." The doctor dried his scalpel with a clean cloth and slid it gently back into its slot in his bag.

"And Victoria, died of drowning?"

"She drowned of her lungs filling up with fluid. The fluid wasn't mucus or blood. It was purple."

Lord Firin's hand spasmed and formed into a fist, almost of its own volition.

"Sir, none of these deaths were natural. They were murdered."

"It wasn't by anyone here, doctor." Lord Firin's teeth clenched and he closed his eyes to try to calm himself. "I think I know who is responsible. It's so hard to believe. When you look at him, he's so beautiful. But he's just a demon wearing that perfect face, that perfect form."

"Sir?"

"Don't worry about it, doctor. I will handle it."

The doctor did not say anything, but having his tools cleaned, rolled up his tools and folded his cloths and carefully stowed and closed his bag.

"I'm glad I don't have to deal with the matter, sir. You have my sympathies. If you will excuse me, I have another patient to see." The doctor quietly and professionally excused himself.

"Sir. We have a murderer on the loose, and you know the king is not going to be happy to hear it." The senior guard in the room spoke deferentially, but Firin would have preferred it if he had not spoken at all.

"I know." Firin bit off, thinking furiously. "We need that young man. We need him alive. An archmage is worth more than a hundred ordinary mages to our program, and given what young Lord Lance has done, I doubt the king would want him running free. We should probably keep him in a cell like the animal he is, but I, I want him." Lord Firin's face contorted, a blend of naked rage and desire that was entirely unhealthy.

The guards did not let their discomfort show. That was not their job.

"Orders, sir?" The senior guard enquired.

"Hunt him down." Lord Firin said. "But, remember, I want him alive."

————

Mobius began the spell without hesitation or doubt. He had already double-checked everything. Doubt at this point was a dangerous distraction. If he had made a mistake in his preparations, worrying about it would not change the predictably gruesome outcome.

As he wrote the runes in Jannis's blood with a small calligraphy brush, they each began to glow, hot and fierce. He felt the pull, like a nagging sense of urgency in the direction she must be. Mobius turned slightly to the right to face her. A slight difference of direction would not affect the spell, but it made it more comfortable to work, with the sensation of magic directly ahead of him rather than to his side.

The magic within him began to well up, urgent to join with the barely forming gateway. Mobius relaxed and held it back gently, slowing the flow but not stopping it. Gates were almost alive, and they would pull the necessary energy from the mages in the working, even to the point of death unless the working were disrupted.

This was the dangerous part. Because Jannis had the stigma notandum written in both his blood and his master's, Aerigard would feel the pull as well, would know what was happening and would react. How would he react? This gate was now protection as well as danger; because Aerigard was trapped in the same working with Mobius, as well as with his niece and nephew. Any disruption of the spell could potentially kill them all, and Mobius was the one casting it.

Mobius counted on the Dark Lord's reason overcoming his fury. The time that the gate was active should give him enough time to cool down, and he probably wouldn't attack while the gate was still active, with the risks involved. *Probably.*

Mobius didn't pause to think again on the consequences. This was all part of the plan, and he was now like an arrow springing from the bow, all action. So many fools in his past had assumed that because he thought long, he could not act quickly. They did not understand--the thrill of long planning was the moment of execution.

He formed the gate nexus effortlessly, blending, pressing, shifting enormous raw energies, both from within himself, and his absent but quickly approaching master. The far terminus of the gate was already bright in his mage sight, the whole focus of his world. Far too bright for the distance that lay between them. It shimmered in a way that was not entirely human. Mobius filed that particular piece of information away.

The door slamming open to his rear left did not disturb his concentration. He tied the energies in a loose knot, feeling the irresistable pull from the gate as it fed on his life force. Then and only then did he turn to the door, and his master.

The Dark Lord Aerigard's face was so dark it would have made thunderclouds ashamed. It was painted with unrestrained fury. Mobius quickly scanned it for a trace of fear, but if the Dark Lord was afraid, he concealed it completely.

Mobius felt a slight dissatisfaction, but displayed none of it. Instead he turned apologetic, knowing it would only enrage the other sorcerer more, but at the same time deflect him from a direct confrontation. Magical combat was not the objective of this game. He was playing for the long-term and there was more than one way to win.

"Please forgive me, master." Mobius babbled, letting his voice break, not with fear, but with shame.

The Dark Lord gazed at him, a deadly serpent's gaze, all trace of emotion stripped from his visage like magic. He could have been a statue for all the feeling in his face. In its own way it was more terrifying than his rage of only moments before, especially in the speed of the transformation.

Was the Dark Lord afraid? He had to know what another sorcerer could do with a vial of his own blood. That it could be used in a dozen different ways to bind, to kill, to enchant... And of course, that if his apprentice could lay hands on his blood once, it could happen again.

A very real threat, very blatantly played, but then, if Mobius hadn't threatened him, Aerigard would have seen even greater threat in the absence of an open challenge. That was the danger of having such an astute master. He saw things others would always miss.

Mobius had calculated this carefully. He had had the blood for over a month, carefully preserved with dark magic, waiting for the right opportunity to make his next move. The fact that he acted with Jannis's benefit as his professed purpose should keep his master from striking him down, even after the gate spell was done.

Mobius did not meet that gaze directly. It would be too much of a challenge for his master to overlook. He kept his eyes toward his master, but carefully lowered.

"I seriously doubt you want forgiveness, and even if you did, I'm not inclined." Dark Lord Aerigard pronounced; his tone cold and ever so slightly amused. "You're no fool. I let you acquire some of my blood to see what you would do."

A bluff? Would the Dark Lord deliberately let his own blood fall into the hands of another, even as a test? Could he possibly set up enough protections and counter-spells to prevent his blood from being used against him? Whether or not the Dark Lord was bluffing, the correct response was still the same—pretend to agree with him.

"Of course, sir. It was quite generous of you." Mobius said smoothly, without hesitation. He let his face grow concerned. "I hope you didn't think I would use it against you. I have far too much respect for you."

"And yet you used it in this gate spell against my wishes."

The other sorcerer drolled, face blank, his tone a blend of amusement and threat.

"Not to harm you in any way, master. I merely wished to help your niece." Mobius paused; then added delicately, "I am risking my own life as well. I did send her my blood. Jannis is completely trustworthy. You don't think your niece would act against you, do you?"

The Dark Lord dismissed the possibility with a negligent wave of one hand. Jannis was probably the only person living who was above suspicion in his mind. A tantalizing blind spot in an otherwise impenetrable paranoia.

Mobius could feel the impending possibility of physical confrontation slowly slipping away, and heaved an internal sigh of relief.

"Get on with it." The Dark Lord commanded, each word a pronouncement that would have intimidated kings. "Don't waste any more of my valuable time." He crossed his arms imperiously across his chest, a deliberate gesture. It was meant as an insult--that Mobius was so dense as to miss any more subtle cue. Mobius flushed with the shame of it, but said nothing.

He turned to the spell crafting, the delicate flows of energy already beginning to reach out to the fixed focus on the other end of what would become a tube of magic joining two distant places.

Mobius could feel the energies of the people on the other side of the gate, flowing into his working. That silvery white gleam was Jannis, cold, crystalline, and beautiful. Fear, faintly, irritation and excitement more strongly, flavored her silver magic. That golden raging fire was Lance--hot, chaotic, and immensely powerful. So powerful it frightened him. He had never realized just what level of ability the young man possessed.

The emotions that flavored that golden fire were

indescribable. Mobius would have to pick the sensation apart carefully later to interpret it.

And a third mage, significantly weaker, and younger. His magic tasted slightly bitter, and was colored blue-green, layered over with intense emotions of rage and self-doubt. Curious. Perhaps the Solarans had had to forcibly recruit a third mage for the working.

Confirmation of what he had long suspected. Both of the Solarans were virgins. He filed away the information. Even more useful a piece of information--despite the enchantment that sheathed Lance from head to toe, he could still be used as a source of power in a spell. And such a source of power!

Aerigard's magic was spicy and dark, like cinnamon and allspice. Despite the strong accents and the faint sensation of burning, Aerigard's magic was untainted by emotion of any kind. There was no emotion on his face either, save for a vague boredom. Almost terrifying, the way that Aerigard could stop feeling anything, going from rage to nothingness in an instant.

To be at the center of that flood, that surging torrent of magical energy was more than exhillerating, it was intoxicating. He felt as if he were soaring through the sky, or riding high on a wave of energy, every nerve in his body tingling, his heart racing.

Was this why Aerigard had kept Jannis and Lance alive? Why he had cared for them? The two of them together had more raw magical power than a dozen sorcerers; a wealth, an excess of power that was almost grotesque. Gateways required an enormous amount of power, and yet, here they were, casting a gate with only five mages, and doing so easily. It was appalling.

And Aerigard. His magic was... so refined. Subtle, and far more powerful than it first seemed. It had an aftertaste of fire and ash, the residuals of the demon-summoning the sorcerer practiced.

Such different magics from all three of them, Mobius would have thought it would take great effort to harmonize them and form a seemless whole. But to the contrary, the magics required no effort at all to join--they simply flowed togther as naturally as water. Mobius filed that bit of information away, too. A side effect of blood magic between blood relatives? Facinating.

The tube of magic energy was changing and shifting, taking form from the two sides of the gateway. Mobius could feel the harmonics. Jannis had chosen a base eight harmonic weave. Very unusual for a human mage. Damnably hard to control, it created echoes and ripples that increased the complexity of the spells significantly.

Mobius was glad he had not chosen to use this gate spell as a way to kill Lance, as he had considered. Working through layers of base eight harmonics as well as Aerigard's spell on Lance would have been virtually impossible.

The pull was stronger now, as the gate finally fused in the middle, joining the two sides, and creating a link between two far distant places in the world. A pulse of power, which if uncontrolled could kill, recoiled into each of them. It was little more than a hiccup. Mobius's spellwork was flawless.

Aerigard drummed his fingers on the top of the worktable. Mobius almost started, he hadn't even heard the other sorcerer move. And then, a shiver, as someone entered the gate from the other side.

"Hello, Uncle, did you miss me?"

Lance stood there, in all of his questionable glory.

Chapter 8

Jannis drummed her fingers on top of a half rotted log near where the gateway opened. She had no idea that she was echoing her uncle, far away, and yet only a few short steps through the waiting gate. Lance had not been gone long, but she was already worried that he was up to no good.

Lance was always up to no good, and she preferred having

him where she could see him. He still got away with a lot, even when she was watching, but far less than he could manage alone.

She deliberately did not look over where the prince was tied up, gagged, and no doubt shooting unpleasant looks in her direction.

The elephant mage, as Lance called him, or Master Emrys as he should more properly be called, was tied up, but not gagged, a short distance away from the prince. Lance had carefully planned so that they could not untie each other.

The gate spell felt... strange. She didn't know how to describe the sensation. It was a part of her, it pulled on her, and drained her energy, but it was not an unpleasant sensation. And she could feel the energies of the other people in the working.

She had never been in a spell-working of this size, though she had done some spellwork with her uncle upon occasion, and even with her brother, before that fateful incident with the hell hound. She had not, however, ever felt Mobius's magical energies before, nor had she ever felt Darien's.

It was unsettling to realize how much weaker the prince was than the rest of them. Lance, of course, was the strongest by far, with their uncle Aerigard next in power, but it was hard to say whether Mobius or she had greater raw magical strength, and neither of them were that far behind her uncle in terms of raw power.

Odd. Jannis mused on these things, still drumming her fingers as she waited for Lance to return.

And then another sensation, which had nothing to do with the gate. Jannis paused, her fingers hovering in mid-air above where they were about to strike the dry wood. She listened, and looked around, with both physical and magical eyes.

Nothing.

What was that?

Jannis frowned, and decided that she was not imagining things. She wasn't the sort much given to flights of fancy.

"Master Emrys, did you feel that?"

"My lady?" He inquired, question in his voice.

"I don't know what that was, but I just felt something."

"The gate, perhaps?"

"No, nothing to do with the gate." Jannis frowned, and her forehead furrowed, as her eyes narrowed suspiciously. She rose from where she was sitting, as silently as she could manage, her leather armor creaking ever so slightly as she straightened.

"I felt something." Jannis repeated, reaching for her sword. She scanned the surrounding dead grass and trees slowly, looking for the source of the disturbance, but could see nothing.

"Perhaps it was just the wind?" Emrys offered, hesitantly.

"Or perhaps I'm just paranoid." Jannis responded flatly. "Not that surprising, considering my family, wouldn't you say? But if I've learned one thing from my brother, it's that letting down your guard is the stupidest thing you could ever do."

"And if it's nothing?"

"Then I look like an idiot. Wouldn't be the first time."

Jannis checked all of her wards quickly, but carefully. Nothing had disturbed or penetrated them.

She bit her lip, wondering if she was in fact jumping at shadows. But then her resolve hardened again. No, there was something, even if it was gone now, there was something out there.

Her fingers tightened on her swordhilt, but she did not draw, not yet. She was no fool, and she would not be caught unawares, not again.

The gentle tap on her shoulder, from behind, made her jump a foot in the air, and bite down hard on a startled yelp. Lance stood there, grinning like an idiot, and handed her a well-worn and very welcome sword. It was her own sword from back home. She had been so sad to leave it behind, but what kind of message would it send for a new queen to come carrying a sword?

"Mobius enchanted it." Lance added helpfully. "He's been working on enchanting our gear ever since we left home."

"Why would he do that?" Jannis replied doubtfully.

"Because I asked him to." Lance reassured. "You know how

persuasive I can be."

"Persuasive, right." Jannis concluded, amused.

"The armor was a lot harder than the swords, at least according to Mobius. Something about our swords being made with mostly Faerie metals instead of iron or steel. I think he was just being lazy."

Lance turned and walked back into the gateway, leaving behind the pair of swords and pair of helms he had been carrying. Presumably it would take several trips to bring all of their gear across the gate.

Jannis examined her sword minutely. She could see the energies penetrating the metal, but didn't recognize all of them.

"Lance," she called, as he came back through the gate, "Did Mobius say what kind of enchantment he put on this?"

Lance gave her a flat look, and slowly set down the enormous pile of metal armor pieces he had been carrying. He took longer than he strictly needed to, arranging the armor carefully next to their saddlebags.

"What's the matter, sis? Didn't study enchanting with the same enthusiasm as all the rest? Don't tell me you can't tell what it is just by looking at it."

"Lance." She repeated warningly, gripping the swordhilt in both hands. The other, ordinary sword, still hung at her hip, forgotten. "If I could have enchanted my sword, don't you think I would have done it myself?"

"So what you are saying is that you are useless. Good to know. Not really new news." He was not even looking at her, already moving back towards the gate to fetch another load.

Jannis stared at her sword with irritation, trying to puzzle out the enchantment laid on it. She really did know some things about enchanting, but not this. It wasn't something that she generally worked at, enchanting metal. She had learned other variants, how to enchant paper, how to enchant cloth, that sort of thing. Metal was different. It wasn't something she liked to work with magically. It was actually quite surprising that Mobius could enchant metal. It was a fairly rare talent among mages.

"I really would like to meet this Mobius," Master Emrys mused from the ground where he sat, staring at the sword in her hands, curious.

"You really wouldn't." Jannis replied, sighing. "He's a sorcerer. And, well, I think that says enough."

"Lady, isn't your own uncle a sorcerer of most fearsome reputation?"

"Exactly." Jannis sighed again. "Take it from someone with experience, sorcerers aren't very pleasant company."

"I'm sorry you feel that way." The voice, soft, smooth, without menace, still sent a shiver straight up her spine. Mobius stood there in the gateway. Lance smirked, and continued carrying metal armor past them both. He had a gauntlet in one hand, and a vambrace slung over his left shoulder.

"I didn't mean..." Jannis stammered, flushing.

"Of course not." Mobius replied, reassuring. "Do not fear, I will not be accompanying you. Your brother assures me he has your safety in hand." The look he dropped on Lance was hard to describe, and Jannis found it disturbing.

"I hope you are well," Jannis said finally, awkward in the silence.

Mobius looked at her, a heavy, mysterious gaze, and smiled.

"My lady," Mobius said softly, bowing slightly. "I am ever concerned for your safety. Be well."

He turned and slipped back through the gate, and Jannis suppressed a shiver. Sorcerers.

The gate energies slowly began to fade, and the resulting rush as her energy returned made the hairs all stand up on the back of Jannis's arms. As seemless a gate working as any mage could want. Mobius really did know his stuff. Even if he was incredibly creepy. Sorcerers. She rubbed the goosebumps on her arms, or at least tried to, with the leather bracers covering most of them.

Mobius returned to the castle through the gate as quickly as he could without alerting the Solarans to his need to leave. He kept his face deliberately smooth, and turned away from Aerigard as soon as he was back inside the gate to give himself enough space to close his eyes and grimace for a moment.

Aerigard chuckled behind him, clearly amused.

"Appalling, isn't it?" His master asked as Mobius gathered himself quickly.

"What do you mean, master?"

"Harderior's blood sickness. All mages lower than archmage suffer from it to one degree or another, it's true. However, the severity of the hermetic anemia in Harderior is simply appalling." Aerigard had taken on a lecturing tone, but Mobius did not find it offensive. He had sought out this man as his teacher specifically because of Dark Lord Aerigard's vast knowledge. Aerigard paused, briefly contemplative, and a sour look came into his face. "When King Eduardo first approached me, I truly believed he wanted help dealing with the symptoms of the blood sickness all of his mages have been dying from. How altruistic of me. I really need to stop thinking the best of people."

Mobius allowed his grimace to show openly, at least a little.

"I must admit, master, I did not expect that hermetic anemia could be so severe. Why is it so much worse in this one particular kingdom?"

"A number of reasons," Aerigard waved one hand, loftily. "Iron deposits in the ground near major populated areas mean that there is a lot more exposure. More exposure means that mages suffer from more nausea and eat less red meat, which causes a deficiency. Harderior has a major cheese industry and the people there consume a lot of calcium, which can in some instances inhibit the body's ability to absorb iron. But more tellingly, in Harderior there are high rates of tannins in their wines and teas."

Mobius's brow scrunched up, and he did not bother to conceal it. "Tannins? You mean the substance extracted from oak trees that they use to tan leather? I am sorry if I am having trouble following, master."

Aerigard shrugged.

"What, wine making and tanning not glamorous enough? All knowledge has value. Tannins are a major problem in some areas in wine making. Yes, they are the same substances used for tanning leather, but they also cause that dry feeling in the mouth from a particularly dry wine." The Dark Lord paused, his eyes boring into Mobius's, and smiled, faintly, before continuing.

"The tannin content in Harderior wine is very high. And tannins, when consumed, inhibit the body's ability to absorb iron. Lower iron absorption means more cases of anemia. And as far as I know, local custom in Harderior encourages a lot of drinking."

"Forgive me for saying so, master, but you seem to have made quite a study of the matter."

"As I said, I was expecting King Eduardo to ask for my assistance. I made sure to do my research."

"And you found a solution?"

"Of course." Aerigard's smile was dark and mysterious. "It's too bad he was more interested in breeding stock than saving lives, wouldn't you say?"

Duke Tellis toyed with the parchment on his desk absently.

The Lady Solaran's abrupt departure had worried him a great deal, but with the king apparently undisturbed, he could not let his concern show.

The king had made a point of sending a highly encrypted message by carrier pigeon to the army on the front, but only so much could be said in such a message. Pigeons were frequently intercepted, and any code could be decyphered. If the message got through, General Frederick would be expecting Prince Darien and Lady Jannis. If the message was intercepted and decoded, the enemy would be expecting them. But an archmage should be able to handle herself. He hoped.

Tellis frowned for a moment at his empty glass, and reached for a decanter of wine on a side-board. He really should have had a manservant or a page in here to refill his glass, but he valued his privacy too much while thinking, and he got precious little privacy at all.

His study was elegant, comfortable and rich. It was decorated with the intent to overwhelm a guest, which is why he frequently used it to meet people. But underneath the calculated opulence, he had a good solid desk and a soft cushioned chair, which was a good thing, since he spent a great deal of time here.

As he put the decanter back on the side-board, his eyes fell on the empty box that had once been full of weyrstone and he scowled. It was painful to think of.

Could Jannis be as much trouble as her brother? A terrifying thought.

What had the king's bargain with that damnable sorcerer cost them? Would they know until it was too late?

He lifted the parchment from his desk as if seeing it for the first time, examining it for any clue. Distance writing was a Fae enchantment, and for the Lady to have enchanted this particular piece of paper, which had been sitting on the king's writing desk, she would have had to handle it herself.

When she was first brought to the castle, he knew, she had been put into the king's study to wait for him to finish with his war council. She had probably handled the paper then. Had she been planning this from the start?

He leaned back into his chair, still holding the parchment and frowning in thought. The beautiful mahogany brown velvet doublet he wore was just a little too tight for comfort. He had been putting on a little weight of late, possibly due to all these late nights. It was hard not to have an extra glass or two of wine when one was working until nearly dawn.

He pulled on the velvet, making it settle right as he shifted in the chair, finally setting the parchment back on the desk again in frustration. It yielded no more clues now then it had when he had first seen the writing appear on its surface.

He sighed, and knowing he was safely alone, voiced the thought that ran through his mind.

"What have you gotten us into this time, your Majesty?"

———————

Jannis glared at Lance. She didn't know why she was glaring at him, yet, but knowing him, she would have good reason within minutes.

Lance shrugged, trying not to let her suspicion bother him, or at least not to let it show. And it did bother him, a little, that she would think so poorly of him. It bothered him more that he got away with much less when Jannis was around. She was worse than a jailer.

"What's wrong with you, sis? Did you wake up on the wrong side of the boulder?" He smirked.

They had had a rough night of it, despite the supplies Jannis had brought from the palace and the supplies Lance had brought from Lord Firin's estate. Jannis had elected to go without blanket, giving hers to the young prince, who was much the worse for wear since the gate weaving.

Master Emrys was suffering from some kind of malady old people deal with, arthritis, which apparently made it painful to even move, and the expected spectacular bruises from his Lance-propelled flight through the air yesterday had appeared on schedule.

All four of them were miserable, tired, cold, and hungry. Which meant Lance was even more cheerful then usual. He knew how much people hated that.

"All I want--all I need--is some coffee." Jannis said, longingly. She ran the tip of her tongue across her lips and her eyes took on a distant, foggy look, as she imagined the turkish coffee she and her uncle adored.

"Don't suppose you brought any with you?" Lance asked offhandedly, and Jannis scowled.

"Oh well, none of the rest of us care about your coffee. At least we have some water. And some, what are these? Field rations?" Lance held up a withered, leathery piece of meat of dubious origin, and examined it minutely, as if it were the most interesting thing in the world.

"Hey elephant mage, do you recognize this?" Lance asked, happily, shoving the strip of dried meat at the other man. Master Emrys and the prince had been released from their bonds after the gateway had closed the evening before.

"Eat it or not, I really don't care." Master Emrys replied flatly, rubbing his swollen hands and wrists. Whether the swelling was due to his arthritis or to the injuries from the day before, or both, was unknown. Master Emrys had a somewhat lower opinion of Lance now, after the rough treatment the prince had endured.

The prince was a sight. Not a good sight. He was weak, and wheezing, and his face was pale and wan, waxy colored with yellowed overtones. He was still lying in the heap of blankets where he had slept the night before, only stirring to drink the water Jannis had brought him. Master Emrys had bandaged his bleeding hand carefully, with some herbs in the bandage to keep away infection.

"What about you, your royal Sickliness? Want some?" Lance proffered the pathetic strip of meat towards the heap of blankets, and Darien's eyes were the only thing that responded. They rotated towards Lance in his silent, motionless face and stared, accusingly.

"Guess not." Lance shrugged, oblivious. "More for me."

"Darien isn't feeling well, Lance. Do you have to pester him?" Jannis asked, finally having reason for her earlier glare.

"We could just leave him here." Lance said hopefully. "Let him get some rest."

"Abandon a sick little boy in the middle of the wilderness?" Jannis asked, disgusted.

"Surely I've done worse things." Lance replied dismissively.

"Your past performance isn't any kind of measure I would want to use." Jannis countered.

"Do you two ever shut up?" Master Emrys grumbled, still rubbing his aching joints, elbows this time.

"Why do you put me in a category with him?" Jannis said, glancing at her horrible brother.

"Aww sis, you say the nicest things. Obviously, I'm in a category all of my own. There is no comparison." Lance said grandly, puffing out his chest and almost sounding serious.

"Goddess, I would almost sell my soul for some coffee." Jannis said longingly, putting her head in her hands.

"Careful with that one sis: don't sell yourself short, I am sure there are plenty of, well, demons in the market. You could do a lot better than some coffee."

"Mmm... Yeah, you are right, I could do a lot better than selling my soul for some coffee; I bet I could trade my brother for some coffee. There has to be someone, somewhere that wants you, Lance."

"Ha ha, your pitiful mockery disturbs me not. I know there are plenty of demons that would give an awful lot for all of this." Lance gestured at himself with both hands, and grinned.

"I'd take the coffee."

"You have an unhealthy obsession with coffee." Lance commented dryly, his face resisting the urge to twist into a roguish grin. "There are so many more important things we could be talking about—like me."

"And who is talking about unhealthy obsessions? Do you ever stop talking about yourself?"

"Speaking of unhealthy obsessions, I have to tell you about this guy, Lord Firin. Now, I've gotten used to the mindless admiration of the masses over the years, irritating as it may be—it's really unavoidable considering how spectacular I am—but he took the admiration to an uncomfortable level."

Jannis raised one eyebrow at her brother and pursed her lips.

"Lance… you don't mean…"

"Goddess, you have a filthy mind. No, I don't mean that. He was just a little excessively interested in me."

"Lord Firin has been dedicated to King Eduardo's mage breeding program for years. It is hardly unexpected that he would take interest in an archmage, any archmage, when we have been trying so hard to find them for so long." Master Emrys commented, still rubbing his arms.

Lance ignored Master Emrys, and continued.

"I suppose I might just have to get used to this celebrity, now that we are out of the swamp. More people are going to know we exist, and that means, once they realize just who I am, they are going to start worshiping me. This is going to be very tiring."

"Normal people don't talk like that, Lance." Jannis commented wryly, taking a drink of water from her flask.

"That's *why* they are normal." Lance said disparagingly. "Why would I want to be ordinary?"

He stretched a little, and tossed the scrap of meat back in the supplies.

"I don't know what your problem is. Why would you want me to have some kind of false modesty? I mean, I know exactly how great I am, and everyone else who encounters me immediately recognizes my greatness. Well, except for you, sis, you seem to have been born with some kind of mental defect that prevents you from recognizing it." He sighed and shook his head. "And all this despite the fact that I give you plenty of opportunity to see my greatness in action. I've almost given up hope for you, sis."

"Then how do you explain how almost everyone that meets you, hates you? How many people have tried to kill you?" Jannis asked, sweetly.

Lance sighed again.

"I'm afraid that the admiration people feel when meeting me is just too great for an ordinary mind to contain. It overwhelms them within a very short period of time. And eventually, inevitably, turns to uncontrollable jealousy that such a perfect being as I could exist. I've learned to live with it. That almost everyone I meet will eventually hate me, no matter what I do."

"I'm not jealous of you, Lance." Jannis said.

"No, you're special. Horribly flawed, and probably brain-damaged, but at least I don't have to suffer that same uncontrollable jealousy from you, sis."

"I think there is one thing we can agree on then, Lance." Jannis paused, for emphasis. "The more people who know you, the more people are going to try to kill you."

Lance opened his mouth as if to respond, then closed it again, silent. He paused, contemplative.

"For once, I think you're right, sis. This could be a serious problem."

"You do realize we are heading for a battlefield, Lance." Jannis added. "Pretty much everything they have there is designed to kill people."

"And what if one of them gets lucky? It would be a crime beyond imagining if the world were deprived of me..."

"You might have to... conceal your greatness a little, Lance." Jannis concluded, smiling internally, even as she wore a mask of concern.

Lance sighed. "I'm not an idiot, sis. I can dampen my brilliance so that I don't blind random passersby. I even cleaned the floors when I was at Lord Firin's estate!"

"What a horrible imposition that must have been." Jannis said, trying to keep a straight face.

"You have no idea."

At that moment, Darien passed out. His eyes rolled back in his head, and Master Emrys came to his feet and rushed over to the prince's side in distress.

"His heart is racing!" Master Emrys exclaimed, checking the prince's pulse at his neck. "And he's having trouble breathing!"

The prince's chest rose and fell in short, rapid gasps.

Jannis hurried over, and fell to her knees at the prince's other side, unsure how she could help.

"What can we do?" She asked, helplessly.

"Elevate his legs. I wish we had some kind of medicine…" Master Emrys said, leaning down to listen to the prince's breath with his ear near to the boy's lips.

Jannis pulled over one of the saddlebags and pushed it under Darien's knees. She grabbed a second saddlebag and pushed it under his ankles. Then she stood there for a moment, feeling helpless, completely unsure of what to do.

"I warned you, lady, I did." Master Emrys spoke harshly, maybe more harshly then he had intended, because of his concern for the boy. "He was already weak, and you two had to cut him open."

Jannis bit her lip, but Lance just rolled his eyes.

"He'll be fine." Lance said flippantly, dismissing the matter. "He's not that big, we can tie him to the horse and keep moving."

"Oh that tears it," Jannis declared, stalking towards Lance and reaching for him. Lance fended off her emotional strikes almost gently, still talking as he snagged her wrist and pulled her into a bearhug, holding her arms immobile.

"Calm down, sis. You always did get worked up over nothing."

"How can even you be so cold, so uncaring? He could die, Lance!"

"So what if he does?" Lance asked, ruthlessly. "I really wouldn't care."

"I care!" Jannis declared, struggling against his arms.

"Well, you should! Its your fault he's out here. If you hadn't drug that poor, sick child along, he would still be in his soft, warm bed! If he dies, it will be because of you."

"Lance, how could you?" Jannis sobbed, gasping.

"I'm going to let you go now," Lance replied, ignoring her struggling and her tears. "So get ahold of yourself. I'm going to go scouting around, see where we are and the best way to go. You two can stay here and obsess over the boy."

Lance didn't just release her, he shoved her, so that she staggered away from him, and he had enough room to turn and start walking the other direction.

"Lance!" Jannis shouted, but he just waved back at her, without turning around.

"Don't expect me to dig the grave if the boy dies. I did enough grave digging already."

Lord Firin stood, surveying the line of cloth-wrapped bundles awaiting burial with his lips pursed into a thin, tight line.

Fortunately, they hadn't had any more "special" deaths after the first three, but the renegade archmage loomed large in Firin's mind all the same.

The guards had quickly found his trail leading away from the estate, and just as quickly, lost it. Lord Firin didn't realize it, but Lance had long ago mastered the art of disappearing--the result of a lifetime being doggedly chased by an annoying and overbearing older sister bound and determined to ruin his fun.

Firin stared at the row of bodies, irritated and aggravated. He felt so helpless sometimes. He would have given anything to keep them from dying, and they still died. He breathed deeply of the crisp autumn air, the last lingering traces of summer still scented the wind when it fitfully gusted by.

The guards were scouring the countryside looking for Lance Solaran, and the news from the palace was little better: his sister had similarly disappeared. The king was, by all accounts, taking the news quite well, but Firin doubted that Eduardo was nearly as calm as he appeared to be. Firin was right. Eduardo had his own plans in motion, and one of them chose that moment to ride up to him, armed and armored, with a squad of similarly armed and armored men from the palace guard.

"Lord Firin?" The man asked deferentially, handing down a sealed letter from where he sat in his saddle. "I'm Lieutenant Flemming from the Royal Guard. His Majesty has placed me in charge of the force being sent to protect his future wife and the future king, Prince Darien. I was instructed to detour here to get magical support."

It had been a rough couple of days for the poor lieutenant. In the flurry of activity searching for the missing Lady Solaran, he had been so busy that he hadn't bothered to check on the new recruit, Lydia, that he had sent to guard the prince's quarters until nearly three hours later. That had not been a pleasant surprise. The sight of the empty room had been accompanied by the most horrific sinking feeling in the center of his chest. For a very brief moment, very brief, he had considered saying nothing, or even fleeing the palace discretely, but then military training had kicked in.

He promptly reported his discovery to Captain Schrander. The captain was displeased, but did not reprimand--sitting quietly, a tight, sour expression on his face. The captain politely but firmly dismissed him, and went in person to report the new information to His Majesty.

Lieutenant Flemming had waited in restless anticipation for the captain's return, turning his pent-up frustration to handling all the minor administrative hiccups that inevitably ran through the guard in the captain's absence.

It was more than an hour after that, that Captain Schrander returned and informed the other man that the king wanted a word in private.

"You spoke with my wife." The king said to him, the moment that Flemming had knelt before him in the king's study. "Do you have any insight into what is going on in that pretty head of hers?"

The lieutenant hesitated, and considered his words carefully before speaking.

"She seemed... lonely, my lord. Perhaps she was pining for the company of her brother."

The king paused, irritated, as if the words were nothing what the king was hoping for.

"Any idea why she would have kidnapped my grandson and gone harring off to the front line to take on Kalen single-handed?" The king barked.

"No, sir. I have no idea."

"That fool woman. I've already told Captain Schrander this, but I need some good men to go after her, and I thought, given your exemplary past service, you might want to make up for your stupidity earlier this evening." The king looked pointedly at the lieutenant, who blushed furiously in response, both in shame and anger.

"Of course, your Majesty." He said, standing and saluting the king.

"Get out of here. You don't have time to dally," the king gestured, and one of the everpresent pages ran up to Lieutenant Flemming with three sealed letters, and another unsealed scrap of parchment. He took the papers without even glancing at them, backed up a couple of steps out of respect, and then turned and ran for the door.

Three hours later he was in the saddle with a good-sized squad of men, waiting in the courtyard outside of Lord Firin's estate. Lord Firin was a small, sickly man, who dressed in dark, somber clothing. He was a wretched, twisted spider, who had helped poison His Majesty's mind with this unreasonable hunger for ever more magic. Flemming did not like the man. What's more, Lord Firin seemed the kind of person who without even trying makes everyone else around him miserable.

Lord Firin examined the letter for only a moment before breaking the seal. He was quite familiar with the king's messages. He scanned the page for a long minute in complete silence, while the horses snorted, and shifted their feet, leather saddles creaking. The waiting men said nothing to disturb him.

Finally Lord Firin folded the letter in his hand and turned his attention to the still-mounted guards.

"You want someone right now, I expect?" He said, slightly offended that they did not even bother to dismount in his presence.

"Forgive me, sir, but this is a matter of some urgency." Lieutenant Flemming said softly.

Lord Firin scowled, but gestured, and several men in the yard went running for the main building.

"I'm coming with you." Lord Firin declared, unexpectedly. Flemming blinked but did not bother contradicting him. It was well-known that Lord Firin was a mage. Flemming did not have the authority to demand a different, more amiable mage.

Flemming gestured to his men, and one of them led a horse,

already saddled with tack, to Lord Firin.

"Your selection is limited, I'm afraid, guardsman. Not many of our mages can endure a hard ride." Firin said, by way of explaination as soon as he was in the saddle.

Two more mages were rushing from the building, one of them an older woman, wrinkled as a prune, her hair heavily grey with only a few streaks of its original golden-brown color. The other mage was a young man, too young to shave, thin as a stick and looking like he would break in two with a single good blow. Each accepted a horse from a guardsman.

The entire group gathered and started moving as soon as the mages were settled, Lord Firin taking pride of place at Flemming's side. The lieutenant said nothing. The man might be tedious, but it was far better to humor him in any way possible. Firin was the kind of person who remembered a slight, and just might try to find a way to repay it later.

The group hurried out the road, heading, ironically, back towards the king's castle. It was faster to take the road than to cut across country, and with the direction of the enemy encampment, it made more sense to go that way, before taking another road several miles further on.

They moved at a good pace, but with the even road and good light it was still quite possible to carry on a conversation while riding.

"Did you meet him at the palace?" Firin asked.

"Meet who?" The lieutenant inquired politely, unsure what Lord Firin was talking about or why the dark little man was feeling so talkative.

"The brother. He's an archmage, you know. They both are."

"I never had the pleasure. I saw the wedding party when they rode in. He seemed a handsome sort of fellow, tall, blond, clean-shaven, not much muscle on him. I never would have guessed he was an archmage."

Firin had a sour expression on his face. Fleming politely

ignored it and continued.

"He was out at the estate for some time, wasn't he? After he assaulted his sister, I heard the king sent him out there to cool his heels a bit."

"He did." Firin snapped, irritated. Flemming wondered why the man had chosen a topic of conversation that caused him such discomfort and debated changing the subject. But then Lord Firin spoke again.

"Lord Lance ran off. He stole a number of valuable books from the library, kidnapped one of my most trusted, reliable mages, and ran off. He also raided the pantry, took supplies, horses, and who knows what else. There were things missing from the magic stores."

Ah. Firin's irriation made more sense now, as well as why they were talking about this.

"You think he would go looking for his sister." Flemming said. It was not a question.

"I do." Firin's face twisted in a scowl. "And I intend to retrieve my man, my books, and that two-faced bandit of an archmage on this little mission of ours."

"The prince's safety has to come first." Flemming warned. "And that of our future queen. But you have my support if we come upon the lady's brother. If a thief, he at least deserves to meet the king's justice."

"Good." Firin said, with finality. The dark little nobleman pulled up a bit, and let Flemming take the lead, falling in behind to give them both room.

———

"Lance is right." Jannis said miserably to Master Emrys, as they both tried to do whatever they could to make Darien comfortable.

"I'm sure that's a novel experience for him." Master Emrys commented, shifting the blankets around Darien slightly to cover him better. His face was pained and concerned.

"I never should have taken him from the castle."

"If you are looking for comfort you are talking to the wrong person. I agree: You never should have taken the prince."

Jannis huddled miserably in a ball on the ground next to Darien.

"You know what your problem is? You don't recognize other people's limits. Darien was struggling for quite a while before he finally got this bad. But you kept pushing."

"I thought he would be alright." Jannis said lamely. "He wanted to come. He wanted to help."

"We often want what we can't have."

"I mean, I know he was only seven, and sick, but... When Lance was seven he could fly, he could take down grown men... He even almost destroyed the world, once." Jannis paused, perhaps realizing what she was saying. "But Darien isn't like Lance, is he?"

"Lady, no one is like your brother, and that is a blessing I think I will fervently thank the goddess for."

"How could I be so stupid?" Jannis moaned.

"Lady, you aren't stupid. You are ignorant, which is dangerously similar. How could you know how bad the blood sickness is for us? You've never experienced it before. But maybe you should have listened to those of us that have." Master Emrys sat back with a heavy sigh that seemed to deflate the man as she watched. He absently rubbed at his lower back, but his eyes never left the prince.

"Maybe you could tell me about it," Jannis suggested.

"There isn't much to tell. All mages in Harderior suffer from it. All the mages in the world, really, but we seem harder hit here."

"Really? That seems odd, do you have any idea what causes it?"

"It's a blood sickness. Causes a yellow cast to the skin, weakness, difficulty breathing, irregular heartbeat..." Master Emrys sighed again, and placed his fingers beside the prince's neck.

"His heart is still racing. I pray it doesn't give out on him."

"I was thinking when I first heard about this blood sickness, that it was caused by iron, or the lack of iron, in the blood."

"You mean hermetic anemia?" Master Emrys' forehead furrowed. "Yes, that is entirely probable. There isn't anything to do about it, though. Mages have a very strong averse reaction to iron. Giving them more only makes them sicker, even though the lack of iron is what is making them sick in the first place. You just can't win."

"But it doesn't affect everyone equally. You don't seem that bad, Master Emrys."

"No, and I wish I knew why. I was thinking perhaps that the severity of the bloodsickness in Harderior is due to some kind of flaw in the bloodlines here. I wasn't born in Harderior; I moved here when I was eight. Maybe that is why I don't suffer as much."

"You mean you came from another country? Which one?" Jannis asked, genuinely curious.

"Kalen. I try not to advertise it much, given that we are at war. People can get strangely paranoid sometimes."

Jannis shuddered. "I can imagine." A thought occurred to her. Suddenly everything that wasn't quite fitting clicked into place. "Is that why you were off on some estate instead of at the front lines? What exactly did you do to get off of battlefield duty?"

Emrys chuckled. "You really are sharp, I'll give you that.

Most mages are... unsettled by the sight of blood. Lots of people are, but it's worse for mages because of the iron in it. I just... exaggerated my reaction a bit."

"You pretended to be hemophobic?"

"I might have passed out a few times at the sight of blood, yes. Enough to make my move to Lord Firin's estate where I could constructively assist the war effort in my own way. Without killing my former countrymen."

"Why on earth are you telling me this? Considering the level of crazy paranoia and just general crazy in this country, you could be charged with treason if someone found out!"

Master Emrys sighed.

"It's the reason Prince Darien is so important. His Majesty has... unusual views about mages and magic in general. They have strained what were once mostly peaceful relations with Kalen. I believe the prince will turn it around, when he finally comes into his own--that he will heal these wounds between our nations."

Master Emrys leaned over and brushed aside an errant lock of hair that had slid onto Darien's unconscious face.

"Did you tell Prince Darien? That you were from Kalen?"

"Of course not. It would make things much harder for him. The prince respects me, and if he knew I was from Kalen it might change the way he thinks about the people. It's a lot easier for him if he sees them as the Enemy, faceless, and nameless. If he starts seeing them as people, with families and children of their own, he might lose his nerve. He might not be able to kill them."

"It's disgusting." Jannis pronounced. "Probably more disgusting than treating people like breeding animals. I mean, sending children out to a battlefield and making them kill people. And how does it make any sense that you avoided the battlefield so you wouldn't have to kill, and yet a little boy like Darien has to?"

Emrys sighed heavily, pain in his face.

"I can't argue with that, lady, that I cannot."

They sat there in awkward silence for a few moments.

"Maybe you can make a difference, put an end to the war somehow. I mean, if diplomacy fails, there is always subterfuge and sabotage--we can just set Lance on the Kalen army. Goddess knows, that maniac is like a living weapon. It's almost inhumane to even think of it." Emrys smiled darkly as he said it, but there was still pain in his face.

Jannis caught a glimpse of a blond head over the tall waiving grasses, still somewhat distant.

"Maybe I should go see what he is up to." She offered, already rising. Having Lance out of sight for any period of time made her very nervous.

"I'll stay with the prince." Master Emrys said in reply, not even looking at her, all his focus on that tiny, fragile body.

Chapter 9

"Oh there you are, sis." Lance said, without turning as Jannis came up.

"You couldn't possibly have finished scouting around already, Lance."

"Oh no, I was waiting for you to get over your girly hissy-fit so we could talk. Privately."

A surge of sudden apprehension ran up Jannis's spine. She swallowed.

"What have you done now?"

"Why do you always assume I am up to no good?"

"Mostly because you always are up to no good!"

"Always, always. Never, never. You see the world in black-and-white instead of seeing it for its possibilities."

"I see enough of your possibilities that I have trouble sleeping at night."

"Sometimes you say the nicest things, big sister."

"Are you ever going to get to the point?"

"How is his royal Sickliness? Dead yet?"

Jannis resisted the urge to strangle Lance. Barely.

"Prince Darien isn't going to die!"

"So touchy! You really are getting attached to that annoying little brat, aren't you?"

"And why should you care, Lance?!"

"I don't care. I thought I already said as much: I don't care if the brat lives or dies or grows wings and runs off to become a hippogriff."

"Then why are we even having this conversation?"

Lance rolled his eyes and raised his hands skyward as if pleading for patience from some unseen diety.

"Because. Obviously. You care."

"And when has that ever mattered to you?"

"It's always mattered to me! Goddess, you can be so dense sometimes. Look, whatever, just take it." Lance wasn't even looking at her, but he had lifted a small bottle of dark, thick, bubbled glass. Whatever was inside was some kind of thick liquid just a few shades darker than the bottle itself. Even if it hadn't been offered by Lance it looked dubious. In Lance's hands, it looked positively villianous.

"Lance..." Jannis said warningly, her eyes narrowing.

"Oh for the love of... something. Just take it. I can't stand acting noble. It makes me nauseous. Now take this damn bottle so I can go out in the boulders somewhere and heave my guts up."

Jannis covered the short distance between them slowly, hesitantly. If there was one thing you could be sure of with Lance, it was that he was unpredictable. And there had been those rare, precious occassions when he had done something truly wonderful. Probably just to let her know that yes, he really was being that annoying on purpose.

She took the bottle and squinted at it dubiously.

"What is this, Lance?"

"Does it matter? Just get your lil sick prince to drink it. And it tastes absolutely disgusting. Trust me."

Jannis stared at the strange bottle in her hand. The glass was thick, and a dark brown, with bubbles and flaws throughout. The bottle itself was sort of squat, squarish, without ever actually becoming square. There was a cork in the top, sealed with some wax. There was also a slight odor hanging about the bottle that promised a far more disgusting scent as soon as the bottle was opened. By the time she looked up to thank Lance, he had already vanished, presumably to be violently ill somewhere private.

As she carried the bottle back to the prince and Master Emrys, she was equally torn by two different questions: What on earth was in the bottle? And where had Lance gotten it?

"Master Emrys, do you have any idea what this is?" Jannis asked, handing him the bottle, and sitting on the other side of Prince Darien.

He pried at the seal and the cork with the tip of a small knife, and recoiled at the scent. She recoiled as well, and she was farther away.

"What unholy...? No, I have no idea what this is," he gagged, pulling out his handkerchief and pressing it desperately to his face. He handed her the bottle in desperation.

"Lance said to give it to Darien." Jannis said, holding her nose with one hand, and the bottle in the other.

"You can't possibly be considering..."

"You don't know my brother. He is more madness wrapped up in one skin than any creature on earth... but every once in a great while, he pulls a miracle out of nowhere; perhaps just to thumb his nose at fate."

"My lady, please... You can't risk the prince's life on a feeling."

"Isn't that what we are all doing? Risking our lives on a feeling?"

"It isn't the same, not at all. Darien is Harderior's hope."

"And he's dying." Jannis concluded with relentless certainty. "Sometimes you have to take a chance."

Master Emrys seemed torn, he eyed the bottle as if it might bite him.

"You're right. But I'm not risking the prince's life on a feeling. I'm taking the first sip. If it is poisonous, my life is worth less than his."

"Master Emrys, I..."

"Just give me the bottle."

Jannis complied, handing the bottle back. Emrys scowled, glancing at the prince's unconscious form, and sighed. Then he pulled the cork the rest of the way out, and took a swallow of what was inside.

The effect was immediate, although whether or not it was actually helping wasn't obvious. Emrys gagged violently, his whole body shaking and heaving, and Jannis hurriedly took the bottle back before they lost its contents.

Emrys was gagging, wheezing, coughing, and heaving for at least a minute while Jannis looked on. Finally, he took a deep breath and let it out again.

"That stuff... You think the smell is bad, but the taste is worse."

"Do you feel any different?"

"Not really, but we couldn't really expect a reaction that fast. Let's wait an hour and if I haven't fallen over dead, you can give the rest to the prince."

"I guess its a good thing he's unconscious, if it tastes that bad."

They waited an hour, and nothing happened to Master Emrys, either good or bad. Whatever effect the potion had, it was apparently either slower-acting or more subtle than they could determine.

Master Emrys gave her the go-ahead to give the rest to Darien, and Jannis slowly trickled the concoction down his throat, stroking the sides of his throat to make sure it went down. She didn't give him the entire bottle, keeping a little bit left over in case they needed to douse him a second time.

At some point, Lance came back. He didn't say anything and gave the two of them a wide berth. Jannis took that as a good sign, or at least a sign that Lance was uncomfortable. Lance was never uncomfortable about making other people miserable.

The sun rose slowly, and Master Emrys took the time to rub some herb-smelling cream into his aching joints, while Jannis checked and cleaned her armor. The two of them took turns watching Darien. Lance appeared and disappeared from the camp, silently and irregularly.

It was almost midday when Darien finally woke up. He

looked better. Jannis couldn't quite put her finger on what had changed, but he looked better.

"Aha, and his royal Sickliness returns. You do realize you made us waste an entire morning of travel time while you were passed out?"

"Lance!"

"Do you have any idea how many people could die on a battlefield in four hours?"

"Lance!" Jannis repeated, an edge to her voice.

"What?" He asked, irritated. "Excuse me if I'm the only one here actually focused on our goal. While you two were fluttering around like mother hens, I did some scouting. It's pretty obvious why there isn't a main road through here. And I'm not talking about the rough rock and the hills."

Jannis felt a sinking feeling.

"What now, Lance?"

"Gwyllion."

Jannis groaned. "Are you sure?"

"Pretty damn sure. And they are roaming around looking for something. Probably stirred up by your stupid gate."

"What are gwyllion?" Darien asked, his face still pale and wan.

"Mountain fairies, your Highness." Emrys supplied for him, with a bob of his head that suggested a bow without actually becoming one. "They have a bad reputation. People have the tendency to disappear when gwyllion are around, the bodies found later."

"The females are the ones you have to watch out for," Lance supplied helpfully, "Just like with people. Not that the males are particularly friendly, but a little less vicious."

"I'll pretend I didn't hear that," Jannis said, glaring at him.

"Gwyllion females are incredibly ugly, even uglier than her, and twice as vain. When you first see one, your instinct is to shrink back, but they take that as a deadly insult." Lance continued, ignoring his sister. "Our best bet to deal with them, is to stay put. Let them come to us. You can't avoid gwyllion in their own territory."

"At least this gives his Highness a chance to rest." Master Emrys sighed, and stood from where he was sitting. "I suppose this camp is as good a place as any."

"Good enough, I suppose." Lance said, glancing around. "I'd like a little more cover personally, but that also makes it harder to sneak up on us."

The area they were in was mostly clear, and the grass was short immediately around them though it lengthened on the other side of the hill. They had a fairly good view of the path in both directions. There was little in the way of trees this far up in the hills, only some scrub brush and the odd stunted tree. A couple of flat boulders imbedded in the dirt had provided a place to make a fire.

"I wouldn't be too sure about that, Lance. Gwyllion, like most Fae, have some strange magics. They might be able to turn invisible, or move without sound, or cast illusions to blind us." Master Emrys pointed out. Lance scowled.

"Gwyllion do have magic, sure, but it's mostly earth magic, not illusion magic. Don't get me wrong--they can do some damage-- but they aren't illusion experts like elves, or shapeshifters like the selkie. Just think of them like really skinny, ugly dwarves, and you won't be too far wrong." Lance corrected. Emrys looked around as if expecting the gwillion to pop out at any moment.

And, as if on cue, the ground began to shake.

Tiny mounds of earth bunched up on the ground, and finally

each split to reveal a very angry, scrawny and wrinkled little man.

The faerie standing in front, presumably the leader of this group of gwyllion, spat vehemently on the ground at Lance's feet in disgust. He was barely tall enough to reach Lance's waist.

"Your Highness. And what is a thrice-bedamned Prince of the Summer Court doing slumming in our neighborhood?"

Lance's face squirmed as he resisted the different ways it tried to twist, but his violet eyes sparkled with sudden, terrifying merriment. Jannis interceded bodily, placing herself between the two of them and glaring Lance down.

"No. Lance. You are *not* going to impersonate a lord of the Seelie Court."

"But, sis," Lance complained, as he saw a golden opportunity snatched away by his sister yet again. "It's not my fault I get mistaken for an omnimage."

"Ignore him," Jannis said, addressing the ugly little man and turning away from her brother. "I'm Jannis Solaran, and this is my brother Lance Solaran. We are the niece and nephew of the sorcerer Aerigard."

"Solaran?" The mountain faerie said, face scrunched up in confusion. "That's not Dark Lord Aerigard's surname, and who might your father be?"

"How is that your business?" Lance countered. "And how exactly do you know Uncle's surname? He doesn't advertise it."

The gwyllion shrugged. "He don't. But there be ways to find things out if you knows the right folk ta ask." He pondered, and asked again, "But that be not the answer to my question. Where be you come by the name Solaran, m'lady?"

"I really don't know anything about our father." Jannis said, exasperated. "But Solaran is our surname. We're not bastards–our parents were married before our father disappeared."

"At least that's always the way Uncle has told it." Lance commented darkly. "Makes you wonder though. Kinda a personal topic for a conversation with a person you just met."

The mountain faerie grunted again, and waved a hand horizontally in front of him in an almost dismissive gesture.

"No offense good sir, good lady. I likes to knows who I deals with. And I am much pleased you are no a stinking Prince of the Summer Court. Thems prissy bastards should stay in their own realm and leave me and mine folk in peace."

"How long have you been in the middle realm?" Jannis asked curiously.

Our world, sometimes called Earth and sometimes called Terra, is also called the middle realm because of where it is situated between the different worlds. Imagine different worlds are like pancakes in a stack, some higher and some lower. Of the nine known realms, Earth is the fifth, which places it smack in the middle.

"Four generations." The mountain faerie replied proudly, and the others nodded with various degrees of enthusiasm.

The realm of the faerie, the world above the middle realm, is close enough to our world that temporary doors between the two worlds sometimes open of their own accord, when the conditions are right. It is also possible for a skilled mage from either side to open a temporary gateway.

As such, there are a number of creatures and persons from the middle realm living in the realm of the faerie, and vice versa. The Fae are generally shy, and normally live away from human habitation in mountains or forests, or out in the oceans, but there is a noteworthy population of them on Earth.

The Summer Court, also known as the Seelie Court, is an alliance of the different Faerie species, a council formed of the rulers of the major races. Primarily they try to impose order and get into everyone's business. There is also a Winter Court, an Unseelie Court, a counter-alliance composed primarily of those races who refuse to join the Summer Court, and generally a far darker and more feared organization.

The Summer and Winter Courts do have some limited authority in the middle realm, but both groups generally perceive their power as far greater than it actually is. The seat of their power is in the realm of the faerie. Faeries emigrate to the middle realm for various reasons, but many do so to escape Faerie politics, or the wars that occasionally break out between the Summer and Winter Courts.

"Impressive." Jannis said approvingly. " I can see you've had time to develop a pretty effective intelligence network, too."

The gwyllion puffed a little. As a species they were particularly vulnerable to flattery. "Knew the Dark Lord had young ones out in that swamp. I doubts most would know that, but I gots some friends in thems parts. Always figgered it was the sorcerer's bastards. Niece, huh. Then the sister was your mother. Ciara, I think. Poor girl."

"Is it possible for you to waste any more of our time?" Lance snapped, tapping one foot.

"Can you maybe, be a little less like yourself before you mortally offend a Fae you just met, Lance?" Jannis said, irritated.

"Bah, I'm not one of those common mortals who don't even know Fae customs." Lance said, rolling his eyes. "And he is entirely too interested in us for my comfort. You aren't spying for Kalen, are you?" The last was directed at the wizened little man.

Who promptly spat at the ground at Lance's feet again.

"Serve mortals? Never!" The gwyllion puffed up with righteous rage. "I gots me pride, after all."

Some of the other gwyllion in the group were eyeing Master Emrys and Prince Darien with cruel, cold eyes. They were inching ever closer, from multiple sides.

"An what is the kin of the Dark Lord doin in these parts? With two common mortals?" The lead gwyllion asked Jannis, with a glance at its fellows.

"Do I have to kill you all?" Lance snapped, shoving his sister aside and towering over the gwyllion. "Our business is our business. We're not easy prey. We did cast a damn gateway, after all. I presume that's why you are out here: chasing the tail of the magic you could feel from miles away. It's all her fault," Lance indicated his sister with a negligent wave of one hand. "I told her she would attract any Fae for miles. Not that she ever listens to me."

"Archmages of some skill..." The gwyllion mused. "Considering you is relations of the Dark Lord we mights be willing to grant you safe passage through our lands." There was a scheming look in his eyes.

"But?" Jannis asked, knowing that there had to be a 'but.'

"But that's not me choice, that be Hildegard's decision, you hears me?"

"Hildegard?" Jannis repeated, with a sinking feeling.

"Matriarch of me clan, me mam's mam."

"Obviously, sis. Gwyllion tribal leaders are all females, remember?" Lance commented, unsurprised. "Let me handle it. You keep the two of them alive." Lance indicated the prince and the old mage with an almost rude hand gesture. "I'll be back before dark. Don't go and die on me. I would be really put out."

———————

Lance followed the band of wizened little faerie men out into the grassy hills and broken stones, leaving his sister and the other two behind. The terrain was rough, and sound carried strangely over the tops of the boulders, the wind twisting through the patches of tall grass, and making the tops of the grasses bob and weave.

Strangely enough for Lance, he did have a plan. Female gwyllion were terrifying, not only to travelers, but to their own kind. If he could get the matriarch on his side, Lance knew the entire tribe would obey her. And there was one sure-fire method: flattery. Gwyllion were hideously ugly, but incredibly vain. Vanity was one thing he understood intimately.

They came around the side of a rugged hill, covered in scrub brush, to a mass of boulders. The gwyllion deftly manuvered between the enormous stones, each taller than a man, and tilted at crazy angles. Lance followed with equal agility, no small feat considering he was twice their size.

Deep in the jumbled stones was the mouth of a cave, dark and forboding. There was the faintest flicker of light deep within its depths. Lance smirked and stooped inside.

It wasn't that far into the hill before it opened up into an enormous single room with other tunnels leading out of it in other directions. The roof of the cavern was high enough for even Lance to stand upright again. He stretched out, lazily and arrogantly, and cocked his head from side to side to pop his neck.

In the middle of the cavern, on an almost-throne made of dirty bones roped together with bits of animal hides and skins was what had to be the most terrifying sight he had ever seen in his eighteen years alive. And growing up in the castle of a sorcerer, that was saying something.

She was... indescribable. Stooped, but he had expected that. Hunchbacked, wrinkled, with leathery skin of a sinkening yellowish-brown- yes, he had expected all that. Gleaming red-rimmed too-blue eyes teeming with madness- yes he had expected that. The warts, the open, pus-leaking sores, nothing too surprising there. Maybe it was the drool leaking from the corner of a horribly twisted mouth filled with rotted, sharp canines. Maybe it was the breasts hanging like empty, aged sacks under her red-brown dress. A red-brown that reminded him strongly of dried blood.

"What wretch have you brought me?" Hildegard howled, her face twisting in manical glee at the sight of him. A lesser man would have wet himself, screamed in senseless terror and ran in the opposite direction. Lance smirked, and executed a perfect, courtly bow to her.

"No wretch, beautiful lady, I am Lord Lance Solaran. Words cannot express how deeply honored I feel to be in your presence." He said smoothly, gazing at her with an almost predatory stare.

Hildegard blushed. She arranged the folds of her dress in her lap, and squared her shoulders.

"I see, my lord. And what brought you out to our distant mound? I doubt you are a simple traveler."

"If I had heard tales of your beauty, it would be the only thing that brought me, but truly I was ignorant of your people's presence in these mountains until earlier today. May I approach, great lady?"

Hildegard shot him a sharp glance, as if not sure she could believe a word, but the steadfast sincerity on Lance's face persuaded her.

"You may approach," she said grandly, relaxing. The other gwyllion grumped and grumbled, but made way as Lance approached the grotesque bone and skin throne.

As soon as he was within reach, Lance reached out and took that gnarled, filthy hand in his own, placing a delicate kiss on the back.

"Sweet lady, I fear you lack for adequate company in this distant place, though I know you value your privacy and scorn the company of lesser beings." He spat the last in comtempt for the absent masses. "Please give me the honor of your company for just a while. I have a similar problem. It is so trying to be traveling with *humans*." Lance twisted the word as if it were horribly distasteful.

"You poor dear," Hildegard breathed, patting him consolingly on one shoulder. "Of course you can stay and talk to me. You are so right, my boy, it is so hard to find good company."

"And it's so hard to believe that more Fae wouldn't travel here to enjoy your company! Since coming to the middle realm, the other Fae must have grown too callous for simple courtesy." Lance replied smoothly.

"You have no idea! My own granddaughter doesn't bother coming to see me. Ever since she traveled to her own mound, I haven't seen a hair of her head. All I get is a letter or two, scrawled in haste." Hildegard scowled, and sighed.

"Poor Hildegard, that your own young would have so little time for their kin."

"That is exactly what I told that brat. But she doesn't appreciate me, no she doesn't."

"I can't imagine how frustrating that would be. But at least you have other family here. Your grandson led me here." Lance waved at the gwyllion he had followed from the camp.

"Brats, the lot of them." Hildegard grumped. "Have to scream and yell to get them to do anything. Lazy sots." She shifted on her throne and Lance's sharp eyes noted it.

"Maybe a softer seat would suit you better. Surely there is somewhere where you would be more comfortable?"

"Yes, indeed. Help me down, would you, sweet boy?" Lance complied, his strong wiry arms holding her hideous old form steady as she climbed down.

"I can't believe you were enduring that just for the sake of formality. Here let me help you get more comfortable." Lance fussed, moving bits of this and that out of Hildegard's way, settling her in a comfortable pile of blankets and furs, plumping her pillows and putting up her feet.

"It's sad really," Hildegard mumbled, with satisfied viciousness, "That a stranger has to show me own kin how to treat a lady."

"Even if we just met, surely you don't consider me a stranger." Lance said, his tone hurt. "I'm a guest in your house, at least for a little while."

"Oh you poor boy, I didn't mean it that way." She said consolingly, and then with a quicksilver transformation, snapped viciously at her fellow faeries. "Bring your poor dying grandmam something to drink! I'm parched and ignored by me own kin!" A young gwyllion darted off to obey her instruction, but she was not finished.

"And I want some proper hospitality for this sweet boy. Bring him a drink as well. Bring me something to eat while you are at it! I'm famished as well as parched. How you could treat me this way; I should skin the lot of you!" Several gwyllions jumped and ran at her order, the rest milling about anxiously.

"Twist, Grindle, Hector, you stay and help keep me company. The rest of you sorry lot, get back to work! You have far to much to do to be gawking at your grandmum's guest and drumming your heels!" The attendant troop of gwyllion that had milled around her throne all immediately dispersed, as if by magic, the three called out to 'keep her company' looking as if they wished they were somewhere else. One of the three was the same mountain faerie who had led Lance here.

He gave Lance a dark, wordless glare.

All three of them sat, forming a circle with Lance and Hildegard, finding a comfortable seat on piles of fir needles or furs or homespun blankets.

"Why don't you tell me about your travels?" Hildegard asked, with what she intended to be a winning smile. It was... indescribable. Lance wondered if he would see it in his nightmares in years to come.

"Of course! Ever since I left my uncle's castle, I've been wandering around in mortal lands, dealing with all their tedium and trouble. If it weren't for my sister, I think I would have already gone mad. She is wholy rediculous most of the time, but at least having her around I'm not alone."

"I see, I see! And what is your sister's name? Who is your uncle?"

"My sister's name is Jannis, and our uncle is Aerigard. We've lived in his swamp most of our lives."

"Kin of the Dark Lord?" Hildegard asked, surprised and impressed.

"Ciara's younglings." Her grandson supplied, glancing at Lance.

"That's something in your favor at least. Your uncle is hardly human. A mark in his--and your--favor. And what about your father, lad?"

"Funny," Lance said carefully, "Your grandson asked the same question. I never knew the man--he left when I was very young. He could be dead for all I know."

Hildegard smiled. It was not a pleasant smile. There was something dark in her eyes, very dark.

"You don't really believe that, do you, lad?"

Lance thought quickly and carefully before responding, deciding to give her the unvarnished truth, though it galled him.

"No, I think he's still alive."

Hildegard smiled again, secretively, as if Lance had confirmed something significant.

"And what makes you think that, lad?"

"My uncle won't talk about him. Not at all. And the way he reacts when asked about it. It's not an old wound, it's fresh. That tells me he hasn't managed to kill my father yet."

"And why would your uncle want to kill your father?"

"Because he blames my father for my mother's death. Obviously. Uncle and mother were supposed to be close. Sorcerers tend to deal with heartache through bloody retribution."

"Something sorcerers and gwyllion have in common." Hildegard said pleasantly, comfortably lounging in her pile of furs. "There is something terribly... satisfying about it."

Lance sensed there was an undercurrent in the conversation. Hildegard knew something about his father she wasn't interested in sharing. Something significant, and she was trying to extract information out of him. Infuriating. Lance decided it was time to take back control of this conversation.

"You must have a hard time up in these mountains with the armies getting so close," Lance commented in an off-hand way.

The gwyllions' reaction was immediate and violent. Their bodies tensed, their foreheads creased, their eyes narrowed, and they hissed and spat with rage.

"A curse be upon all their mother's sons!" One of the gwyllions spat, with a sharp gesture.

"Thems mortals and their problems, like an infestation of rodents," Hildegard's grandson agreed, and his grandmam nodded sagely.

"True, true, Twist, and I pray to the headless god that the worms feast on all their innards." She spat with emphasis.

"If they enter our hills," the gwyllion to Twist's left said grimly, "We will leave a pile of bodies so high that the carrion birds will be too fat to fly."

"Damned humans." Lance cursed, convienently ignoring his own origin. "Maybe I can help you in that regard. I was traveling in that direction anyway, planning on heading towards the border with Kalen. I might be able to raise some mischief."

"And how might you do that, omnimage, spell-bound as you are?" Hildegard asked shrewdly.

Lance rolled his eyes.

"This spell? My uncle's work. He got a little jealous of my ability. It doesn't matter." Lance said dismissively. "I can cause more trouble with these two hands than a dozen archmages." Lance gestured significantly with both hands.

"Boy, you are far too clever for your own good." Hildegard said approvingly. Gwyllion, like many species of faerie, treated the pursuit of mischief like an art.

"Then you grant us safe passage across your lands?" Lance asked, in an off-hand way, as if it were a question of no importance.

"How many filthy humans am I permitting in our land?" Hildegard countered, her eyes narrowing in consideration.

"Only two. My sister and I have a servant, an old man who is almost useless, but she seems to have taken to him. The boy is an orphan my sister picked up. She's always picking up trash like that, wounded animals, human children, that sort of thing. You can call it compassion. I call it being soft in the head."

"You shouldn't be so critical of your sister," Hildegard corrected. "She sounds like a lovely girl." Lance reminded himself that the gwyllion were ruled by females. They had a different view of gender roles.

"You are completely right, of course, Hildegard. I'll try to be more understanding of my sister and her human pets. And may we continue traveling as we have been?"

Hildegard considered. The other gwyllion glanced at each other, their eyes dark. Lance knew that whatever their personal feelings, Hildegard's word would be law. He met her eyes, and smiled winningly.

It took her far too long to think the matter over, but finally she turned and gave the barest nod of her head to the gwyllion to her side. He sighed, and it almost seemed like he deflated.

"Just you and your sister and her two pet humans?" Hildegard considered aloud.

———————

"It's all taken care of." Lance declared as soon as he was within reasonable speaking distance.

Jannis heaved a heavy sigh of relief. She had not been entirely sure Lance was up to handling this, and had been expecting him to come back with a pack of enraged gwyllion on his heels.

"Any trouble here?"

"They've been lurking around, but there haven't been any actual attacks." Jannis said, glancing at the hills around them. "I kept a pretty close eye on our friends."

"You mean your friends. Any one who wants to be my friend is welcome to apply, but the application process is pretty grueling. Isn't that right, elephant mage? How are the bruises?"

Master Emrys debated glaring at Lance, and decided it was not worth the effort.

"How did you take care of it?" Jannis asked, suspiciously.

"I lied." Lance said serenely.

"Well, you are an expert," Jannis noted, her voice edged with scorn.

"I strive for excellence in all I do." Lance declared.

"Even lying?"

"Especially lying. It's one of life's most critical skills."

"Sometimes I wonder how you ever made it to adulthood with your warped notions." Jannis commented.

"Sometimes I wonder how you made it to adulthood without realizing the most basic truths about the world. It should be a crime to be so naive."

"We should get moving." Jannis said, ignoring Lance's last barb. "We've lost too much daylight already. How do you feel, Darien?"

"A lot better, thank you." The prince said, as he levered himself up into the saddle with Master Emrys.

Chapter 10

Gregor awoke to the sounds of shouting, the clatter of horse's hooves, the clanking of metal and thudding feet, and the strange flicker of light as torches moved across the opening to his tent. He was still groggy with sleep and half in the dream, but that didn't stop him from rising from his cot, or throwing on his clothes and boots. Any experienced military officer learns to get ready at a moment's notice when needed, whether half asleep, barely conscious from blood loss, or staggering drunk.

He staggered to the tent flaps, and nearly ran into a young man carrying a bucket of water. The soldier stammered an apology, nearly bowing to the ground, and moving backwards in his chosen direction, clearly horrified by the near collision. Gregor was positioned high enough in the army to ruin the life of anyone who displeased him. That he had never done so, or even been tempted to do so, did not change the near-reverence the common soldiers treated him with. At least Frederick had to put up with it too.

Gregor did not bother stopping anyone to ask what was going on. It was pretty clear that whatever had happened, it wasn't another night attack by Kalen. The troops were all running in a completely different direction than the enemy army. That implied assassins or sabotage more than anything else.

He moved in the same direction as the other troops, though at a far more sedate pace, and gathered himself, shaking off the last lingering traces of sleep. He yawned widely.

It was about an hour before dawn, the perfect time for any kind of subterfuge. Gregor considered going back to bed, since he was not directly involved with the combat actions of the army, but he thought maybe there was a chance there would be unusual medical or logistical issues that might come out of whatever it was, so it might be a good idea to be awake and available if he was needed.

The shouting was louder now, and he was near the edge of the camp. This side of the camp had very limited security and guard coverage, because it was butted up against the mountain range between them and the capital, a no-go zone that was considered too dangerous for movement. Both armies had lost scouts in those hills. No one was entirely sure what was out there because none of the scouts had ever returned.

Gregor desperately hoped that whatever was in those hills had not decided to come out.

As he came around the last row of tents he was greeted with a strange sight. He was not entirely sure what he was seeing, because of the poor lighting. Pools of torch light poorly illuminated the scene before him, most of it was in the deep shadows in between.

A knight, or what might have passed for one, as he was not currently mounted, but in full plate armor and with sword sheathed at his side, was assaulting a group of soldiers near where one of the watch checkpoints had been established.

Gregor could not make out the man's face beneath his helmet, but the knight's body seemed stretched out, distorted. He was incredibly tall and painfully thin, but moved with an inhuman grace and incredible strength.

As Gregor watched, one of the Harderior soldiers charged the knight with blade raised. The knight did not bother to draw his own sword, instead deflecting the blow with his right vambrace and sliding snake-like underneath the blade to strike a sharp blow with his other gauntlet at the weak place where the shoulder guard connected to the helmet. The soldier went down, but the strange knight didn't even bother looking back, as he was already rolling to avoid a massive battle axe swinging right for the middle of his torso, and struck the instep of yet another soldier, who pitched forward and got between the knight and the axe-wielder.

The strange knight slipped in close as the axe-wielder swung again, catching his left wrist and twisting. Despite the gauntlets both of them wore, there was a brief tussle, and then the axe dropped to the ground. It had not even hit before the strange knight head-butted the soldier, and he dropped unconscious to the ground.

Gregor took a quick count of the bodies on the ground, then scanned the shadows to see if there were any more attackers. There were easily two dozen soldiers lying scattered on the ground.

Because he had torn himself away from the scene playing out in front of him, he caught the slight movement in the shadows, rapidly moving towards him. Gregor opened his mouth to raise an alarm, but then the shadow resolved itself into a familiar, a very familiar form.

"Prince Darien! What are you doing here?"

"Time for explanations later. Would someone please tell your men to stop attacking my brother?" The voice was high, imperious and irritated. A woman, just as tall and painfully thin as the strange knight, and most ridiculously of all, dressed similarly in full plate armor, had come up behind Prince Darien.

She was walking, but leading two horses behind her. Another, older man followed behind her, also leading two horses.

"And you are?"

"Jannis Solaran." The woman said flatly, squaring her shoulders.

"Archmage." The older man added.

"Grandpa is gonna marry her," Darien added.

Jannis rolled her eyes. "First let's stop a war, and maybe stop Lance from killing our own allies. He's just playing with them now, but if he feels his life is at risk, he won't hold back. It's not like Lance has any kind of moral restraint."

"Or any restraint." The older man added mildly, raising one eyebrow.

"Or any restraint." Jannis agreed.

"Come on Gregor, let's go tell the men to leave Lance alone." Darien said, grabbing the officer's hand.

"I don't know that that is appropriate," Gregor deferred, but did not resist as the prince tugged him towards the ruckus a short distance away. "You seem to have made a remarkable recovery, your Highness. I don't know that you were ever this energetic before."

"Let's just get Lance back under control." Jannis said in short, clipped words.

The other, older man with them was just chuckling, shaking his head and following behind them all.

An hour later, in the command tent, Gregor stood before General Frederick, who had just awoken, trying to explain just what had happened. Prince Darien and the woman were there with him, but the other two were with the medics. The old man had had some serious bruising and a back injury; the strange knight hadn't been hurt, but had insisted on staying with the other man.

"And you are our future queen?" General Frederick asked, his voice carefully neutral as he looked at the odd woman.

She was, to be sure, a beautiful woman: high, delicate cheekbones, pale satin skin, silken silver hair, intense violet eyes. It was an eerie, almost inhuman beauty. Not the kind of beauty that makes a man's mouth dry with desire, more the kind of beauty that haunts your dreams, and raises the hair on the back of your neck.

And despite her delicate features and delicate frame, she was wearing full plate armor. It had to have been made especially for her, because it wouldn't fit anyone else. The breastplate had been contoured to her chest, the gauntlets were so dainty that a child would have had difficulty fitting into them, and she wore it easily, despite its massive, metal weight.

No one wore armor that easily unless they trained in it constantly. Even large men had difficulty carrying all the extra weight if not on horseback. It changed the body's balance, and made movements harder, more sluggish.

What a mage would be doing in armor was incomprehensible to him. An archmage even more so. Most mages couldn't even stand the touch of metal, and certainly wouldn't have the strength to bear the weight of it.

Her violet eyes narrowed at the question. The general had

not explicitly expressed his considerable doubt in her identity, in case her claim was true, but even the carefully neutral question implied it.

"That's right, General Frederick." Darien pipped, grinning at the woman. She softened at the prince's smile, and winked at him.

"I heard a rumor that you were the Dark Lord's niece."

"Yes, well, it's no rumor." The lady said finally, shifting her feet slightly as she shrugged her armor into a more comfortable position. "I'm not anywhere near as skilled as my uncle, but I do know a little magic. I prefer the sword, like my brother, but only a fool casts aside a weapon because it's not her first choice."

"An archmage... swordswoman? That's an unusual combination." Gregor said. The biggest understatement Frederick had ever heard.

"I was raised in a swamp by an evil sorcerer. Nothing in my life is exactly what I think you could call normal. I do my best to fake it, but I know I'm not really fooling anyone."

There was an awkward silence in the tent as they considered her words and didn't really know what to say or how to respond. Finally, Frederick spoke.

"Can you do magic with all that metal on? Doesn't it make it harder?"

Jannis shrugged. "A little, I guess. The metal isn't really touching my skin, because of the underpadding, and I've got good enough control of my magical energies that they stay really close to my skin. The magic actually stays underneath the armor. Then all I have to do is make sure I have at least one hand free." She unstrapped and pulled off a gauntlet, displaying a shapely, pale hand.

"The armor has one very real benefit," she continued. "As long as I am wearing it, no one can tell magically that I'm an archmage. The metal acts to prevent any delvings or scrying spells, as well as any direct magical attacks on me."

Gregor and Frederick were both nodding now, they could see the tactical benefit of that.

"And that means that unless Kalen has one heck of a spy in our camp, they have no idea we have an archmage, and no way of finding out." Gregor said, still nodding.

"Two archmages." Jannis corrected. "Though my brother is worse than useless most of the time. He doesn't do magic."

"How is it that an archmage can't do magic?"

"He 'doesn't' do magic. Whether or not he can doesn't really matter."

"Forgive me if I don't understand." Frederick frowned.

"Believe me it's a discussion that makes most people's heads hurt. If you want to think of my brother in a tactical sense, do it this way: a master swordsman who doesn't obey any orders, is completely immune to all magical attacks, and who takes great pleasure in causing any trouble he can imagine. Be warned, he has a very good imagination."

"It sounds to me like I should just lock him up now."

"You can try."

Frederick was frowning pretty heavily now, and rubbing his chin with one hand. "Why would you bring someone like that with you?"

"He's my brother. Besides, he can cause just as much damage to the enemy as his allies. We just have to point him in the right direction."

Gregor was thinking furiously now and he latched onto something the lady had said.

"How is it, that he is completely immune to all magical attacks?"

"Not just attacks, he can cancel protection, locking and binding spells, healing spells, warding spells, curses, Fae magic, demonic or elemental magic, any kind of magic really." Jannis said, shrugging.

Everyone in the tent was staring at her.

"How is that even possible?" The general whispered.

"It's complicated." Jannis sighed. "Everything about Lance is complicated."

"Well, try to explain, if you can." Gregor coaxed.

"I guess... Lance... just nullifies magic, he stops it like it was never there in the first place. Any magic, any source, any purpose, if he touches it directly. Even the most complex spells just... unravel."

"I've never heard of anything like this... anti-magic... before."

"I doubt anyone else has the skill. I certainly couldn't do it. It's a spell my uncle cast."

"So THAT's what that spell does!" Prince Darien declared. "But, then, why didn't he destroy the gate when he went through it?"

"Umm, I really don't know." Jannis offered weakly. "Maybe because uncle was in the spell?"

"Gate? You were responsible for the gate our mages sensed three days ago?"

"Yeah," Jannis shrugged, again, shifting her armor, and pulled her gauntlet back on.

"You couldn't have cast it by yourself?"

"Of course not! Lance, and my uncle, and my uncle's apprentice, and Prince Darien, they all helped."

"You cast a gate with five mages?" Gregor asked, aghast.

"Well, technically, four archmages and a mage."

"Gregor?" General Frederick asked, dropping into a folding camp chair and nearly knocking the damn thing over.

"Sorry sir, my head is still spinning. I don't know what to say."

"I guess our miracle appeared on schedule. Miracle or curse, or the influence of a trickster god."

"My money is on the third option. But, I guess it doesn't matter how ridiculous it is. I would gladly shake a mad god's hand if he can get us out of this mess."

"Hmmm." General Frederick appeared preoccupied by something.

"Sir?"

There was a long pause as the general quietly contemplated whatever was on his mind and Gregor waited in the painful silence.

"I was wondering if we should go on the offensive. As you said, Kalen is not aware of this new development, and will not discover it until it is too late. With their raw military superiority, they won't expect a sustained assault. Sure, they might expect one last desperate attempt on them, but they won't expect us to have any kind of chance of winning. It may be the best strategy."

Gregor carefully contemplated the general's idea. "Sir, while I think you may be correct--Kalen won't expect any kind of coordinated and effective offensive from us at this time--how do you plan to utilize our new archmage most effectively? And do so without seriously risking her life? Remember sir, that this is our king's future wife we are talking about, and given the difficulty he has had thus far recruiting archmages, he might take it very personally if we get one killed."

"The thought had occurred to me, Gregor." General Frederick said mildly, smiling.

Gregor half-inclined his head towards the general, in a gesture of vague subservience. Of course, Gregor had known that the general would have thought of that, but he felt obligated by matter of his position to mention the matter aloud. They both understood.

"And what about the brother," Gregor continued, "Are you planning on doing anything about him?"

"According to Lady Jannis, Lord Lance plans to call a parley and demand the surrender of the enemy." General Frederick commented, his voice still bland.

"Do you plan to stop him?"

"No. If the fool gets himself killed, it will only save us the trouble of dealing with him later. If he confuses or confounds the enemy, that only benefits us. On the absurd chance he can actually convince the enemy to surrender, that also only benefits us. He isn't a part of the Harderior army, nor is he one of our citizens, so if he embarrasses himself, it doesn't reflect on us or our nation. If he assassinates the enemy commander, we can claim complete innocence, since he isn't even one of our men and we don't even pretend to control the man."

"You've given the matter some thought."

"That's my job. We're losing this war. Let's take advantage where we can."

Lance stood imperiously, a lone man on a lone horse, before the great host that gathered before him. There was malice in the glistening spears, the shining armor, the stomping hooves of horses, the silent glint of eyes. Lance wasn't impressed. He was impressed by very little.

He stood alone in the field, in the no-man's land between the two great armies, painfully vulnerable on his little horse, the white flag of truce hanging sullen in the still air from the pole thrust into his stirrup.

The whole of the Kalen army had stirred itself to watch this single idiot ride out from the other camp with the white flag. There was the outside chance that he would be shot down, but common courtesy demanded that the Kalen commander at least acknowledge him.

Lance hadn't really expected the Harderior general to let him do this. Military men, especially experienced, hardened leaders, certainly wouldn't let him do what he wanted. Lance felt quite gratified that this general Frederick seemed singularly open-minded. Perhaps he was just desperate. It was pretty apparent to anyone with eyes that the Harderior were the worse for wear. They were losing.

So here he sat, out in a field, waiting for an arrow to come hurtling out at him, or maybe a crossbow bolt, or perhaps an enraged and bored soldier, while he sat, quiet and still, shoulders squared and posture relaxed, waiting for the enemy to respond.

This wasn't his war, and it wasn't his sister's, but he was more than willing to adopt it for her, if only to relieve his boredom.

Sitting out here in the field was not, however, relieving his boredom. He had been out here for almost an hour. It showed the worst kind of manners on the part of the enemy commander. Though the fool did not know it, making Lance wait, fume, plot, and scheme, was one of the worst possible things he could do.

Finally, some motion in the enemy camp. There was a rustling and a stirring among those waiting there, as the line parted to allow a single rider to pass. It was not the enemy commander-his second mistake.

The man rode down, resplendent in his full plate armor, the flag of truce stuck in his stirrup as well, and arrogance set full in his shoulders. He had no idea just what he was up against.

Lance considered the figure that approached him with care. He rubbed his chin with one gauntlet, and a smile slowly grew on his face. It was not a pleasant smile. He had been taking lessons from the gwyllion.

"I am ready to accept the immediate surrender of the Harderior forces on behalf of General Frances Hamilton," the Kalen soldier said as soon as Lance was within range. Lance considered a moment before he replied.

"Can't help you with that, I'm not part of the Harderior army. If you want them to surrender you're talking to the wrong person."

That brought the man up short. He glared back.

"Then who the hell are you?"

"None of your business." Lance said loftily. "I came out here to talk to the commander of the Kalen army, not some riff raff."

"I can assure you the commander doesn't have time for any of your nonsense!"

"Tell him that if he doesn't get out here to talk to me, I'm going to personally cut his head off, after I destroy his army!"

The soldier snickered nastily. "Sir, whoever you are, you don't have any army."

"I don't need an army." Lance said with complete self-assurance. "I can whoop both your army and the Harderior army at the same time, single-handed."

That absolute self-assurance told the soldier that Lance was not bluffing, which left one other possibility.

"Our army doesn't deal with madmen." He said dismissively, turning to ride back to the waiting throngs.

"All soldiers are madmen, including your commander. As such it seems fairly ridiculous to claim your army doesn't deal with them." Lance shouted at his back.

When Lance rode back to the Harderior army, frustrated and impotent, Jannis was there waiting.

"Now what, Lance? He won't even talk to you."

"I'm going to kill them all."

"Lance..." Jannis said warningly.

"Well, I'm going to kill them until he finally comes out to talk to me. Are you coming?"

"I'm fairly sure the Harderior general would have something to say if he knew I was going to attack the Kalen army." Jannis responded.

"Then you better not let him know." Lance concluded, shrugging.

"Do you have any idea how incredibly stupid it is for the two of us to attack the army on our own?"

"Sure I do. It's a lot smarter than taking these idiot Harderior soldiers with us. They would just get in the way, and then get killed. By the way leave the brat here, the same goes for him. I want the elephant mage though."

"So you what, want to leave Prince Darien here, and take Master Emrys with us?"

Lance rolled his eyes. "I'm pretty sure I didn't mumble. Let's get moving, I don't want to lose the element of surprise."

"Lance, you surprise everyone you meet."

"I haven't met this general yet, so we better get moving!"

Master Emrys was remarkably amenable to the suicide mission, for which Jannis was grateful. They avoided Prince Darien wanting to come along, by the simple method of not letting him know they were leaving. He was in the tent near the medics assigned to the army's mages, which was close, but conveniently far enough away that he didn't see them preparing for their epic attack.

"Do you have a plan, Lance?" Jannis asked doubtfully.

"Of course I do! You think I would attack an army without a plan? There is something I've always wanted to try."

Jannis felt immediate and deep apprehension at Lance's words. An apprehension that only strengthened as Lance broke into an angelic smile.

"I'm afraid to ask."

"Well that's pretty silly, since my plan fundamentally depends on you and the elephant mage to work. It's all about this." Lance held up one hand and clenched his fist, still smiling.

"Your fist?" Jannis asked doubtfully.

"Uncle's spell!" Lance snapped back, irritated at how dense his sister could be. "It isn't field-limited."

"Meaning?" Jannis asked.

"Meaning the spell can be spread out." Master Emrys inserted, comprehension dawning on his face.

"Exactly! The spell is centered on my body, and that part can't be changed, but the range of the spell can be expanded beyond just me."

"What good would that do, Lance?"

"Are you a complete idiot, sis? It means that Kalen won't be able to use any magic on us at all, or on the Harderior army for that matter. In fact, Kalen's mages will be pretty useless for quite a while."

"Kalen's army has a whole lot more than just mages, Lance. They've got soldiers, and weapons, and siege equipment."

Lance shrugged. "I've got a sword. So do you."

"You've got to be kidding me."

"Would you just shut up for a change and listen?" Lance asked, conveniently ignoring the fact that Jannis had been listening to every word. "I need you to create a link again, like you did for the gate. Take control of all my magic, then reach out and link with your boyfriend and uncle. The power of all four of us is easily more than enough to spread the effect of this spell across several miles."

"How, by the goddess, do you expect me to link with Mobius and uncle?"

Lance frowned. "Come on, any idiot can form a link using a blood-based connection like you did for that gate. But there are other ways to link magics."

"I don't have any blood, Lance!"

"You aren't listening! You don't need it! Use their feelings for you! You are the single most important person in either of their lives, though I doubt either would admit it and even contemplating why makes me ill. Form a soul-bond."

"Lance, soul-bonds are Fae magic!"

"And? You do lots of Fae magic, like that stupid note-writing thing you do, or the illusion cantrips."

"I never learned how to form a soul-bond! Do you have any idea how advanced a magic they are??"

"By the goddess, you are even more useless than I thought. Well, I guess we'll just have to work with the power the two of us have." Lance concluded doubtfully. "Right well, link with me and then pour my magic directly into uncle's spell. Don't try to unravel it, or mess with it, just feed the spell as much power as you can. Not exactly what I would call elegant work, but very effective, trust me."

"I have serious doubts about this." Jannis protested, but complied. She formed the link with Lance. Their bond was so intense that it didn't even require direct physical contact. Gently,

Jannis touched their uncle's spell on Lance with a small thread of power.

The effect was immediate. The spell blossomed outward, the intricate fabric of the magic stretching out effortlessly in a sphere with Lance as its center. That thread of magic vanished, devoured by the spell.

"Told you." He commented smugly.

Jannis bit her lip. Even that small amount of power had easily doubled the physical area the spell was affecting, but it wasn't anywhere near enough to make a difference. She wondered if the power the two of them possessed would be enough.

Lance was a powerful archmage, the most powerful she had ever heard of. Easily powerful enough to justify the gwyllion's earlier mistake. There were no human omnimages. They were rare even among the Fae, or even among the jinn, rarer than archmages among men. That much raw power might be enough.

She took a deep breath and plunged her will into the raging torrent of magic that was Lance.

It probably would have killed almost anyone else. They had a very special relationship, though Jannis didn't really realize it. If she had bothered to think about it, she might have remembered that even their uncle hardly ever resorted to tapping Lance's raw magic power. There was something visceral about it, something unstable and horribly dangerous.

This was far more difficult, far more chaotic than the gate had been. There, careful preparations had aligned the flows of magic, shaping them in the direction that Mobius had intended. Jannis had been essentially a passenger in the gate spell just as Lance and Darien had been, even if she had been the union point, the nexus, of her end.

This was madness unleashed. The magic twisted and writhed

like a thing alive, burning and freezing at the same time--piercing and slippery--furious and filled with a hollow, cold menace. How she manipulated it, she did not know— it was instinct more than anything else.

The power she funneled, a golden gleaming torrent, edged with the barest coating of Jannis's own silver-white, directly into the intricate spell-work that the Dark Lord Aerigard had wrought. Jannis held her breath, certain that this would all go horribly wrong somehow, but the spell responded exactly as expected.

That painfully complex spell ballooned outwards until it covered the entire field and beyond. Lance was shimmering brightly with the traces of magical energy—he was difficult to look at, like a heat haze on desert sand—light and air seemed distorted around him.

"I guess you can't screw up everything," Lance commented approvingly. "Let's get moving."

"I... can't... fight like this." Jannis mumbled, her attention still fully focused on funneling the massive flow of energy. It took an immense amount of concentration; it was almost like juggling lightning bolts. She was dizzy, and the ground seemed to be dipping and rolling.

"I knew playing pretty princess was going to make you unbearably lazy! Can you ride at least?"

"Probably. I wouldn't be much good in a fight."

"Like that's a change." Lance's head turned towards Master Emrys, and Jannis followed it and found herself staring. Master Emrys was on the ground, barely conscious, and almost incoherent. "About what I expected, really." Lance commented, taking a few steps towards the mage and toeing him in the side.

"What's wrong with him?"

"Powershock."

"He's not even in the spell!"

"Are you a complete moron? Mages can suffer from powershock from residual exposure to enough magical energy!"

"That's only theory! No one has ever proven archmage Diagras right!"

"Field spells are concentrated at their center. Out on the edges, mages probably won't even feel sick, but close to me...." Lance looked incredibly smug. "Not only will they be incapable of doing any magic, but they also will fall over like little rag dolls."

"Is that the whole reason you wanted Master Emrys here, just to test your theory?" Jannis asked, aghast.

"Well I needed to know if the effect was lethal. It would have... changed my strategy."

"Every time I think I've taken the measure of your depravity, you surprise me again. You would have killed what probably amounts to the closest thing you've ever had to a friend?"

Lance shrugged. "Should we have brought your little prince instead?" Lance pulled himself up into his saddle and settled himself with the metallic clink and scrape of his plate armor rubbing against itself. He was still hard to look at—Jannis couldn't see his face very well, even when she looked directly at him—he shimmered and distorted. It was nauseating.

But Jannis just turned away and pulled herself into her own saddle. She dipped a little as she settled herself. Holding onto a magical flow of this magnitude was something like being intoxicated, her reactions were slowed, her mind fogged, and the whole world seemed ever so slightly out of whack.

"Stay close to me." Lance instructed firmly. "I'm not entirely sure what will happen if we get too far apart. It might have... unexpected consequences."

When Lance was worried about something, it made Jannis doubly worried. Who knew what would happen to the spell?

Jannis kneed her horse into a gallop, following Lance closely as he directed his horse to stretch out into a full charge towards the enemy camp. Jannis could only imagine what they must be seeing, a pair of horses charging towards them, with one man shining like a fallen star.

The Kalen army didn't delay-they recognized a threat. With magic out of the question, the first attack that came was a hail of arrows as soon as they were within range. Lance fared far better than she, because he was hard to look at, he was hard to aim at, and none of the arrows struck him or his horse.

Jannis, on the other hand, suffered a hail of blows. Whatever enchantment Mobius had put on the armor and sword, it was not currently effective due to the spell field. Instead, Jannis was forced to deflect whatever she could with her shield. Ordinary arrows couldn't penetrate her heavy metal armor at this distance. The horse wasn't so lucky. A number of arrows struck it, and the poor beast stumbled and fell with a horrific death scream. Jannis was thrown, hard.

She rolled, the metal shell protecting her and hampering her at the same time. It took a precious few moments before she was oriented enough to get back on her feet, shield held ready to deflect the rain of blows that had not stopped while she was in mid-air.

An arrow glanced off of the vambrace protecting her right forearm, and ricocheted dangerously close to her neck. Jannis instinctively flinched even though the armor guarded her skin. She was barely aware of a thudding thunder very close, the heavy hoof beats of Lance's horse as he barreled towards her from the side, leaning impossibly and irrationally out of his saddle to reach down and grab her from behind where her armor was segmented at the shoulder.

"What the hell do you think you are doing!?" He shouted over the horse's heavy thunder. "Don't get separated, remember?

Bad things happen!" Lance's voice was heavy with disgust even at full volume.

The horse had slowed with the weight of both of them, and Jannis wondered how Lance had been able to lift her in all that armor one-handed. She didn't have to wonder long though as he let go and let her crash to the ground in a loud series of metal clangs.

"Get yourself together, princess! Good goddess, how much weight can you gain in two weeks of fluttering around a damn castle?"

Lance had positioned himself between her prone form and that incoming hail of arrows. Once again, because of his distorting effect, the arrows started to fly wide, either short or long of their position. Jannis slowly staggered to her feet, an effort tripled by both the added weight of all that metal and the need to maintain the spell. All she really wanted at that moment was to empty her stomach of anything and everything in it. The nausea was overwhelming.

Once upright, Jannis began plodding towards the enemy army in Lance's wake. She wasn't charging so much as moving in a cross between a run and a stagger. Lance didn't bother to wait for her, though he seemed determined to stay within a certain distance. He turned back and forth, moving serpentine towards the enemy, who had started to move forward on their position. It appeared that the Kalen soldiers weren't particularly interested in letting the archers finish off this skirmish.

As the first of the light cavalry approached, the arrows stopped falling in a rain, and only the occasional carefully aimed shot whistled towards them. Only an idiot would shoot at his own troops, an idiot, or a marksman who could be sure of missing them and only striking the enemy.

Lance already had sword out, and reached out almost casually to sever another man's arm at the elbow joint, sword and arm clad in leather and metal plating dropping useless to the ground like a chunk of meat. His longer than average arms were a big advantage, and that distorting effect of magic an even bigger advantage. A second Kalen cavalryman barely avoided losing his head to one of Lance's vicious backhand side sweeps.

Lance was losing his forward momentum as he began to trade blows with the light cavalry. They weren't doing much damage to him, but they had effectively blocked any way he could have taken towards the enemy lines. Jannis found herself wishing that the null magic field effect weren't preventing her from using magic just like everyone else. She didn't have very long to worry about it though, because Lance wasn't the cavalry's only target, and she was on foot.

A pair of the Kalen light cavalry were charging directly towards her. Somehow they had skirted around Lance and the melee there, and were gaining speed quickly, with the obvious intent of running her down, or hacking her head off if she evaded. So she did neither.

Jannis ran right straight for them, sword ready, her wrist flexed, and her shield raised. She aimed at a point just to the right of the first rider, and as he veered slightly to try to run her down, she leapt into the air, coming down hard, not with sword, but with shield, and not on the rider, but on the horse's exposed head. The force of her shield bash caused the beast to lose its footing and crash sideways to the ground, pinning its hapless rider beneath, and the poor beast had lost little of its forward momentum. It was a good thing Jannis was already airborne, for she used her own momentum from the impact to throw her just far enough out of the way to avoid a possibly fatal collision with the collapsing horse and rider.

She rolled on the ground, sword arm and rapier extended above her head to prevent slashing herself. The other rider went wide of her because of it, and had to circle his horse back around.

That didn't buy her any advantage though, because he was behind her now, and was being joined by two more riders coming from the Kalen army. She was flanked.

Jannis took a deep, shuddering breath and tried to make the ground stop moving. She didn't bother glancing at Lance, he was too pinned down to help. She could trust him to get out of it, but probably not in time to provide any support.

Jannis made it to her feet just in time to meet their pincer charge. The two in front of her galloped their horses directly at her, and the one behind did the same. The first to reach her, only seconds before the others, came down with a vicious sword stroke that she just barely managed to block with her shield. The force of the blow combined with the momentum of horse and rider was enough to throw her bodily. Jannis didn't try to stop that momentum, instead she moved with it, exaggerated it and went hurtling to the side.

It was a foolhardy move to make, probably fatal if they were the only two combatants, but they weren't. Jannis flew to her right and smashed into the horse of the rider coming up from behind, as she had expected. She had flown too low to hit the rider directly, but the sword in her hand took a nasty swipe at his legs, opening up his calf, and more tellingly, gashing the horse's side and partially severing the belly band keeping the saddle on the horse. That was the advantage of a rapier- so much more agile of a weapon at close quarters. It was a miracle she didn't get stepped on. She rolled again, under the horse as it went crashing forward. The rider who had swung at her was still there and still mounted, but he had lost a lot of his speed as he came around the other rider. The one with the leg wound was trying to stay on his enraged horse.

Jannis came up into a crouch, not bothering to come all the way to her feet. Those swords had a limited reach from horseback, one of the major disadvantages of cavalry. Even a sizable sword couldn't easily reach all the way to the ground unless the rider leaned heavily to one side. She was just lucky none of them had pikes. The biggest danger right now was being trampled.

The enemy realized it to. With her so low to the ground, the best way to kill her was with hooves not swords. Both of the approaching riders picked up speed, staggering their horses slightly so that she could not avoid both. Jannis's eyes narrowed. The other rider had finally gotten his horse under control, but was not yet attacking. The man down under his horse had managed to get out from under it, but he was not moving very fast or preparing to attack.

They still did not seem to realize that their horses were their biggest weakness. Jannis had realized it in a sudden flash of inspiration the moment her horse had gone out from under her in that rain of arrows.

Jannis hunched down, her shield and sword readied in front of her, staying as small and close to the ground as possible. The forward approaching rider shouted out a bloodthirsty warcry and urged his horse to go forward even faster. He still did not understand.

Jannis smiled at his sudden startled cry, as the horse gathered itself and leapt directly over her head. The horse understood even if the rider did not. She wasn't a target to the horse, she was an obstacle. A heavy metal obstacle complete with edged blade that was perfectly capable of slashing legs. Thanks to the rider's urging, the horse was already moving with enough forward momentum to easily leap such a low obstacle.

The rider was quite a distance away before he managed to turn his horse back into the battle, but Jannis was already dealing with the other rider in a very different manner.

She whistled. Very loudly. Jannis had learned this particular whistle from one of the swamp Fae she had befriended, and it was hair-raising. More specifically, it was unexpected, and unusual. These horses may have been conditioned to deal with combat, with the sounds of combat, and the sights of combat, but they had not been conditioned to this. The horse charging at her shied back, turning to the side and narrowly avoiding her. The horse with the slashed belly spooked and took off with his rider who was trying fruitlessly to get the animal back into the fray.

The two riders still threatening her tried to haul their horses back towards her, but both animals were resisting. They didn't like this new creature. Jannis whistled again, and one horse reared. It didn't buy her much time though- these were trained riders with trained horses. A few moments of urging and they had their horses pointed at her and charging again.

The horses, however, were nervous enough about her that they would not run her down. They each swerved slightly to the side as they came within range.

Jannis elected to be more conventional this time. She pirriueted, slashing the nose of the first oncoming horse, and followed through to hack into the exposed side of the second rider, while simultaneously throwing herself to the side to avoid his own attack.

He paused, motionless for a moment and then toppled sideways, falling to the ground with a thud. The first man had been crushed by his own horse when the beast went flying, and his unmoving form suggested that something vital had squished under the substantial weight of the beast.

Jannis surveyed the field. The one rider whose horse had spooked was gone, the first rider was staggering back towards his lines, it appeared he had a broken arm and probably some broken ribs. The other two were probably dead. Lance rode up beside her and surveyed the damage.

"Pretty pathetic if you ask me." He commented, lifting his visor. "I took on like thirty, and you didn't give me a lick of help. And you nearly got killed by three guys?"

"Four," Jannis grumbled. "One of them got away."

"I really wish I could have left you behind."

"How could you have made the spell work without me?"

"That's the only reason I didn't. Girls are so useless."

"Would you shut up already?!" Jannis finally shouted, irritated out of her mind both at the close call and Lance's criticism. "Your stupid spell is throwing my balance all off, and at least you still have a horse! If you didn't notice, we still have a whole bloody army to take on!" She gestured wildly with her sword-arm, sword still in her hand, at the new batch of approaching Kalen soldiers, this time foot soldiers and pikemen.

Lance eyed the oncoming horde, contemplative and rubbed his chin with his right hand. "Not really worth the effort, are they?"

"Lance, would you please stop being such an idiot and get on with your so-called brilliant plan? Being able to completely cancel magic on the battlefield won't matter much if we get skewered!"

Lance sighed, and dismounted, slapping the horse on the rump to make it take off back to the other side of the field where the Harderior army was camped.

"What do you think you are doing?" Jannis demanded furiously.

"Well, with all those pikes coming... I don't particularly like the idea of my horse rolling or throwing me. You might have wanted to kill your horse, but I don't." Lance grinned again, his eyes flashing and his face villainous. "Besides, if I don't keep your sorry butt alive, someone might start hurling fireballs this way."

"Goddess help me, if they don't kill you, I might."

"Promises, promises. You haven't followed through with that particular threat yet, and you've been saying you would kill me since we were kids."

"You're still a child!"

"Only at heart, sis, only at heart." Lance drew his sword and examined the edge for a moment, completely ignoring the pounding of feet and shouting as the enemy drew near. He laughed, and thrust his visor back down, turning to face the oncoming mass.

Jannis turned and stood back-to-back with her brother, two against a hundred. Poor fools, they thought they had the advantage with their superior numbers- they had no idea how horribly outclassed they were.

Lance waited until the best possible moment, and then lunged forward at the enemy. Jannis, expecting him to go on the attack, followed at a slight distance, walking backwards and trailing him.

Anyone in front of Lance was cut down quickly and precisely. Those few who tried to come at him from the rear met with Jannis's smaller but similarly deadly rapier. Jannis preferred the rapier, her sword was thicker and heavier than a dueling rapier, but still a far lighter weapon than a broadsword, the more so because it was made of Fae metals rather than steel. Even with its lighter weight she could feel her arm aching from the effort of the battle. She didn't bother blocking blows with her thinner sword blade, instead deflecting them or using her shield.

She found herself carefully stepping behind her, searching with the toe of her boots for the bodies Lance was leaving in his wake. Suddenly she found herself bumping into Lance's back. He had stopped suddenly.

"We've got company," he muttered, loud enough for her to hear over all the noise of clanging sword blow, pained cries, and clanking metal.

Jannis glanced over her shoulder after she slid her blade free of where she had rammed it into a soldier's neck in the gap between breastplate and helm. The body tumbled to the ground.

"What?" She asked, glancing quickly to each side for the next incoming attack. The soldiers had withdrawn a couple of steps out of reach of their swords, but still pressed in a great circle around them.

"I don't believe I've ever seen a spell like that." A rich, commanding voice from behind her commented.

"Jorander?" Jannis blurted, as she recognized the voice.

"You would think," Lance commented, his voice heavy with sarcasm, "That the damned Harderior would have warned us Kalen had an archmage."

"Oh my, my. Is that Jannis and Lance? I never would have expected Aerigard's brats to be here. Thought he never let you out of your swamp?"

"And I would never have expected you to be here, vermin. When did you join the Kalen army? I thought you were with Lorenica." Lance retorted, his whole body tightening.

"I haven't joined the Kalen army. This is just... a matter of mutual convenience."

"It's convenient for me, too. Here you are, facing my sword without your magic to protect you." Lance smiled, his eyes sparking flame.

"Such a hard decision. Do I want you alive, to drain your magic and ransom the husk back to your uncle, or do I kill you slowly for what you did to my familiar?" Jorander was smiling too, and it was an ugly sight.

The soldiers were still milling about just barely out of reach, but apparently didn't want to disturb Jorander's conversation. Probably a smart decision; even if he was without magic right now, angering an archmage had frequently fatal consequences.

"Why," Jannis asked, her voice pained, "Do you have to torture and kill every familiar you can get your hands on?"

"That's a stupid question. You know I hate magic." Lance replied flippantly, and then turned his attention back to the enemy archmage.

"Come closer, Jorander, and taste my steel! Or are you too much a coward, crouching behind all these little fools with their swords and spears? I'll just cut my way through them to get to you!"

Jorander looked down at Lance and their eyes seemed aflame. He might just have responded to Lance's taunt, but then someone else came up beside the enemy archmage, all puffed up with importance, and peered down at the temporarily interrupted battle.

"What," he asked Jorander, "Is that?"

"That," Jorander remarked, gesturing at Lance, "Is the closest you will ever find to an abomination in human skin. I'll give you a thousand gold pieces and an elixir that will add ten years to your life if you deliver him to me alive." He paused, and then added, as if an afterthought, "And I'll give you five hundred for the girl."

"I think I just figured out why uncle kept our existence a secret." Jannis commented dryly behind Lance's back.

"You're just jealous I'm worth twice as much as you are." Her brother remarked in a tone just as dry.

The new arrival glanced around the field aghast. There were bodies scattered everywhere, mostly human, and all belonging to the Kalen army. "Are you trying to tell me the two of them did all this damage?"

"Indeed. And they are also responsible for the sudden strange lack of magic." Jorander supplied.

The Kalen officer stared for a moment at Jorander and then bellowed, "Send a rider for reinforcements! Get the mercenaries over here!" A man ran for a horse and galloped off back behind the hill as soon as he had finished shouting.

"Find your courage, men! There are only two of them! Take them alive if you can, or kill them if you have to!" The officer shouted, as more men came up over the hill to join those already there.

Jorander stayed well back on the hill, watching them intently, but clearly out of range of any danger. The officer stayed with him, as streams of armed men came rushing past them directly towards the surrounded Solarans.

Chapter 11

Lynx had been a mercenary for almost eighteen years, and had been the leader of his own particular little band for the last decade. It was strange, there was a very high fatality rate among mercenaries with less than five years of experience, but after that initial horribly deadly learning curve, you learned how to stay alive. Which fights to pick and how to pick them.

When the call went up that there was a fight brewing, his interest was immediately piqued, and at the same time, his survival instincts started calculating. Something wasn't right. Why were so many men being mobilized for such a small skirmish?

"Dyr, get the band together, looks like we've gotta earn our lunch today." He commented to the tiny woman next to him in her dull grey robes.

She nodded, and vanished, without a word, probably going to find Ginger. That was the fastest way to get everyone up and ready.

Lynx was already in what amounted to armor for him, a chain-mail shirt over a leather gambeson, sturdy reinforced boots that were good for both running or riding, and a leather helm reinforced with metal plates and studs. He had never understood the appeal of heavy plate armor - leather armor was heavy enough if it was properly hardened and reinforced, and so much easier to move in.

The Venturi were a small band, less than forty members, and would probably have been slaughtered in such small numbers if they were a typical mercenary band. They were anything but typical. Lynx was a disenfranchised nobleman, with a rather unique worldview, and he had the habit of attracting extremely talented folks who for one reason or another reason were rejected by society.

Dyresse was one great example. An extremely talented mage, trained for years at one of the best academies in Ren, she had been expelled and stripped of her licensure, then banished from Lorenica. She was probably the best mage in the entire army when sober.

Lynx already had a brace of long knives, his even heavier long dirks and his stilettos strapped on, but he slung a hunting bow and a quiver of arrows over a shoulder as he moved, at a sedate pace, in the direction of the chaos.

It didn't take long for the first couple of members of the Venturi to fall in alongside him, an apostate priest turned theurgist who had barely escaped being burned alive for heresy, and a poor ex-guardsman who had nearly been hanged for hacking the hands and feet off the guy who had slept with his wife.

"Trouble?" Krael enquired, without even glancing in his captain's direction.

"Always." Lynx replied, his tone bland. "Aren't we just a bunch of murderers and sellswords? We attract trouble."

"We don't attract it, it finds us. Or we find it."

"And this from the guy who talked me into taking this job."

"Well. I can't say I approve of Harderior's rather skewed approach to magic, and those kinds of ideas have a nasty habit of spreading." Krael stroked the smoky crystal embedded in the top of his dark-stained walnut staff; it was a habit he had when he was worried.

"What is it?"

"Dyr didn't tell you?"

"You mages all have a bad habit of answering questions with questions, is it something they teach you in school?"

"I think we learned it from our commander. Didn't you just answer my question with one of your own?"

Lynx grunted, and raised one eyebrow at the smaller man. That was saying a lot, Lynx was fairly short, slightly below average in height, but Krael was even smaller.

The theurgist took the hint. He stroked the edge of the crystal on his staff with his thumb unconsciously, but answered the question.

"There is some high level magic going on over there. I can't identify it, but really, really high level stuff. The kind of stuff regular mages don't even dream of touching, and even archmages take deadly serious."

Lynx grunted again. "Jorander involved?"

Krael shrugged. "Maybe. I can sense him in that direction. I didn't think he had the stomach for something this powerful..."

"Or the nuts," The ex-guardsman Roger interjected. Most of the Venturi had a low opinion of Jorander.

"...but there could be other archmages involved." Krael concluded.

"Where's Dyr?" Lynx asked finally, as more of his men fell in behind him.

"As if he doesn't know." Someone snickered from the group in a lowered voice, and there were a few rolled eyes.

"Would someone please go collect her?"

They all stopped for a moment and everyone glanced at each other, but then Dyresse ran up to the group. She was, Lynx noticed, now wearing a rather concealing cloak that draped all around her.

He took two steps and then reached out and grabbed her shoulder as she got within range. She flushed angrily, and opened her mouth to speak, but Lynx calmly and efficiently began to pat her down in a search. Only a few seconds later, his left hand emerged from the small of her back with a leather flask twice as long as his hand. She flushed even redder, in embarrassment, and refused to meet his eyes. Lynx sniffed the flask. Brandy. He tossed it overhand behind him to the waiting group of mercenaries, and someone caught it.

"Let's get going, we've got work to do." Lynx said, turning away from her, and picking up the pace.

"And you have no idea what's up?"

"No. But something doesn't smell right. Something's off. Everyone, be careful." Lynx said flatly. "Roger, take Martin and Cedric and go get the horses ready, we might want a ready escape if things get dicey." Three bodies peeled off the group and started running for the horse lines. He hardly noticed. As more of the Venturi arrived, the group around him was getting larger and louder.

"Ginger's already packing up." Lorynn commented as she fell in beside Lynx. He grunted again. A very bad sign. His wife had a certain instinct for trouble, and if she was packing up their gear, something was definitely up.

"I may not be the genius some of you mages are, but I can count. And things are adding up to big trouble." Lynx said to Dyresse. "Can you fill me in?"

She was still flushed, but nodded and cleared her throat. "Massive magical energy over there, more than I've ever sensed before. I don't think I could even get too close. Not me or any of the other mages. And we won't be able to use our magic at all-- something is preventing it."

"You have got to be kidding me."

Krael was already shaking his head furiously in agreement.

"Oh no, I can't cast even the smallest spell, haven't been able to for the past quarter hour no matter how I try."

Not good. One of the biggest advantages the Venturi had over other, larger mercenary bands was their rather large and skilled complement of mages, in addition to other specialists, their trackers, siege engineers, and a former cat-burglar and thief who may-have-been involved in espionage under the orders of an unspecified royal before things went sour.

"Right, Dyr, you better stay back then. All the rest of the mages, too. But be ready in case your magic starts working again, we might need you. Lorynn, stay with them and protect them while their magic's gone. All right everyone, it's about to get real. Don't get killed."

———

Lance continued his relentless but painfully slow advance towards where Jorander sat safely back behind the ever-increasing hordes of Kalen regular troops and miscellaneous mercenaries. Kalen had invested a considerable sum in both its own army and in various irregulars to beef up the army's fire-power.

It was all Jannis could do to keep up with him. It didn't help that the particular form the battle had taken meant she had to walk backwards all the way, trying not to trip over rocks, holes in the ground, and all the bodies Lance left in his wake. She knew she wasn't doing nearly as much damage as her brother, but he had a triple advantage over her- being able to walk forward, having that spell distortion that made it so hard to hit him, and, of course, his greater strength, endurance and reach of arm.

It made her feel singularly sour that Lance was once again stealing all the glory for himself, and dragging her reluctantly along in his wake. It didn't occur to her that the only reason he was able to wreck such incredible havoc was because he didn't have to watch his own back.

"Lance...." She whined, sounding both pathetic and demanding, and not particularly caring, "...there's too many of them. I can't keep this up much longer!"

"Oh please, there are only what, another twenty or thirty thousand more to cut through? Think about how many we've already killed; I'm barely winded, and don't have a scratch on me. We'll be the first brother-sister team in history to wipe out an army of this size!" He punctuated the sentence with a deep lunge that let him thrust his blade deeply through someone's chest, piercing both heart and lung. The soldier fell back, blood spurting from his mouth.

"You're a monster, a freak of nature! I can't keep up with you! I'm still maintaining the spell, remember! It's exhausting!" She parried a thrust from a spear with her rapier, and ducked under a massive swing of a war-axe.

"You have no idea how much I wish you were my brother instead of my sister. It's such an incredible burden to have to come out here and fight an entire army virtually single-handed because the only help I have is from a weak-willed little girl." Lance said it casually—he really was barely winded—and he killed two more men even as he was speaking, sweeping his sword in a low arc to hack off a man's leg near the hip, and pulling it back in a backhand sweep to take off another head. It was a miracle he even had a decent grip on his sword, the blood drenched the blade and was even running down the hilt onto the grip.

"I hate you!"

"Save your breath, sis, and keep up!"

She gasped in a heavy lungful of air, and dodged a heavy war-hammer, sliding under the guard and plunging her rapier into the man's throat. A second man swung high at her own exposed neck, but she rolled back, nearly overbalancing in her armor, and evaded the blade. Lance was leaving her behind, damn him.

She scurried to catch him before the surrounding enemies could split them off and envelop her. He didn't even look back.

"I hate you!" She repeated for good measure, panting.

Jannis couldn't see it underneath Lance's helm, but he was rolling his eyes.

Lynx came up behind Jorander and cleared his throat, loudly. It wasn't meant to be offensive, it was just loud so that it could be heard above all the clang and clatter and ruckus of battle. Still, Jorander's shoulders tensed up, whether in apprehension or offense, it was hard to tell.

"You took your sweet time getting here." The archmage commented, without turning around. "Hadrian's Vandals and Grady's Swordsworn are already down in that mess."

Lynx shrugged. Jorander wasn't the one paying him. Jorander was just another hired thug, like the rest of them, archmage or not.

"I didn't come to listen to your delightful conversation, archmage. I came for information. Rumor is you know something about the enemy and I think you should share. Odd that, you knew them on sight, you knew their names, even though no one's ever seen them before."

"My offer still stands, even to you. A thousand gold pieces for the man, and five hundred for the girl. That's enough money to feed and equip your pitiful band of murderers and thieves for more than a year, and buy yourself a little thieves' den to hide in."

Lynx grunted, but didn't bother to take offense. Jorander had an inflated opinion of himself, and he didn't like the Venturi, not one bit, with Dyresse taking a lot of the glory he wanted for himself, casting advanced spells the army needed, that really only an archmage should have been able to pull off. It irritated Jorander no end that a 'mere mage' was given more credibility than he was.

"Who are they, and what are they?" Lynx asked instead, evenly.

"If you're implying that they might not be human, I've had my doubts. They're just a couple of jumped-up kids though, brats. Their uncle spoiled 'em rotten, and Lance was rotten to begin with. Even a cretin like you has heard of the Dark Lord, I presume?"

Lynx grunted again. "A sorcerer's brats? Are they archmages?"

"Indeed. Don't wet your drawers, mercenary, just go earn your pay. And I will make it well worth it. I'll pay good gold to have that brat in my hands."

"You do realize, I work for the kingdom of Kalen, not for you." Lynx commented lightly as he walked away from the archmage.

"Mercenaries work for whoever pays them." Jorander retorted darkly. Lynx wanted to slap him. The Venturi were very selective about who they worked for.

The rest of the Venturi were waiting for him, not very far away, observing the melee a hundred yards down the field.

"Impressive," Phil was muttering to himself, stroking his chin and that ridiculous red beard of his. "I don't think I've ever seen this much damage done by two fighters."

"You would think someone would have gotten lucky by now,

an arrow, a knife in an armpit... something." Someone else added.

"Look at that blow, beautiful." A third man commented as a Kalen swordsman swung overhand, avoiding Lance's blade and shield, and coming down hard on the vambrace protecting his upper arm.

"Hardly, he didn't even stagger, it should have thrown him on his rear." Someone else commented.

"That's some nice armor if it's taking blows like that and not even taking a dent!"

"War's not a spectator sport." Lynx commented to the group, raising one eyebrow at the lot of them.

"Come on, Captain, we're just taking Krael's advice. What does he always say, 'know your enemy'?"

"It's good advice, but we're not here for entertainment. Don't want the others to call us cowards." He said it with a grin, to soften the words, and they all laughed. Only a fool would call the Venturi cowards.

"Ya gotta admit though, those two are really something." Phil was still saying, stroking that beard of his.

Lynx shrugged. "Everyone has a weakness. Everyone. But I'll be damned before I hand them over to Jorander. Let's go bag us a pair of renegade archmages, whadaya say?"

Phil laughed. It was a rumble deep in his massive chest. "Poor lil' doves, they may make mincemeat of the Kalen regulars, but the Venturi haven't hit the field yet. Do you want them alive?"

Lynx considered. "Whatever works." He shrugged again. "We've our own hides to think about."

———————

Lance really was a monster, Jannis thought, glaring up at

him. She was panting heavily, her vision blurred, staggering with every step and he had only just broken a sweat. At least the brutal press of enemies all around them kept him moving very slowly forward, for if it hadn't, he would have left her behind a while ago.

And then, as sometimes happens in the flow of battle, the press lightened, and the encroaching Kalen forces backed up a few paces to ring the pair of them and contemplate their next move. Lance pulled his blade from the chest of his latest victim and slung the flat of it over his shoulder.

"Come on," He demanded, raising his visor, "There has to be one or two of you that can put up a decent fight. This is embarrassing."

"Shut up!" Jannis shrilled. "It isn't enough for you that we're out-numbered and surrounded, you want to go picking fights?"

"Well," Lance said, sounding hurt, "Jorander won't come and play. I want to kill someone with some, I don't know, challenge or something."

"We wouldn't want to disappoint." A raised voice said over the noise all the crowd was making. "Not when you came so far for a decent fight."

"Make a hole!" Another voice shouted, "Push the rabble back!"

And with that, the wall of Kalen troops buckled back to make room for a group of about thirty mercenaries. These particular mercenaries were, if scruffy, at least clean, and with very well-made and well-kept armor.

"Nice armor," Lance commented at the really big guy near the front with bright red hair, "Dwarven-made?"

"Seriously, Lance? You want to talk about armor now?" Jannis panted from behind his back.

Lance shrugged. "It's like I was telling the prince, if you want to stay alive, you invest in good armor."

"I'd almost think you were a mercenary, thinking like that." A man of average to below average height said from beside the big guy. He was in a mail shirt, darkened to charcoal with a coating that prevented rust, and had dark green dyed leather under it.

"Nah, I don't fight for pay. I just kill people cause it's fun." Lance replied, favoring the crowd with one of his devilishly cheerful grins.

"I'm sure we'll both enjoy this, then." The man in the chain mail said, stepping forward. He turned to the big guy as an aside, "Keep the crowd outta my way. Some random soldier taking an opening could get me killed."

"Will do, Captain."

"You really think you're good enough to take me on?" Lance asked incredulously, slapping his visor back down and hefting his sword.

"Is this the part where I'm supposed to brag about my training? 'Good enough' works." The mercenary said.

Even while he was speaking, he was drawing a pair of what could be called short swords or really long knives. They were a form of heavy stiletto, with a stronger spine for piercing and to support the longer length. If anything, they were just short rapiers, and he took one in each hand.

"You won't even be able to reach me with little blades like that," Lance snorted, and advanced without warning, darting across the few feet between them.

Lance's biggest advantage had always been his speed--that and his longer reach which allowed him to carve up his opponent while remaining out of reach of counter-attack. While Lance retained and increased the advantage of reach against Lynx's shorter blades, he completely lost the speed advantage. Where Lance was viper-fast, Lynx was lightning-quick, and he had two weapons instead of one.

It was hard to tell which of them would have been faster if they had been fighting out of armor, but in this contest, Lance's heavier armor also meant slower movement. Lynx avoided Lance's attack almost contemptuously, and slid under the other man's guard with his own attack, which Lance barely managed to deflect in time with his shield.

"Lance!" Jannis shrieked, darting forward to try to stay close behind him.

"What the hell do you think you're doing?! I'm going to trip over you!" Lance shouted at her, and shoved her to one side even as he deflected one of the stilettos with his sword.

"This isn't a duel, you moron!" Jannis shouted back at him. A very timely observation, as she deflected the heavy blow one of the other mercenaries launched at her. They had used the first few blows between Lance and their captain to neatly encircle the Solarans.

"Whatever happened to a nice, brutal, one-on-one fight to the death?" Lance whined petulantly as one stiletto screeched across his shield, leaving a thin silver line in the enamel. His wrist whipped his sword blade in a blur to block the other stiletto and an incoming pole-ax.

"Take the girl." The mercenary captain grunted, shoving aside the man next to him. "I need room to move."

He had barely finished speaking before he was darting at Lance again. Their blades both moved so fast that Jannis couldn't follow the blows let alone the counters.

And she had her own problems to worry about. About a dozen of the mercenaries had formed a loose outer ring, keeping back the Kalen regular troops from the melee in the middle, but another dozen were circling her, and unlike the regular army, these men were quite skilled in blocking, reflecting, deflecting or parrying her blows.

Jannis whirled, blocking one attack and evading another at the same time. Her only real advantage in this was that they did not seem that interested in killing her, or at least not yet. A quick flick of her rapier tore open one man's thigh and he danced back, biting off a curse.

"Do you really think you can beat me?" Lance was taunting the short mercenary in the dark chain-mail shirt as they grappled with one another, blades locked tight.

"Keep talking. I'm not dead yet." He replied flatly, sliding sideways out of the metallic knot they had made with their weapons.

They circled each other, darted at each other again, and Jannis was once again distracted by a near miss as a throwing knife sizzled through the air an inch from her face. The second knife she barely managed to block with her shield as she ducked behind it.

She sensed more than saw the rapid approach of another two mercenaries from behind, and rolled violently forward towards those in front of her, head first, shield blocking an attempted attack of opportunity. She spun to face the mercenaries who had charged her from the rear before the others could react, and gently deflected the thrust of a sword blade with her own, thinner rapier.

Her counterattack skewered the man through the neck. He sputtered blood and toppled over. Another mercenary grabbed him by the shoulder and drug him out of the action. She didn't bother watching, as her attention was already on the next attack.

These mercenaries were disturbingly coordinated. They didn't present many openings, and worked as one unit. She was already tired, and they were fresh.

"Lance! Hurry up and finish your new friend! There is no

way I can take them all out by myself!"

"Shut up, princess!" Her brother replied, his response muffled by effort and metal visor. "Stop distracting me!"

"Listen to your sister, boy. She's almost done for, and so are you." The short mercenary had a bored expression on his face, and though flushed, he was not breathing hard at all.

"The arrogance of some people." Lance rolled his eyes, blocking one stiletto near the base of his sword blade, and then rapidly pressing forward so that the stiletto slid up into the guard near his hand. A flicker of movement from the wrist, and the stiletto went flying through the air.

The mercenary danced back, flexing the fingers of his now-empty hand, but he still had another blade.

"Ready to surrender?" Lance smirked, twirling his blade.

"Funny, I was just about to ask you that." The mercenary replied, pointing with his empty hand.

"Sis!" Lance said contemptuously, frustrated, as he looked in the indicated direction.

"'Tis alright, lil' dove. Dun move." Phil said, from where he was pressed behind Jannis's back, her left arm twisted up behind her, and his dirk at her throat.

"I didn't see him." Jannis said in a small voice.

Someone laughed.

"He's a pretty big guy to miss." One of the other mercenaries commented.

"You have got to be kidding me." Lance said with disgust, throwing his blade to the ground. It was so soaked in blood you could hardly see the metal at all.

"Take the spell down." The captain ordered. One of his men ran over and retrieved the stiletto that Lance had disarmed and returned it to him. The mercenary captain didn't even glance down as he sheathed his stilettos. His attention was entirely focused on Lance.

Lance sighed. "Go ahead, sis."

The mercenary didn't look at her, but a brief moment of surprise, quickly concealed, showed that he had thought Lance the spell-caster and not her.

Jannis cut off the connection to Lance's magic abruptly, and they both felt the recoil. She probably would have fallen over if she hadn't been tightly in the grip of the big mercenary with the red beard. Lance just expressed his feelings with some choice words that probably should not be repeated.

"Get them back to the camp before Jorander shows up." Lynx ordered, glancing behind him.

"You know, Captain, fifteen hundred is a lot of money." Someone commented from behind Jannis and to the right.

"We're working for the Kalen Royal Army, not that puffed-up archmage. The real question is what General Hamilton wants to do with them. Jorander can go suck an egg."

Lynx saw an army officer approaching and quickly moved to intercept him.

The mercenary captain shouted back over his shoulder, even as he was leaving, "Remember, get them back to the camp, and don't let anyone try to take the prisoners. Kalen regulars would never be able to handle those two, even unarmed and bound. Get Dyr. I bet she knows how to immobilize an archmage."

―――――――

"I believe you have the honor," the general paused and looked up at the short, ordinary, rather-unimposing man in chain shirt and leather that stood before him before continuing, "Of being the commander of my smallest and yet most expensive band of irregulars. Are you really worth what we are paying?"

Lynx shrugged. He didn't see the point in trying to defend their fee. It wasn't his fault that most mercenary bands didn't keep a former imperial magistrate on the payroll for delicate negotiations, like contracts. Besides, the Venturi were worth every coin.

And he didn't need to defend himself. For the general's own aide rushed to remind his superior just how much the Venturi contributed. Including a master siege engineer who had been training the less-experienced siege engineers that the army had brought. It made Lynx smile inside, though he kept his face carefully neutral.

The general was not amused. He waived away his aide.

"And just what were you thinking, claiming these renegade knights for yourself?"

Lynx shrugged again. "I was securing them, sir. They had already demonstrated the extent of their threat. I thought extreme measures were necessary to ensure we had them contained. If you want them, sir, you have only to give the order."

The general waived vaguely, and his aide rushed to supply him with a polished tin mug of coffee.

"Just what exactly do you have in your custody?" He asked, stretching himself in his folding camp chair and glancing at the report sitting on the portable desk before him.

"Two archmages trained as swordsmen. They aren't part of the Harderior army by any account, and they both deny any connection with the enemy, even though they were clearly seen leaving the enemy camp by multiple witnesses."

"Two combatants. Unknown affiliation, may be with the enemy." The general summarized for himself. "Why do I care about two combatants? That doesn't even count as a skirmish."

"Archmages." The general's aide reminded him. "Who managed to completely nullify all magic for at least a mile in all directions."

"How many losses?"

"I lost one. Girl took Dmitry in the throat. Your regulars lost almost two hundred before we got there." Lynx supplied.

"One hundred and ninety-two." The aide supplied, glancing at a report.

"I have thousands of men to worry about, and a war to win. Why are you wasting my time with this?"

"What do you want done with them?" Lynx asked.

The general shrugged. "You caught them; they're your problem now. Kill them; keep them in chains. Do whatever you want with them. Just keep them off my battlefield. The last thing I want is archmages on the other side."

"As you wish, General." Lynx bowed and left as quickly as he could without appearing to rush.

Things were looking decidedly up. With the general's permission, he now had legitimate custody of two archmages. That opened up several different possibilities.

"And?" Queried a harried-looking man in the uniform of a Kalen Army officer as Lynx came into view.

"General Hamilton is leaving them in my custody."

The other man let loose a string of inappropriate comments that Lynx ignored.

"What is the general thinking?" The other man asked, falling in next to the mercenary as Lynx continued on towards his camp. "These are archmages. Possibly with Harderior. They should be interrogated, they could have valuable information!"

"We'll question them, don't worry."

"No offense: you're a good man, Lynx, but you're still a mercenary. The army should have those prisoners."

"I'm used to it. We're just the rabble, anyway."

"That's not what I meant and you know it! We both know what you built with the Venturi, and how much you do for this army. I don't lump you in with the rest of the mercenaries."

"You just did."

The officer paused. "You're lucky I like you so much, because sometimes you don't know when to keep your mouth shut."

Lynx shrugged. "Oh, I know. Sometimes I just don't care."

"Whatever. I want one of my men in on the interrogation. They may be your prisoners, but this is our war."

"Depends on who it is. You know how my wife is. One of our prisoners is a girl. She will not let Lyler or Paisley near a female prisoner, and you know it."

Ginger was religious about making sure the women in the Venturi were protected from possible predators. Many times regular soldiers were a little too eager to get too close, especially when they had been drinking off-duty. Most mercenary bands didn't have very many women specifically beause of that fact. The Venturi were the exception.

"Don't worry, we all know how you are tied to your wife's apron strings. How such a tough warrior could let a woman boss him around, I don't know."

"If you had ever slept with my wife, you would understand. But don't ever try: I like you too much, and I don't want to kill you. Besides, Ginger does all the real work; lets me focus on fighting and killing, and that's just fine with me."

"Keep telling yourself that."

"Like I care. Send your man over whenever; my people have

already been interrogating the prisoners, from the moment we took them."

"Do you ever rest?"

"What's that old saying, 'no rest for the wicked'?" Lynx smirked and waived, continuing on, as the other man fell away and started going in a different direction.

Chapter 12

"Interrogation" was perhaps too strong a word for what had actually happened. Lynx's wife Ginger had bustled out of the camp as soon as she had seen the massive group of Venturi returning and had promptly taken charge of Jannis, with a couple of female mercenaries in tow, and Dyresse of course, just in case the prisoner tried to escape.

There was only one of Dyresse, and two archmage prisoners, so they dealt with Lance in the most rational way possible: A solid clout to the head. Besides which, as Dyresse had expressed to Lynx in an aside, Lance would be able to undo any spell she cast to contain or suppress him. The Venturi, being fundamentally practical people, decided to try to pry some information out of his sister first, and leave Lance unconscious.

Lynx left shortly after arriving, to go and speak with the general and deal with the Kalen regular army. The rest of the Venturi stayed back at their camp, now sparse and stark with all their gear and tents packed away. Ginger stoutly refused to unpack the gear; she was still convinced something big was coming.

Lynx's wife was something akin to a force of nature. Sweet-tempered most of the time, she also had a way of rolling right over any resistance. And a serious temper when pushed. Most of the

Venturi just followed their captain's example and humored her most of the time.

Jannis, exhausted by her recent ordeals, and shaken by too many close brushes with death, didn't stand a chance. Ginger had stripped her out of her armor, wrapped her in a warm blanket, and plied her with some hot apple cider fortified with apple brandy.

While Dyresse stole glances at the mug in Jannis's hand with a haunted look on her face, Ginger gently but persistently pulled the story from her hapless prisoner.

"You kidnapped him?" She asked with mild surprise, leaning back on the cart wheel behind her.

Jannis flushed. "I don't know if I would call it that: Prince Darien wanted to come out here. I just… helped him get here."

"And you left him at the Harderior camp?" Ginger persisted.

"Well, yes, that is where he wanted to go…"

"So why didn't you stay there? Do you feel any loyalty or allegiance to the Harderior forces? You seem to have some kind of affection for this prince."

"I don't know. I had to help my brother. He wanted to attack an army by himself!"

"How is attacking an army thousands-strong with two warriors any better than one?"

Jannis flushed again. "I don't know. I guess I just thought it would work out."

"You mean you hoped your brother wouldn't get you both killed. But even if he did, you didn't want to watch him die alone."

"Maybe," Jannis said in a small voice. Ginger reached out to pat her on the shoulder consolingly.

"Family has a way of making us do things we wouldn't otherwise. I understand. I have a brother, too. Though thank the goddess he hasn't gotten me into this kind of situation."

"Where is your brother now?"

Ginger smiled sadly. "I don't really know. We lost touch after I became a mercenary. It's not exactly a glamourous or desirable kind of job. I think I embarrass him."

"Are you from a noble family?" Jannis asked, interest piqued.

"Merchant, actually, but quite well-to-do. In some circles, the merchants are just as self-important as the nobles. And they have just as delicate of egos."

"I think I've had enough of egos." Jannis replied tartly.

"It's a male thing." Ginger shrugged. "And you can't escape it, no matter where you go."

"Mages are every bit as bad as nobles or merchants." Dyresse offered, finally joining the conversation after a long silence. "Though I don't know that egos are a male thing. I knew some ladies with raging egos in Ren, and they were worse than the men. Some of the instructors at the academy. They had a way of undermining their enemies. Just relentless. It was brutal."

"That's academia for you." Ginger offered. "Competitive in the same way as war, or politics, or business. In a lot of ways, I prefer war. At least it's honest in its brutality."

And that was the moment that her husband returned and quietly walked up to them. Ginger harrumphed and winked at Jannis before levering herself to her feet and taking her husband to the side, within sight but outside of immediate hearing.

"And?" Lynx asked quietly, his eyes fixed on the unearthly, silver-haired woman.

"Well-educated, conscientious, loyal. Ridiculously loyal. And naïve, terribly naïve. She just followed her brother out here, risked her life without any real reason. And before that was walking into an arranged marriage just on her uncle's say-so." Ginger muttered under her breath so that only her husband could hear.

"Another problem. We should keep that particular fact between us."

"You didn't tell the Kalen regular troops she is affianced to the enemy king, I take it?"

"They never would have let us keep her if they knew." Lynx frowned, contemplative. "Is there any chance she's lying to us? How reliable is the information you are getting?"

Ginger laughed.

"I'm sure she could come up with a believable lie given enough time, but she didn't have that time, and doesn't seem the sort to lie on impulse. I've kept her off-balance and developed rapport. Yes, everything she's said is reliable. You know me."

"Indeed I do." Lynx replied with a friendly leer. They were married after all. Ginger blushed.

"Behave yourself. Later. We have work to do."

"Slave-driver." He mocked back, winking. "I'm going to go get our ace in the hole, and then it will be time to wake up our sleeping prince charming. Any additional thoughts?"

"That you are devious beyond words, love. Get moving. I'll keep an eye on Phil's 'lil' dove.'"

It hit them like a fist, the sudden lack of magic. For Lieutenant Flemming it meant little: only the warning of dangerous magic being worked. But for Lord Firin and his mages, it was more than just their livelihood: they shared the king's almost religious fervor about magic. It was like to watching the sun vanish from the sky. One of them started crying.

"And you don't know what is causing it?" Flemming asked Firin again, firmly maintaining his calm.

"I can guess." Lord Firin said sourly, suppressing his own rising panic.

"Just who, or what, is this archmage you are chasing if he can do magic like this?" The lieutenant asked, not really expecting an answer.

Firin ignored him and urged his horse forward.

They had been following the trail of the Solarans and the missing prince for several days now, though they had broken off at Lieutenant Flemming's insistence yesterday, and took the longer, but faster route that the supply trains followed, after the trail went into very dangerous territory.

"Local folk speak of evil mountain fairies," Flemming had assured Lord Firin. "But no one knows for sure, because no one comes out alive to speak of what they have seen. In any case, we know where they are going if they keep going the way they have been. We will actually gain ground on them by going around and taking the supply route."

Lord Firin didn't really give much stock to rumors of evil fairies, but was quite willing to take a detour if it meant catching up to their quarry.

"You better pray we don't lose them." He had retorted, and that had been that.

Now, however, Lord Firin's cold and unshakable resolve was being shaken to its foundations. What could take the magic out of the world? It was more than uncanny, it was unnatural. In all his study, Firin had never heard of a spell that could do this.

The only good thing out of this whole horrible situation was that they were very nearly to the current position of the Harderior Army, where it was engaged with the enemy. It hadn't taken the lieutenant or Lord Firin long to figure out what the Solarans' goal was after they had seen the direction of the trail. There wasn't a whole lot out in this direction at the moment besides two large and aggressive armies trying to destroy one another.

"Jacob!" Lord Firin demanded, turning his head to shout back over his shoulder.

The young man in question, one of the two mages Firin had brought, too young and more elbows and knees than one person should have, came trotting up without delay. His horsemanship was just barely passable.

"Yes, m'lord." The young man blurted, attempting a sketchy half-bow in the saddle that Firin ignored.

"How far are we from the encampment?" Firin asked. Jacob had been with the army until he was worn into exhaustion about a month ago and was sent back to the compound to recooperate. He had just barely gotten back up to something approaching fighting condition when the lieutenant had arrived.

"Not very far. It would have been about two days ride when I was there, but they were already planning a retreat. I bet it is only two or three hours now." The young man offered hesitantly, fidgeting with his reins. He was a mage too, and felt deeply the loss of not being able to touch his magic.

"Let's hurry. We're almost there." Firin said instead, not allowing the slightest trace of the discomfort he felt to show on his face.

"Pick up the pace!" Lieutenant Flemming shouted, taking his own direction and urging his horse into a canter. The road was broad and flat, to allow the passage of large supply wagons, and besides the deep ruts to the side where heavy wheels cutting into mud had torn the earth, was clear of obstructions.

Their horses were not fresh, but not near exhaustion either, and readily moved into the ground-eating lope, ears pricked forward. The packed earth was ideal footing, and the light was good. Perhaps they sensed that rest, and food, was near.

In a little over an hour they were there, thundering up to the checkpoint that the soldiers had established along the road at the outer edge of the Harderior army. None of the guards on duty recognized them, but the uniform of the Royal Guard, and the royal orders that Lieutenant Flemming carried, were more than enough to get them through the checkpoint in record time.

Unfortunately, however, that did not extend to getting an audience with General Frederick. He was currently embroiled in strategic planning with his senior commanders and officers and could not be bothered to see them until he was finished. Lord Firin was not amused. Lieutenant Flemming shrugged. Sometimes you just had to wait to see someone when that person was important and had other important things to do.

They were waiting, as a courtesy to Lord Firin and the other mages, in the part of the camp where the army mages were housed. It was a strange sort of place to be, Flemming mused, looking around him. There wasn't any metal to be seen anywhere. Anything you would have made of metal in another part of the camp, here was made of light, jointed hardwood or ceramic.

It all made Lieutenant Flemming painfully aware of the metal he was wearing on his own person: his sword and scabbard, his belt buckle, the buckles on his boots, and the crest on his hat. Strange, the things you think of, that you had never noticed before.

Lord Firin favored him with a sour smile, as if he could read the other man's thoughts.

"The guard said they were over here!" A young voice

chirped loudly, and suddenly the tent flaps to the tent where they were waiting opened.

In darted a small boy, which neither of them could recognize for a moment, though both of them thought he looked very familiar.

"Prince Darien?" Jacob asked, incredulously, from where he was seated in one corner on a wooden box of supplies.

At that point of course, both Lieutenant Flemming and Lord Firin recognized the child, who looked dramatically different from how they both remembered him. But while they were registering this new development, another man followed the prince through the tent flaps.

Though it was a large tent that they were waiting in, there were now seven people inside it, and it was fairly tightly crowded. All but one of the royal guards were waiting outside, but between Lord Firin, the lieutenant, the other two mages they had brought, Prince Darien, and the newcomer, the tent was getting decidedly stuffy and claustrophobic.

"Lord Firin." Master Emrys greeted, with an abbreviated bow in the small space. "I'm surprised to see you out here. Pleasantly surprised."

"We have to save Jannis!" Darien demanded, interrupting whatever Firin would have said in reply.

"Save?" Lieutenant Flemming asked immediately, all his attention rivetted on the prince.

"Her crazy brother talked her into attacking the Kalen Army and they both got captured!"

"I myself only just woke up a few minutes ago. Lance knocked me out before he executed his mad plan. Prince Darien and I came to find you as soon as we heard you were in the camp." Master Emrys clarified.

"This is a disaster." Lord Firin complained needlessly.

"Lord Lance tends to drag disaster in his wake." Master Emrys commented, dryly. "It's a miracle he's still alive. While Prince Darien is determined to rescue our wayward comrades personally, I've expressed to him several times that his own safety is of upmost importance."

"Of course it is." The lieutenant agreed flatly. "That's why we're here. You can have faith in me, your Highness. I will rescue the lady and her brother. But I must ask you to remain here at the camp with one of my men to protect you. You simply can't risk yourself. Harderior needs you."

"That isn't fair! I can help you. I'm not as weak as I was. My magic can help you!" Darien protested.

"I have to say," Jacob commented from his place in the corner, "You do look remarkably well, your Highness. I could hardly recognize you. What happened?"

"This isn't the time to be talking about that." The lieutenant shot the mage a significant glance.

Lord Firin quickly overruled him.

"Yes, what happened to you? How did you get better?"

Master Emrys flushed and glanced away quickly, clearing his throat, before replying.

"Well, ah, our renegade archmage gave the prince a questionable potion, and you see the results."

"You look different, too, Emrys." Firin commented flatly, eyeing the man.

"I refused to let that man give the prince anything without testing it first. It could have been poison for all I knew." Master Emrys explained, flushing slightly with embarrassment.

"A very rational decision given what we know about that archmage." Firin said coldly, furiously, his face alight. "Yet another reason why we need to get our hands on Lord Lance: apparently he has the cure to our sickness." Firin pierced Master Emrys with that look.

"I don't suppose you know what was in that potion?"

"No, sir."

"Or where that maniac hid my books?"

Master Emrys flushed again.

"No, sir. I'm sorry."

Lord Firin's eyes were filled with a quiet, cold intensity that Master Emrys found quite unsettling.

"Lieutenant, after you ensure the safety of the prince, I think we need to plan a rescue mission."

———————

Lance smiled. He smiled frequently, and had a hundred different smiles to choose from. Lance had learned early in life that a smile was a particularly flexible and potent weapon. It could disarm, confuse, distract, or infuriate an opponent, all depending on the type of smile, the situation, and the timing.

But Lance only occasionally smiled a genuine smile, as he did now, an honest, slightly malevolent smile as he saw all the possibilities laid out before him.

"That... is sheer genius." Lance said finally, smiling. "I don't think I could have come up with a better plan myself, and that is saying something."

"I can't think of a higher compliment." The mercenary captain called Lynx replied, carefully neutral, rolling up the sheaf of papers on the folding desk between them. "This plan does expose you to some substantial risks. Can you handle your part?"

Lance rolled his eyes dismissively. "What I can't manage on

sheer talent, I usually manage on extraordinarily good luck. And I have a really high pain threshold. Helps a lot when being tortured."

"Your sister probably isn't going to approve." Lynx added.

"That's why we aren't going to tell her. Sis hasn't figured out yet, that life is a game where everyone cheats, and you have to cheat to win. She's got that whole nose-in-the-air, holier-than-thou problem."

"My wife called her naive."

"Great goddess, what an understatement."

"So you can handle your part?"

"I'm pretty sure I said I can."

"And no qualms about what you have to do?"

"I'm a cold blooded killer, give me some credit."

"Thought you said you weren't a mercenary." Lynx offered, a cocky half-smile appearing on his face.

"I think I said I don't get paid to kill people, I do it for fun."

"You are one sick bastard."

"I get that a lot. Most people don't understand."

Lynx grunted agreement, and turned to go, the papers rolled up in his hand, when Lance stopped him.

"Who are you, anyway? You aren't a common mercenary."

"Who, me?" Lynx smiled. "I'm nobody. But I do have a certain ability to find and attract people of extraordinary talent. People who don't fit in with the common throng. People who aren't understood, because they are bigger, stronger, smarter or better than everyone else. And extraordinary people often have extraordinary problems. It can be a major headache. Worth it, but still, a headache."

"And you consider me a headache?"

"I consider you extraordinary. Take that how you will."

"Insightful, for a sellsword and a thug. I think I like you."

"I'm honored."

"I find myself actually hoping that I don't have to kill you someday."

Lynx smiled and winked, sketching an elaborate, remarkably accurate court bow. "And I also, find myself hoping that I don't have to kill you someday."

"Who the hell are you?" Lance asked again, irritated at being put off.

"Nobody." Lynx answered again, ducking out of the tent where they had been talking, and effectively cutting off the conversation.

Ginger was waiting just outside the tent, Dyresse in tow. Jannis was with Lorynn, discussing rapier technique, within eyesight but out of earshot, and it seemed the best way to handle the matter with both Solarans awake at the same time.

"And?" His wife asked significantly, as Lynx emerged from the tent.

"Good to go."

"Be careful with that one, love. He's every bit as devious as you are."

"I know, I like him already. Arrogant sot, but such a mind."

"Just be careful. A lot can go wrong."

Lynx grunted agreement. "Love, go tell Abrius to pen that letter to Jorander. It's a good thing you already packed, because I think we'll be moving out shortly."

———————

Jannis had spent an unsettlingly pleasant afternoon in the company of the mercenary troop. The one called Ginger, a medic by trade, and apparently running the operation of this particular band, was very friendly, almost motherly, and the wife of the mercenary captain. Many of the other mercenaries were also women, including a remarkably well-educated mage from Ren named Dyresse, and another woman who used rapiers in battle, Lorynn, who also used long knives like her captain.

It was fairly obvious they were keeping their eyes on her, and also pressing her for information, but they did it in such a gentle way that Jannis really couldn't fault them for it. And it was really quite unexpected, especially given that she had killed one of their number.

All in all, she was pleasantly surprised with the results of her capture, which she had been certain would involve torture or death, or both.

There were a thousand things she was worried about still, but she had no answers to most of them, and so carefully avoided thinking about all her problems, instead enjoying this respite while it lasted. She avoided thinking about all of her problems, that is, except one. She was worried out of her mind about her brother. She hadn't seen him since their capture.

Worrying about Lance wasn't something new. It seemed sometimes that all he did was make her worry.

Ginger came up to where Lorynn and Jannis were sitting on some boxes of supplies. The two of them had been talking as the other woman sharpened her stillettos. Ginger seemed harried, worried somehow, and that made Jannis and Lorynn trail off their conversation and turn their full attention to her.

"Jannis, my husband has made... an arrangement. I know it may not be what you want to hear, but, well... you'll just have to make the best of it." She harrumped, placing her hands on her hips. Jannis's mouth felt dry.

"What...?" She began, but Ginger cut her off.

"You can hear about it from the source." She gestured at a group of mercenaries heading in their direction, and Jannis realized with a sinking feeling that Lance was in the middle of the pack, unarmed, stripped out of his armor, and tightly bound and manacled. Lance usually seemed larger than life, but he seemed singularly fragile in that moment, just a painfully thin man with a shock of blond hair.

In moments they were there, and Lance smirked at her. Jannis felt a sinking sensation in the pit of her stomach.

"They're giving me to Jorander." He said to her without preamble, and Jannis paled.

"How can you be so calm?" She demanded, furiously, but Lance only shrugged.

"You can't blame them--it's a lot of money. Here's the deal: I go quietly, and they keep you safe here from Jorander, the Kalen Army, the Harderior and anybody else. Being a mercenary isn't so bad, sis. I bet you could make a good life of it. Better than getting married to some psycho anyway."

Jannis choked. "Lance, you can't..."

"For goddess' sake, you are such a pain. I can take care of myself. Don't make a fuss and don't do anything stupid. You know that's my job."

"Lance, please..."

"You worry too much. You'll be fine." He had the nerve to wink at her, and then the mercenaries were dragging him away.

She choked back a sob, and Ginger placed a consoling hand on her shoulder which she violently shrugged off.

"How could you?!" She demanded.

"It's not just the money. Jorander has a lot of influence

around here, and he isn't too fond of the Venturi already. Trying to keep both of you would have been too large a risk. If your brother had stayed here, Jorander would have probably acted against us directly." Ginger explained patiently. "I don't really know why he hates your brother so much, but it's not something we can risk."

"Just go away. Leave me alone!" Jannis curled into a ball, hiding her tears behind her knees. Ginger raised one eyebrow at Lorynn, who nodded. Ginger harrumphed again, and crossed her arms across her chest.

"Alright, I'll give you some space. Try to pull yourself together." Ginger stalked off.

Lorynn remained where she was, watching Jannis unobtrusively out of the corner of her eye as she ran an oiling cloth across the blade she had just sharpened.

"You're an archmage, too, right?" She commently neutrally, sheathing the blade. "They're pretty rare. Kalen was offering a lot of money, but Jorander was the only one they could find. The Harderior don't have even one. About the only place you find more than one or two, is at the academies in Ren."

"Just leave me alone."

"Are you any good?"

"Leave me alone!" Jannis repeated, still curled in a ball with her face in her knees, and her arms wrapped around herself.

Lorynn went silent, pulling another blade from its sheath and slowly running her sharpening stone along its length. It made a soothing whisk whisk sound as it slid across the metal. A familiar, comforting sound.

They sat there in silence for a long while. Lorynn finished sharpening one knife, ran the oiling cloth along it, sheathed it, and started on another.

"We never should have gotten a mage as skilled as Dyr. Not

in a mercenary troupe. She was the dean of one of the academies in Ren before, you know, her troubles."

Jannis looked up at Lorynn accusingly, irritated at the interruption, but unable to stop her curiousity all the same.

"What troubles?" She asked, after a long moment.

"Being stripped of her licensure and getting banished." Lorynn said flippantly, examining the edge of her blade. She didn't even look in Jannis's direction.

"For what?"

"Magic is, as I'm sure you know, something of a delicate art, that requires a precise touch. Dyr has something of a drinking problem. She had too much one night... and the rest is history."

Jannis shuddered, intrigued despite herself. "What happened?"

Lorynn shrugged. "An explosion. And a fire. That spread to the city, and engulfed several blocks. There were some injuries. And some casualties. Then came the investigation. Dyr doesn't like to talk about the details. But the end result was that she was sent packing, with almost nothing. There were some large restitutions she had to pay out, and she had nothing left over when she was banished. It might have been more humane to just kill her. I'm surprised she didn't kill herself. Over the guilt, if nothing else."

"And she became a mercenary?"

"Lynx has this way of finding people. Odd people, like her, like you, that don't fit anywhere else. Like me, like Ginger, and Phil and Krael and Abrius, and well, all of us."

Jannis was silent for a while, thinking. She sat thinking, with her knees pulled up to her chest, while Lorynn finished sharpening her last blade.

"What about you?" Jannis asked finally.

Lorynn shrugged. "I don't talk about my past with anyone outside of the Venturi." She said flatly, but not meanly. "So if you ever want to know, you'll have to join the company."

"I see." Jannis replied, noncommittally.

"Abrius, now he used to be an Imperial Magistrate." Lorynn continued. "Until he discovered that his superior was embezzling money from the Empire. When he reported it, he was framed for it. He barely escaped execution. He's got a somewhat skewed view, excessive cynicism, but you can't blame him. And he's still completely loyal to the Empire, even though they threw him away like trash. Lynx calls him our 'secret weapon.' Abrius writes all our contracts and negotiates all our fees. The man has an incredibly sharp mind; I would almost call it devilish."

"I know what you're trying to do." Jannis said finally. "But how could I really stay here, how could I ever belong here, when you turned my brother over to a monster like Jorander. He's as good as dead. You have no idea what Jorander will do to him."

"Actually, I have a very good idea." Lorynn said, and there was heat in her voice. "This isn't the first time we've tangled with Jorander."

"Then how could you..." Jannis put her head back down on her knees. She was worried sick about Lance. And not just Lance. She had left Prince Darien back at the other army camp. Had he really recovered from his illness? He had looked a lot better when she had last seen him, but he could have a relapse. The whole reason she had come out here was to help defeat an army that she was now sitting a prisoner of.

What was wrong with her? Couldn't she do anything right?

Lorynn sighed and sheathed her last blade. She leaned back against the stack of supplies, stretching her arms out behind her head.

"You think too much." Lorynn said finally. "Mages always think too much. I doubt archmages are any different."

"I guess this is better than being dead." Jannis said bitterly.

"If your brother hadn't surrendered when we took you captive, Lynx would've had to kill him on the battlefield. At least this way he gets to protect you. Has to make him happy."

"Lance isn't the self-sacrificing type."

"It's not a type."

"Just shut up."

"If you don't want to stay," Lorynn said. "You can always leave once we finish with this current job. We can drop you off somewhere along the way. Maybe you can enter one of the academies in Ren or something. There is always work for an archmage, pretty much anywhere."

"I don't care. I hate magic, anyway."

"Suit yourself."

And with that, Lorynn gave up on her attempts at conversation. Jannis sat alone in her misery, alone except for the ever-watchful mercenary who was so obviously guarding her morose captive.

Chapter 13

Lance, on the other hand, was entirely too busy to be worrying or morose.

The mercenaries, lead by their captain Lynx, and with Dyresse and two other mages in tow, were dragging him across the Kalen camp to where Jorander had set up.

An archmage, he wasn't content with a tent, and had caused

trees to grow together into a living building resembling a miniaturized estate house. Despite the fact that he was with an army in the field, he was not content to go anywhere without a real bed and a real roof.

Jorander's vanity did not, however, extend to real windows. Glass was not only extremely fragile, it was also heavy and difficult to transport, so he made do with thin sheets of silk covering the openings in his living treehouse, which let in a light breeze, but kept out the bugs. He had heavier coverings of leather to drape down over the openings as it got chiller during the night, but the days were still quite warm.

It was late afternoon by this point. There was still daylight, but it was approaching sunset, and the gnarled tree almost-house had a surrealistic appearance. Some of the mercenaries muttered, but Lynx did not hesitate, nor did he allow any of his feelings to show on his face.

Instead he laughed, carefree, at a joke someone had whispered behind him, and grabbed his hapless captive by the sleeve on one side, shoving him forward.

One of the mercenaries knocked on Jorander's door. It opened to reveal a strange creature, seemingly made out of roots, a magical construct that Jorander used for cleaning and to pack and carry his extensive magical supplies in the field. He had a number of these servants. The thing had no eyes or face, but the upper part of it, what you might call a head, turned towards each of them, sensing.

Another mercenary muttered. Lance was not impressed. Lesser treants were something he had seen before. They weren't particularly fast or clever, but they used less magical energy than a simulcrum or a homonculus, so he could understand why Jorander used them.

"Can we please get this over with?" Lance said finally, as they all paused outside the door.

Lynx grunted and shoved the younger man through the doorway, past the treant, and moved deeper into the house. The treant led the way, past a sitting room to where Jorander was seated on an almost-throne, growing up out of the floor, with bark covering it, and with vibrantly colored maroon silk cushions. Dyresse and one other mercenary followed them in, the rest remained outside.

"You got my letter?" Lynx asked neutrally.

The archmage looked up from the book in his lap and smiled. It was not a pleasant smile.

"I was quite surprised to see you came to your senses. I certainly never expected it. Did your greed finally overcome your stupidity?"

"I told you, we work for the Kalen Royal Army. I had to confirm that General Hamilton didn't want the prisoner before I could do anything else. Do you want him, or not?"

"So callous. So unprofessional." Jorander oozed out of his seat, like a serpent uncoiling. "But I'm used to your rough ways. And I believe we have business to conduct."

Jorander grabbed Lance's chin in one hand, forcing his head forward. The mercenary holding Lance from behind pushed him forward slightly. Jorander turned Lance's head slightly to the right and then to the left as if inspecting him. He was still wearing that malevolent smile. Lance just looked bored.

"I still haven't decided if I'm going to kill you, yet. But I don't think I need to make that decision right away. Either way, I am sure you can entertain me for a long while, boy."

Lance didn't bother to respond, he just looked at Jorander with a bored expression.

Jorander's hand clenched on his face, and one fingernail cut into the skin just below Lance's mouth, a tiny drop of blood welling up.

Lynx cleared his throat noisily, and Jorander scowled, distracted from his prize.

"Oh yes, I didn't forget the sellswords. Take your money." Jorander gestured, and one of the treants handed Lynx a bound brass chest. It was heavy enough that the mercenary commander took hold of the brass ring hanging on one side of the chest, and gestured at the other mercenary holding Lance to take the other side.

"Now get out." Jorander said. Dyresse however had something to add.

"Aren't you forgetting something? The drydalius potion?" She said sweetly.

Jorander scowled. The potion in question was made with some extremely rare ingredients, and he had been hoping the mercenaries would overlook it in their eagerness to secure the gold. He stepped back from Lance and went over to a cabinet on the other side of the room, carefully pulling out a tiny glass bottle. He handed it to the waiting treant, who carried it to the other mage.

Dyresse secured the potion in the pocket of her robe and then all three mercenaries started to leave the room.

"Wait," Jorander said suddenly, and they all paused. "What about the girl?"

"We're keeping her." Lynx said bruskly. "An archmage is worth more than five hundred gold pieces."

"Are you bargaining with me, mercenary?!" Jorander demanded, suddenly furious.

"Just making a statement of fact." Lynx replied. Jorander might have said something else, but Lance decided to interject.

"Come on, Jorander. You know me. Do you really think this mercenary trash could have kept me prisoner without a hostage?" Lance said it so simply, so plainly, like a statement of fact. "I could have killed them all on the way across the camp. Besides, I'm worth more than a thousand gold pieces. You're getting one heck of a bargain."

"In this, I think we can agree." Jorander breathed, moving back towards Lance, and wrapping one hand around the other man's throat. "I can't think of anything I want more."

"Then if our business is concluded, we shall leave you two alone to get reacquainted." Lynx said neutrally, slightly stooped to the side with the weight of the chest he had in his left hand. "It was a pleasure doing business with you, Jorander."

"Just leave." The archmage snapped, his attention again fully focused on Lance. The mercenaries vanished as quickly and quietly as they could while carrying a heavy chest filled with gold. There were a couple of thumps on the way out.

"Wow, you are almost as bad as Lord Firin." Lance said, raising one eyebrow. "I know it can be hard, living in a world with a being as fabulous as I am, but this obsessive jealousy can be very trying."

"You have no idea how hard it was deciding what I was going to do with you, once I had you. So many options..."

"You know Jorander, most of the time I ruin people's lives accidentally or incidentally, but you are one of the few who I genuinely enjoyed watching suffer."

"Me, suffer?" Jorander laughed. "That's a drop in the ocean compared to what I have planned for you."

"Promises, promises. You always did talk big. Why don't you prove it?"

"Oh, I intend to." Jorander stroked one side of Lance's face, almost gently.

"Wow, awkward. I don't think our relationship is ready for this level of intimacy. Why don't we just start with the torture?" Lance asked flippantly.

"Time is precious. But, taking the time to savor one's pleasures is just as important."

Jorander's dark smile sparkled in his eyes as he turned away. The treants crowded around, their gnarled root hands clutching Lance firmly and forcing him forwards after Jorander as the archmage left the room.

They meandered through the strange living house until they arrived at one of Jorander's workrooms. The archmage carefully unlocked the arcane wards on the room and the more mundane lock on the door, and the treants forced Lance into the room.

He scanned the workroom, noting the pentacle engraved into the floor and the black and red candles, the smell of something rotting.

"Really, Jorander, demons? How nausiatingly predictable. Aren't you even going to try siphoning off my awesome magical power to increase your own?"

"You would like that, wouldn't you? How stupid do you think I am?"

"Do you really want me to answer that?" Lance asked hopefully.

"No. In all the years you lived with him, how many times did the Dark Lord tap your magic?"

"I don't know," Lance hedged. "Not that often, a few times."

"Magical energy is finite. Do you really think the Dark Lord would have left a vast resevoir of magical energy virtually untapped, unless he had good reason?"

"So what you are saying," Lance mused, "Is that you don't have the skill. Jeez, my own sister can do it, and she is practically incompetent. I've really lost respect for you."

"Your pathetic attempts at baiting me are really quite quaint.

I'm fully aware of my own limitations, and I doubt any human mage, even an archmage, could safely siphon off your magic against your will."

"I bet you are wishing you offered more for Jannis, now, huh?"

"Oh your sister shall be joining us, soon enough. But that can wait for another day. For now," Jorander smiled and paused in his spellwork, "Let's get you comfortable."

At his gesture the treants started unlocking the chains that had been binding Lance, but Lance didn't have any opportunity for escape. The magical constructs stripped away the chains, true, but also his shirt, and drug him over to the center of the room. Treants were slow, yes, but incredibly strong. And there were too many of them there, four of them, for him to be able to overpower or escape. Not that Lance struggled much, it would have given Jorander too much pleasure.

There were iron manacles embedded in the wooden floor, and the treants strapped him in, lying spread eagle on the floor. He was feeling decidedly vulnerable.

Jorander ignored him, lighting candles, fidgeting with his spell materials. Lance tugged gently at the manacles, but they didn't give at all.

"Comfy?" Jorander asked finally, his preparations complete.

Lance shrugged. "I'm getting a little bored down here. You sure take your sweet time. I've never been a big fan of demon-summoning. It's entirely too much work."

"You know blood magic is more art than science. In a lot of ways it's more about quality than quantity. You can drain a body dry of blood, and still not have enough raw magic to work with. You can slaughter hundreds and still not have enough magic to work with."

"You can get to the point any time." Lance said, his tone bored.

"I guess it's about purity. Not in the religious sense, but in the sense of concentration of magic. In the blood of most, magic just runs entirely too thin."

"I'm pretty certain I know where this is going. Stop orating and just cut me, if that's what you want. I'm really getting tired of listening to you blabber."

"One thing I had seriously considered was cutting out your tongue. But then I would miss out on the screams and the pleading for mercy later. It was a hard decision."

"Me, plead for mercy? Some delusions are incurable. Screaming, however, is probably likely. I have very delicate skin."

Jorander scowled. He started chanting malevolently in arcane tongue, a wicked, curved dagger inscribed with runes in one hand, and the other hand making passes through the air above it.

Lance sighed. "And people wonder why I hate magic."

Jorander paced slowly across the room towards him, still chanting, the dagger now alight with an unnatural fire that licked up the blade, red and purple-blue. His voice rose in pitch and intensity as he brought the point of the dagger to Lance's wrist and slashed across his exposed inner forearm with one clean motion. The blood began to well up almost immediately, and formed a thin rivelet running down Lance's arm to pool on the floor.

The light dimmed in the room, as all the candles went out, and the unnatural flame that had licked at the knife blade began to dance from the floor.

"I hope you know what you're doing." Lance commented, opening and closing both hands, and shifting his wrists slightly in the manacles to try to get more comfortable. "Demons eat amateurs for breakfast."

The thing that began to materialize in that room was enormous. It was like a dark cloud swirling, hovering in mid-air. A low keening sound began, as the air in the room was slowly sucked into whatever hole in reality was forming above them. But it was becoming more and more solid by the minute.

Demons, being spirits, did not normally have physical form in the middle realm. Thus, when a sorcerer or other mage summoned one, that mage also had to provide enough magic for the demon to take physical form, or, alternatively, provide an adequate host body for the demon to possess.

This particular demon was materializing rapidly. Lance felt weakened, and knew it was not from blood loss, he hadn't lost enough blood for that. The thing was feeding off his magic and his life-force both. Fortunately for him, Lance had power to burn. Weaker sacrifices tended to die. Whatever Jorander was summoning, it was big, that it would require so much power to materialize.

When it finally finished taking form, and Lance could see it clearly, he whistled his surprise. Jorander was definately in over his head. Lance should know, he'd seen this particular demon before, several years previously.

"Welcome to the middle realm." Jorander intoned to the new arrival, full of pompous arrogance.

Demons were from the world below the world below the middle realm. The world immediately below our own was inhabited by a variety of natural forces and spirits and was controlled primarily by the djinn. The world below that one was a place of unspeakable horrors, of which demons were only one.

The demon, more specifically an archdemon, a thing of horns and dark leathery skin and firey eyes, glanced at Jorander, and almost immediately dismissed him as unimportant. It's attention was instead riveted on Lance, still manacled to the floor.

"Nice to see you again, Dark Lord Harutinabi. Can I call you Haru?" Lance said, smiling. "I'd bow, but you know, kinda tied up right now."

The archdemon immediately turned back to Jorander.

"Name your price, mortal."

"Excuse me?" Jorander sputtered, surprised.

"I'm flattered, really." Lance said from the floor.

"For that creature," the archdemon said, gesturing at Lance, "Name your price, mortal."

"Told you you got a good deal. Don't you know everyone wants me? It should be a mortal sin to be this desirable." Lance commented from the floor.

"He isn't for sale." Jorander said finally, his mind working rapidly, "At least, not right now. I have a different proposition to make, however."

The archdemon's eyes narrowed, considering.

"Speak." It commanded.

"The magic within this... creature. I propose we divide it." Jorander said, gesturing at Lance. "But don't drain him to the point of death. As long as he's alive, his magic will regenerate and we can drain it again."

The archdemon considered. "Split evenly?" It asked finally, after a long moment. Jorander nodded.

"Agreed." The archdemon said, and reached for Lance.

―――――――――――

"The general is occupied." The senior army officer named Gregor repeated patiently, in response to Lord Firin's continued prodding.

"I don't think you comprehend the gravity of the current situation." Lord Firin pressed. Lieutenant Flemming sighed. The man was bound and determined to be a nusiance.

"I do, in fact." Gregor said, insulted. "I've been with this army from the beginning, and I met in person these two strange archmages of which you speak. The fact that we haven't recieved a ransom demand, or a head in a basket, means that the enemy army probably doesn't even know exactly what they have. It would be substantially unwise to advertise that their captive is the king's fiancee."

"How can you really know that they are still alive?" Firin pressed further. "Kalen could have killed them already!"

"They were taken alive, therefore they are probably still alive. Kalen wouldn't kill a pair of archmages out of hand just like we wouldn't, were our positions reversed." Gregor replied, stuffily. "I doubt they are comfortable, but you can be assured, most likely alive."

"But you don't know for certain."

"In battle, nothing is certain. For all we know, one or both of them could have been wounded in the fight, and died later from blood loss or toxic shock. But Kalen wouldn't kill them."

"If they are still alive, then we have to rescue them!" Firin concluded. Gregor sighed, and rubbed his temples.

"Lord Firin, I insist that you return to the mage area and rest. Your long ride has clearly placed a great deal of stress on you."

"But!"

"I insist." Gregor said, and there was poorly concealed steel in his voice. Firin's lip curled into a most undignified snarl, but he obediently turned and left Gregor's tent, offended pride set into his shoulders.

Lieutenant Flemming rose to follow him, but Gregor stopped

him.

"Stay." He said, rubbing his temples.

"Of course, sir." Flemming was part of the royal guard and not the army proper, so he did not answer to army officers directly, but military protocol required deference, and Gregor outranked him.

"I appologize for his manners," Flemming continued, indicating the now-absent Lord Firin. "He's had a rough week."

"He has the king's ear and his confidence, and that makes the man dangerous as well as insufferable. He is always overreaching himself, and there are far too few that will call him on it."

"Don't you worry about your own position if Lord Firin chooses to undermine you?" Flemming asked, concerned.

"Hardly." Gregor replied. "My family has extensive connections in the royal court, including with the royal family. I might get a stern talking-to for putting Lord Firin's back up, but it won't go any farther than that. But that isn't what I wanted to talk to you about." Gregor paused, and drummed his fingers on the top of an empty supply crate that was doing duty as his desk.

"Do you have any information about the Solarans?" Gregor asked.

"I wish I did, sir." Flemming answered sincerely, and Gregor sighed. "I mean I don't know if this would help at all, but I did meet Lady Jannis at the castle briefly and we spoke."

"Anything." Gregor encouraged.

"She seemed... I don't know, vulnerable. Lonely and isolated, and trying too hard to appear strong. I think she is really just a sweet, innocent girl underneath it all. But goddess knows, being a sweet girl would only get her eaten alive in the royal court... or on the battlefield for that matter. Maybe it's better she puts up a front."

"That poor girl." Gregor sighed. "I met her, too. It almost made me uncomfortable being around her- beautiful, brilliant, but slightly... off. I don't know, it felt like I was talking to a being that didn't quite fit in the real world, something that didn't really belong in a smelly canvas tent, with mud, and blood, and sweat. Something that belongs in a dream."

"Those eyes, they seem to stab right through you, stripping away all illusions." Flemming mused. "Not exactly the most comfortable experience."

"I hope it all works out for his Majesty. It probably won't be the most comfortable of marriages." Gregor commented. "Still, archmages are rare enough that he can't really be choosy."

"Very true." Flemming replied, because he knew it was expected of him. Still he couldn't help but wonder if the pending marriage would be just as hard on Lady Jannis as it would be on his Majesty.

"Thank you." Gregor said, as a way of dismissal, as they both stood. "For keeping an eye on Lord Firin. He may be insufferable, but he's also irreplaceable. I, at least, understand what you must endure in support of your king. He isn't pleasant company."

"Thank you, sir. Please let me know when the general is available. I'm sure Lord Firin would appreciate it." Lieutenant Flemming bowed, and left the tent quietly.

"Captain." Dyresse said by way of greeting, falling in beside Lynx and gazing out at the encampment as he did.

Lynx sighed. "Out with it."

"Sir?" She asked, innocently.

"You are as bad as Krael, fidgeting everywhere. Something

is bothering you. So out with it."

"Well, I, had a premonition."

Lynx groaned.

"The last three times you claimed you had a premonition, it didn't go so well, if you will recall."

Dyresse flushed, and grabbed her own upper arms. It looked strangely like she was hugging herself.

"That isn't my fault." She said pointedly. "'Premonitions of doom' are a seperate ability from 'classic premonitions' that see both good and bad futures. If I have a premonition, you already know it's going to be bad."

"So what did you see?" Lynx asked, sighing.

"Glowing red eyes, fangs and claws... death screams... blood running like a river..."

"I freaking knew it."

"I also saw Jorander's body, it looked like it had been burned horribly, it was barely recognizable..."

"Jeez. I think I know why you started drinking. That is one crappy ability to have."

"Doomseers have a high suicide rate. Some go mad, too." Dyresse supplied. "All in all, I think I handled it pretty well."

"I love the excuses. You're a great mage, Dyr, but I'm still keeping you off the bottle."

"You're a heartless bastard."

"I'm a mercenary, comes with the territory."

After a long pause, both of them staring out over the camp, Dyresse continued.

"Are we going to do anything?"

"Dunno, sounds like Jorander's going to tangle with something beyond his ability. Not really a big shock, and he deserves what's coming."

"Demons that kill the one who summons them are a thorny problem though," Dyresse commented. "The easiest way to send them back the way they came is for the mage who originally summoned them to do so. Once he's dead, it gets more interesting. A demon can stay in the middle realm as long as it has a host or enough magic to remain materialized."

"Makes demon-summoning sound like a fool's business."

"It is. Anyone who practices it uses wards to protect himself from the demon. If you ask some religious orders, just the practice itself should be banned, and anyone who practices it, executed. In Ren, it's strictly regulated, for academic purposes only, and in the northern part of Lorencia, it's banned completely."

"So what you are saying," Lynx said, pulling Dyr back on topic, "Is that bastard is about to unleash a demon on the army, us included."

"If he hasn't already." Dyresse clarified. "My premonitions don't usually hit until right before the disaster."

"Lovely. Is that part of the 'doom'? So you don't have time to stop it before it happens?"

"Exactly."

"Let's keep the casualties to a minimum. Who do you want?"

"Krael, for sure. Phil, to counter direct physical attack. I'd like the girl too. She's probably out of her mind with worry for her brother, and an archmage's raw power would be a big help even if she were completely untrained."

"If she and her brother get together, and turn on you though, do you think Krael, Phil and you could counter them?" Lynx asked.

"Probably not." Dyresse conceded. "The brother is a lot stronger than she is, magically speaking. I don't think Jorander could handle him either. Of course, he is spell-bound, but if anyone were stupid enough to break the spell..."

"Could you?" Lynx asked. "Break the spell, I mean."

"I could, but I wouldn't. It's an incredible piece of spellwork. Would be like smashing a stained glass window in a church, and besides, whoever built it did so for a good reason. Not just any mage could break it, though, only one with extensive training, or an archmage."

"You're afraid Jorander might."

"We already know he's a moron."

"I'd love to come with you..."

"But you are going to be establishing an alibi, right? So we don't get blamed for this particular coming disaster?"

Lynx smiled.

"You're learning. Abrius is a wonderful influence, don't you agree?"

"Then I'll take Lorynn and Roger. Oh, and Linaloe, if you allow."

"Just tell her to keep the hat pulled low. The last thing we need is for the Kalen army to find out we have a Fae in our troupe. Take Zalapa with you, too, they are both probably stir crazy from being cooped up in the tent all the time."

Linaloe had grown up in the other realm of Haerg Nerue, to a good family, and had promptly rebelled upon reaching early adulthood, hired a mage of questionable repute to open a gateway and fled to the middle realm. She was extremely young for an elf, only one hundred and twelve years old. Zalapa was a sylph of the desert winds tribe, a wind elemental and archer of the highest ability.

Either of them could, in the wrong place and time, get the entire band lynched or chased out of a town by a rampaging mob. The average citizen viewed the Fae as something akin to pretty-looking monsters. Though technically a sylph is not a Fae, coming from an entirely different world, the average citizen would hardly make that particular academic distinction.

"I'll do my best to keep them out of trouble." Dyresse said doubtfully. "At the very least we just kill anyone who recognizes them."

"Casualties to a minimum." Lynx ordered, sighing. "I'm going to see some people I know. Get moving. I don't hear screaming yet, so you might have a minute to get everyone together before it starts."

Chapter 14

Lance didn't really remember much. Which was probably a good thing. At some point the pain had started, at some point it had gotten so bad he started screaming and at some point he had passed out from the pain, drifting into blessed oblivion.

A mage's power isn't like water in a bucket that you can just dump out; it exists in layers, for protective reasons. The first portion of power is easily extracted, even by force. Deeper layers are far harder to access, and are removed with increasing physical and mental pain. It happens that way for the same reason that a blade piercing the body causes pain: as a mage's power is drained further, it causes damage to the body and spirit, and that pain is a warning of the damage, and the amount of damage being done. It is possible to kill a mage by draining all of the magic from the body, and it is a very painful death.

With discipline and training, mages learn to overcome pain,

to be able to access deeper layers of the inherent power they already possess, but there is a price in recovery for overextension. And of course, magic extracted by the mage's own will is significantly less painful than magic extracted by external force.

Lance felt sore all over, and it was a wierd sensation, because the soreness wasn't really in his muscles. He experimentally flexed one or two, and felt no corresponding increase. He also felt weak, which was a very novel experience for him.

"Good morning!" Jorander said from somewhere on the other side of the room. "Sleep well?"

"Like a baby. Can't say much for your hospitality though, leaving a guest chained to a floor all night." Lance replied flippantly. "Where's Haru?"

"He'll be back shortly. Are you that eager? Maybe I underestimated your sheer lack of sense."

"You do realize you are going to get screwed. Demons aren't known for fair play, and Haru has a pretty dark reputation even compared to his own kin."

"Demons aren't known for their gentleness, either. Did you have a pleasant night, Lance?"

"Gotta give it to Haru, he's got skills. So how long did I last before I passed out? I wasn't really keeping track of time."

"A lot longer than I expected, but not nearly long enough. I could listen to your agonized screams all day and night."

"Sorry I couldn't accomodate you, but everyone gets tired sooner or later. And I did sorta take on an army and fuel an area-effect anti-magic spell yesterday. I was already a little tired before I got here."

Jorander didn't say anything in response, and Lance didn't have a very good view of him from the floor. He wriggled a little on the floor, it wasn't very comfortable not being able to change position.

"So did Haru actually give you your share of my magic like he promised?" Lance asked. Jorander didn't respond. Lance continued after a long moment of silence. "You really are an idiot, you know."

"I will get what was promised." Jorander snapped. "Unlike you, I know how to be patient."

"Hey, I'm patient. I spent two weeks chopping wood and digging holes just so I could gather some intelligence. I bet you've never done an honest day's work in your life."

Jorander ignored him.

Resummoning the archdemon was considerably less work than the initial summoning had been. At this point, Dark Lord Harutinabi was under contract to return, and already had all the power he needed to materialize.

He materialized rapidly, almost popping back into the room, and it caused a sudden change in air pressure to have all that demon appear in such a small space without sucking some of the air out first. There was a wooshing sound as air was forced out through the tiny space under the door.

The demon however, looked surprised to have been summoned.

"Draining him again this soon will not yield as much power." Dark Lord Harutinabi pointed out to Jorander.

"Perhaps not." Jorander mused. "But I enjoy seeing him suffer. And besides which, you still owe me the power promised."

"Indeed..." The archdemon purred. "I would not want you to feel cheated."

It reached out one clawed hand towards Jorander, who to his credit, did not stumble backwards, but stood firm.

Upon physical contact, the demon began pouring magical energy into the archmage. As Jorander had previously noted, demons were not known for their gentleness. He had to noticably brace himself against the flow of magic to keep from toppling over.

Lance sighed heavily, and closed his eyes. He wasn't really sure he wanted to watch what was coming next.

Jorander cried out.

"Stop... please..." He mumbled, falling to his knees.

"I would not want you to feel cheated." The archdemon repeated in a purr, "Half the power is yours. As agreed." His clawed hand clenched tightly around the archmage, as Jorander struggled to pull away.

"Too much! Stop!" Jorander pleaded, and you couldn't make out anything after that but screaming. Jorander screamed for a very long time, his voice rising in intensity until it finally broke off in a sputtering gurgle and the room was filled with the smell of burning flesh.

Lance glanced over at the charred corpse that had once been the archmage Jorander, and sighed heavily. Now he would have to deal with the demon. Why couldn't his sister help clean up the mess? She wasn't good for much else.

"And now you..." The archdemon paused and turned his full attention on Lance, placing the same clawed hand that had killed Jorander on Lance's exposed chest, one long clawed finger reaching alongside Lance's neck, "Are mine."

"Hey, Haru. I can call you Haru, right? Rip out my heart and eat it, or get me out of these manacles, whichever way you feel, but I really am sick of being chained to this floor. I'm getting cramps."

The demon chuckled, genuinely amused.

"As if I would slaughter an omnimage for a tiny snack, no

matter how delectable."

"Archmage, actually. I've been getting that a lot lately. You haven't been talking to any mountain faeries have you?"

"Archmage?" The demon repeated, distainfully. "Do not insult my intelligence, mortal."

"There aren't any human omnimages." Lance replied with some heat. "It's impossible, in any book I've ever read. The raw magical power of an omnimage can't be contained within a human body."

"Of course not, it fries to a cinder if you attempt to." The demon said, politely.

Lance glanced over at Jorander's body. "Oh."

"Oh." Lance repeated, suddenly at a loss for words. It was definately going to be a bad day.

The demon chuckled again, settling itself in a curl on the floor around Lance.

"I find this amusing. You genuinely believed you were human?"

"Well, yeah. If I'm not human, then what the heck am I?"

"It doesn't matter. Very soon you shall be a demon."

"Excuse me?"

Dark Lord Harutinabi chuckled deep within its chest, and smiled, a distinctly disturbing smile.

"With an omnimage as my vessel, I can enslave the entire middle realm and lay waste to all its nations. Together, we shall be unstoppable."

"Not gonna happen." Lance said flatly, pulling at the manacles that still held him firmly on the wooden floor. "I'm not really keen on being possessed. I'm quite flattered though. And I'd be more than happy to help you find an alternate host body, if you get me off this floor." Lance smiled winningly.

"The real question, omnimage, is how long your will can resist mine, drained and weakened as you are. Shall we find out?"

"I can't talk you out of this, Haru?" Lance asked hopefully. The archdemon smiled even more deeply and stroked Lance's chest with the clawed hand still pressing down on him. "It's really getting tiresome being this incredibly desirable." Lance concluded. "I hate magic."

———————

Sylphs, the most well-known of the wind elementals, who originate in the realm of the djinn, belong to seven distinctly different tribes. The northern wind tribe is frost-pale, with pasty skin, platinum blonde or white hair, and piercing blue eyes. The southern wind tribe is golden, with golden-brown skin, gold or brown hair and brown or green eyes. Zalapa was neither of those. He was from the desert wind tribe, and that meant he was dark. Dark hair, dark eyes, and brown skin. If you were to compare his tribe to humans, they might be easily mistaken for turks or saracens.

In size, sylphs are large enough to be mistaken for humans, though they run on the small side as humans go. Sylphs can remain solid when they wish to, though their most noteworthy ability is to turn their body completely into wind and rematerialize elsewhere in a moment. This makes them silent, deadly assassins, who can quite literally appear and disappear like the wind.

Sylphs can also listen to the wind, and hear things that happen from miles away, which makes them adept trackers.

But being a wind elemental, used to the freedom of the skies, made being trapped in a tent nearly unbearable. Especially with such immature company.

The elf was young, in her defense. Elves are frequently self-centered and vain, and when young, have not yet learned the necessary degree of tact.

"Zal," Linaloe repeated, ignoring once again his request not to shorten his name, "What do you think?" She paused, as he remained silent, and then raised one delicate eyebrow above her beautifully sloped green eyes at him.

Zalapa sighed. Again. "Your hair is always lovely."

"But does it look better this way?" She asked, turning in front of the mirror to try to get a clearer view of the back.

"It looks lovely both ways." Zalapa said, tactfully. Truthfully, he didn't understand this fixation with appearance. She was lovely, was that not enough?

"You aren't helping." Linaloe huffed, running the fingers of one hand through her hair, and adjusting it in some way he couldn't fathom. It looked exactly the same to him.

"So should I wear the silver clip or the rose-gold?" She asked, irritated.

Finally, a question he could answer.

"The rose-gold, of course."

"But the silver might go better with this dress..."

Zalapa sighed. Again.

"Zal, stop that."

"Stop what?"

"The sighing. I would almost think you don't enjoy my company." She smiled as she said it, her eyes twinkling at him. "But I know that can't possibly be the case."

"If you do not wish my opinion, then why do you ask?" He asked instead, puzzled.

"Well, if you feel that strongly about it, I'll wear the rose-gold. Of course that means I can't wear the velvet cloak with it, so I'll have to change my slippers."

Zalapa had no idea how that particular set of wardrobe changes came out of a hairclip choice.

Linaloe opened a trunk and pondered slippers for a few moments.

"The dark brown silk, I think. Subtle, but elegant." She changed her slippers. And then changed her mind. "Actually I think the dark rose would be better, I like the embroidery." She changed her slippers, again.

"Zal, what do you think?" Linaloe asked, twirling around, her eyes sparkling merriment.

"That you look lovely." He replied neutrally, not asking the obvious question: why she bothered taking such elaborate pains with her appearance, when there was no one there to see or admire her. He was old enough, and knew through experiences with his sisters, that such a question would be taken badly.

"But do I look better in this than the blue-green silk?" She pressed, turning to the mirror again.

How should he answer?

"Yes." He said finally, considering.

"Do you really think so?"

"I said so, did I not? It suits your coloring admirably."

She frowned at the mirror.

"Are you sure? The blue-green silk makes such a statement..."

Zalapa sighed.

"Zal, stop that."

"Zal is not my name."

"Is that what this is about? You can be so sensitive sometimes, Zalllaaaappaaaaa."

She laughed as she exaggerated the sounds of his name, as if it were some form of joke.

Zalapa sighed again.

"You can be such a stick-in-the-mud." Linaloe said, swirling a fine wool cloak around her shoulders.

"I am just... uncomfortable in such a small space."

She laughed. "This isn't exactly a small tent, and there's only the two of us in here."

"It is alright if you do not understand, you are not a sylph."

"I'm not exactly thrilled to be trapped in here either you know, sylph or not. But I'm making the best of it. You know, I should totally give you a haircut!"

"A what?" Zalapa asked, suddenly wary. "My hair does not need cut. See?" He gestured at his head, where indeed it did not need cut.

"Oh it doesn't look bad," Linaloe began. "But just think, we could make you the most stylish sylph around! I could..."

At that moment, blessedly, the tent flaps opened, interrupting whatever the elf would say next, and the human mage called Dyresse came in.

"You are most welcome here, my lady." Zalapa said with relief. "How can we aid you?"

"I had a premonition," Dyresse began. Linaloe groaned. The human glared at the elf, and continued.

"Jorander is summoning a demon, and he's not going to survive the attempt. You know what that means."

"Time to hunt." Zalapa said, a satisfied intensity setting into every muscle. Sylphs considered demons their mortal enemies and took great pleasure in hunting them down and casting them back into their own world.

"Do we have to?" Linaloe whined. "I'll ruin my slippers."

"Then put on some boots. But hurry up, we need to get going!" The human mage instructed her. Zalapa had already collected his bow and arrows and was standing, fidgeting, by the tent flaps.

"And for goddess sake, put a hat on, Linaloe! Hide those ears!"

"This is totally going to ruin my hair." She complained, but complied, first pulling on a hat, and then pulling up the generous hood of her woolen cloak.

Dyresse paused, and turned to look at him, considering.

"Zalapa," she said. "You aren't going to do anything stupid this time, right?"

"No." He said, without protest. Though how wind-walking to stop a fleeing opponent was stupid, he did not understand. Dyresse still held it against him that the Venturi had been driven by force from that village once the villagers had seen he was a sylph. But he had had no choice! It was wholly unfair.

She pursed her lips at him. The woman held a grudge. Zalapa said nothing, and simply met her gaze quietly. Finally, she turned back to the elf. Linaloe winked at him. And then, they were all outside.

The touch of the wind was sweet, he inhaled deeply, his eyes closing in pleasure, though only for a moment. They were already running, a moderate ground-eating lope that he kept up with easily.

The winds caressed him as he moved, the air around him alive and vibrant. It whispered to him of things both near and far.

And the wind spoke of a demon, his foul scent upon the air. Zalapa turned instinctively, and both women followed him.

"You scent it already?" Dyresse asked, surprised.

"Yes." He answered, completely fixated on his target.

"I hope the others can catch up," Dyresse said doubtfully. "Slow down, or they might not see us."

Dyresse's fears, however, were unfounded, as Roger, Lorynn, Phil, Jannis, and Krael spotted the three of them and moved to intercept.

Lorynn smiled broadly as soon as she saw him. She waved and called out, "Good to see you out of the tent! Get some fresh air!"

This particular human female was attracted to him, and while Zalapa was indeed quite lonely for female companionship of his own kind, she was not his species. He was no more attracted to her, than she might have been to a horse or a frog. But since he could not think of a tactful way to tell her this, the sylph instead simply smiled awkwardly at her and let her believe he was shy.

Roger however, decided to thump him heartily on the back at this interchange.

"I wish I had your way with the ladies, sylph!"

A joke? Or just blind ignorance? Zalapa decided on the first, and laughed appreciatively.

"I think it will take a hundred lifetimes to fully understand your human women." Zalapa offered honestly, and Roger thumped him on the back again, grinning. Ah, the correct response.

"We all feel that way." Roger agreed.

"Speak for yourself." Phil laughed.

Jorander was the only archmage currently in Kalen's employ. As such, there were some tasks that only he could perform. When someone asked, someone else noted that Jorander had not yet left his residence that morning. And thus, a couple of hours after Jorander was supposed to be out doing his job, someone sent a small squad of soldiers to collect him from his living treehouse.

Jorander was not strictly speaking lazy, but he had his own priorities, and had neglected the priorities of the army before. As such, the soldiers who pounded on the door were irritated and not particularly concerned by his apparent disappearance.

There was no answer. The door was opened anyway. Soldiers are like police in that way. They then promptly began searching the house for the missing archmage. Whatever fear they felt at intruding upon an archmage was overcome by the explicit nature of the orders that had sent them.

The house was empty, except for one locked door they could not open. Jorander, like any sensible archmage, closed and locked the door behind him when he went into his workroom, using both a mundane lock, and an arcane lock to prevent untimely interruptions.

The soldiers pounded on the door, and shouted through the door, to no response. At some point there was a discussion about whether or not to try to break down the door. Then, mysteriously, the door that had previously been locked slowly inched open, not much, certainly not enough to see into the darkened room on the other side.

And then a voice they did not recognize, hoarse and flat and full of amused irony, said from the darkened room, "Whoever you are, you really don't want to come in here."

Which had the exact opposite effect. The soldiers shoved open the door and piled into the room, despite or perhaps because of Lance's warning. And that's when the screaming started.

While the demon had already expressed the fact that it wanted Lance whole, for the purpose of possessing his body, it had no compunctions whatsoever about ripping the Kalen regulars limb from limb and plopping choice morsels into its fang-encrusted maw.

The last soldier in the door was the first one out, running as fast as feet could move, limbs heaving, and heart thumping. He almost made it, breaking out of the outer door into the sunlight, when the clawed hand whipped out of the open door behind him and dragged him screaming back inside the house.

Dark Lord Harutinabi was a little too large to fit through the door openings that Jorander had created, but that didn't stop him or even slow him down much. He crashed through the wooden doorframes, sending splinters flying.

Lance, however, didn't get to enjoy much of the show, still being strapped to the floor of Jorander's workroom, which was now smeared with blood and various other bodily fluids.

Still the distraction was a most welcome one, as he was rapidly approaching the end of his strength; his body pale and soaked in sweat; vision blurred. Haru was one tough customer, and dozens of attempts to possess his body, while he in turn pushed with all his will to keep it out, had taken their toll.

So he just took a moment to rest, a sweet moment of relief--and ignored the frantic screams and sounds of battle right outside, just as he ignored the blood splattered on his shoulder. Lance took a breather, and bided his time.

Lieutenant Flemming looked out over the Kalen army encampment from where he was nestled between three large branches in a large, and still leafy tree, all the leaves edged in brown and gold where they were slowly dying as summer became a memory.

Master Emrys, Lord Firin, Jacob, and the rest of the royal guards, minus two who were keeping Prince Darien safe in the Harderior Army encampment, were all waiting a short distance below and behind him, under cover of some brush.

The problem did not resolve itself just from looking at the enemy encampment. The Kalen encampment was very large, consisting of over ten thousand soldiers over a wide area. And they had no idea where Lady Jannis and her brother had been imprisoned. Wandering blindly in looking for them would be like looking for a needle in a haystack.

There weren't any obvious locations where prisoners were being kept, and it seemed that the encampment was actually a number of seperate, smaller encampments all closely grouped. Some were probably individual companies and regiments of the Kalen regular army. Others were probably bonded and free mercenary companies. Kalen had not been discrete about hiring out for their war.

Lieutenant Flemming climbed down from the tree quietly, and returned to the others. It was still very early morning. The group had come up close to the army encampment under cover of dark, but the night was ending.

"I don't see how we are going to find them." The lieutenant said simply. "It's not possible to search all those tents. And there isn't a central area where they are keeping prisoners, at least not one I can see."

"We don't have to search all the tents." Master Emrys replied mildy. "If we get close enough I can sense their magical energies. Archmages aren't exactly subtle."

"Getting close enough is the problem though. There is a lot of ground to cover." Lieutenant Flemming pointed out.

"So what do you suggest?" Lord Firin snapped, irate.

"Infiltration. Steal uniforms and try to get information. If we can identify where they are being held, we can plan a rescue. Right now we just don't have any information."

It was quickly agreed, and they paired off, one guard and one mage in each pairing. The extra guard waited where they had hidden in the brush, to be the communication link between the groups as they checked in.

And thus, three pairs of Harderior snuck into the Kalen Army's camp.

The scene as Jannis and the mercenaries came into view was nightmarish or hilarious, depending upon how one's sense of humor ran. Dark Lord Harutinabi had smashed his head through the roof of Jorander's strange living treehouse in the room near the front door. And he had gotten stuck there. He was attempting to free himself from the tangle of brush and branches, while simultaneously tearing the Kalen regular army to shreds.

An archdemon's primary weapon is not claw or fang, though it might relish the feel of tearing flesh; an archdemon is primarily a mage. And this particular demon was killing the Kalen regulars with magic more than claws, calling down lightning, burning them alive, turning the ground into pools of acid, and whatever else it thought of.

Who knew how much damage it could have done if it had its undivided attention on the poor mortals surrounding it, but fortunately for all of them, the archdemon had a good deal of its attention focused on the house it was stuck in.

That did not last. The house burst into grudging flame, being made of green wood, that angrily smoked and crackled as it attempted to resist the fire. The demon's magic fire was hot enough however, to alight even the living wood of Jorander's treehouse, and it was soon burning merrily, thick grey-white smoke billowing everywhere and whipping around in the breeze.

Jannis' attention was immediately drawn, however, to the

tiny, dark mercenary with a bow, who rather than pausing a moment to survey the scene, had continued on relentlessly towards the demon, until it was within range, and started firing. He was using a hunting bow made of horn or bone rather than wood, of about fifty or so inches in length, not long enough to be a long bow, but with enough length to put some force behind his shots.

He was remarkably accurate, but the missles from his bow didn't seem to be doing much damage, lodging themselves into the demon's thick neck and shoulder muscles. She noticed the swirl of wind magic around him with her mage sight and put two and two together.

Not human. An elemental? Wind elemental, but what kind? He was a lot darker than any of the slyphs she had seen. Maybe a djinn? There weren't many that were wind element, but there were a few.

"Hey!" She called out, sprinting the distance between them, despite her heavy armor, which had been temporarily returned for the battle.

He ignored her, his entire attention focused on the demon and his bow, at least until she nearly barreled into him. Then he turned, shocked, as if surprised to see her there.

"Let me help," Jannis said impulsively, grabbing his quiver. Zalapa opened his mouth to object, but did not have time to, surprised by her bruskness.

She pulled an arrow out of the quiver and quickly stroked the arrowhead alongside her face near her jaw, making a minor cut, and leaving the barest trace of blood on the arrowhead. A hand would have worked better, but it could be a pain getting those gauntlets back on once she had them off!

A few short phrases and a dusting of magic later, she handed the enchanted arrow to the wind elemental archer, who eyed it doubtfully. Jannis could have screamed. It was only sheer luck that the archer had been using horn arrowheads instead of metal, which she would not have been able to enchant in any case.

"Silly thing to do," he said at last. "You should have asked first if I poisoned my arrows. Sheer luck that I grabbed this quiver, not the other, otherwise we would have a significant problem."

He said nothing else to her sudden shocked expression, but drew back on the bow and fired the arrow at the demon.

The demon screamed fiercely as the arrow pierced it, and the whole arrow began to glow with a hot, pale blue flame.

He held out a hand to her for another shot without even looking in her direction, all his attention riveted on the demon, and Jannis flushed, pulling another arrow from the quiver and repeating the process.

The second arrow struck home in the demon's neck, and dripped flaming bits of pale blue fire down onto the demon's shoulder. The demon reached up and ripped the arrow out with one massive clawed hand, its hand smoking at the arrow's touch.

Dark Lord Harutinabi's attention was now fully fixed on them, its eyes pulled to the direction from which the arrows flew.

"Run." Zalapa said calmly, accepting a third arrow from her. He pulled back, ready to fire.

"What?" She demanded. "Hardly." Jannis pulled off a gauntlet, irrititated. They were so hard to get back on! She shoved the gauntlet in the belt that held her rapier at her side.

"Avant re sepris," Jannis chanted, her hand glowing pale blue, as Zalapa fired his last shot, which barely missed striking the demon in the eye, skittering along its temple.

The archdemon howled, and pulling itself free of the remains of the house's front room, pushed its way out of the front door, sending splinters flying in its wake.

"You really should run." Zalapa said, gathering his quiver from where she had set it down between them.

"What kind of coward do you think I am?" She retorted. "Besides, you can't escape from an archdemon of corruption by running. They can fly."

And indeed, the archdemon did have a pair of hideous bat-like wings which up until now it hadn't bothered to use. Wings don't give much advantage inside of a building.

"Restese phir khra," Jannis continued, the ground at her feet beginning to shimmer with the same pale blue light. Zalapa released another two shots, which struck with unfailing accuracy, but without enchantment doing little damage.

The demon was heading in their direction when it was struck by a massive fireball from the side fired by the other mercenary, Dyresse. The Venturi had finally gotten into the fight.

Dyresse and Krael had taken the opportunity to move around the demon so that they could attack from multiple sides, Phil and Linaloe were with Dyresse, and Lorynn was with Krael. There were now three seperate groups, each spaced a distance apart, with a mage, and the ability to attack at range.

The demon hesitated for a moment, glancing in the direction the fireball had come from, reconsidering its choice of target, before turning back toward Jannis and the wind elemental.

But that distraction had bought Jannis a few precious moments to complete her enchantment. Blue light rippled through the ground, spreading rapidly, past the demon, past the other mercenaries. She felt the recoil like a slap in the face--it dazed her for a moment. She closed her eyes, pausing for a moment to take a few deep breaths.

"I hope whatever you just did helps." The wind elemental said doubtfully, glancing around, and seeing no response.

"Of course it did! That was a demon ward, it temporarily blocks a demon from using its magic. I guess there are some advantages to living with a demon-summoning sorcerer." She retorted, and paused as an outrageous thought occured to her. Was a demon ward the basis of the null-magic spell that her uncle had cast on her brother?

"I've just never cast a spell like this over such a large area before." She finished stupidly, weaving on her feet.

Dark Lord Harutinabi paused as it came closer and got a better look at her.

"I was wondering when Aerigard's other brat would show up," The demon said, its voice a deep, smooth rumble. "You shouldn't leave your brother alone; we both know what kind of trouble he can get into."

"It knows you." Zalapa pointed out rather accusingly. Jannis sighed. What a life fate had dealt her, that demons recognized her on sight when none of her fellow humans did!

"In honor of the long, fruitful working relationship I have with your uncle, I'll give you once chance to dispell the paritta warding, and I might let you live. Otherwise..."

Any kind of response was precluded by a second fireball slamming into the demon's head, followed by a storm of what could only be called arrows of ominous red magical energy. Phil used the distraction of the combined magical attack to close quickly with the demon and ram his heavy spear-tip through the demon's clawed foot and into the ground below it before rolling rapidly out of the way.

Jannis was distracted by the demon, to be sure, but not so much so that she didn't notice the strange shimmering, warping in the air immediately in front of her. She opened her mouth to point it out to the wind elemental, but before she could, the distortion materialized into the form of the hooded and cloaked girl from the mercenary troop.

"Zal..." Linaloe said warningly, grabbing Jannis's wrist. "You should know better."

"I told her to run." He said, confused. "Twice."

"Not that: you didn't bother to stay and find out what Dyr wanted you to do, you had to go right for the demon. We fight as a team, remember? Dyr said to go find the brother. You're the only one here we are sure can get past the demon. And don't forget your *other* orders. Remember?" The girl was almost humorous in the way she tried to stare down a man, well, elemental, who was probably hundreds of years older than her.

A giant clawed hand slamming down on the ground entirely too close to any of them finally motivated Zalapa into action, darting to the side towards the house. Linaloe was already pulling Jannis in the opposite direction, as fast as her little legs could move.

"It's after you!" The girl screamed over the demon's frustrated and pained roaring. "Paritta wards can be dispelled by the death of the caster!"

They darted away as fast as they could, with the demon in close, but frustrated pursuit, due in part to its wounded foot, and in part to the fact that it was now unable to use magic and hence, unable to fly.

Demons, like many magical creatures that fly, use elemental wind magic to fly faster, higher and better than their wings would be able to without assistance. In some cases, creatures' wings are too small to be able to launch the creature into the air without magical assistance, as was the case for Dark Lord Harutinabi.

Without his magic, he thrashed about, entirely too fast for a creature of his size and weight, but less maneuverable without flight.

His whole attention was fixed on the silver-haired girl in armor who shimmered pale blue in time to the faint shimmers that shot through the ground all around them, subtle visual manifestations of the paritta ward she had cast.

Chapter 15

Zalapa wind-walked as soon he was out of sight of any onlooking soldiers, swirling into a dark brown cloud of dust that whipped immediately out of sight. It was relatively easy to trace back the demon's path, and not just because of the intensity of its horrid stench. Blood, various other fluids and bits of flesh, and splintered wood marked the path so easily that a small child could have tracked it back to its source.

Not that any sylph would subject a child to the sights he was forced to endure. Demons were... abberations to the natural way, and they wrecked destruction wherever they walked. He was not surprised. Disgusted, as any sane creature of sound heart would be, but not surprised.

In a very short period of time he was deep inside the house, approaching a room that positively reeked of demon and death. And there was another scent there, one he could not identify. Almost human, but with strange overtones.

Like the girl in metal, he decided. Probably the brother.

He wind-walked into the room, and surveying the damage, materialized, his wind turning dusty brown and swirling into man-shape.

A cough from the floor.

"Aren't you a bit dark for a sylph?" Lance asked hoarsely from where he was still manacled spread-eagle on the wooden floor.

Zalapa sighed. It was not his fault that his tribe was not nearly as well-known as the Northern Wind Tribe or the Southern

Wind Tribe. The Desert Wind Tribe was smaller, for one thing, and for another, not inclined to glory-seeking or dramatic displays for the benefit of the curious. This was a common problem for him, even among those who correctly identified him as a sylph. The question had lost all novelty.

"Perhaps you still wish to rest?" Zalapa asked lightly. "Or you are ready to leave?"

"Nothing would give me greater pleasure than to get off this damn floor." Lance said with feeling.

Zalapa gusted over, melting instantly into a puff of brown dust and reforming on the floor beside Lance, unlatching the manacle on Lance's right wrist. As soon as it was free he gusted over to the other side, while Lance flexed his stiff arm.

"You took your sweet time." Lance grumbled, while Zalapa freed his first leg.

"The plan is actually ahead of schedule. We had to move up the timeline when Dyresse had a foreshadowing of this disaster."

"I guess it just feels later than it really is. When you are personally entertaining an archdemon, time moves very, very slowly." Lance's second leg was now free and he sat up and started looking around the room for his missing shirt.

"I am surprised you survived this long. Usually an archdemon would just drain your body of magic and then eat your heart." Zalapa commented, taking the chance to check his quiver quickly before they had to start moving again.

"Just my irresistable charm. Even demons aren't immune."

Zalapa didn't bother responding to that. Lance pulled on his shirt. It had been left, neatly folded, in a corner by one of the treants, and now, apart from a couple of drops of splattered blood, was exactly as he had last seen it.

Lance rubbed one hand on his chin irritably. He

momentarily wished for a chance to shave. Not that any observer would have noticed the tiny stubble when it was such a pale blonde against his skin, but Lance was very vain that way.

Lance sighed.

"I doubt there's time for a break with a demon running amok, huh?"

Zalapa again did not respond to that. It did not deserve an answer.

He vanished in a swirl of brown dust, and Lance staggered through the open doorway, the door splintered and shattered on the floor. He wished for his sword. It was an inconvenient time to be unarmed.

The two of them made their way through the house, Zalapa gusting here and there, vanishing and reappearing at will. Lance plodded, stripped of his normal agility by exhaustion, using the walls to hold himself up when he needed to, and staggering in the sylph's wake.

It wasn't long before they were standing near the front of the building, the sounds of Dark Lord Harutinabi's battle more than just audible, since they shook the walls and floor.

"I hope you do not plan to go out the front door." Zalapa said reprovingly.

"Just what kind of moron do you think I am?" Lance asked, raising one eyebrow.

"The kind that 'entertains' demons."

"That's fair." Lance said after a moment. "You will note, however, that I'm still alive."

Zalapa nodded. "Yours is a cunning folly."

"I think I like that." Lance strode over to the side of the front room and peered out of the opening covered by a thin sheet of white silk.

"I bet we could get through here, and the demon isn't visible from this side of the house." Lance pointed out, looking back at the sylph.

"I will scout." Zalapa vanished in a swirl of brown dust, the wind drifting past Lance and out the opening in the wall.

The sylph quickly reappeared on the other, outer, side of the opening.

"Can you fit through?" The elemental asked, eyeing the opening.

It was a good question, as the openings were tall and thin, designed to let in light, while not letting in other things, but Lance was extremely thin for a man of his height, and while he never would have fit through with his armor on, that was currently not an issue.

"Probably." He said, and suited words to action, shoving the silk covering to one side, and squeezing himself through. It was a tight fit, but he didn't lose any skin in the process. "I've been in tighter places."

And Lance had. To pull off some of the pranks he had perfected over the years required squeezing into very small and inconvienent locations.

"We have a problem." Zalapa continued, "Your sister currently has the demon's attention. In order to collect her, we will either have to destroy it or deceive it to get her away."

"This is my not-surprised face." Lance said, pointing to an exaggered expression of irritation and boredom. "Sisters."

Zalapa sighed. "A feeling with which I can sympathize. I have sisters."

"You have my condolences."

"I favor destroying the demon." Zalapa said, getting right to the point.

"And I favor deceiving it." Lance responded. "You do know what kind of demon we are dealing with? This is an archdemon of corruption, the Dark Lord Harutinabi. I call him Haru. And Haru is currently running with a massive degree of raw magical energy which makes him insanely dangerous and virtually indestructable."

"Except for the paritta warding your sister cast."

Lance started swearing profusely. If Jannis had cast a paritta warding she now had Haru's complete and undivided attention, and the demon would not stop short of a kill. Where the heck had she learned a paritta powerful enough to use on a demon of Haru's degree anyway?

"I guess we go with Plan B, then..." Lance said with disgust.

"Destroy the demon?"

"Destroy the demon."

Jannis was getting seriously winded. Heavy armor was not suited for running and she had been running in hers for entirely too long already. How she wished for her poor, dead horse. The girl Linaloe darted effortlessly over the ground, more a wisp of wind than a living thing, and Jannis plodded desperately after her, every step burning in her calves and thighs.

The demon was still relentlessly trailing them, and would have caught them a dozen times if not for the magical attacks still being launched from two sides by the mages Krael and Dyresse. Lorynn's throwing knives and Phil's spears similarly did little damage but added to the confusion and slowed the demon's progress.

It screamed its frustration, as Jannis narrowly evaded its claws once again, rolling to the side as the ground shook with the impact.

"I'm... seriously... rethinking... this... armor..." Jannis panted heavily, pulling herself back upright and staggering forward into a run. Linaloe grabbed her wrist and pulled at her, as if somehow able to make her move faster.

And then a sudden shove in the small of her back, pushing her violently forward.

Jannis staggered, but did not fall, moving with the unexpected momentum, as another close impact shook the ground.

And Lance was there. The shove she had felt was his arm around her waist, pushing forward.

"You know," he said, in that irritating, condensending way. "Whenever I think things can't get worse, you show up and find a way to make it worse."

She started to retort, torn between angry response and the intense relief she felt at seeing him alive, but instead said, "You look like hell."

"It's his fault." Lance gestured vaguely with his other hand at the demon still in hot pursuit behind them.

"And I'll have you know, I consider this a win." Lance said, offended pride in his hoarse voice. "I challenge you to find anyone who survived the personal attentions of a demon that powerful for that long."

"I doubt you were entertaining him with your clever wit."

"So cynical."

"I don't really want to know what you were doing. I have to sleep at night." She shuddered, still running to stay out of reach of the demon. "I'm just glad you're still alive."

Lance smirked. She would have slapped him, but she was too happy to see him.

"Right, so, we need to put Haru down, and fast, before he splats both of us." Lance summarized, as the demon once again swiped at them and barely missed, leaving deep grooves in Jannis's vambrace with two claws. The sound of shrieking metal filled the air.

"Elf." Lance addressed the girl, Linaloe. "Tell crazy mage lady to use the Galdrastafir rune with the fourth high paritta chant. Use salt, silver, cinnamon, and olive oil. Go!"

"Elf?" Jannis asked, as Linaloe vanished.

"Start paying attention, sis."

"And since when have you been an expert on demon banishing?"

"It's not for banishing. Obviously. It's a binding spell. Why the heck did you cast a paritta warding without a binding?" You could hear Lance's exaggerated eye-roll in his voice.

"I've kinda been busy! It's not like I had time!" She shrilled at him, irritated.

"Well, it's not like you would have the skill anyway. This Dyr character seems to know her stuff."

"Excuse me?!"

"Just run, sis. Unless you want to go splat." The heaving of the ground beneath them emphasized his statement, as Harutinabi threw himself bodily towards them, slamming into the ground with enough force to throw them forward.

The Solarans darted back and forth, randomly changing direction as they led the demon around, but in the general area of the ground that Jannis had enchanted with the paritta ward. It would have been decidedly uncomfortable if they had led the demon too far and it had started using magic.

Krael kept up the barrage of magical attacks, primarily the

tiny red missiles of magical energy, but the fireballs vanished. Dyresse was, presumably, working on the binding spell.

"I hope you know what you're doing!" Jannis panted, as Lance shoved her yet again out of Harutinabi's reach.

"Always." Lance said smugly.

And then the crashing and thrashing stopped. Jannis staggered forwards a few more steps, leaving Lance behind, where he had similarly stopped.

She had to run back as he turned and started walking towards the demon.

"Lance, what are you doing?!"

"Just relax, he's bound now. Isn't that right, Haru?" The last was addressed to the demon, whose eyes narrowed.

"The only thing that exceeds your arrogance is your luck, mortal." It grumbled.

"Go ahead, sis, release the paritta ward."

"Are you crazy?"

"He's bound. And he can't cast the spell to transfer back to his own realm if he can't cast magic. Isn't that right, Haru?"

"I will not underestimate you when next we meet, omnimage." The demon growled, its voice low and hard.

"I'm blushing, really, Haru. I won't say you are pleasant company, but I still look forward to seeing you again."

"A sentiment I share. And be certain of this, omnimage: we shall meet again."

Jannis released the paritta ward, and a few moments later the demon was disappearing into a rift in the air.

"Tell me what the heck was going on in your head, sis...." Lance commented, without looking in her direction. "That you would cast a paritta without a binding."

"I didn't have any spell components, Lance!"

"It would be wise," Linaloe said, suddenly appearing again out of a distorted place in empty air in front of them. "To disappear now, while the Kalen soldiers are still in disarray. That will not last."

"Cast an illusion, sis, to swap your appearance with hers." Lance supplied, when Jannis didn't respond.

"What? But..."

"Ignore her, she has always been slow on the uptake." Lance said to Linaloe. "Can you cast invisibility on me?"

Linaloe whispered something and made a sign with her hand, and Lance vanished.

"I don't understand what's going on." Jannis complained, casting an illusion of herself over the elf, and an illusion of the elf's appearance on her own form.

"Like that's a change." Lance commented, his disembodied voice hovering in the air.

"Zal's waiting for you over there." Linaloe, wearing Jannis's form, but still her own voice, pointed. "I will mislead the regular army as to your intended direction, but you will not have much time."

The elf ran back towards the rest of the Venturi and Jannis stared after her.

"Time's wasting, sis." That voice coming from nowhere was very disorienting.

"Would you please tell me what is going on?" Jannis said plantively.

"Start moving and I'll explain." Lance provided encouragingly, and Jannis started walking in the direction Linaloe had indicated.

"I made a deal with the mercenaries. They wanted to let us go, but if they did, they might have been accused of treason and been executed. So we figured if Lynx handed me over to Jorander and I escaped from him, Jorander would get the blame for it. And the mercenaries would get the money. And since we all hate Jorander, it seemed like a great idea."

"Until Jorander summoned an archdemon." Jannis commented.

"You can't plan for everything." Lance replied dismissively, his disembodied voice hanging in the air.

"I suppose I really shouldn't be surprised, given your past performance. Outrageous, dangerous, poorly planned -- it's really your typical way of doing things."

"You will always find something to complain about. So, as soon as we catch up with the sylph, we need to take the general hostage."

"Wait, what?!"

"Good grief, sis, just listen for once. We take the general hostage, and force a parley. A cease-fire. I thought the whole reason we were out here is because you were fighting your little princey's war for him?"

"The general isn't going to just agree! What do when he refuses?"

"Kill him." Lance said dismissively.

"I take it back, this plan is definately more outrageous and dangerous than usual."

"It's not my fault. He's the one who ignored me, and sent a subordinate."

"And what about the mercenaries? Won't they turn on us too,

when they find out what you are doing?"

"Of course not. Lynx thought it was a great idea."

"You've got to be kidding me! He thought it was a great idea when you told him you were going to kidnap his commanding general?!"

"He's a very pragmatic person. I actually kinda like him."

"This is insane. This can't be happening..." Jannis said, shaking her head in disbelief.

"Just shut up, relax, and do what I tell you. It will all work out."

They found Zalapa easily enough. He was waiting behind some unoccupied tents, just a small dark figure sitting patiently beneath a scraggly tree. As soon as they got close, and without a word exchanged, he stood and started moving. Jannis followed a short distance behind him, and couldn't help the occassional futive glance back to see if they were being followed.

"You look suspicious; stop it." Lance instructed from thin air, and nearly giving her a heart attack.

They moved easily enough through the camp, keeping a safe, but not noticeable, distance from the soldiers moving, guarding, or working around them. It was late morning, and no one was anticipating immanent attack. The armies were in a period of regrouping before the fighting started again.

Zalapa paused again, and as she came up to him, he nodded once, glanced to the side, and then vanished, a swirl of dust in the wind where he had been standing. She froze, her mouth open in shock, as an invisible hand rested on her shoulder.

"Don't worry, sis. This is where we part ways. He's going back to his camp. The general's tent is over there. And you should probably change your disguise. We don't want anyone mistaking you for an elf. Regular folk are kinda wierd about fae."

"Speaking about fae, what was a elf doing with those mercenaries? And how did she cast an invisibility spell on you without it being undone?"

"If I had to guess, I would say that uncle's spell isn't that powerful right now, since Haru massively drained my magic, and my magic fuels the spell. Plus which, she didn't cast it on me, exactly, but on my clothing. What kind of idiot are you? Basic magic theory dictates that invisibility spells are localized field spells..."

"And that they can't be cast directly on a living thing. Thank you, Lance, for telling me what I already knew."

"As for why an elf is with them, my guess is she wanted to be a mercenary, and Lynx is probably the only mercenary captain enlightened enough to be taking in fae and sylphs. Goddess only knows what other kinds of freaks are in that company."

"Is that admiration in your voice? Will wonders never cease."

"Hey, we have a standing invitation to join once this nonsense with Harderior and Kalen is done with."

"You're thinking of becoming a mercenary now?"

Lance shrugged. "I dunno. It makes sense from their perspective though. Archmages are hard to find."

"Enough. I already know everything that comes out of your mouth is garbage. So let's just get this madness over with and find someplace to take a bath."

"And shave." Lance added with feeling.

Jannis rewove the illusion on herself, giving herself back her own face, but turning her hair a plain mouse brown, and reshaping her clothing until it matched that of the Kalen soldiers everywhere around them.

Then she examined the spell on Lance, and carefully unwove

it, before placing her own illusion on him, so that they appeared to be a pair of Kalen regulars. It never occurred to her how hard it should have been for an ordinary human mage to unweave pure fae illusion magic cast by an elf.

"Tolerable." Lance said, observing her work. "Let's just hope we don't get spotted by a mage. Cause you know any mage is going to be able to see we have illusions distorting us."

Lance helped himself to an unattended sword leaning against the outside of a tent, and the two of them began circling together towards the tent, large, noticable and guarded, of the general.

"Should we try to sneak in?" Jannis whispered. Lance shrugged.

"Why bother? Let's just go in the front."

"They aren't going to just let us in, Lance."

"You have so little faith."

Lance walked straight up to the pair of guards outside of the tent. "Report from the field for the general, sir. There was a large demon at archmage Jorander's residence. It wrecked a significant amount of damage before it was put down by one of the mercenary troupes. Casualty numbers are still pending, but there are at least two dozen dead."

Lance turned and walked away before the startled soldier had time to really respond.

"Wait," The soldier said, holding out a hand to forestall Lance, who was already moving away with a purpose. "Do you know if the archmage is alive or dead?"

Lance stopped and turned, looking distracted and irritated to be questioned. "Dead."

"Confirmed?" The soldier pressed.

"I saw the body. Demon burned him to a crisp." Lance said

emotionlessly.

"Report to the general directly." The soldier replied.

"But..." Lance protested, glancing the way he had been traveling.

"Whatever you need to take care of can wait." The soldier replied, exasperated.

"Sorry, looks like we're stuck here." Lance said to Jannis.

"But we have to get back! I told you we should have sent someone else to report."

"It's not my fault!" Lance protested.

"You always say that." Jannis replied.

"Because it never is my fault!"

"If you had just talked someone else into coming over here we could be back at the tents fixing our broken chest straps right now."

"But..." The soldier guarding the tent entrance tried to interject.

"You know we aren't going to have time if we get stuck here, I have duty tonight! And there's no telling when we will have the chance to get more. They always run out of supplies so fast out here."

"The only reason the chest straps broke in the first place is you didn't clean them right away after they got soaked, and then the leather dried out."

"And why am I responsible for cleaning your gear?"

"Just get inside and report to the general!" The exasperated soldier at the tent opening said, and pointed inside.

The two of them ducked inside, and Lance winked at her.

"Sir, we have a report." Lance said stolidly.

The general was deep in discussion with two other men, all three of whom looked up at the newcomers in the tent. The general frowned slightly, and his forehead came down like a billowing thunderstorm.

"Whatever it is, it better be important." The words were delivered quietly, but there was a silent kind of menace about them.

"Archmage Jorander's dead." Lance supplied.

The general bit off an explicative, and the other two men quietly excused themselves, slipping away from the tent like well-mannered shadows.

"Confirmed?" The general pressed, turning slightly to face Lance.

"I saw the body, sir."

"I suppose it was that demon we heard about a few minutes ago?"

"Yes, sir. The demon has been neutralized. Some mercenaries took care of it."

"What a mess. Do we have casualty reports yet?"

"No, sir. But there are at least two dozen dead."

"Is there any sign that the demon was summoned by the Harderior?"

"No, sir. It's uncertain where the demon came from, but most likely was summoned by Jorander for some reason. The demon was too powerful for a common mage to summon. And the Harderior don't have any archmages."

"Weren't there some archmages of unknown affiliation captive in the camp?"

"Yes, sir. But by all accounts they were bound and blocked, unable to use offensive magic."

"Guard!" The general shouted, and immediately the two guards outside the tent flaps poked their heads into the tent.

"I need casualty reports from that mess over by the archmage's residence. It sounds like the demon's been taken care of, start getting the wounded treated, and counting bodies. I want a confirmation of Jorander's death. This soldier says he saw the body, let's confirm it."

The guards poked their heads back out as fast as they had poked in, and one went off to find an officer to pass the orders on to.

"What about you?" The general asked, glancing at Jannis.

"What?" Jannis responded, surprised.

"What do you have to report?" The general asked, as if it were obvious and he was greatly indulging her by tolerating her momentary distraction.

"Actually, sir," Lance supplied, "She's one of the 'archmages of unknown affiliation' you were referring to."

The general paused, looking at Lance skeptically, before he opened his mouth.

Jannis just reacted, jumping forward to put her hand over the general's mouth before he could call out. Lance was already moving, grabbing the general's wrist, and twisting his arm behind him. There was a brief scuffle, thankfully muffled, which did not attract the attention of the guard still outside.

In short order Lance had the general bound and gagged in his own tent.

"Now what, Lance? Someone's going to come in here very soon, either to report or to talk to the general about strategy or something. Presuming the guard doesn't poke in just to make sure the general doesn't need something."

"Honestly, I wasn't thinking beyond getting inside the tent."

Lance shrugged.

"I can't believe you!" She hissed at him. "Why do I always have to clean up your mess?"

"Less rhetorical questions, more cleaning." Lance ordered.

"I am Jannis Solaran, and this is my brother Lance." She said to the bound general. "We came here as neutral third parties to negotiate a cease-fire between Harderior and Kalen, until my idiot brother got mortally insulted by your subordinate and decided to attack your army."

"Oh, thanks. Somehow it's always my fault."

"Because it always is!"

"Ok, look, General Hamilton, we both know that your ability to make war on the Harderior is damaged by the loss of your only archmage." Lance smiled winningly as he said it, leaning forward and inviting confidence. Jannis rolled her eyes and crossed her arms in front of her.

"You've been waging a very expensive war out here, hiring mercenaries, losing equipment, men, supplies... It's in Kalen's best interest to take a breather. The Harderior are weakening, yes, but we both know they are also becoming more desperate, and that means they will fight even harder." Lance said it so simply, so logically, that his argument was hard to deny.

"I mean, is your fight really with the Harderior Army? Isn't the insult to Kalen the result of one man? One lunatic, who just happens to wear a crown?" Lance snorted, and an edge came into his voice.

"Honestly, I share your opinion. I was in the Harderior royal palace for only a couple of days, and the king's lackeys were throwing women at me. Eddy's a nut job. He even slapped me!"

"Guys like that don't stay in power for long. Sooner or later, someone says 'enough!', and they get removed from power. Don't you think the Harderior people have the same opinion of their king and what he's been doing? Kidnapping and killing children? Starting a war?" Lance paused and stared at the bound and gagged man in the tent.

"But I don't expect you to believe me. How can you trust someone who sneaks into your tent and ties you up? That's why I'm going to let you go."

"Lance..." Jannis said warningly.

"Oh right, sis, because it would be sooo easy to sneak out of this massive encampment with a valuable hostage?" Lance took his borrowed blade and knocked the general on the side of the head with the hilt. His eyes slid shut. Lance quickly unbound and ungagged the general.

Then the two of them walked out.

Jannis's heart was in her throat; she had to forcibly resist the urge to look behind her. She kept waiting, agonized, for the shout from behind them, for the sign that they had been recognized. It didn't come. They walked down past row after row of soldiers and tents, and the horse picket lines. Near the edge of camp, they came upon Lorynn, who was standing beside Lance's horse, his armor and sword neatly tied atop it.

"That's the sign of a good leader--attention to detail." Lance said approvingly. He reached for his sword, drawing it from its scabbard to check the blade.

They stopped there long enough for Lance to put on his armor and mount his horse. It was an excruciating experience for Jannis, waiting for them to be discovered while Lance nonchalantly strapped on vambraces and greaves. But all her worrying didn't amount to anything, because nothing happened.

Now, Jannis's horse was dead, a casualty of their initial battle. But the mercenaries had also supplied a replacement, a lovely grey who danced nervously to the side and tugged on its lead with the scent of demon on the air. It took a moment for Jannis to calm the nervous horse, while Lance was strapping on armor.

"I cannot believe that worked." Jannis said finally as they rode out of the encampment towards the Harderior line, under cover of some trees and brush along the edge of a ridge.

"You have no faith."

"Consider past experience."

"How critical. And patently unfair, I might add."

"You need a shave."

"Harridan."

"Scruffy mercenary."

"Manipulative witch."

"Lance?"

"Mmm?"

"I'm glad you didn't get your fool self killed."

"Right back at you, sis."

Jannis paused, and they rode along in silence for a minute. Finally, however, she couldn't help but share what was on her mind.

"Did we actually accomplish anything, Lance?"

"I suppose it would have made you feel better to kill the general?"

"No, that's not what I meant! Did we really make a difference at all? I mean, how do we know if we got through to him?"

"We don't. The real question is, would any other course of action have given a better result? I could have killed him, but that would have... certain consequences. We could have taken him with us... other consequences. We could have just snuck out of the camp without trying to talk to the general at all. Which would have been stupid, but it was an option."

"So what you are saying is that you nearly got us both killed for nothing."

"You mean *you* nearly got us both killed for nothing. This is your war, not mine."

"And when did it become my war?"

"You're the one gonna marry the king of Harderior who dragged me out here to help your new grandson-to-be."

"It's impossible trying to talk to you. Your reasoning twists in strange ways."

"My reasoning? The only reason I haven't left you behind to die a hundred times is because life would be too boring without you in it to give me problems to solve!" Lance retorted, snorting.

"I'd almost think that was complementary." Jannis said, rolling her eyes.

"I bore easily. The curse of an active mind. And just for the record, we did accomplish something. Jorander is dead. That alone will let me sleep well tonight."

"What exactly did he do to you to make you so hostile? I mean I know what *you* did to him, but I have no idea what *he* did to you."

"None of your business." Lance said abruptly. "It's all water under the bridge now anyway."

"Whenever you get evasive, I get worried."

"Is that why you worry all the time?" Lance glanced at her sideways. "Just out of curiousity, Uncle never mentioned anything about our father that you haven't told me, has he?"

"No, and why the sudden interest?"

"Those gwyllion were entirely too interested. It makes me wonder..."

"Now you've got me really worried, Lance."

"We know next to nothing about our father except his name."

"Uncle doesn't like to talk about it, and you know it. We've tried before."

"Which makes me wonder why he doesn't want to talk about it."

"Does it ever occur to you that maybe its painful for him to remember?"

"Please. He's a sorcerer; they have pretty thick skin. But if Uncle isn't inclined to share, I'll just have to find someone else to ask."

"Like who?"

They rode in silence after that, because honestly, neither of them had any idea where to begin on that particular subject. Their uncle may have information that they didn't, but he was not inclined to share.

And Jannis had no idea why Lance was suddenly so interested in this particular subject, which they had pursued when younger, but had not seriously thought on for years. Yes, the gwyllion had been surprisingly interested in their parentage, but Jannis could not think why.

Chapter 16

Lieutenant Flemming and Master Emrys started their survey of the enemy camp by stealing laundry.

It is amazing how many historically significant infiltrations and covert operations begin with the simple theft of enemy uniforms. It is similarly amazing that military leaders don't take greater measures to ensure the control of their uniforms, as they already do for weapons and food supplies. Stealing the uniforms was almost laughably easy.

Disguised as enemy troops, they were able to move fairly freely through the camp. Due to the mixed nature of the camp, with so many different mercenary groups and regiments, there weren't a whole lot of challenges to them in particular.

The Kalen regulars were almost under siege in their own encampment, and spent most of their time watching the mercenaries warily and keeping them out of the areas where the regulars were camped.

Mercenaries come in a wide variety of skill levels and degrees of trustworthiness, some almost regular soldiers, some better than regular soldiers, and some little better than the kind of cutthroat thieves you find in back alleys.

Kalen had cast its net wide when recruiting, and while some of the mercenary troupes were solid, reliable and trustworthy, the majority were not.

Hence, disguised as Kalen regulars, Lieutenant Flemming and Master Emrys were mostly ignored by the regulars, and watched warily by the mercenaries, as all the rest of the regulars were.

And there was another consideration that aided in their disguise.

Lieutenant Flemming had been afraid that Master Emrys, despite his impressive magical prowess, would be quite useless on a covert information gathering mission. He was pleasantly surprised to find that Master Emrys was actually quite valuable in maintaining their cover.

"Where are you from?" One of the three regulars they were

talking to asked Master Emrys.

"A few miles south of Coverrich, have you heard of Havenfort?"

"Yeah, we have a couple of guys from that area in our regiment. Do you know Martin Wright?"

"Any relation to Trevor Wright?" Master Emrys enquired.

"That's his cousin."

"Oh, *that* Martin." Master Emrys responded, rolling his eyes.

"So you do know him."

"Sweet goddess, I hope the boy has matured. If he is anything like I remember, you have your work cut out for you."

The soldiers all laughed appreciatively.

A few careful questions about recent events revealed that this particular regiment hadn't been involved in the wierd skirmish the day before with the two armored archmages. They had heard some interesting things, and were quite willing to gossip about it, but knew little detail.

A few minutes later, Master Emrys and Lieutenant Flemming excused themselves and kept moving.

"How do you know so much about Kalen?" Flemming asked, deciding the direct approach was best under the circumstances.

Master Emrys pursed his lips and took a deep breath. He had known the question would come out eventually. It was cleaner to address it now.

"Well, I have family there. We wrote quite a lot back and forth before the war started. Nothing in the last three years, of course." Master Emrys paused and met the lieutenant's eyes.

"It's not something I advertise. Sometimes people jump to

conclusions."

Flemming nodded. He could see that.

"This war must be very hard on you."

"It's hard on everyone. War always is."

"I mean with your personal situation though, it must be even harder."

"I try not to make judgements about what my betters decide." Emrys said carefully. "I just try to do what I am told. Some questions, and some opinions, are better left unsaid."

"Very wise. I can't count the number of people I have met who have not learned that particular lesson. And it usually ends badly."

"Something I have seen as well. And mages are not exempt, perhaps given slightly greater leeway, but not exempt."

"And you work quite closely with Lord Firin."

"Not because of any excellence on my part. The ranks of Harderior's mages have been somewhat depleted. I was simply available. I'm sure Lord Firin would agree."

"But you were also the prince's tutor at one point?"

"Again, coincidence. There was no one else."

"He has spoken well of you." The lieutenant offered.

"Has he? I feel quite honored. Working with his Highness was an honor of which I was unworthy. I am very pleased that he found my instruction valuable."

"Touching the lives of such important people, I can well understand your... reluctance to advertise your connection to Kalen."

"Then perhaps I am not being too bold, in asking you to keep this in confidence."

"My first loyalty is and always has been to Harderior. But, if this information causes no harm, I see no reason why any other should know it."

"I see you, too, have some experience."

"Not enough." Flemming sighed. "I was a fool not to recognize Lady Jannis, even if she was disguised. I recognized that she was out of place; I knew she wasn't like the rest of the guards. But I made an assumption, and for that I am a fool."

"Ah." Master Emrys supplied. "But if there were others there, did anyone else recognize her? You aren't a mage, that you would be able to see the signs of magical disguise."

"I suppose not. But I am an officer, and I did recognize that she was out of place. I just never asked the next question. I never confirmed whether she was a new member of the royal guard or an impostor."

"Why not?"

"I spoke to her, and she didn't seem like an assassin or a thief or any other kind of bad element. There was an... earnestness about her, a quiet intensity. The kind that the best men I ever served with possessed. I guess I was just trusting my instincts."

"Not such a serious lapse of judgement. I think the lady is one who can be trusted. She does have her faults, but I would not count integrity among them."

The lieutenant did not reply. One of those awkward silences that fall sometimes in conversation descended.

Nothing further was said on the matter. They both continued the search for information on the whereabouts of the missing archmages.

When Lieutenant Flemming and Master Emrys returned to

the rendevous point, Lord Firin and the hapless guard who had accompanied him were already waiting.

The five of them settled in and waited for Jacob and the last royal guard to return from their own reconnisainnce.

As soon as the last two returned, they all compared notes. Their efforts were sadly inadequate.

Lord Firin had discovered that the archmages had been taken captive by a mercenary troupe called "Venturi."

Master Emrys had learned that the Venturi were not native to Kalen, but were considered almost as reliable as regular troops by the regular army; a high compliment indeed, considering the terms which were used to describe the majority of the mercenary troupes that had been hired. Efforts to learn the location of their camp had come up short, however, as the regulars generally did not have much contact with the mercenary troupes and preferred it that way.

Jacob had discovered that a demon had been rampaging on one side of the camp, a fact that seemed at first irrelevant until he pointed out that a strange girl in armor had cast a warding spell on the demon.

Everyone agreed that anyone casting spells in armor was almost certainly the missing Lady Jannis. Mages did not wear armor.

But when pressed for details as to where this had occurred, Jacob had no information. As for the current location of the missing archmages, they still had no idea where within the camp to begin searching.

Lord Firin was not pleased. The longer they stayed this close to the enemy, the greater the chance for detection. It was critical that they find the missing archmages and extract them quickly. Discovery would infinitely complicate things.

The sound of crunching leaves and breaking twigs warned

them that there were people approaching. They collectively crouched further down behind the brush to reduce the chances of being seen.

"Are you sure they're over here?" An imperious voice demanded. It was a voice anyone would have recognized had they heard it once.

"Maybe if you used your mage sight you could confirm it, instead of asking stupid questions." An irritated female voice replied.

"I don't *do* magic. Remember?" The first voice replied, condescendingly, and then continued, increasing in volume.

"Elephant mage, if you are out here, you are damned lucky Kalen's archmage was crispified this morning by a demon, or the Kalen army would have found you by now. Jorander may have been self-absorbed, but he would still have set proximity wards to detect enemy mages approaching the camp."

Master Emrys immediately stood up from behind the brush and smiled ruefully.

"So sorry. We didn't know that Kalen had an archmage."

"What a coincidence, neither did we, until we saw him." Lance supplied. "Jorander is so massively incompetent though, probably the Harderior army didn't even notice that there was an archmage over here."

"Let's just get moving." Jannis said, looking back over her shoulder nervously. "We are still entirely too close to the Kalen army to be sitting around chatting."

"In this I must agree." Lord Firin added imperiously, straightening from behind the brush.

"Yes, we should go." Lieutenant Flemming seconded, and that was the end of it.

Jannis and Lance were on foot, leading their horses, to get through the dense shrubbery and brush that the Harderior had been concealed in.

"I do admit to some curiousity as to how you managed to escape." Master Emrys whispered.

"My unparalleled cunning, of course." Lance supplied, smugly.

"Sheer luck." Jannis retorted.

"Of course, I am not only massively cunning, but also unnaturally lucky." Lance agreed. "Though I admit, even I was worried when I saw the demon that Jorander summoned."

"You, worried? Will wonders never cease."

"No ordinary demon would have worried me," Lance corrected. "But Haru's something else. Totally not in Maliad Heriophant's league."

"Dark Lord Harutinabi." Jannis clarified. "Archdemon of corruption. As you can see, Lance's charming habit of assigning nicknames isn't limited to humans."

"At least it isn't 'elephant mage.'" Master Emrys pointed out lightly.

"I'm sure I could come up with something worse." Lance offered. "Maybe a homage to the sound you make when you fly through the air, or have your head smashed through a wall."

"This is why you don't have any friends, Lance." Jannis noted.

"Hey, I can't help it if I am just a little too much for most people to handle. And not just people--demons, fae, djinn, elementals, sorcerers... I'm too much for almost anyone."

"That isn't something to be proud of!"

"Of course it is." Lance replied innocently.

"And are you proud of being a murderer?" Lord Firin asked harshly, injecting himself into the conversation.

"Lance. You didn't kill any of the guards when you were breaking out of that compound they sent you to, did you?" Jannis asked accusingly.

"Of course not! A total waste of my time, the lot of them." Lance paused as a thought occurred to him. "Although I suppose the Kalen army was pretty much a waste of my time, too, and I killed a lot of them. Over a hundred, I lost count. Not particularly proud of that though, it was like squashing insects."

"You did have an unfair advantage." Jannis added.

"That's true, being me is a terribly unfair advantage."

"I meant the spell distortion." Jannis retorted. "It made it almost impossible for anyone to accurately see you."

"So where, thief, have you hidden my books?" Lord Firin demanded.

"Sorry, don't remember. My stupid sister interrupted me to save some dying prince, and I completely forgot to write down where I buried them."

"Lance!" Jannis admonished.

"Good grief, even when I'm not doing something wrong, you still hassle me. See sis, this is why I'm never getting married. Women are just too much trouble."

"And you are like trouble incarnate, like total chaos walking around wearing skin. It's a good thing you don't plan to get married, because I doubt any woman would have you."

"Come on, sis, there are a lot of stupid women. Wait, that came out wrong."

"Ah, so you do make mistakes from time to time." Master Emrys said, hiding a smile.

"Life is a social experiment. You can really only determine a mistake after it's already happened. Because you can never perfectly predict the consequences of any action." Lance said stiffly.

"And is that your justification for doing whatever the heck you want?" Jannis asked.

"Everyone does whatever the heck they want." Lance said condensendingly. "Most people just gloss it over with nonsense and rhetoric, like duty and honor, or looking towards the future. It's how they soothe their consciences when their decisions hurt others."

"And you don't have that problem." Jannis said nastily.

"Heck no, I don't have a conscience, and I pity the lot of you that do."

"I sometimes wonder what kind of miraculous things you could accomplish if you used your powers for good instead of evil." Master Emrys mused.

They were almost back to the Harderior camp, and so Jannis and Lance never got to finish their conversation. That was probably a good thing, as Lord Firin had much more to add on the matter of the missing books.

Prince Darien practically jumped for joy to see them alive and safe. He did throw himself at Jannis in a huge hug, which considering she was encased in metal armor, probably gave the prince a couple of bruises.

The consensus of the people whose opinions mattered; that is, Lord Firin, Lieutenant Flemming, Master Emrys, and Lady Jannis; was that they should return to the royal palace as soon as possible. The royal guards' horses had rested the night before, and while a full day of rest would have been preferable, were ready to ride.

Prince Darien vehemently resisted leaving, as he still wanted to help the army, with or without his grandfather's permission, and

Lance supported him, because Lance liked causing trouble for everyone else. And although Lance would never have admitted it to anyone, especially not his sister, the kid was starting to grow on him.

It was hard not to like a seven-year-old who wanted to single-handedly defend his country and defeat an army. It was the same kind of often-dismissed 'thinking big' that Lance himself indulged in.

The biggest surprise came right as they were preparing to leave. Senior staff officer Gregor found them as they were mounting up.

"I don't suppose we have you to thank for this reprieve?" Gregor asked, raising one eyebrow and handing Jannis a small sheaf of parchment.

She glanced at it curiously, and then eyebrows rising, handed it to her brother wordlessly.

"Ha!" Lance declared. "Reason wins the day again."

"And an audacious mid-morning personal assault on an enemy general." Jannis added. "Explain where reason came into any of this."

Lance handed the papers to Master Emrys, who immeditely handed them to Lord Firin.

"A cease-fire?" Lord Firin asked incredulously.

"I talked some sense into General Hamilton." Lance explained pompously. "After I tied him up and gagged him."

"Are you really that surprised, considering who you are talking to?" Jannis asked patiently.

"No, not really. Your brother has the devil's own luck. I'm beginning to wonder if he is even human."

Lance laughed weakly, mostly succeeding to conceal his discomfort at the statement. "Yeah, I get that a lot."

Lord Firin handed the document back to Gregor, and they all mounted and rode out of the Harderior army encampment.

They followed the road, and unhampered by a sick child, as they had been coming this way before, were able to make very good time, only pausing to rest and water the horses.

Lance was on his best behavior on the ride back to the castle. That is to say, one of the royal guards developed a strange rash no one could explain, Lord Firin started uncontrollably burping the second day after lunch, and Master Emrys' reading glasses disappeared and were found crushed.

None of these incidents could be connected to Lance, although his sister challenged him at each. He demanded to know why everything that went wrong had to be his fault. There had been guards posted continuously and no one had seen anything.

Prince Darien was thoroughly enjoying the entire ride, and was getting into everything and asking questions about everything like any healthy seven-year-old would. The cease-fire had relieved a substantial conflict within the young prince, between the desire to return home, and the desire to stay and fight with the army.

But with a two month cease-fire in effect, Prince Darien was more than happy to return home. It was a bittersweet kind of feeling because he strongly suspected he would be returning to the battlefield all too soon.

Jannis was preoccupied. She recognized the royal guard with Lord Firin from the castle, and the guilt she felt at decieving him still bothered her. She avoided it by avoiding him for the first day, but the second day he approached her and she could not avoid it any longer.

"Lieutenant." She greeted stiffly.

"...Flemming." He supplied with a smile.

"I remember." She said curtly.

"Still sour, ice princess?" He teased gently.

"I just don't know what to say."

"Start with 'sorry.'" Lieutenant Flemming responded. "I got in a lot of trouble thanks to your little disappearing act. The king was very worried about you. And his grandson."

"Everything turned out alright in the end." Jannis protested lamely. Flemming raised one eyebrow at her and she flushed.

"I'm sorry. Really. I didn't mean to cause you any trouble."

Lieutenant Flemming sighed.

"Well, I guess it was worth it. I was really looking forward to doing a little sparring with Lydia, too, you know."

It took Jannis a moment to recognize the fake name she had given when they first met. She flushed again.

"I don't suppose queens get to do much arms practice." She said sadly, fingering the hilt of her rapier.

"That's the king's decision, not mine." Flemming said simply. "But there's no harm in asking, is there?"

He glanced to the side as if looking for listeners, and then leaned over in the saddle to whisper to her: "And there is always that illusion spell, isn't there? Even if queens can't do arms practice, Lydia can."

She smiled at him and he winked back.

"Ah, there's that smile. I don't know why you don't use it more often."

"Yeah, really." Lance added, inserting himself into the conversation just as he rode his horse in between them. "You really should smile more. Like me! Everyone should be more like me."

"A homicidal maniac berift of conscience?" Jannis asked.

"Elegant." Lance answered for himself. "Poised. Undaunted

by any challenge. Unafraid to defy norms. Cunning. Clever. Handsome. And yes, if you must, that bit about being a homicidal maniac as well. The world needs more."

"It does?" Lieutenant Flemming asked politely from Lance's other side.

"Indeed it does, Lieutenant Flem. The world is entirely too boring." Lance replied. "A few more maniacs would do the world good. Stir things up a bit."

"What do you plan to do after the wedding?" The lieutenant asked Lance. "Will you stay in Harderior?"

"I hadn't really given it much thought."

"I think Lord Firin has a well-nurtured grudge against you regarding some books."

"Lord Firin needed a good shake-up. He's one of those people who thinks they can control everything around them. I should post a notice: You can't control anything, and trying is just madness."

"And how will you address the charge that you are a thief and stole priceless books from the royal collection?"

"Stealing implies I intend to keep them or sell them."

"And you don't?"

"I just appreciate a good book. I like knowing more than everyone around me."

"And what about when we were still on the battlefield? Lord Firin called you a murderer."

"I seriously doubt a Harderior judge is going to try me for killing a hundred Kalen soldiers. That should earn me a medal, it's the sort of thing war heroes do."

"And what about that potion you gave the prince?"

"I don't know what you are talking about." Lance replied evasively.

"The potion that you gave to your sister to give to the prince." Lieutenant Flemming corrected himself. "The one that cured the mage sickness. We heard about it from Master Emrys."

"Are you implying that I would do something altruistic?" Lance asked in mock dismay. "Haven't you figured out yet that I'm a monster pretending to be a man? I would never do anything so noble."

"I seriously doubt either Lord Firin, or the king, would accept that answer." The lieutenant said simply.

"What they are willing to accept is really irrelevant as far as I'm concerned. I'm not a cooperative person by nature." Lance supplied.

"And the fact that you are an archmage is going to make it pretty hard to leave Harderior if you wanted to. Archmages are hard to find; they aren't likely to let you leave now that they have you."

"Actually, about that. I just recently discovered that I'm not an archmage at all. I had no idea."

"Where would you get an idea like that, Lance?" Jannis interjected from his other side.

"Haru told me." Lance answered.

"The demon?!" Jannis sputtered.

"Archdemon, actually." Lance corrected, gently.

"And you believe him? Wait, I don't even believe that he said it in the first place. But even if he did, why on earth would you believe a demon?"

"Credibility is a funny thing. Let's just say that while I would not believe just anything that he said, he demonstrated this particular fact in such a way that I am convinced it is the truth."

"You aren't an archmage?" Jannis repeated doubtfully.

"Nope, not at all." Lance replied serenely.

"But you are a mage." Flemming pressed. Lance pursed his lips.

"Of one kind or another, yes. Though I don't *do* magic."

"Then you better resign yourself to staying in Harderior. If that sounds unbearable to you, it might be wise to disappear before we get back to the castle."

"I do believe you are offering me an out." Lance said delightedly. "Very kind of you, but I can usually find my own way out, once I want to leave."

"I just don't want Lady Jannis's brother falling into Lord Firin's hands." The lieutenant said simply. "The man can be... hard to work with."

"Oh you mean all that stuff about Eddy's mage breeding program, and the noticable shortage of adult mages?"

"Please do not speak of his Majesty with such disrespect, but yes, that is what I was referring to. It seems to me that it would be for the best, for you, for your sister, and for the entire kingdom if Lord Firin did not try to hold you here against your will."

"This one is remarkably insightful, isn't he, sis?" Lance asked, thumbing at the lieutenant.

"Indeed." Jannis replied, her face carefully neutral.

"Well, Flem, despite your horrible name, I think I like you. Therefore, I will do you the great honor of killing you, if we ever cross blades."

"You really think a lot of yourself, don't you?" The lieutenant asked, his face neutral. If Jannis hadn't known better, she might have thought he was trying not to laugh.

"Lance is very good." Jannis said, slowly, looking at the

lieutenant. He met her eyes and nodded slightly.

"Ah, well, then I hope we never have to face each other in combat. While you may consider it a great honor to die by your blade, I would prefer to keep living. If it's all the same to you." Flemming said lightly.

Lance sighed.

"Terribly unfortunate. I don't find enough decent opponents. It almost makes me want to go back to the Kalen Army and find that mercenary captain. Best fight I've had in a very long time." Lance glanced at Jannis. "And I would have won if my sister hadn't gotten herself caught."

"Have you ever considered that maybe it's better things turned out the way that they did, Lance? Those mercenaries would have slaughtered us if we hadn't surrendered."

"Which company?" The lieutenant asked, frowning.

"Venturi." Jannis supplied.

He whistled and shook his head.

"No wonder you were overwhelmed. They have something of a reputation. I don't know how Kalen got them, they are usually pretty selective about the jobs they take."

"What have you heard?" Jannis asked, interest piqued.

"Well their captain, his real name isn't Lynx by the way, that's an assumed name, was a disenfanchised nobleman. Rumor is he surrendered his birthright voluntarily in favor of a relative better suited. And supposedly, they have the former dean of one of the acedemies in Ren."

"Dyresse." Jannis interjected. "Her name is Dyresse."

"Really?" The lieutenant asked. "They are also rumored to employ fae and demons and djinn."

"An elf and a slyph." Lance corrected. "At least that we

saw."

"Sylph?" Jannis asked, confused.

"A desert wind sylph. Most people mistake them for djinn because they're so dark."

"Oh, I see. I've never seen a desert wind sylph before." Jannis said awkwardly.

"They're pretty rare. You don't see one outside their realm hardly at all." Lance offered. "And I wouldn't be at all surprised if Dyr dabbled a little in demon-summoning. She's a little crazy, if you know what I mean."

"Well their leader has to be a little crazy if he offered to take you in, Lance."

"Standing offer. I explained I was too busy right now."

"Even more than a little crazy, then."

"I'm almost sorry I missed it." The lieutenant commented. "Harderior offered them a job, but they turned us down. Although, in hindsight, I don't know if the offer was completely genuine, or if Lord Firin had set it up to try to lure them in. They do have a well-known complement of mages. Far more than the average mercenary troupe. And of higher quality."

"Lynx attracts all sorts of wierd talent." Lance said.

"It almost sounds like you want to run off and become a mercenary, Lance." Jannis teased.

"I wouldn't leave right before your wedding, sis. What kind of guy do you think I am?" Lance asked, the very picture of hurt innocence.

"Riiight." Jannis said skeptically.

"Of course, if you decided you didn't want to get married; I mean, if you got cold feet at the last minute, if I wasn't here they would just force you to go through with it anyway. So it's a good thing I'm coming along, because I'm the only one who would be there to help you escape if it came to that."

"That is surprisingly considerate of you, Lance." Jannis said. "I do admit to a certain degree of doubt about this whole marriage thing. I don't know if I ran off with Prince Darien just to buy myself more time to think it over."

"That's probably the most sensible thing I've heard you say all day."

"I guess I had just never really thought about getting married before uncle told me about the engagement. It didn't even occur to me. And when I got to the castle, there were so many strange expectations. It felt like everything I did was wrong." Jannis warmed to her subject.

"I mean what is so strange about asking about the castle accounts?"

"Most women aren't very good at math, or care about where the money comes from." Lieutenant Flemming supplied sadly.

"And why should it be strange that I asked political questions?"

"Those who know the politics already know the answers, and so never ask. And you were probably asking the wrong people, at the wrong time." The lieutenant continued.

"And they knew I was an archmage, so my interest in discussing magic shouldn't have been a surprise."

"Most of the mages would be out on the battlefield or at Lord Firin's estate. Of the handful that his Majesty keeps on hand at the palace, I doubt any of them could hold his own in a conversation with an educated archmage." The lieutenant concluded.

"They treated me like I was made of glass! I couldn't breathe trapped in those rooms all the time!"

"Most mages in Harderior are terribly ill. And no matter how healthy you appeared, that didn't mean you wouldn't get sick as well, or get injured. And most women don't, as I'm sure you are aware, practice swordfighting, unless they have an occupation that requires it, like being a guard or a soldier."

Lieutenant Flemming glanced back at the other mages in the group, trailing at a significant distance and added, thoughtfully, "And all that metal you are wearing really does put the mages off-balance. You are about as far from a normal mage in Harderior as it is possible to be. Look at them, they won't even get close to you."

"You know, sis, it didn't occur to me at the time," Lance said slowly. "But when your princeling got really sick after the gate spell, it may have been because of all the armor we brought through and started wearing, not from the cut on his hand."

Jannis paused and thought about it. Lance did make sense from time to time. That could very well have been what triggered his collapse, though the strain of the gate may also have contributed.

"So what you are saying, is that I just don't fit in." Jannis said sourly to the lieutenant.

"No, what I am saying is that since it is impossible to meet their expectations, you should just ignore them completely. I mean the only person's opinion that counts is your future husband's, the king's. Everyone else's opinion means less than nothing. You should just do what you want, and let them all talk. Gossip is going to happen no matter what you do, anyway."

"So what about the king? Do you think he would let me practice swordfighting, or go out riding, or wear pants?" Jannis countered.

"I would think that would depend on how charming you can be, and good you are at flattery." The lieutenant said. "A smile can be a very potent weapon. And a beautiful woman's smile even more so. And," here the lieutenant paused, and glanced quickly around. "As we are all aware, the king has a certain... weakness for mages. Of which you are one. And a rare and valuable one. Archmages are very hard to come by. Think about it."

"It's too bad you didn't bother to take lessons from me on manipulation. " Lance said jeeringly. "You could wrap him around your little finger. I doubt you have the skill to, though. You always looked down on my offers to teach you the art of social lying."

"Like you are any kind of expert." Jannis said dismissively.

"I *have* to be an expert. Do you really think anyone on earth could be this annoying by accident?" Lance said proudly.

Jannis started to answer, then thought better of it, and closed her mouth instead.

Chapter 17

Once they reached the royal palace, things were painfully predictable. They were all seperated, Prince Darien returned to his room, Lady Jannis to her suite of rooms, the guards to their barracks, and Lance was given his own suite, with around the clock guards 'in honor' of his service to the country, but really just because the king wanted him under house arrest.

They were three days late for the wedding. That meant that much of the food had to be redone, and the floral arrangements, to great additional expense, much to the chatelaine's distress.

The date was reset for three days after the bride's return.

Lord Firin decided to stay at the palace for the wedding, both in response to the king's personal invitation, and in keeping with his desire to stay close to Lance. Master Emrys similarly stayed at the palace for the wedding, and spent most of his time teaching Darien magic.

Jannis decided to take Lieutenant Flemming's advice, and since she was trapped in her suite, she lounged around in tunic and leggings, reading books she had ordered retrieved from the library to the handwringing and distressed stares of the ladies-in-waiting.

She only bothered to put on a dress when the king came to see her. Fortunately for both of them, he always sent word rather than just showing up unannounced.

And that was the state of affairs, when the night before the wedding, she heard a tapping on her window.

It was Lance, of course. Hanging outside the window from his signature rope, the rope looped around his leg, and one hand loose to knock on her window. The downside of windows this high up in a castle, was that they didn't open.

So Jannis did what she did last time, and ran one finger around the ouside of the glass window pane chanting a cantrap under her voice, until the pane slid free of the window and nearly took her fingers off with its weight. She kept forgetting how heavy glass was.

Lance swung into the room and landed with the grace of a cat on the floor, letting the rope swing back out the window on its own weight. It dangled a foot from the wall, right outside of her window.

"I don't suppose I should ask what you are doing." Jannis said, rubbing her fingers.

"Last chance." Lance said without preamble. "If you want to run, I've already packed."

"That's really sweet, but I..." Jannis began, the words catching in her throat as Lance pulled her rapier, still in its sheath from his belt. He held it out to her with both hands, the blade parallel to the floor.

Jannis started to reach for it, and her hand dropped. What could she do?

Lance's face hardened, and he hefted the sword in one hand,

still in its sheath.

"You know what your problem is? You don't know how to be happy. You can't choose something for yourself. You just want to drift and follow the rules, let someone else tell you what to do, instead of making a hard choice where you know your happiness comes at the expense of someone else."

"I'm not like you, Lance. I'm not going to hurt someone for my own benefit."

"And what about your feelings? Don't they matter, too? Do you really want to get married, or are you just too afraid to deal with the consequences of saying no? Are you that determined to sacrifice yourself for everyone else?"

"You don't understand."

"Oh I don't?" Lance reattached the rapier to his belt. "You are always telling me to get serious. Well I am serious. As serious as an arrow through the heart." Lance paused and drilled into her eyes with his own, before continuing.

"You drive me more kinds of mad than there are words to describe. I don't know what is going on in that head half of the time, and you can irritate me more than I can stand. But you are the only one. You are the only one in the whole world I would die for. And if your husband-to-be doesn't feel the same way, he doesn't deserve you. It's as simple as that."

"Lance..." Jannis said, momentarily overwhelmed.

Lance turned away from her, and reached back out the window for his rope, tugging on it to make sure it was still secure.

"Last chance, sis." He said without looking at her.

Jannis stood there, with her heart in her throat, trying to decide what to say to him, what to do.

"Lance, I..." She hesitated. "I'm just not like you."

He sighed, and heaved himself up onto the windowsill without a word, and started climbing the rope outside her window.

Jannis realized she had finally gotten the last word. Lance had always had the last word, every time she could remember. But there was no pleasure in the victory. She felt dead inside.

———————

The day of the wedding dawned picture perfect, like something out of a fairy tale. The sky was blue, the sun shining brilliantly, only the slightest scattering of clouds, and only the barest breeze. It was neither too hot, nor too cold, and Jannis lounged across her featherbed in leggings, staring sourly at the elaborate wedding dress she would have to get into.

And that was quite a task. It took three ladies-in-waiting to lift the gorgeous confection of silk and crystal and pearl beading up over Jannis' head and fit it around her limbs. The dress was so stiff with embroidery that it could have stood up on its own!

After all the effort of getting into that dress, Jannis then had to endure the primping and priming of the ladies-in-waiting as they swirled around her with jewelry, make-up and hair adornments. It was starting to play on her last nerve. Jannis was not someone who liked to sit idly in one place for long, at least not without a book to distract her active mind.

Jannis' delicate features twisted at the sight of her own reflection in the mirror, and siezed by a sudden irrational desire she whispered a quick cantrap under her breath.

The illusion took effect and beautiful, brilliant blue butterfly wings unfolded from her shoulders. Jannis preened, turning in the mirror to see herself better.

The ladies-in-waiting all just stared at her with identical expressions of shock and horror. Jannis sighed at their expressions.

It totally took the fun out of it.

"Too much color, I suppose?" Jannis asked rhetorically, glancing from the dress to the wings. The blemishless white-on-white of the dress seemed harsh and unforgiving against the rich blue of the wings.

She rolled another cantrip off her tongue, and the butterfly wings folded back and morphed into white feathered wings two feet long. Jannis preened again, turning to get a better look at the wings. They were patterned off of cherub wings she had seen in paintings in religious books in the library, too small for her body's size, but still so charming, nonetheless.

The ladies-in-waiting were trading unreadable looks now. Two of them turned away to whisper at each other. Lady Charlotte seemed as if she were gathering all her courage, and then she cleared her throat deliberately.

"My lady," she said carefully, as if to a small child, "We are all very impressed with your magical skills, but is this really the time to play such games? Surely you wish your wedding to be as perfect as can be. Put them away. Please."

Jannis sighed, and glanced at the mirror again, sourly. She muttered something and the wings vanished.

The ladies-in-waiting paused a moment, politely restraining sighs of relief before once again cheerfully working on Jannis' hair, braiding strings of crystal and pearl into the silver locks, collectively ignoring the unexpected interruption as if it had never happened.

Jannis sighed heavily and just stared blankly at the mirror, resisting the urge to scowl, and endured their presence and all their preparations.

Chapter 18

When the bride finally entered the great vaulting hall that made up the chapel in the royal palace, there was a great intake of breath. She really did look like something out of a fairy tale. Like something that could scarcely be real, hardly human at all. A perfect gleaming statute of ivory flesh, silvery hair, crystal and shimmering white silk. Even her violet eyes were cold and piercing.

It made shivers run up more than one spine to see her. She was so breathtakingly beautiful, but it was not the kind of beauty to inspire hunger or lust. Watching her was like watching a fierce snowstorm, or the violent crashing of waves against a seacliff. You marveled at the beauty, beauty even more breathtaking because it was untouchable. A force of nature, without malice, but deadly all the same.

She stood poised within the door for a long moment and when she strode into the hall, it was with a firm step. The waiting crowd remained fixed on her, and not a word was spoken, though somewhere some musician took a cue and pleasant, familiar music began to fill the silence.

The room was enormous, and yet seemed small for the waiting crowd which had been crammed within it. The ceiling rose over a hundred feet high in the air, with elegant arching spans of wood and bronze holding the roof aloft. Tall windows let in a massive amount of light through paned glass windows, edged in brilliant colored glass. The dominant feature of the room was one enormous colored glass window depicting the goddess in all her glory with her worshiping children arranged at her feet.

And that is where the king stood, before the altar to the goddess where the attendant priest and priestess waited. Jannis took her time, taking deliberate measured steps towards where he waited. She didn't bother glancing to either side.

Lance wouldn't be here. She knew him too well. He would never admit it, but he would be deeply hurt by their exchange the night before. He could be so childish sometimes.

So many eyes on her. Why didn't it disturb her? Shouldn't she be nervous? She just felt empty inside, as if she was waiting for something. What was she waiting for? She pondered it for a moment, and then dismissed it as rediculous. It was just a fancy.

So cold. How could the room be so warm and she feel so cold? She wasn't sweating with the press of all those bodies; she was resisting the urge to shiver.

Jannis found herself wishing for her brother. Lance was so aggravating, but the world seemed warmer when he was around, more alive. There were hundreds of people all around her, but she felt alone.

What was wrong with her?

Jannis came to a stop silently next to her husband-to-be and turned to face him. Her face was a perfect mask of queenly elegance, controlled and serene. His face too was a perfectly controlled mask of royal authority. A quick flick of his eyes up and down her was the only indication that he had examined her appearance and approved.

Someone started speaking. Jannis wasn't really paying attention, it was all part of the background. Time seemed to slow.

And then a massive crash as the beautiful stained glass window directly behind the altar went flying in thousands of brutal glass shards.

Jannis fell to the ground instinctively, not even thinking or caring what was happening. The numbness inside her seemed to dull her reflexes. Her mind was moving at a crawl.

There was screaming. There was shouting. She crouched there on the floor, her movements hampered by the elaborate white wedding gown, her eyes fixed on the black and white marble tiling on the floor beneath her.

It fixed strangely in her attention, the swirling of the black and the white in the stone. It meant something. She was sure of it. But the meaning slipped away.

With an effort she ripped her mind from the mesmerizing swirl of the marble beneath her feet and back into the chaos of the present.

"Lance..." Jannis whispered in horror.

And it was.

Lance had, with characteristic flair, used his rope and wall climbing ability to repel off the roof of the chapel, building up enough momentum to go smashing through the giant, glorious stained glass window that was the chapel's greatest pride.

To prevent death or serious injury while smashing through sharp glass at high speed, he was quite rationally garbed in his full plate armor, with his sword strapped to his back. The sword on his back momentarily confused her, for he always wore his sword at his hip, but that was quickly explained by the empty rapier sheath at his side, her sheath.

Shock still slowing her mind she turned, to where her own rapier hilt stood out of the king's chest where he was slowly dying, still half on his feet.

It wasn't rage or fear that painted the king's features, it was confusion. As if he could not understand what had happened. And his next words confirmed it.

"I... can't die...." Eduardo gasped, dazed. "Not even an archmage could break the wards that protect me."

"I'm sure you're right." Lance said evenly, and his hand reached out like a snake to rip the blade from the king's chest. "After all, there is nothing in the world as powerful as magic. You were wise to gamble your life on it."

The king toppled over, his breath a harsh gurgle as the blood filled up his lungs, and Lance reached down to the train of Jannis' beautiful, gleaming white wedding dress to wipe the blade.

It left harsh streaks of red, vibrantly red on the white silk.

Lance glanced at her, his face empty, his eyes hard, and said nothing. Jannis was still in shock and could not seem to find something to say. But there were others who were not bound by shock. The royal guard quickly surrounded him, swords and pikes drawn.

Lance smiled, a smile that never reached his eyes, and dropped Jannis's rapier, raising his hands in a gesture of surrender. He was wise to do so, for they would surely have killed him had he resisted even in the slightest.

They siezed him, binding his arms harshly behind his back and striking him hard in the temple to knock him unconscious.

Jannis then did something that she would quite violently deny later. She fainted.

In the aftermath of the ruined royal wedding things moved so quickly it sometimes seemed as if the ground itself were shaking. Lance was thrown into the dungeons. It wasn't clear whether he would be imprisoned for life, held for trial and later executed, or if something else would become of him.

Eduardo died of his wounds later that same night, despite the frantic ministry of both doctors and mages.

The next in line to the Harderior throne was a seven-year-old, Prince Darien. There was a brief power struggle behind the scenes as different noble houses vyed for control, and then Duke Tellis emerged as the official Royal Regent until the Prince achieved his majority   Strangely enough, Kalen sent an official emmissary shortly after the king's death, ratifying and extending the cease-fire, and tentatively opening up talks to officially ending the conflict between the nations.

Master Emrys agreed to remain at the palace as the Prince's tutor in magic and foreign relations, at the king-to-be's special request, and several other skilled tutors were appointed to fill in all the other skills needed to rule a nation.

Jannis remained in her rooms under house arrest until careful investigation cleared her of any involvement in the king's death. Even after she was cleared, the palace staff kept a careful distance. The only person who was still willing to speak to her was Lieutenant Fleming and even he was distant with her.

Lord Firin oversaw Lance's interrogation personally. In addition to identifying any accomplices in the murder of the king, he had a vested interest in discovering the location of the stolen books and the cure to the Harderior mage sickness.

All of Lord Firin's efforts to pry information out of Lance were in vain. Lord Firin resorted to torture after the first couple of fruitless days of questioning, but in response, Lance started speaking only in Jorse, an ancient language known only to a handful of scholars. Lord Firin was forced, to his frustration, to bring in an expert from the local university to sit in on the interrogation and translate.

Most subjects, while trying to conceal information, say nothing. That was not Lance's temperment. He talked nonstop, until he lost his voice, first in the common tongue, and then in Jorse, telling stories, singing songs, and lecturing as if he were a professor on a dozen different unrelated topics.

Lord Firin was starting to develop a number of strange habits, talking to himself, staring fiercely at walls, and mumbling something in Jorse, when Duke Tellis directed him to cease the questioning. Lord Firin had been trying to pry information out of

Lance for almost four weeks, and Duke Tellis, at least, understood the futility of wasting any more time on the effort.

Lord Firin protested violently, and was told politely to return to his estate, and begin the dismantling of the former king's special project.

The mage children would be transfered to a special "school" in the capital, an idea Prince Darien originally came up with, and Duke Tellis cheerfully adopted and improved, so that their special medical needs could be met, and they could still grow up in a relatively normal environment. Many of them had been on the battlefield at a very young age, and were still bearing the scars of those experiences. They wouldn't fit in well with other children in an ordinary school.

Jannis was at loose ends. She mostly read books and worried frantically about her brother, when the word finally came. She was summoned to Duke Tellis' office.

———————

She put on a dress to meet with the duke. Jannis didn't like dresses as a rule, but she understood also the expectations of nobles in Harderior.

Duke Tellis looked up, mildly curious, when she came in the door to his study, and then glanced back down at the pile of paperwork in front of him. He scrawled something on the bottom of a page, pressed a seal into the pool of melted wax on the page, and pushed it to one side, then looked up and gave her his undivided attention.

"I imagine you must be running out of patience at this point. I'm sorry it took so long to work through this issue." Duke Tellis said carefully, smiling sadly at her.

"I, yes, of course, sir." She muttered, meeting his eyes briefly, and then looking away.

"Your brother's crime is not exactly treason, since neither of you are citizens of Harderior, but the murder of our king is still a serious matter, for which death is an appropriate punishment." He paused to see the effect of his words on her.

Jannis tried to shrink into the plush chair she was sitting in. She did not know of anything she could say to help, so she said nothing.

Duke Tellis nodded thoughtfully and continued.

"We originally planned to hold a pubilc trial and execute him, but then the negotiations with Kalen over the end of hostilities took a strange turn. They demanded Lance's release as part of the conditions of a peace agreement."

"What?" Jannis asked, genuinely surprised and confused.

"That was my reaction, too." Duke Tellis agreed. "It almost made me wonder if Lance had some form of agreement with the Kalen to kill our king, but both the Kalen emmissary and Lance have denied working together, and there is no proof in any case."

"So what are you going to do?"

Duke Tellis paused and looked contemplative for a moment. "King Eduardo was my personal friend, and I loathe the idea of his murderer walking free, but I also have to weigh the good of an entire nation. Peace, at the price of one life, is cheap. Especially when you consider how many lives have already been spent."

"You don't seem very distressed." Jannis commented, bluntly.

Duke Tellis stared at her, his eyes cold and his face flat.

"Excuse me," he said, his voice hard, "But I am very distressed. As I said, Eduardo was my personal friend as well as my king. I would have died in his place if I could have." Duke Tellis visibly tried to calm himself, and forced a smile.

"But I know you had nothing to do with his death, and I can't shove blame upon you just because your brother is an out-of-control monster. Don't mistake politeness for a lack of concern."

"Of course. I apologize." Jannis said awkwardly.

"What I need from you is an assurance that you will do everything in your power to ensure that your brother never sets foot on Harderior soil again. And if you fail, be warned that the next time he falls into our hands, there will be no mercy."

"I understand."

"Good. Then I suggest you go and collect your monster and get on the road as soon as possible. Not everyone agrees that our king's murderer should be allowed to escape justice."

———————

As Jannis left Duke Tellis' office and turned to walk down the hall, Lieutenant Fleming caught her arm from the side. She hadn't even seen him standing there.

"You could stay, you know." He said, his voice low. "The new king knows you had nothing to do with what happened. He even seems to have taken a liking to you. I doubt I could keep an archmage in the castle guard, but I don't think they would turn you away either."

Jannis stood for a moment, torn, her face anguished, her eyes following the rapidly disappearing back of her brother as he was forcibly escorted away.

"I…" She began, and stopped.

"You are one deceptive lady." Fleming commented, his voice

hard, shaking his head.

"Deceptive?" Jannis retorted, hurt.

"How can a woman who carries herself with such arrogance, such steely self-assurance, be so unsure of herself? Do you even know what you want?"

"Doubt is weakness, and doubting oneself the greatest weakness of all," Jannis said, her heart aching. "You don't show weakness to your enemies."

"And who here is your enemy? Me?"

Jannis paused, steeling herself.

"The world is my enemy." She said finally, her voice cold.

Fleming reached out and traced her chin with one finger, wonderingly.

"How can a woman so soft be so hard? How can a woman so beautiful be so cold?"

"In the swamp, the most beautiful flowers were the most poisonous. I would have thought you would have learned that lesson already. Haven't you met beautiful women before?"

"Vipers. But you aren't a viper, even if you pretend to be one. So, just what are you?"

"My uncle would say that I'm a child; my brother would say that I'm a pain."

"No man would mistake you for a child, and I haven't met the boy who didn't consider his big sister a pain, mostly because she always got in the way."

"Please, stop. You don't understand."

"Understand what?"

"I can't leave him."

"Who, your brother?"

She nodded, closing her eyes.

"You do realize he's a man grown. He doesn't need you to take care of him."

"No one needs to 'take care' of Lance," Jannis said darkly. "I just need to watch him. He's dangerous."

"You didn't stop him from assassinating the king." Fleming pointed out, quite reasonably.

"And do you think that is the worst Lance is capable of?" Jannis replied, her voice foreboding.

"You can't hide in his shadow forever." Fleming said finally, after a long pause. He withdrew his hand.

"As I said, you just don't understand."

"I wish I did."

"Goodbye, lieutenant. Maybe if the Goddess is generous, we'll meet again under better circumstances."

"I'm not very devout, but maybe I'll offer a prayer or two. You never know, it might help. And if you ever change your mind, you're always welcome here."

"I don't belong here. I wish I did. But thank you for the offer. I do appreciate your kindness. Goodbye."

Chapter 19

Jannis collected her "monster" at the dungeons. Lance was remarkably cheerful for a man who had spent the last several weeks being tortured for information, and had a death penalty hanging over his head.

"I was wondering when you would show up." Lance said by way of greeting. He was mostly clean, which was a testament to the sheer obsession he had with his personal appearance, for it was quite difficult to remain clean in a dungeon for any period of time.

"This is all your fault." Jannis said with finality. Lance rolled his eyes.

"If you hadn't agreed to marry that monster, I wouldn't have had to kill him."

"One monster to another?" Jannis asked coldly. "And this had nothing to do with him slapping you?"

"Well, it was just a nice bonus."

"Do you feel any remorse at all?" Jannis asked cynically.

"No. Did you expect me to?"

"And what if they had killed you for it?!"

Lance shrugged. "We already had this discussion. You are the only person in the world I would die for. So, really, I wouldn't have minded."

"You are insufferable! I suppose you thought you were doing me a favor!"

"Well, yeah. He didn't deserve you."

"I can't believe you! You do realize you ruined my wedding and killed my fiancee. That is not what I would call a favor."

"We can't always see eye-to-eye. I'm used to being unappreciated. You are my sister after all."

She slapped him. All-in-all Jannis considered it a very measured response to that particular comment.

Lance and Jannis didn't talk much on the ride back to Aerigard's castle. Jannis was still fuming at Lance for being so... Lance, and Lance was uncharacteristically contemplative. What horrors lurked within his mind no man could guess, but the net effect was a very silent ride through forests and swamps, interrupted only by the bite of the early winter wind, promising snow.

They made one detour, which took several hours, and resulted in a dirty saddlebag that Lance strapped with ceremony to his horse but without further explaination.

Jannis almost considered apologizing for being so ungrateful for his efforts, but the audicity and violence of his recent behavior stopped her. He deserved to be unappreciated in this. Even if, she realized, she was vastly relieved that she had not had to marry Eduardo.

And that was the state of things when the two of the rode up to the gates of an imposing black stone castle deep within a cursed swamp.

Jannis and Lance dismounted, still silent and walked into the keep.

Their uncle sat, in pride of place, at the head of the massive wooden table that filled one side of the collective dining room. A silver mug of Turkish coffee steamed gently at his side, and there was a scroll unrolled before him that had been reading when they came in.

The dreaded Dark Lord, sorcerer known and respected by demons and djinn sighed heavily, and put one hand to his brow.

"Back already?" Aerigard asked, his voice and face carefully blank, but his eyes hinting at tortured resignation.

Lance didn't bother responding, instead dropping the extremely heavy leather satchel he had been carrying on the table in front of his uncle and taking a nearby seat. Jannis was already sitting in one corner, desperately gulping down Turkish coffee. It had been too long.

"I heard what happened in the kingdom of Harderior. Good riddance. That Eduardo was too persistent for his own good; he would have been coming after me too, sooner or later."

"Eddy would have been no match for you, Uncle, and we both know it. But I'm always glad to amuse myself at someone else's expense. And killing people is fun, too. You might want to open the bag. I have a surprise for you."

"I'm afraid to open it. Had too much experience with your 'surprises' in the past."

"Now, now, I'm hurt, Uncle." Lance assumed an expression vaguely like a pouting child. "How little you trust me, and we are family after all."

Aerigard drank his coffee and glanced at the bag. "Indeed we are family. And I know you are just as bad as I am. Don't think I'm that stupid."

Lance grinned ferally. "You know you want to. You can't resist."

"No." The sorcerer drank his coffee, unmoved.

"No?"

"No."

"The temptation is killing you. The mystery of it all; the dark and forbidden secret."

"Your nagging is killing me. I've been researching a new spell that tears out tongues, just in case you were foolish enough to come back here."

"Threats, already? That bag really must be tempting you. What could it hurt? Just open it."

"I'll open it." Jannis declared, frustrated and infuriated at her brother and her uncle. "For once, this isn't one of Lance's nasty surprises."

She stormed over to the table, unbuckling the top of the satchel, and pulled a thick, old, musty book out of it. Another thinner, but older book followed. The odor that came from them was mold and dust and made you want to sneeze like mad. A third book joined the pile-- this one bound in gilded leather, but worn and spotted with age. Jannis kept pulling books out of the satchel until a small pile sat on the table, and finally threw the now empty satchel to the floor and stalked back over to her chair.

Aerigard pursed his lips and lifted the top book off the stack, opening it carefully. With one eyebrow cocked quizzically, he thumbed through the book, then set it aside, lifting the one beneath it. He repeated this process, thumbing through three more books and making a second neat stack on the table.

Aerigard paused, and a possessive joy lit his eyes from within. He caressed the spine of one particularly old tome, the title obscured by centuries of wear.

"Well," The Solaran's sorcerer uncle licked his lips and smiled. "I never thought I'd say it, but I'm actually glad to see you, Lance. Welcome home."

"Don't worry, it won't last." Lance retorted with a smirk.

70516473R00200

Made in the USA
Lexington, KY
12 November 2017